MAFIA MISTRESS

The Kings of Italy Book 1

MILA FINELLI

Cover: Letitia Hasser, RBA Designs

Editing: Sabrina Darby

"Hell is empty and all the devils are here."
—William Shakespeare, *The Tempest*

CHAPTER ONE

Francesca

Toronto, Ontario

I MET the devil the morning after my eighteenth birthday.

Hungover and tired, I rolled over in bed, where my toes brushed against warm skin and crisp body hair. A friend of mine held a graduation party last night at her pool and my boyfriend, David, slept over after. We usually hooked up at his apartment, but I was too drunk last night and insisted on coming here.

It hadn't been easy sneaking him into the house under the watchful gaze of the cameras monitored by Papà's men, but I was a pro. I'd been outsmarting the guards and the cameras for years now. The one thing the guards loved? Routine. Once you learned the routine, you could get around it and do whatever you wanted.

Papà was the head of one of the seven families of the 'Ndrangheta in Toronto, a criminal network that stretched from Canada to South

America to Italy. My father's business was dangerous, so my two sisters and I weren't raised as typical teenagers. Wherever we went, we were trailed by guards with guns inside their jackets—including to school. Our extracurricular activities were severely limited, our lives kept under careful scrutiny.

Which was why I couldn't help but occasionally sneak out.

I was the responsible one, the big sister who began caring for my two younger siblings when our mother died. I deserved a break every now and then.

A knock sounded at my door. "Frankie. Are you awake?"

My father.

Shit. Panic filled me. The first night I dared to have my boyfriend sleep over and my father was outside my door. This could not be good.

Hangover forgotten, I grabbed David's shoulders. "You have to get out of here," I mouthed silently. "Like, now."

David nodded and hurried to dress, while I handed him his clothes. I looked at the door. "Papà, don't come in. I'm not dressed."

"You need to get up and look presentable," he said from the hall. "We have guests."

Guests? It was barely nine o'clock. "I'll need at least an hour," I said.

"You have ten minutes."

I could hear the command in his voice. "All right," I called.

David zipped up his jeans and threw on his t-shirt. I opened the window and looked down. My bedroom was on the second floor, so it was high but not a death-defying jump. "Hang down from the window ledge and you should be fine."

A rough hand slid over my bare ass. "Maybe it's time for me to meet your family, babe."

The idea almost made me laugh. My father would strangle David with his bare hands for daring to touch his precious daughter. "You have to go. Keep to the side of the house and out of sight. There is a path on the left and it leads to a wall. The cameras won't see you there. Hurry."

He pressed a hard kiss to my mouth, then crawled out the window. I watched as he slowly lowered himself down, his biceps bulging with the effort. Before we graduated last month, he'd been one of the most popular boys in our senior class and captain of the hockey team. I was going to miss him when I left for college in August.

David dropped to his feet and then gave me a salute. I blew him a kiss and shut the window, my mind already racing to Papà and the guests.

After a quick shower, I braided my wet hair and dabbed concealer under my eyes. A swipe of mascara later, I threw on a prim dress that covered most of my body, as my father preferred. Instead of flats, I put on a pair of heels. I was tall, but I liked the way I looked in heels. Like nothing could stop me. Intimidating. Fierce.

The house was quiet, my sisters still asleep. The sixteen-year-old twins, Emma and Gia, usually stayed up well into the night, watching movies and talking to their friends online. I would miss them when I went away to school, but they didn't need me as much these days. They would be fine after I left.

My heels popped on the marble floors as I approached my father's office. I rarely went in here, seeing as how I'd rather not know what Papà was really doing most of the time. Ignorance was bliss when it came to having a family member in the mafia, let alone running it.

I knocked and waited until I heard my father's voice telling me to come in. He was seated behind his desk and the room was full of men in suits. Some faces were familiar, like Uncle Reggie and my cousin, Dante, but the others were strangers—and they all stared at me.

"Francesca, come in." My father stood and buttoned his suit jacket.

Swallowing my nerves, I approached his desk. "You wanted to see me?"

"Yes. This is Fausto Ravazzani."

A man unfolded from the armchair and my heart leapt into my throat. I'd never seen such a handsome man before, one with such thick, wavy dark hair and piercing blue eyes. He was trim, with a chiseled jaw and broad shoulders, and his suit fit him perfectly. He looked to be in his late thirties, and under any other circumstances I would have guessed him a former model or actor. No one looked and dressed like this unless they were dependent on their looks for a living.

But this was no prima donna. Power rolled off his taut frame in waves, like he was in control of everyone and everything around him. The men accompanying him clearly weren't his friends, they were guards. He was someone important, someone worth protecting.

And he seemed... dangerous.

I nodded once. "Mr. Ravazzani."

His eyes drifted over my face and down my body, as if I were a horse he was considering purchasing. Tingles broke out along my skin wherever he looked, but I couldn't tell if it was from excitement or embarrassment. Even more confusing, my nipples hardened in my thin bra, which I hoped he wouldn't notice.

The smirk on his face when he met my gaze told me he was aware of the state of my nipples.

"You are eighteen?"

The words rolled out of his mouth with an Italian accent and my heart gave an ominous thump in my chest. Were these men from Toronto? I doubted it. No one in my father's employ had an accent this thick. "Yes, sir."

He nodded once to my father. "She'll do."

She'll do? "Do for what?" I asked.

My father shot me a quick look before addressing Ravazzani. "Excellent. We'll plan the wedding for next month."

"Wedding?" I screeched. No, no, no. I was supposed to go to college first. My mother made my father promise that all three of their daughters would be educated before marriage. I was counting on it. "What wedding?"

"Quiet, Francesca," my father hissed.

I glanced at my cousin, hoping to find answers, but Dante wouldn't meet my eye. Which meant this was bad. Really bad. Normally he relished my unhappiness.

One of Ravazzani's men entered and leaned down to speak in his ear. The edge of Ravazzani's mouth curled as he listened, then he waved the man away. Returning his attention to my father, he said, "No. The wedding will take place at my home in Siderno, where Giulio resides. We leave tomorrow."

Giulio? And wait, Siderno? As in Italy?

What the fuck was happening?

Lines deepened on my father's forehead. "But what about me and my family? We have a right to—"

Stiffening, Ravazzani glared at my father, and the mood in the room went arctic. "Be very, very careful, Roberto," he said softly. "You lost your rights when you lost my shipment."

Yikes.

No one moved and the moment stretched. I'd never seen *anyone* put my father in his place before. No one had ever dared. I held my breath until my father finally put up his hands. "*Mi dispiace*," he apologized.

This appeared to appease Ravazzani, but I still had no idea what they were talking about. "Will someone please tell me what is going on?" I blurted, unable to hold back any longer.

Ravazzani moved quickly, stepping closer, until he towered over me. His irises were so blue, with hints of gray, but they didn't seem angry. Instead, he appeared amused. "You have spirit. That's good. You will need it, *piccolina*."

Walking around me, he went to the door, trailed by five of his men. "I expect her ready, Mancini," he said over his shoulder.

Anger burned in my chest. Expected me ready? Like I was a piece of luggage? No one was carting me off to Italy. I was going to school in New York City, not getting married to some scary Italian man who was most definitely in the mafia.

When the door closed, I rounded on my father. "Papà, what is this all about?"

He dragged a hand down his face and dropped into his chair. Uncle Reggie and Dante didn't move, but the rest of my father's men left the room. "Sit, Frankie."

"I'd rather not. I'd rather stand until I know what's happening."

Papà slapped a hand against the surface of his desk. "For fuck's sake. Do as you're told!"

I hated when he spoke to me so coldly, like I was one of his men. Dante shook his head, clearly indicating he thought I was an idiot, and Uncle Reggie wore his usual frown. Pushing away the hurt and confusion, I slid into a chair. "There. Now please explain what is happening."

"You have been chosen to wed Ravazzani's heir, Giulio. It's a good match, Frankie. An honor, really."

An *honor*? I stared at the man who'd promised I would receive a college degree before marriage. Who said I could have my choice in a husband. Empty lies. Every single one. "Absolutely not. I won't marry some stranger in Italy. I don't want a mafia husband. I'm going to school in the fall."

My father's face hardened into a scary expression, one I'd never seen before. I suspected this was his *'ndrina* face, the mafia leader who did terrible things with no remorse. "You will do as you are told or people will die. People in this family. Is that what you want?"

The threat hung in the air between us and I thought of my twin sisters upstairs, asleep and trusting. With no idea I was being forced to choose a life I didn't want to secure their safety. *It's no choice at all.* I would do anything for them.

Though I was just two years older, I had been the one to care for them after my mother's death. I taught them about boys and periods. Helped them buy bras. Dried their tears and managed their screen time. The backs of my eyelids started to burn. "Why is this happening?"

"Alliances through marriage are a part of our world. There is nothing anyone can do to prevent this. I expect you to do your duty and make Giulio happy."

I pressed a hand to my stomach, trying to ease the sudden cramping of my insides. How had my future changed so drastically? "But you promised," I said weakly, fighting tears.

His expression didn't budge. "My promises to the 'Ndrangheta come first. Now, do not dishonor me. This is an opportunity for us to gain more power through your husband's family. Ravazzani is one of the wealthiest men in Italy, the head of one of the largest clans, the *'ndrina* which bears his name."

Power. Wealth. Was that all anyone cared about? I rubbed my eyes, uncaring if I smeared my mascara. "This isn't fair."

"Grow up, Frankie," Dante sneered. "Ravazzani is one of the high-est-ranking men in all of the 'Ndrangheta. You'll be married to his son, who will inherit everything one day. Any woman in our circle would kill for this chance."

"Screw you, Dante. I don't want to marry a boss," I snapped. "I want to go to school and get a degree." Like I had been promised.

College meant freedom from my father and his men. It meant living in New York City and going to clubs and bars, dating boys and drinking too much. I would study and have a career and live a normal life before I had to marry.

It was all my mother had wanted for her girls.

Be your own woman, Francesca. Don't make my mistakes.

She was a top Italian model before she met and married my father. While their marriage had been a love match at first, she said she always regretted giving up her career for him.

"Stop," my father said. "You're acting childish. It's been decided. Go up and pack your things. I expect you to be ready first thing tomorrow."

"But—"

"Not another word, Francesca. You are leaving with Fausto Ravazzani and that is final."

I pressed my lips together and rose. The men said nothing as I left, thinking I'd agreed. That I'd willingly cross an ocean and marry a man I hadn't met, just because my father screwed up with some mysterious shipment.

They should have known better.

CHAPTER TWO

Fausto

THE CAR TURNED into the warehouse lot. The place hadn't been used in years by the looks of it, which was perfect for this errand. When the wheels stopped, I opened the door of the rented car and stepped out. Marco got out and unlocked the trunk.

The boy was yanked out and thrown onto the ground, where he crumpled in a pile of limbs covered in cheap clothing. My men caught the *stronzo* crawling out of her bedroom window this morning. I stared at him, wanting to see what she saw. Why would a woman as beautiful as Francesca Mancini ever waste her time on such a pathetic and ordinary creature like this?

She was glorious. The rumors of her looks weren't exaggerated. All three Mancini daughters were said to resemble their mother. Sofia Mancini had been a famous model before marrying Roberto—I remember jerking off to her photos as a teenage boy—and Francesca was the spitting image of her mother, except with bigger tits.

Dio, how I would love to fuck those tits.

Stop. She's marrying your son.

Angry at my inappropriate thoughts, I transferred that fury onto the man on the ground. "So you are the boyfriend."

His frightened eyes darted between me and my men. "Who are you? Why am I here?"

I nodded at Marco, who gave the boy a swift kick in the ribs. "I ask the questions," I said when the boy caught his breath. "And I want to know if you fucked her."

The boy's brows rose. "What?"

After another kick from Marco, the boy wheezed for two full minutes. I sighed. "David, I grow weary. Just tell me if you have fucked her."

"Wait, are you talking about Francesca?"

Marco lifted his leg to kick again, but David held up his hands. "Stop, stop. I'll tell you anything you want to know."

Finally. I bent and looked him in the eye. "Did. You. Fuck. My. Son's. Fiancée?"

My tone seemed to impart the gravity of the situation on David. His brows flew up and he started babbling. "I had no idea she was engaged. Really. I'm sorry. She never told me. I never would have slept with her if I'd known. Please, you have to believe me."

"How long, David?"

He licked his lips. "We've been seeing each other for seven months."

I rose and gestured to Marco, then put my hands on my hips. Seven months this *brutto figlio di puttana bastardo* had been putting his dick in her. *Cazzo*, what had Mancini been thinking, letting his incredibly hot daughter loose on the streets of Toronto?

Marco put some effort behind this kick and David curled up in a tiny ball, gasping. "Please, no more," he begged. "I think you broke a rib."

I exchanged an amused look with Marco. We both knew he'd been holding back. "Get him up," I ordered.

Marco and Benito each grabbed an arm and hoisted David to his feet. The boy moaned, his head hanging, so I snatched his hair and tilted his face up to meet mine. "Listen to me carefully. Forget she

exists. If she contacts you—today, tomorrow, a year from now, whenever—ignore her. If you don't I will peel the skin from your body while
you watch. Do you understand?"

He whimpered and I could smell the piss now staining his jeans.
Cristo santo, I wanted to go home. "Are we clear?" I repeated.

David wisely nodded. "Yes."

"Good." I stepped back and headed for the car. "Leave him."

I heard David drop to the ground as I opened the door. Marco and
Benito, both my second cousins, got in and we drove off, leaving David
to find his own way home. I rubbed my jaw and stared out the window.
Mancini had clearly let his daughter run wild. She'd probably slept with
a handful of men. Did I care? Even though we retained most of our
traditions in Siderno, the old way of insisting on a bride's virginity was
dying out. The bloody sheets ritual was practically archaic these days.

My wedding twenty years ago had adhered to all the traditions, the
things that were supposed to bring a couple good luck. Yet my bride
died after just five years of marriage, a young son left behind. There
hadn't been good luck. Only heartache and regret.

I hadn't loved Lucia. We'd both been young, the marriage arranged
as an alliance with the Lombardo 'ndrina. I thought she understood
her role as my wife, tolerating my long absences and the mistress I
kept in town. After all, these things were common in our world. Giulio
had been born after our first year of marriage and I always assumed
we'd have many more sons and daughters. How foolish I'd been. How
naive to think the violence of my world wouldn't extend to my family.

"You think Giulio's going to like her?" Marco asked. "He wasn't
happy you were coming here to select his bride."

"Giulio will marry whoever I tell him to marry." To be honest, I had
no idea of Giulio's taste in women. Even at eighteen, my son was secre-
tive—a trait he learned from me. But who wouldn't want Francesca
Mancini?

And it didn't matter. The marriage would forge a strong bond
between our families, as well as settle a debt. A win-win.

Marco glanced at me in the rear-view mirror. "Should we go back to
the hotel?"

"For a bit. But she's going to run, so we need to be ready." Mancini had given his daughters too much independence, clearly, with no discipline or consequences. The manner in which Francesca had spoken to her father and to me meant she didn't know her place. I almost envied my son for his task of bringing her to heel.

I liked women with spirit. They were much more fun to fuck, and having a strong woman bend to my will always got my dick hard.

Benito turned around. "You think she's going to run?"

A smile tugged at my lips. "Oh, you can bet on it. But we'll be waiting. Tell the pilot we leave today."

Francesca

LATER THAT AFTERNOON, I threw my makeup bag into a satchel. I couldn't bring much when I ran, but I would take my very favorite things, like the earrings Mama left me. A photo of me, Gia and Emma at CN Tower. The leggings that fit my legs and ass perfectly. And, of course, my passport and money.

"This is a bad idea," my sister, Emma, said. "How are you going to live?"

"Forget about that, how is she going to escape Papà and the guards?" Gia turned the page in her magazine, barely paying attention. "You'll never even reach the street, Frankie."

"Yes, I will."

Two years ago, I discovered the cameras didn't cover one sliver of the stone wall surrounding our house, so I chipped footholds into the stone, which allowed me to come and go as often as I dared. It was how I snuck out to lose my virginity to David last November.

My sisters didn't know this, however. That escape route was too dangerous for anyone but me.

Gia made a noise in her throat like she didn't believe me. "Papà's going to be totally pissed when you're caught."

Bag packed, I went and sat on the bed next to them. "I hate to leave you both, but I have to do this. I cannot marry some stranger and become a mafia wife, trapped at home with a zillion kids while my husband fucks a mistress on the side."

"The Ravazzanis are loaded," Gia said. "I Googled them. They live in a castle, Frankie. An honest to God *castle*. And the son is a total snack. I don't know what you're bitching about."

God, Gia was so spoiled. She had no idea how bad it could truly get for mafia wives. "Mama gave up her modeling career for Papà and she always regretted it. You don't remember her as well as I do, but I can't give up the chance at a normal life. Not for any amount of money. It's not worth it."

"I understand," Emma said, always the level-headed twin. "And I don't think you should agree. The man who came here, his father? They call him *il Diavolo*."

The Devil.

I could well believe it. No one rose to the top of the Calabrian mafia without being evil and terrifying.

Emma touched my hand. "I have a thousand dollars saved up in my room. Do you want it?"

I felt like crying. Again. I threw my arms around her. "I can't take your money, Emma. You might need it someday. But it's very kind of you to offer." I had five thousand plus some gold coins in my satchel. It wouldn't last long, but it would be enough to disappear. I hoped.

Next I hugged Gia, who embraced me almost reluctantly. "I'm just going to see you again in an hour or so when Papà's men drag you back inside," she said.

"Well, in case you don't, please give me a hug."

That got Gia's arms to tighten ever so slightly. "Good luck, Frankie."

"I love you both. Use these next two years to figure a way out. He won't marry you off before you're eighteen."

"He might," Emma said. "Gabriella Pizzuto's father arranged her marriage when she was only thirteen."

Gross. I stood and grabbed my satchel. "You can both come with me, you know."

Gia frowned. "That would only make it easier for us to be caught. Besides, they won't hurt us in retaliation."

I hoped that was true. Women and children were supposed to be off-limits in any mafia conflict, but I would never forgive myself if either of my sisters were harmed because of me. "Convince Papà to honor his word about allowing you each to go to college."

"Go," Emma urged. "It's dark enough now that you won't be seen."

She was right. I needed to get going. The guards were eating dinner for only another twenty minutes.

I looked at my phone on the dresser. Not taking it with me felt very strange, but it would be too easy to find me if I kept it. I needed to leave it behind, as I always did when I snuck out.

After opening the window, I took the rope I kept under my bed, secured it to the bedpost, and unrolled it over the windowsill. I tossed my satchel to the ground and then climbed down into the yard. My sisters watched me safely descend before pulling the rope back up. I blew them a kiss then sprinted for the trees. Papà had no idea David existed, so I'd start there tonight. In the morning I would come up with a plan. Perhaps I'd go to Vancouver. Or Colorado. Somewhere I could hike and ski. I couldn't stand being cooped up inside, not since I'd accidentally locked myself in a closet as a girl.

It had taken four hours for someone to find me, and I was nearly catatonic with fear by then. After that I hated the indoors, and Mama used to let me follow her outside to her gardens. She grew vegetables and flowers, and it always seemed like everything around her was beautiful. Ever since then, I've loved dirt and rocks and fresh air.

First I had to escape the estate. Then I would need to stay hidden, change my name, and never contact my sisters. I couldn't allow Papà to find me, not until the threat had long passed. Still, I could do it. No, I *had* to do it. I had to leave all this behind and become my own person. Find happiness for myself, as my mother had urged me.

Never settle, Francesca. Be your own woman.

She said those words when I was a young girl, and I hadn't understood them at the time. But I did now...and I would heed her advice.

I followed the well-worn path to the wall and into the trees, where the cameras couldn't see. I chucked my satchel over the wall first, then

I used the footholds to climb up. At the top, I threw my legs over and held on with both hands so I could jump the rest of the way down.

Except fingers wrapped around my legs, startling me. They didn't let go.

I kicked—hard. But it did no good. The hands only tightened. "Stop it! Let me go."

"Not a chance, Francesca."

No, no, no. This couldn't be happening. How had Ravazzani found me here? It was *impossible*.

I struggled to get away but my arms weakened and I was quickly forced to let go of the wall. I fell into a hard, male chest, arms folding like steel bands around me. "Get your hands off me. I'm not going with you."

He didn't budge. "You are coming with me. Even if I must drug you to do it."

I gasped. "Drug me? Is that what you Italians do to unwilling women?"

His lips met the edge of my ear. "I could not say. There are no unwilling women in my life, Francesca."

Was that...sexual? My mind remained confused, but my body must have been on board because it went up in flames. I was close enough that I could smell him—lemon and mint and maybe green apple—and my nipples tightened. I shut my eyes, humiliated. Why was I having this reaction, especially when this man wanted to kidnap me and force me to marry his *son?*

Using all my strength, I bucked against him. "Get off me, you dick."

He gave a soft chuckle. "Drugs it is."

I tried to push away to see his face. "No, please. Don't—"

A sharp prick in the back of my neck was followed by a cold rush in my veins. "What was that? Are you seriously....?"

And the world went black.

CHAPTER THREE

Francesca

THE DREAM WOULDN'T LET GO. As I struggled to wake up, my brain felt as if it was swimming through molasses, sticky and thick. Where was I?

I heard murmurs and a rumbling underneath me. Was I in a car? My body felt heavy and my limbs were cement. I couldn't seem to open my eyes.

What was my problem?

Then I remembered. The wall, Ravazzani, the needle. Shit! He drugged me. That *asshole*.

I concentrated on my breathing and willed the drugs out of my system. I needed to fight whatever was happening to me.

"Good. You are awake."

I would have started if I'd been capable of moving my limbs. Was he spying on me while I slept? Just my luck to get kidnapped by a murderer *and* a creeper. Great.

I was on a mattress, the sheets crisp and cool beneath me. "You...kidnapped...me," I forced out. "And...drugged me."

Large fingers brushed the hair off my face. "I retrieved my son's fiancée by any means necessary. Let that be a warning to you."

A tiny shiver went through me. None of this made sense. Ravazzani could choose any woman to marry his son, and most would probably come willingly. "Why...me?"

"Don't you know that you and your sisters are legendary? Your mother was very beautiful and famous. Tales of her daughters have been spread across the globe."

I swallowed against a dry throat. My mother hadn't wanted this for me, for any of her daughters. *Have your own life, Frankie, and never give it up for any man.*

I knew I looked like her. Everyone told me as much and I had seen enough of her modeling photos online to notice the resemblance. Still, that wasn't a good enough reason for ruining my life.

Blinking, I finally pried open my lids. Ravazzani's gorgeous face filled my vision, his lips twisted into a smug smile as if I amused him. As if my resistance was nothing but a joke. I held his gaze steadily. "I will never marry your son."

The smile dropped instantly. "Never is a long time, Francesca, and don't forget you are at my mercy. You'd be wise not to make an enemy of me."

The threat rolled so easily off his tongue, and I didn't doubt him for a single second. Even still, I would not bend. He could try to break me, try to force me into a marriage I didn't want, but I would never stop resisting. "What will you do, threaten to shoot me? Torture me?"

"That depends on you, *monella*. Because if you refuse, I will consider the debt unsettled. I'll be forced to retaliate against your family. Is this what you want?"

Brat. I knew that word, one I had been called before by Papà's men. "You won't hurt my sisters."

A dark brown brow shot up. "No?"

We stared at each other, and I tried to see inside his head, to figure out if he was bluffing. I couldn't tell. The man was too good at concealing his thoughts. But even if he promised not to hurt Emma and Gia, he might kill Papà. "What does your wife think of you kidnapping a woman to marry your son?"

"My wife died many years ago."

A lump settled in my stomach. Had he killed her? Or had she been killed by a rival family? The mafia was violent and cruel, which was why my mother tried to protect us from it. "I'm sorry," I murmured.

Avoiding my eye, he pushed to his feet and straightened his cuffs. "It was a long time ago. Giulio is my only son, which is why he will have the best wife, the daughter of the famous Sophia Romano Mancini. A woman to make all other men envious."

"And if I won't marry him?"

"Do not make me answer that, Francesca." He strode to the door. "Two hours before we land. You should sleep."

He had a lot to learn about kidnapping if he thought I could possibly sleep right now. "I need a bathroom and my satchel."

"Through there," he pointed to a small door in the rear of the bedroom. "I'll have the hostess bring in a tray. I'm sure you are hungry."

I wasn't about to thank him, so I repeated, "And my satchel."

"You won't have your things returned until I find you cooperative."

I glared at him and tried to burn holes in his skin with my eyes. "There are people who will be worried about me. I need to somehow let them know I'm okay."

"Do you mean David?" he sneered, sending a bolt of cold fear through me. "He's not worried, Francesca. You no longer matter to him."

"Oh, my God. Did you kill him?"

He had the gall to look down his nose at me. "You watch too much American television. He is alive and well—for now—but you will not see him again." At the door, he paused and pinned me with a dark stare that scared me down to my toes. There was no feeling there, no sympathy. Just a man always used to getting his way. "Oh, and do not bother looking for a weapon. I made certain you won't find one."

I waited until he disappeared before ignoring his advice. I jumped off the bed and started searching. There had to be something in the bedroom or bathroom to defend myself with once we landed. Papà had reluctantly let us take self-defense classes, and the instructor said many ordinary objects could be used as a weapon.

The bathroom yielded nothing. The medicine cabinet was empty and the shower contained only plastic bottles. I quickly used the facilities and washed my face, then found that a tray was waiting for me on the bed in the other room. I dug in, knowing a hunger strike would only weaken me, and I had to keep up my strength to fight when we landed. I hardly tasted the food, though, my haste and fear overriding everything else at the moment. Unfortunately, the silverware was plastic, as was the wine glass and water bottle.

I kept looking. The desk contained nothing but blank paper, while the nightstand just had condoms. Extra large, naturally. Disgusted, I slammed the drawer shut and then dropped down to check under the bed.

Tucked into the carpet along the wall, I spotted it. A pen. I snatched it up and slipped it into the pocket of my jeans.

As a weapon, it wasn't much but I just had to wait for the right opportunity to use it.

Fausto

I HEARD the bedroom door open and my body went on alert. I didn't want to admit it, but I had been listening for any sound of her back there. Eager, like a schoolboy. I shook my head, disgusted with myself. Even if I weren't too old for her, she was engaged to my son.

I needed to pull my head out of my ass.

All my men turned to watch as she picked her way to an empty seat, her tits bouncing with each step. Long legs and shapely hips, with waves of blond hair that reached down her back, and a face that could make angels weep. *Dio*, she was hot.

When I looked away, I found Marco smirking at me. Had he read me so easily? When my father died and I became *capobastone* ten years ago, I appointed my cousin my right-hand. In fact, there was no one I trusted more. We'd grown up together, killed together, and risen through the 'ndrina ranks together.

But that didn't mean he had the right to smirk at me.

"You have something to say to your capo?" I asked him.

He didn't appear chastised in the least. "Are you going to shoot me if I say it?"

"Probably, once we are on the ground."

Marco held up his hands and remained silent. I went back to my phone, to the emails and notes I was reviewing. These were for the legal businesses, the ones I used as a public front for my family's wealth. My cousin, Toni, handled most of the Ravazzani corporation for me, but I kept involved. After all, I had to provide answers if the Guardia di Finanza paid me a visit.

Earlier, I texted Giulio to ensure he remained home tonight. I wanted him to meet Francesca as soon as we arrived. The sooner the two of them met, the sooner she would accept the marriage. In the meantime, Giulio could look after her well being, acclimate her to life in Siderno.

Though my son was only eighteen, I needed him settled and married. The time had come for Giulio to fulfill his role as my heir, which meant producing heirs of his own. I was an only child, as was my son. Therefore, until I had grandsons, the future of the Ravazzani 'ndrina would remain at risk.

That brought my thoughts back to Francesca, who was staring out the window at the night sky. Was she on the pill? I'd need to inform Giulio about her former boyfriend and the possibility she might be carrying another man's child. Best to wait until she bleeds before the wedding.

Her gaze met mine in the window's reflection but she did not cower. I liked that about her. Most women feared me, or at least my reputation. Francesca didn't seem to have that problem. In fact, she showed more spirit than most had dared in the last ten years. Would she show that same spirit in bed?

I had to stop. These thoughts weren't productive and I could not afford the distraction. Besides, even if she weren't marrying my son, she was too young. I had a mistress already, one who gave me no hassle whatsoever, and I wasn't interested in replacing her.

Resolved to ignoring Francesca, I returned to my phone. For the rest of the flight, Marco and I talked business, going over all that needed my attention after this trip. The *crimine* in San Luca was coming up in two months, where all the leaders gathered every year to discuss our operations. Even the Toronto capos, like Mancini, would attend. This meant that profits needed to be up, all our debts collected. We would need to pull some men off other jobs to clean up the 'ndrina books.

I rubbed the back of my neck, exhaustion pulling at me. I closed my eyes, but I couldn't relax on planes or in hotels. It was why I rarely left the *castello* in Siderno. At least there I was safe.

"You should sleep in the back," Marco said. "Now that she is awake."

"We are close. I'll wait until I'm home."

"Too bad. I bet the sheets smell like her."

"Fuck you."

Marco chuckled. "You think Giulio can handle her?"

I cracked one eye. "Are you saying he is soft?"

"No, but he's not like you. He doesn't have them eating out of the palm of his hand. Never seen a meaner bastard get more pussy than you."

I had a temper, for sure. Giulio was more even-tempered, like his mother. "She will come around," I said about Francesca.

The pilot announced our landing. A silent Francesca put on her seatbelt as I secured my own. Her quiet demeanor bothered me. Shouldn't she be yelling and panicking right now? Throwing something at my head? Trying to overpower the pilot? The instinct that had kept me alive for nearly thirty-nine years screamed inside me, telling me to be on my toes around her. She was up to something.

I smothered a grin. Whatever she planned, I would be ready. She didn't stand a chance.

Minutes later, we touched down. As I descended the steps to the ground, I made certain Francesca was directly behind me with Marco on her tail. My car was waiting, so I clasped her arm to pull her toward it—and felt a sharp pain in my hand.

"Cazzo!" I hissed. She'd stabbed me with a pen, the point now embedded in my flesh. I snarled and ripped the thing out of my skin, tossing it to the ground. That *stranza*.

Francesca darted off the second she had the chance but she was no match for Marco, who still jogged daily. I hadn't even finished cleaning up the blood on my hand before she was dragged back to my car.

"Help!" she shouted to the crew I employed at the private air strip. "Help! I'm being kidnapped."

My men snickered. No one in a fifty-mile radius would aid a person complaining of a kidnapping here. They all knew better. I jerked open the rear door of the car. "Get the fuck inside, Francesca."

I walked around to the other side, fury boiling inside me until I nearly choked on it. She had embarrassed me in front of my men. Drawn my blood and made me look weak.

She would pay for this when we arrived home.

She fought Marco, but it was in vain. Soon she was pushed inside next to me and the car sped off. "I won't apologize," she said, like a petulant child.

For once, I didn't try to appear civilized. Instead, I let her see the darkness I normally kept hidden. "Good, because I am looking forward to punishing you."

She swallowed and focused on the scenery. Fifteen minutes later, we arrived at my home, Castello di Ravazzani. I loved every bit of the estate —the olive groves, vineyards, farmland and pasture—but I couldn't appreciate any of it at the moment. And this only increased my fury.

When the car stopped in front of the stone entry, I didn't move. "Leave us," I told Marco and my driver. The doors closed and Francesca jumped, a frightened little rabbit. I angled toward her slightly. "Do you know my favorite part of owning a castle?"

"No," she said, her voice breaking.

"Not even a guess?"

"The turrets?"

Smirking, I got out and came around to her side. Once I pulled her from the car, I leaned down. "My favorite part of this castle is the dungeon."

She gasped. My patience thin, I didn't give her a chance to run. Instead, I hauled her over my shoulder and started walking toward the back entrance that led below ground.

She instantly began thrashing, her legs kicking frantically. "Put me down! Stop, please."

I ignored her and kept going.

"No, please. I can't go into a dungeon. Don't take me down there. Please, Signore Ravazzani."

Signore? That was new.

But I was mad, beyond rational thought. We used the dungeon for business, though I preferred not to kill people on my land. It made too much of a mess. Francesca could stew in one of the dank cells for a few hours, then she might be more amenable to my hospitality.

By the time I threw open the heavy door, she was weeping. Good. Perhaps this would help her learn her place.

"Please, signore. I can't... You cannot put me down here."

The soles of my shoes scratched against the old stone as I descended. Hopelessness rattled off the walls, while blood and despair hung in the air—two familiar scents that never failed to please me. I had done terrible things in this place, and my son would do countless more. The legacy of the Ravazzani 'ndrina would continue here through fear and intimidation, through wrath and torture.

Grabbing a ring of keys off the peg by the door, I strode to the nearest cell. The iron bars were impossible to escape, though many had tried. Chains were embedded into the wall, but I didn't think those were necessary with her. Not yet, at least.

I set her on her feet. Tears tracked her cheeks and her eyes were wild as she clutched at my jacket. "Please. Don't do this. I will literally freak out."

This generation. So damn dramatic.

I shook her off and stepped back, my intention clear. A capo never changed an order once it was made. We never showed weakness or remorse. I would gain the upper hand with this woman and she would fall in line.

I stepped outside the cell and swung the heavy metal door shut before she could slip through it. When it closed, she shook her head, panic causing her to shake. She clutched the iron bars. "Please, signore. Don't do this. I'll do whatever you want. I'll be good."

The words made my dick twitch as I imagined her on her knees being *very* good for me.

Minchia! There had to be a special circle of Hell for a man who had impure thoughts about his son's fiancée.

With a furious twist of my wrist, I locked the door with the old key. Above ground, we may have gone high tech but medieval worked perfectly well down here. "Perhaps this will teach you who holds the power in this house, *piccola monella.*"

She rattled the bars with a pained cry and for a brief moment I reconsidered, something which I almost never did.

A capo cannot show weakness.

My father had drilled this into my head for years, almost from birth. It was in our blood, our history. After all, the word "'ndrina" was derived from the Greek, meaning "man who does not bend."

Which meant there would be no mercy, not even for her.

I spun and started for the exit. "Enjoy your stay."

CHAPTER FOUR

Francesca

I SCREAMED until my throat ached, raw from the strain. It made no difference. The door remained closed, darkness all around me. I was locked in and no one was coming to save me. *Oh God.* I couldn't survive it.

My throat was dry and my lungs burned. This was my worst nightmare. Caged in below ground, where no one would find me. Was there even air down here? Chest burning, I fell to my knees. How long would it take to suffocate? A few hours?

I could feel hysteria edging out the plain old panic in my mind. The therapist I saw for my claustrophobia had said to breathe and to count to one hundred, that remaining calm was the key.

I closed my eyes and began to count.

I tried to focus on the numbers, on the rate of my breathing, but the musty air reminded me of where I was, of who had imprisoned me. How many men had died in these walls? Has Ravazzani killed anyone here?

Of course he has, Frankie. He is the capo of one of the most legendary mafia clans in Italy.

Were there ghosts in this dungeon?

Oh, fuck. I curled my hands into my palms, nails digging deep into the flesh. It stung but I welcomed the pain because it reminded me that I was still alive. I wasn't dead yet. He would retrieve me eventually. I had to marry his son, after all.

Bitterness filled my mouth. By the time they let me out of here, my mind will probably have snapped. I'll be stark raving mad by then. I gave a hollow laugh. Maybe then he would send me back to Toronto, declare me too unfit to wed the precious Ravazzani heir.

Or maybe he would just kill me.

I rocked back and forth and tried not to think about that. How has this become my life? Two days ago I was an eighteen-year-old woman with a boyfriend on her way to a prestigious college. I planned to study botany. Something with plants and science where I could be outdoors. Now I was locked in a dungeon in Italy, being forced to marry some mafia prince I didn't want.

Tiny claws skittered across the stone and I froze. Oh, my God. What was that? A mouse? No, it sounded big, more like a rat. I curled up as tight as I could, holding my shaking knees to my chest. I hoped Ravazzani found my rat-eaten corpse. It would serve him right, the asshole.

My brain must have checked out at that point, because I don't remember anything else until strong arms lifted me off the ground. A warm muscled chest met the side of my face and I didn't fight. I couldn't. I clung to my rescuer, desperate for escape.

"I am so sorry, signorina."

The voice was new, one I didn't recognize, but I didn't care. Someone had come to save me, thank sweet baby Jesus. *And it wasn't Fausto Ravazzani.*

He began carrying me up the stairs. "My father can be a real bastard sometimes." The words were spoken quietly, as if he were speaking to himself.

"You are Giulio." I hiccuped into the rough skin of his throat, tears still leaking from my eyes.

"I am. You must be Francesca Mancini."

I nodded and tried to burrow closer into him, desperate to purge the lingering cold from my bones. "Th-thank you for rescuing me."

"You never should have been down there in the first place. I wouldn't wish that on my worst enemy."

"Your father...."

"Has a temper. And you stabbed him with a pen. Not that I am excusing his behavior."

We reached the top of the stairs and the wide expanse of stars stretched overhead in the dark sky. The knot in my chest loosened and I dragged in my first real deep breath since getting off the plane. I could smell dirt and grass, a balm to my ragged nerves.

You're okay. You aren't locked in any more.

"You can put me down," I told him through my chattering teeth. "I can walk."

"Forgive me if I don't believe you. You were practically catatonic when I found you a few moments ago."

I was? I sighed and rested my head on my arm. "I don't do well in small spaces."

Giulio cursed in Italian. "I apologize, Francesca. I would like to think he wouldn't have put you there had he known...."

The implication was clear—that Fausto Ravazzani was no stranger to cruelty. That he would gladly use a person's weakness against them. Jesus, what a prize.

Before I could comment, we entered the castle. A small room led into a kitchen, which was surprisingly modern for a place with an actual dungeon.

"I'll have Zia bring up hot tea," Giulio said as he continued into the house. "That's my aunt. She lives with us and does most of the cooking."

Calming down, I began to look around—curious about this different type of prison. The contrast with the dungeon was startling. What I could see was light and airy with gleaming wood accents and light plaster walls. Huge oval windows were framed with tasteful draperies and tile covered the floor. It was even nicer than our home in Toronto.

Surprisingly, I didn't see any security cameras. That was information I stored away for future use.

"This is my wing of the house," Giulio said. "My father stays on the other side."

Thank God. I had no desire to see Fausto Ravazzani ever again.

Giulio carried me past several rooms, including a study with shelves of books and a music room. He paused in the middle of the corridor. "That is my room, the large door at the end. This one here is your room."

The room was bigger than I expected, with a king-sized bed that had an ornate metal headboard. An antique chaise longue and vintage dressing table made up the other side. It was both feminine yet classic and I couldn't help but admire it.

As much as one can admire a prison.

Giulio continued through the room to a small bathroom. The size of the room quickened my heartbeat again, so I took a deep breath as he set me on the tile countertop. I was out of the dungeon and never, ever going back.

Giulio stepped away and thrust his hands into his pockets. Messy dark brown hair fell across his forehead effortlessly, a look that actors and rock stars probably paid a stylist a shit ton of money for. He had his dad's jaw and eyes, but his face was longer. More elegant. Whereas Ravazzani was brutally handsome, Giulio was refined and gorgeous. And his body was rangy and thin, not yet filled out with the strength of his father. Various tattoos ran along his forearms. Gia was right—Giulio was a total snack.

"Are you a model?" I blurted, only half-joking.

The side of his mouth hitched. "I could ask you the same, Francesca Mancini. After all, modeling is in your blood and I am told you look like your mother."

"I tried once," I said with a shrug. "I sent photos to a modeling agency in Toronto but they told me my boobs were too big."

Giulio smiled and kept his eyes on my face instead of checking out my chest like most guys. "It is their loss." He shifted on his feet, looking increasingly uncomfortable. "I should let you shower. You must be exhausted." He turned for the door.

This couldn't be it. Wasn't there more to discuss, like how I didn't want to marry him? "Giulio, wait!" When he paused, I said, "Are you okay with this? Us, getting married, I mean. Wouldn't you rather choose your own bride instead of marrying some random?"

His eyes were flat and resigned, hardly the excitement of a man about to be married. "It doesn't matter what I wish. It only matters what *he* wishes."

"That can't be true. You're his only son. We could help each other, tell him we don't suit. You could say that you don't find me attractive or I'm too bitchy. Anything."

"He won't believe me, and furthermore he wouldn't care. He never changes his mind once he decides something."

The walls felt like they were closing in on me and my palms began to sweat. Still, I had to try again. "Giulio, I don't want this. I want to go home, back to Toronto. I'm supposed to go to school in a few weeks."

"I'm sorry, Francesca."

I wanted to scream in frustration but my throat was too raw. "Frankie," I whispered, needing someone to call me by the name I'd heard all my life. I needed a reminder of home, of people who actually cared about me.

"*Cosa?*"

"Everyone calls me Frankie."

"Frankie," he said quietly, his gaze full of pity. "Cheer up. At least we'll be miserable together."

After that cryptic statement, he left me alone in the bathroom.

Fausto

I WAITED at the bottom of the stairs as my son came down the steps. "My office. Now."

Giulio regarded me with a carefully guarded expression, but said nothing as he crossed the marble floor and went toward the other side of the castle. Clamping my jaw tightly, I followed and tried to get a hold of my anger instead of shouting at him.

Once in my office, he went directly to the liquor bottles. Marco was still there, sitting in one of the armchairs from our earlier meeting. No doubt he wanted to make sure I didn't kill Giulio for interfering tonight. I slammed the door behind me, rage burning every inch of my skin. "Sit the fuck down, Giulio."

He did, but not until he held almost a full glass of bourbon in his right hand. "You wanted to see me, Papà?"

I poured my own drink and went behind my desk, breathing deeply to keep my head reasonably clear. As the boss, I strove to be level-headed and calm in everything. It didn't always work, especially around Giulio. And Francesca, apparently. "Who is in charge of this family?"

"You," my son answered.

"And who is your capo?"

"You."

"Then will you explain why you went against my orders and released Francesca from the cell?"

He took a drink before answering me. "She is my fiancée. It's not right for her to be locked up in the dark the minute she arrives."

"I decide what is right in this family, Giulio. Me—not you." I held up my injured hand. "She stabbed me with a pen in front of the men. A few hours down there wouldn't have hurt her."

He shook his head. "You didn't see her, Papà. I think she's afraid of the dark or claustrophobic. She was nearly catatonic when I found her."

I ignored the pang in my chest that might have been guilt. I had to. I couldn't afford weakness. So, was this Giulio's attempt to play the hero? To make me appear the villain?

You are the villain. And she should prefer him to you, stronzo.

I don't know why that bothered me so much. I wanted them to like each other, to find happiness in their marriage. Perhaps they would have good fortune together, more than Lucia and I ever did. And I needed grandsons. Dio, I was losing my mind.

I downed my drink and let the burn alleviate my anger. "I'm glad you helped her, then. No doubt she was grateful to you, which pleases me."

Giulio frowned, eyes so like mine turning suspicious. "I didn't rescue her to earn her gratitude, but now I am wondering if that's why you put her in the dungeon. So that she'll not fight me."

I hadn't been so crafty, but good he thought me capable of it. "She will not fight you. Still, I'll give you a few weeks to get to know one another before we host the wedding."

"I'm surprised you are waiting."

I cleared my throat, knowing the news must be shared but unsure how he would respond. "She had a boyfriend in Toronto."

Giulio sipped his drink, not showing any outward reaction to the news. "And?"

"And she's not a virgin. It would be wise to ensure she isn't carrying another man's child before you marry her, no?"

"Are you willing to let me marry a woman who isn't pure?"

"It's not ideal, but she is beautiful and spirited. Her mother was one of the most famous women in Italy. Francesca will make you an excellent wife. And this settles the debt with Mancini."

"And ensures stronger ties between Siderno and Toronto, should the Canadians ever want to break free."

I smiled at him, pleased. "Correct. The brotherhood first, *figlio mio*. Always. One day you will sit in this chair and issue the orders, as all the Ravazzani men have done. We serve our 'ndrina brothers above all else."

"I know, Papà. I know."

I tapped my fingers on the desk while I studied him. "I'll tell Gratteri you need lighter responsibilities in the next three weeks. This will allow you to ease Francesca into her new role."

He sat up straighter. "That's not necessary. We're working on opening the new nightclub, so I'll be out at night but home during the day. I'll spend time with Frankie then."

"Frankie?"

"It's what everyone calls her. I assumed you knew."

No, she hadn't told me. Between the drugs, the flight and the stabbing, there hadn't been much time for conversation. But then she'd somehow found time to tell my son.

I cleared my throat. "Good. You're excused." I motioned toward the door.

After he left, I leaned back in my chair. "He took that well, considering."

"He is loyal," Marco said. "A dutiful son."

Yes, he was. I stroked my jaw. "It's better that she likes him."

"It sounds as if you are convincing yourself. Are you feeling guilty?"

I was, but I would never admit it. "You are my oldest and closest friend, my family, but even that has its limits."

"No, it doesn't. I'm the only one who will put up with your moods. By the way, Mancini has apologized for letting her escape. Said he's dealt with the security on that part of his wall."

I grunted and flexed my injured hand. Mancini had underestimated Francesca, something I would never do again, now that I knew what she was capable of. "Good. Maybe he'll keep better watch over the other two daughters."

"He also demanded to attend the wedding, whenever it takes place."

Che palle. Mancini was not the one who made demands in our relationship. "I'll consider it."

"He is the girl's father, Rav. No father would like to be kept from his daughter's wedding."

I glared at my cousin. "You have work to do, no?" We had hundreds of operations to oversee, stretching from Siderno to Milan, Sao Paulo to Montreal. We supplied more cocaine and heroin to Europe and the United States than just about anyone else. Marco was instrumental in much of it.

"Not tonight," he said, rising. "I am staying in to watch a film with Maria."

Marco's marriage had been happier than mine, as he'd actually fallen in love with his wife. Their three sons were already powerful members of the Ravazzani 'ndrina. I tried to tell myself I wasn't envious, but that was a lie. "I keep telling you to find a *mantenuta*. Less work than a wife."

"Not necessary. I'll leave the mistresses to you, *cugino*."

"It's not healthy for a Calabrian man to stay faithful to his wife for so many years. Your balls will shrivel up and fall off."

He laughed on his way to the door. "Maria would cut them off herself if I ever kept a *mantenuta*. Good night, Rav."

I shook my head and looked at my empty glass as I considered the rest of my evening. Anger and guilt roiled in my gut, my body tired but pulled taut, like a wire. Sleep would not come anytime soon.

There was only one thing to do. I picked up my phone and scrolled through my contacts. When I found the name I wanted, I started typing.

FIFTEEN MINUTES. BE READY TO GET FUCKED HARD.

CHAPTER FIVE

Francesca

LIGHT FILTERED INTO THE ROOM, streaks of blinding sunshine that roused me from a fitful sleep. I could barely bring myself to open my eyes.

All night I had tossed and turned, convinced the lock on my door would mean nothing to anyone who wanted to enter. Namely, someone with bright blue eyes and a nasty disposition who liked to kidnap and drug young women. The only way I'd been able to relax was knowing Giulio slept a few doors away.

I rolled onto my back and studied the plaster ceiling. If I were going to find a way out of this, I couldn't stay in bed or hide in this room. I had to get out and explore, look for weaknesses. Try to come up with a plan to escape. Even if Giulio had resigned himself to this marriage, I certainly hadn't.

Thankfully, the bathroom had been stocked with every toiletry I might possibly need, mostly high-end Italian brands we couldn't get in Canada. The closet and wardrobe were full of clothes, from yoga pants to designer dresses. Even La Perla bras and panties, though I don't know why they bothered with such sexy undergarments. No one here would see them.

I rose and dressed for comfort, choosing jeans and a t-shirt. The jeans were a perfect fit, though the shirt was a bit tight across my breasts. I decided to leave it on. Maybe my boobs might distract some of the guards from my escape efforts.

After I was ready, I slipped into the corridor. The house was quiet. Giulio's door was closed, but I remembered the way to the kitchen so I started downstairs. Hopefully Ravazzani slept late like his son.

The smell of freshly baked bread made my mouth water. In the kitchen, I found Zia taking something out of the oven. She'd brought me tea last night and I instantly liked her. An older woman with gray-ish-brown hair, she was Ravazzani's father's sister, and had lived in the castle ever since her husband and son were killed years ago. Unfortunately, she didn't speak much English.

"Hello," I said as I walked in.

She smiled at me and held up the tray. "Ciao, bella. Caffè?"

I sat on a stool at the island. "Sì. Thank you."

Soon she set a cup of espresso in front of me along with a basket of croissant-like things. "*Mangia*, bella. *Cornetti.*"

I couldn't resist a pastry, especially a *warm* pastry. I might be a pris-oner, but I wasn't dead.

I was enjoying my third one when Giulio came in, fully dressed and hair styled, looking like a movie star. He kissed Zia's cheeks and then reached for a pastry. "Buongiorno, Frankie. How did you sleep?"

"Like I'd been kidnapped from my home and brought to a foreign country."

"Sounds about right," he said with a half smile. "I'll take you around the estate today. We can even sample some wine and grappa, if you'd like."

"There are vineyards here?"

Giulio smiled at me. "Vineyards, olive groves, animals. Our soppressata is second to none. You'll love it."

"I'd rather go home."

"Come on. You don't want to stay inside all day."

True, plus a tour would help me learn the property. "Okay."

Heels on the tile caught my attention. I looked over to see a tall brown-haired woman stride into the kitchen like she belonged there. She was beautiful and thin, her tiny silver dress showing off a figure any model would kill for. The heels made her legs look even longer. Who in the hell was she?

"Good morning, Zia. Giulio. I just wanted to take one of Zia's pastries on my way out." Her accent wasn't Italian, but I couldn't place it. Eastern European, maybe?

Zia gave the woman a tight smile, but Giulio was slightly more welcoming. "Buongiorno, Katarzyna."

The woman plucked a pastry out of the basket on the island then cocked her head at me. "You must be the fiancée."

"I'm Frankie."

"I suppose we'll be seeing a lot of each other, then."

From the stove, Zia made a noise in her throat that sounded disapproving. Giulio put down his espresso cup. "Our driver will take you anywhere you want to go, Katarzyna."

"I'm aware, Giulio. This isn't my first time." She rolled her eyes, though a smirk remained on her face. Strolling back the way she came, she looked over her shoulder. "Thanks, Zia. Your pastries are the bomb."

When the three of them were alone again, the silence was oppressive. Zia looked murderous and Giulio appeared embarrassed. I couldn't figure out why, but a sinking feeling in my stomach suggested I might. Zia crossed herself and muttered in Italian. Giulio answered her but I didn't understand any of it.

"Who was that woman?" I asked.

Giulio sighed. "Katarzyna is my father's current mantenuta. Do you know what that means?"

I did. Kept woman.

That woman was Ravazzani's mistress. And she had...slept here last night. In his house.

I didn't care that he had a fuck toy. I was just surprised at seeing her this morning. Yes, the hollow feeling in my stomach was definitely surprise.

"Oh. She seems...." I couldn't think of anything to say. "Comfortable here," I finished.

"She's not terrible," Giulio confirmed. "But I never interfere in my father's personal life. Don't worry, she won't last long. They never do."

They didn't? It seemed Ravazzani was even worse than I suspected.

"They never do, what?" a deep voice asked.

My body jolted as the devil himself walked into the kitchen, looking disturbingly sexy and annoyingly refreshed. And why wouldn't he be? He hadn't spent hours in a dungeon last night.

I studied him through my lashes, unable to help myself. His gray suit was all perfect crisp lines and luxurious fabric, and he wore a blue tie that complimented the color of his eyes. Hair wet, he'd obviously just come from the shower. Had Katarzyna been in there with him? Had he screwed her in the shower?

There are no unwilling women in my life, Francesca.

I had to stop thinking about him, stop noticing his looks. I didn't like the way the hairs on my arms stood up every time he walked into a room. An attraction to this horrible and dangerous man—the person who had locked me in a *dungeon,* for fuck's sake—was out of the question.

"*Niente*, Papà," Giulio said, his posture stiffer now that his father was in the room.

Ravazzani bent to kiss Zia's cheek. "Buongiorno, *nonnina*." His expression was soft and affectionate as he hugged her.

Zia smiled but hit his shoulder with her palm as she seemed to admonish him in rapid Italian.

Giulio leaned over to me. "He calls her granny all the time just to get her worked up."

I frowned. I didn't want to see this side of the elder Ravazzani, the one that teased his aunt, whom he obviously loved. I needed him to remain one-hundred percent cruel and heartless.

Ravazzani started to brew a cup of espresso, then he leaned against the counter and spoke to Giulio in Italian. The only word I caught was "blood." I wished they would speak slower. I knew some Italian, but not enough to keep up with this rapid pace.

I would definitely need to improve my language skills in the next few days to aid in my escape.

Giulio's face darkened, clearly unhappy with whatever his father was saying. But he nodded. "Sì, Papà."

"This pleases me," Ravazzani said in English, gesturing to Giulio and me. "The two of you will spend time together and get acquainted. It's more than most of us had before our weddings."

Then he said it again in Italian for Zia, who responded with something that made Ravazzani laugh—and my breath caught in my throat. The harsh lines of his face eased and his mouth curled, all manly charm and Italian beauty, and I felt a tug of arousal in my belly.

I needed to get a grip on myself. I could *not* be attracted to him.

"What did she say?" I asked, desperate to take my mind off his looks.

He sipped his espresso and studied me over the rim. "She said it was intentional, that my ugly face and surly disposition would have scared off any potential bride."

Well, I agreed with half of that description. "Or your dungeon," I couldn't help but add.

The mood in the room shifted instantly. Giulio didn't move, while Ravazzani pinned me with a cold stare that reminded me of a Toronto lake in the winter. I saw him flex his hand, which had a small bandage on it. "Did you enjoy your short stay in the cell, monella? Because I would be happy to escort you there again, should you give me a reason."

The thought of returning to that small damp place sent waves of terror along my spine, and my skin grew cold and clammy. I stared at him with all the loathing I felt in my soul.

"*Basta*, Papà," Giulio said, telling his father that was enough.

Ravazzani carried his cup and saucer out of the kitchen, departing without another word.

"You mustn't antagonize him like that," Giulio warned. "And definitely never in front of the men again."

"I am not here to play nice. I am here under duress, and I want to go home."

Giulio shook his head sadly. "We rarely get what we want in this life, Frankie. It's best you accept your fate now." Before I could ask him to explain, he held out his hand. "Let's go outside and explore, eh?"

After I thanked Zia for breakfast, Giulio and I went through the back door and into the morning sunshine. Somehow I would use today's outing to my advantage and figure out how to escape this nightmare.

THE ESTATE WAS nothing like I imagined.

Giulio was charming and funny, escorting me around the property and introducing me to the workers. We saw the famous black pigs, rare and prized in Italy, and tasted the prosciutto and culatello made from them. There were sheep, cows and goats who were milked to make cheese. Lemon, fig and chestnut trees dotted the hillside, but olive trees were predominant here. When Giulio let me taste some of the Ravazzani olive oil, the number of olive trees suddenly made sense. The oil was better than any I'd had in Canada, even the kind we imported from Italy.

I couldn't stop asking questions of the employees, and Giulio translated as necessary. The workers seemed proud of their connection to the Ravazzani family, many continuing in the footsteps of previous generations who had worked here. I wanted to ask if they knew their employer was a kidnapper who drugged and spied on women, but I suspected Giulio wouldn't translate it for me.

Our last stop was the vineyard, where vines stretched as far as the eye could see. The estate grew Gaglioppo and Greco bianco grapes, which they blended to make red and rosé wines. They also made *nigredo*, a grappa flavored with licorice—and I quickly discovered this was my very favorite thing on earth.

"Easy, signorina," Vincenzo, the vintner, said as I took another swallow. "The Ravazzani grappa is to be sipped."

"Canadians are quickly becoming like Americans," Giulio teased, mimicking someone guzzling a drink. "More, more, more."

"Stop dragging Canadians," I told him as I shoved his shoulder. "We are nicer than Italians."

Vincenzo chuckled, but shook his head. "You will not like how it tastes coming back up, signorina."

I waved that comment away. "I never throw up after drinking. We Mancinis are made of sterner stuff."

Vincenzo and Giulio exchanged an amused look. "No doubt you are, bella," Giulio said and held up the bottle. "Would you like another?"

"*Per favore*," I said, which only made Giulio laugh.

"Your Italian needs improvement."

"I know. Will you teach me?"

"Of course, but there is no rush."

There was, but I couldn't say as much. Giulio was resigned to our marriage, and who knew what he might do if I informed him of my plans to escape? He was becoming a friend, but not an ally. First and foremost, he was a Ravazzani.

Vincenzo left us and I decided to learn more about this man who seemed to fear his father but had saved me all the same. "What do you do in the 'Ndrangheta?"

Giulio choked on his grappa and coughed loudly. "Are you always so forward?"

"I apologize. It's just that you seem different from your father. I'm having a hard time seeing you as a hardened mobster."

He licked his lips and studied the glass in his hand. "It's all I have ever known. I was young when my mother died, and since then it has been Zia and my father, and the 'ndrina. I was inducted at fourteen. There's no other life for me."

"That sounds...sad."

The edge of his mouth hitched, making him appear like a younger version of his father. "Only someone from the outside would see it as such. Being the Ravazzani heir is a great privilege."

"It is—but only if you want it. If you want the same life as your father."

"I have no choice. And it is not a bad thing, being both feared and respected by everyone I meet. My father's reputation is known by many."

"I can't imagine what it is like for a boy in our world. My sisters and I were sheltered from my father's business."

"As it should be," Giulio said. "What we do is men's business, though there are more and more women leading 'ndrine nowadays."

"There are?"

"Sì. In fact, I thought my father would arrange for me to marry the daughter of La Madrina, the head of the Melbourne 'ndrina. But then you came along."

Australia, wow. "Did you want to marry this other woman?"

"No, but that hardly matters. My role is to marry and have more Ravazzani boys to carry on our tradition."

"Not necessarily. Your father could remarry."

Giulio's expression said this topic had been broached and rejected. "He refuses. I think he carries around a lot of guilt over my mother's death."

Fausto Ravazzani, feeling guilt? I couldn't believe it. "Was she ill?"

"No, she was murdered."

I gasped, grabbing the edge of the wooden table as I swayed from surprise and too much grappa. "Shit, that's awful. I'm sorry, Giulio."

"Thank you. I barely remember her, but my memories are good ones."

"How did it happen?"

"She was running on the beach. A South American gang killed her and guards. It had to do with a deal my father made with their rivals."

"No wonder he feels guilty."

"Unfortunately, it is all too common in our world." Giulio heaved a sigh that sounded bone deep. "The only way out of this life is death, Frankie. Each of us knows that."

I finished my grappa while digesting this grim news. "Shouldn't you be trying to convince me to marry into your family?"

He lowered his voice to barely above a whisper. "I told you, there is no need for convincing. This is happening, whether we like it or not."

"I know my reasons for not wanting to marry you, but why don't you want to get married?"

"It doesn't matter, and we shouldn't discuss this here."

I glanced around us, but there was no one else in the old tasting room. Only the wine barrels could overhear us. "We're alone."

"No, we aren't. There is no privacy in the house or anywhere on the estate, Frankie. Never forget it."

"I don't see any cameras." My father's cameras were the clunky old-school type, that whirred as they moved.

"They are sophisticated. You won't see the cameras or listening devices unless my father wants you to."

My stomach sank as I considered my escape plans. Was there surveillance equipment in my bedroom? "At least you have the freedom to leave the estate."

"I wouldn't exactly call it freedom, but yes, I am able to leave." He poured us each more grappa. "I'll take you anywhere in Siderno you wish to go, yes?"

"Sure. How about the airport?"

He chuckled and toasted me with his glass. "You have a sense of humor, Frankie Mancini. I didn't expect that. You also have spunk, as the Americans call it, but I cannot decide if that is a good or bad thing."

"I'm hoping it's good because I don't know how to act any differently."

"That must be why my father reacts to you so strongly."

"It's because he hates me."

"No, he doesn't. You made him very angry last night, angrier than I've seen him in a long time. He was very worked up."

"Must be my special charm at work."

"It's weird. He is usually very polite with women."

"I find that hard to believe."

"No, I mean it. He charms them. Puts them at ease. Women love my father."

Of course they did. He was a gorgeous and powerful Italian man, and no doubt a beast in the bedroom. I remembered Katarzyna and her model-like perfection despite being in her late 20s or early 30s. Were all his girlfriends so beautiful?

"Your expression is strange," Giulio asked, his eyes trailing over my face. "What are you thinking about?"

I was tipsy but not drunk enough to confess my troubling thoughts regarding his father. I went with a partial truth instead. "I've barely thought of escaping today."

"That is good. We'll make a Calabrian out of you yet."

No, they wouldn't. I'd rather die than be a mafia wife. "I like you, Giulio." I shook my head sadly. "I don't want to, but I do."

"It will make it easier, Frankie. I'll be a good husband to you. And some day, this will all be ours."

"No offense, but I honestly hope you are wrong." I finished my grappa and swayed on my feet. "Whoa."

Giulio grinned. "I think it is time to go back."

"Do we have to? I hate being cooped up inside. It was so nice to be out with the plants and trees today."

"I'm afraid it is almost dinner time. My father will be expecting us."

"Your father." I made a dismissive sound in my throat. "He's already put me in the dungeon. What will he do next if he disapproves? String me up on the rack? Strap me to a dunking bench?"

Giulio was unamused, his mouth flat and serious. "You do not want to ever find out, bella. Come on. You need food to soak up all this grappa."

He took my arm and began leading me out of the tasting room. We said goodbye to Vincenzo and strolled along the dirt path to the castle. "I have decided that I love grappa," I declared as I clung to Giulio's arm. "And the estate isn't so bad."

"I am happy to hear it." He was humoring me.

"I will honestly miss it when I go back to Toronto."

"You've got to put an end to those thoughts. Unfortunately for both of us, Frankie, you are here to stay."

My stomach turned over. I ran behind a fig tree and threw up.

CHAPTER SIX

Fausto

I CAME into the kitchen the next morning at my usual time. My son was there with Zia, but Francesca was still absent. She'd been too ill from grappa to eat with us last evening and apparently was not yet awake.

I didn't like it.

Giulio and Francesca seemed happy yesterday in the tasting room. Unable to help myself, I'd watched the security footage, soaking in the way she smiled at him. Studying the curve of her lips when she laughed. It was clear she liked my son, and I told myself that was a good thing. A sign of their future together, a team working toward the common goal of the future success of the Ravazzani family.

I kissed Zia's cheeks and made a cup of espresso. Giulio was on his phone, scrolling through videos of some kind. He'd gone out last night for work and, from the looks of it, was only getting home. "Rough night?" I asked.

Out of respect, he put down his phone and gave me his full attention. "No. I was at the club until around three. Then we had a ship-ment to oversee. Everything is stored."

"Any problems?"

"None."

"You are just getting home now?"

A flush worked its way above his collar. "I was out with friends."

Getting laid, then. "Try to keep your other women away from your fiancée, at least until after the wedding."

"And not in this house," Zia said, pointing at Giulio. "Your father and his women are bad enough. I cannot take more."

I frowned and sipped my espresso. Zia hated that I brought my mistresses into the castello, but I had little choice. There have been many attempts on my life and, after what happened to Lucia, I learned to be more cautious. I was safe here.

Besides, I was the boss. If I wanted to fuck a woman in my own house, I would.

"I won't," Giulio told Zia. "I promise."

"Your fiancée is alive?" I asked. "Not too much grappa?"

"She was sleeping when I left last night. There couldn't have been much remaining in her system at that point."

"Good. Bring her to my office this morning."

Giulio searched my eyes as if trying to read my intentions, but he knew better than to question a direct order. "I'll fix her a tray and take it up."

I nodded, refreshed my caffè, and departed for my office. Marco would arrive soon with verbal updates on business matters. Until then, I would read the emails regarding the legitimate ventures, offering up opinions when warranted.

Truth be told, I liked the legitimate work better, the strategy and moving money around, but I was more suited to the extortion, drug-running, and gambling operations. Not everyone had the stomach for what needed to be done to run an organization like ours, but I did. Some days, I even relished the violence and chaos.

The sun was just rising over the vineyards outside my office window. The sight never failed to please me. All of this belonged to me, as it had belonged to five generations of Ravazzani men. And it would eventually belong to Giulio and his sons after him. Would they appreciate the sights and smells as much as I did? The rich tang of the earth and the slightly salty air from the ocean? I loved this property, this land that was in my bones. I would fight for it until my last breath. I'd murder, cheat, and steal to keep it, if necessary.

Briefly, I wondered about Giulio's *amante*. Who was he seeing? I trusted my son to keep the family's secrets, but not all women were trustworthy. I should learn her name and do a little digging. Better to worry over nothing than regret it later.

Thirty minutes later, a knock on my office door distracted me from my computer. "Enter."

A very annoyed-looking Francesca arrived with my son. She held herself stiffly, the circles under her eyes giving away her exhaustion. She wore a simple sundress and no shoes, her skin red from being outside yesterday. From now on, I'd tell Giulio to insist she wear sunscreen. The Italian sun was stronger than what she was used to in Canada.

I stood and slipped my hands into my trouser pockets. "Thank you, Giulio. You may go."

My son blinked, clearly not expecting to be dismissed, but it was time to deal with some practicalities of the pending marriage. As head of the family, these were my responsibilities to handle for him.

Francesca reached out to clutch his arm, preventing Giulio from leaving. "Can't he stay?"

For some reason, that pissed me off. As if she needed him to protect her from me. Didn't she know that my son would never dare to question or contradict me, no matter what I wished to do in this house?

"No," I snapped.

"I'm off to catch a few hours of sleep," Giulio told her. "I'll see you this afternoon." To me, he nodded once and walked out the door.

"Please." I gestured to the chairs before my desk. "Sit."

Lifting her chin, she lowered herself into the seat. I did the same and folded my hands as I regarded her. "Are you feeling better?"

"If you mean do I still feel like throwing up, then no. But I don't feel remotely human at the moment."

"Perhaps go easy on the grappa next time."

"Why? Wouldn't it make it easier to manipulate me if I were drunk?"

I steepled my fingers and rested them on my lower lip. "I can manipulate you drunk or sober, Francesca. It is your choice."

"God, you are the *worst*." She rubbed her temples, so aggrieved by my presence. It only made me want to rattle her more. "Get to the point, Ravazzani."

"*Suocero*," I corrected.

"What?"

"Father-in-law. You should practice how to say it."

"You know, on second thought the urge to vomit is suddenly back. I think I should go upstairs."

She started to rise out of her chair, but I held up a hand. "Do not move. We have a few things to discuss."

"Like?" She folded her arms across her chest, calling my attention to her tits. The dress pulled tight across them, creating deep, mesmerizing cleavage. She looked like one of those Hollywood pin-up girls from the 1940s.

"Like your wedding dress."

Going pale, she put a hand on her stomach and exhaled heavily. Perhaps her comment about vomiting once more had not been made in jest. I took the empty bin from under my desk and set it within her reach, then waited. She soon regained her color and narrowed her eyes on me. "I don't need a wedding dress."

I didn't bother correcting her. "I have called in a favor with a designer friend in Milan. She will fly in tomorrow with racks of dresses for you to choose from. Then you will be fitted and the dress will be ready in a few weeks' time."

"I won't choose one."

I lifted a shoulder like I didn't care. "Then I will choose one for you. Are you on the pill, Francesca?" I had seen her health reports so I knew the answer, but I still wanted her to tell me.

Her brows shot up and she clutched the armrests. "*What?* How is that any of your business?"

"Until you marry my son, everything about you is my business.

Answer the question."

"I had the shot two months ago. Would you like to know my latest pap smear results, too? How about my weight and bra size?"

That had my gaze dipping to her chest once more and I couldn't prevent the flare of heat from sparking in my groin. Fuck, how I longed to take her over my knee and spank her until she stopped acting like a brat. It would be fun to show her what I liked, teach her how to serve my every need. Break her until she craved my touch. My dick pulsed at the prospect, but I forced myself to lock those unwanted thoughts away. She belonged to Giulio.

"I'd suggest you put more respect in your tone when dealing with me," I warned her. "You do want your things back, no?"

She became very still, suspicion dawning in her chestnut-colored stare. "You are giving me my things?"

"I might consider it, if you stop fighting me."

"I'll pass, then."

I almost smiled. The girl had spirit, that was for certain. Confidence, too, the kind that came from experiencing sadness and death in your life. Like you knew you had faced the worst life had to offer and survived. I knew that feeling well.

"How about this?" I said. "I will give you the satchel if you choose a suitable wedding dress."

"Really?"

"I never go back on my word once a deal is made."

"Fine."

She answered too quickly and now I was the suspicious one. What was she planning? My friend Celestina would provide enough choices for Francesca to find a dress she liked. There would be no way around it. I held out my hands. "See? That was not so difficult."

"I want a phone."

"No."

"Why not?"

"First, because you haven't earned the privilege. Second, it isn't safe. If you need to make a call, Giulio or I can help you. Until you learn our rules and are willing to abide by them, it is too risky."

"I need to call my family."

"I will think about it."

Her nostrils flared and I could see how she struggled not to lash out. After a long second, she asked, "And how am I supposed to earn these privileges?"

"By doing what you are told. Stop fighting me and the marriage to my son. Accept your fate, Francesca."

Gracefully, she rose out of the chair. "I'd rather you kept your privileges. If that is all, capo?"

My title falling from her lips, even in sarcasm, twisted something dark and hot inside me, like the word unlocked a secret fetish I hadn't known until now. I wanted to hear her say it again, but from her knees, begging me to fuck her mouth. Or on her back while I rode her hard. I wanted her to breathe it in my ear and scream it as she came. I wanted it to be both pleasure and pain, the only word she remembered in the bedroom.

I stared at her, breathing hard, an erection growing in my trousers, all the while convinced I was losing my mind. Never had a woman gotten under my skin in such a fashion. This could not continue. I needed her settled with Giulio. She would never be mine.

The best thing I could do was to push the two of them together more often. Starting tonight.

"That is all," I said. "Enjoy your dinner in town later."

Her dark brown brows pinched but she didn't look at me. "Dinner in town?"

"With Giulio. I assume he told you, no?" Giulio hadn't mentioned it because I just decided on the outing, but she didn't need to know that.

"I can't believe you are trusting me off the estate."

Trust never even entered my mind. I had eyes and ears everywhere in Siderno and she wouldn't get far if she tried to escape. Someone would turn her in to me. The wrath of the 'Ndrangheta meant certain death, and not many would be stupid enough to risk their lives to help a stranger. I'd make sure Giulio took some of our guards, as well. "I don't need trust, Francesca, because you know who suffers if you disobey me."

"Me?"

"And your sisters."

Hate blazed in her gaze, her body nearly vibrating with the urge to shout at me, to scratch my eyes out. Anything to ease her suffering. But there would be no relief. I got what I wanted—always.

"You truly are the Devil."

I gave her a sinister smile, the one I reserved for those who cheated or lied to me. "Never forget it, piccola monella."

Marco walked into my office shortly after Francesca stormed out. My cousin did not appear happy, but his news would have to wait. I pointed at a chair. "Sit down. I have an errand for you."

"When? Now?"

"Giulio is taking Francesca to dinner in town tonight. I want you to go with them."

"Sure, I'll play chaperone. That's more exciting than spending time with my family."

I couldn't tell whether he was being sardonic or not. "Give them space. The idea is for them to get close." Even though the thought made my chest burn with an emotion I dared not name. All the more reason I must push them together—quickly. This girl had me contemplating very stupid ideas, and I could not afford to act on any of them.

"Have you informed Giulio of this?"

"No, but he'll do as he's told." I picked up my phone and texted him instructions. "There. He's sleeping but he'll see this later on."

"I hear he was up late dealing with a delivery from our friends down south."

"He told me there were no issues."

"There weren't...until later."

I smoothed my tie, taking a second to compose myself before hearing disturbing news. I was already on edge from my meeting with Francesca. "What does that mean?"

Marco sighed. "Gratteri called. He inventoried the packages today and thought we were light, even though the men at the drop said it was all accounted for when they left."

"How light?"

"Around four hundred grams."

I instantly did the math. "That's almost seventeen thousand Euros worth—and it's missing?"

"Sì."

"Who was the last to leave the storage site?"

"I'm told it was Giulio."

"*Cazzo*." I pounded my fist on the table.

"I know, but what would Giulio want with that much uncut cocaine? It doesn't make sense."

"He said he went out with friends after. Came in this morning as Zia served breakfast."

"Did he look high?"

"No. Certainly not four hundred grams worth."

Marco held up his palms. "Maybe he did go out and met a lot of friends. Maybe they partied all night."

Even so, I didn't like it. Giulio knew better than to take from the 'ndrina. I gave him everything he wanted. Our power and wealth meant no stealing required. And my son had never been into drugs. If so, I certainly would have heard about it. After his mother was killed, I kept a close eye on him, though I loosened my surveillance in the last three years as he took on more responsibilities. This had to be a mistake. "Tell Gratteri to count it again. I want every gram accounted for."

"He's already counted it three times, Rav."

"It's not a lot, but it looks sloppy. Worse, I cannot have Giulio's name associated with any irregularities in our operation."

"Agreed."

"Don't do anything, not until I can speak with Giulio. If he admits to taking the drugs, I'll inform Gratteri that Giulio was acting under my orders."

"No one will believe you need four hundred grams of coke."

"Maybe, but no one would dare question me."

"What will you do to Giulio if he admits it?"

I tapped my fingers on my desk. I never considered that discipline of this kind would be needed with my son. He'd been born and raised in our world, and he knew the consequences for transgressions. He'd even meted out quite a few himself over the last three or four years. The responsibility for punishment would fall on my shoulders...and I honestly didn't know what I would do. "Cristo. I'm not sure."

"Understandable, considering. Whatever happens, we'll keep it quiet."

"Yes, we fucking will—and the sooner he gets married, the better. Then he'll settle down and begin to fulfill his obligations as my heir."

Marco smirked. "I cannot picture you as *nonno*."

I couldn't see myself as a grandfather, either, but it didn't matter. "You won't be far behind me, not with Fabrizio's reputation." Marco's oldest son was sixteen and slept with anything with a pair of tits.

"Bite your tongue. I am not ready to be so old."

"Just wait. I'll be a nonno and still get more pussy than you."

"Go to hell." Marco rose out of his chair. "Let me know when the lovebirds are ready to go out."

The knot in my stomach twisted. "I will."

"Oh, and did you hear? D'Agostino died."

I leaned back in my chair and considered this news. D'Agostino had been the head of the Avellinos, a 'ndrina we'd warred with in the past. My father brokered peace with them when I was a boy, but not until after two of my uncles and six cousins had been killed.

Enzo, the eldest D'Agostino son, was known for his unpredictability. Some said he wasn't right in the head. This would require careful navigation. We had to get along without giving up any of our power, a balance that seemed more and more difficult these days.

"We'll have to arrange a meeting on neutral territory," I said. "Make it appear as if we're willing to work with them."

"Want me to set it up?"

"No. Wait until they contact us. The Avellinos need us more than we need them."

"That is certainly true. With our lock on the southern ports, only the Sicilians come close to doing our business."

"I'll let you know the time for tonight later."

"Are you going to ask Giulio about the coke before he leaves for dinner?"

I thought about it. I needed Francesca to fall for Giulio, to accept this marriage, which meant I needed him charming and happy. If we argued, the evening might be ruined for everyone. "I'll wait until the morning. Tell Gratteri I am looking into it. Let Giulio and his fiancée have fun tonight."

CHAPTER SEVEN

Francesca

EVEN IF I didn't want to admit it, I was excited to go out tonight. I told myself it was because I wanted to see Siderno, to look for possible escape routes. It was definitely that, but it was also the chance to get out of the castle. I hated being cooped up there, and a night in a fancy dress, at a fancy restaurant, sounded like heaven.

That was how far I'd fallen in just a few days.

Giulio was chatty during the drive into town, pointing out places and things, sharing funny stories about his childhood. The more I was around him, the less he seemed like a hardened gangster like his father. Giulio was thoughtful and smart, playful and entertaining—basically everything Fausto was not. If they didn't look so much alike, I wouldn't guess they were related.

At the restaurant, everyone fawned over us like we were Kate Middleton and Prince William. I supposed we were sort of royalty, considering Giulio's last name. We were seated in a private room, the table covered with silver and crystal. The place was cozy and dark, with exposed brick and soft lighting, and rows of wine bottles rested along the walls.

"*Benvenuti a L'Agriturismo,*" the host said when we sat down. Then he started speaking to me in rapid Italian. I looked at Giulio, helpless and embarrassed. It wasn't a feeling I liked.

"*Inglese,* per favore," Giulio said.

The other man nodded. "Do you have any food allergies, miss?"

"No, I don't." I ate just about anything and everything, a trait that used to make my father laugh. A pang of homesickness washed through me, hollowing out my stomach, but I pushed it aside. Papà had given me to Giulio. To Ravazzani and the 'Ndrangheta. I would never forgive him for it.

"*Va bene,*" the man said. "The chef is preparing a special meal for you both, using ingredients from the Ravazzani estate. *Buon appetito.*"

"Grazie, Stefano." Giulio placed his napkin in his lap then looked at me. "Have I told you how beautiful you look tonight?"

I smiled at him. "Only three times, but I am not complaining."

This eighteen-year-old guy was supposed to become my husband. We would be *married*. I couldn't picture it. Giulio was polite and complimentary, but he didn't seem attracted to me. Even weirder, I felt the same. There was no spark, no burning desire. Yet I would be expected to sleep with him, to bear his children. Stay faithful to him until the day I die, while living in the castle as the perfect mafia wife.

My mouth dried out, a scream echoing somewhere deep in my brain. I reached for my water glass and tried to stay calm. There was no need to panic yet. I still had time to find a way out.

"Are you all right?" he asked, brows pinched. "You went as white as this tablecloth for a second."

"I'm great. Never better."

"You really should learn how to speak Italian."

"I understand some, but not enough, especially when it's spoken quickly. My father speaks mostly English, and my mother died before she could teach us more than a few simple words and phrases. So you should feel free to teach me."

"I'd be happy to, though I like practicing my English with you." He grinned, looking so much like his father in that moment that I have to remind myself to breathe.

"Speaking of that, how do you and your father speak such good English?"

"English is spoken all over Italy, so you'll find most people can speak a bit of it. My father and I went to boarding school in Massachusetts, though."

My jaw dropped open. "What? That's wild."

"Yep. From the age of six to twelve."

I couldn't picture Ravazzani as a boy in school. I'd sooner believe he popped out of his mother's womb fully formed, fully evil.

The server entered with a bottle of the Ravazzani rosé. I held up my hand. "I think I'll stick with water, if you don't mind." I didn't need another night like the previous one, ever.

Giulio pressed his lips together, amused. "So tell him. *Acqua frizzante.*"

I look up at the waiter. "*Acqua frizzante,* per favore."

When we were alone, Giulio asked, "Are you feeling better?"

"Yes. I couldn't hold down food until noon." Oddly enough, I was now starving. "Zia seemed disappointed that her *cornetti* went uneaten."

"I had to work last night or else I would have been up."

I picked at a fingernail under the table. For some reason, I didn't want Giulio to think the worst of me. "I should apologize for getting so drunk. I'm sure I was a hot mess, so thank you for helping me."

When I woke up, my hair had been pulled back, my face cleaned, and I was dressed in a t-shirt three sizes too big. Two pain pills and water had been waiting on my bedside table. Best of all, my vomit-stained clothing was nowhere to be found, hopefully incinerated.

"You're welcome. You are a cute drunk. I don't think you stopped talking—between the bouts of vomiting, of course."

"Oh, my God." I dropped my face into my hands. "What did I say?"

"You told me about Toronto, about your sisters. David, who I have to assume was the boyfriend my father told me about. Oh, and you talked about my father. A lot."

My head snapped up, disbelief and horror warring inside me. "I did? About how much I hate him, no doubt." God, please let that be the case.

"It didn't sound entirely like hate. Fear, yes. But mostly fascination. You asked me many questions about him as a father, as a capo...as a man."

As a man? What did that mean?

Giulio wasn't finished, apparently. "You also were very curious about Katarzyna."

I wanted to crawl under the table. How mortifying. Giulio must have assumed I'm jealous, that I'm attracted to his father. Which I was...but reluctantly. Regardless of my out of control hormones, I certainly didn't want his son—my supposed future husband—to know as much. "Isn't everyone fascinated with Fausto Ravazzani?"

"Definitely, especially women. He's like the man from that film. You know, *The Godfather.*"

"Don Corleone?" The elder Ravazzani was ten times more handsome than Marlon Brando.

"No, the don reminds me of Uncle Toni. I meant the young Marlon Brando, back when he was young. Like from *Streetcar Named Desire.* That is more like my father, no?"

I didn't know the movie, so I couldn't say. Wanting to get off the topic of Fausto's looks, I asked, "Is Uncle Toni your mother's brother?"

"He is my father's cousin, but I call him Zio. Like Marco."

"You have a lot of relatives."

"The 'Ndrangheta is all about family. The only way in is to be related to the capo."

How had I not known this? "Really? In Toronto, not all my father's men were related to us."

"Allowances are made for 'ndrine outside of Italy. But we take blood ties very seriously here."

Hence why Ravazzani needed Giulio to start making babies. A group of waiters arrived then, sparing me the need to fret over my role in this patriarchal mafia nightmare. One poured the sparkling water, while the others arranged dishes on the table. The selections made my mouth water. There were three different pasta dishes, fried artichokes, steak with butter sauce, pork chops, bruschetta with ham and tomatoes, and fish soup. When we were alone, I gestured to the food. "Do they think we can seriously eat all this?"

"No. They want to impress us."

We started sampling dishes, and I could not believe how delicious every bite was. I moaned as I swallowed another bite of fettuccine with beef ragout. "This is the best thing I've ever had."

Giulio leaned in, like he was sharing a secret. "Zia's is better."

"Impossible."

He grinned and cut me a piece of his pork chop, putting it on my plate. "Try this. I think you'll love it."

"Wait, is this a Ravazzani pig?" I saw some yesterday on the estate and they were so adorable and sweet. While I wasn't a vegetarian, I felt bad for those little piglets.

"Frankie, you had no problem eating the steak or the beef ragout."

"Cows aren't as cute as piglets."

He shook his head, probably thinking I was ridiculous, and reached to take the piece off my plate. I stabbed his hand with my fork. "I didn't say you could have it, stronzo."

This caused him to throw his head back and laugh. "I see you are picking up more Italian."

"Only the helpful words." I ate the bite of cooked pork and it was delicious, damn it.

We split a tartufo for dessert and drank cappuccino. As much as I didn't want to be in Italy, I had to admit this had been a perfect meal. And I didn't hate my time with Giulio. What did that say about me? Was I giving in already?

The thought depressed me, but even more depressing was the thought of returning to the castle. My prison. I wasn't ready to face Ravazzani and his unforgiving eyes and lush, stern mouth. No doubt he would gloat over his victory of getting Giulio and I to go out together, never mind that he'd blackmailed me to do it.

Stronzo, indeed.

An idea occurred. "Where do you go for fun in Siderno?"

Giulio pursed his lips before taking a sip of espresso. "What are you thinking, Frankie?"

"I am thinking I don't want to go back yet. Sitting in the castle is lame. Let's go have some fun."

"I'm supposed to bring you straight home."

"Orders from your father, no doubt." I rolled my eyes. "Come on, Giulio. I'm sure there is some safe place where you can take me so we can live a little."

"Oh, sure. *Figurati!* Defy my father. You make it sound so easy."

"He won't mind if we are spending time together. That's all he wants anyway."

"True." He exhaled and checked his watch. "I'll take you to one of our nightclubs. No one will bother us there."

I put down my spoon. "I'm ready."

WE PULLED up to the club's front entrance. Marco, our driver for the evening, had been none too pleased about this stop, but we promised to only stay an hour. No doubt he'd already texted the capo to tattle on us, but I didn't care. The bass thumped in my chest as soon as I stepped out of the car. Yes, I needed this distraction.

Ignoring the long line out front, Giulio shook hands with the man at the door and then we were inside. The sound in here was louder, with bright lights flashing above a wide dance floor. Bodies were everywhere, young and beautiful Italians who weren't being forced into a marriage they didn't want. I longed to lose myself in them, even if it was only for one hour.

"Would you like a drink?" Giulio asked over the loud music.

"No, I'd rather dance."

"Come on, then."

Taking my hand, he led me to the dance floor. I'd only been to one other club, a secret outing with a girlfriend from school. Except I'd spent the entire night looking over my shoulder, fearing my father's men would appear at any moment. I hadn't been able to relax and ended up leaving sooner than planned.

Tonight, I'd make the most of this outing. Giulio would have to carry me out of here kicking and screaming.

On the floor, we began jumping and writhing with the rest of the crowd, pressed in with strangers while staying close to each other. He didn't try to grind on me, which I was grateful for. Most guys tried to cop a feel while dancing, thinking the close proximity gave them access to a woman's body.

He'll have access to my body soon enough.

Letting my eyes close, I swayed and tried to forget where I was and why I'd been brought here. For someone who hated tight spaces, I should have been miserable on the cramped dance floor. But there was something about the music and the anonymity that put me at ease. It felt like freedom.

The songs blurred together, one after another. Giulio could really move, and the people around us—men and women—took notice. I didn't feel jealous, though, not even when a woman ran her hands all over his back.

He looked at me, probably to gauge my reaction, so I gave him two thumbs up. "Yes, Giulio," I shouted. "Get it!"

He shook his head, though his lips twitched. "We are supposed to be engaged, no?"

I held up my left hand. "I don't see a ring."

Laughing, he drew in closer. "There's an associate in the VIP area who I need to speak with. Would you like to come or stay here?"

"Definitely stay here." I had no desire to get pulled into 'ndrina business any sooner than I needed to. Hopefully never.

"Don't move. I'll return in a few minutes."

He disappeared and I continued to dance my ass off. I was wearing three-inch heels and my feet already hurt, but I didn't care. If we could only stay an hour, then I intended to make the most of it. I spun and twirled, let the music carry me off to a place where nothing mattered. Where I was *free*.

Many songs later, Giulio hadn't returned. My feet were throbbing and my throat was dry. I decided to take a break and see if I could find him in the VIP section. At least then I could sit and drink some water.

The man guarding the stairs to the VIP section barely gave me a passing glance, instantly dismissing me. "Ciao!" I said loudly, waving my hand in front of his face. "I'm with Giulio Ravazzani. I believe he went upstairs."

The man didn't move a muscle. "Nice try."

"No, I really am with Giulio." Then I forced the hateful words out. "He's my fiancé. I'm Francesca Mancini."

The man blinked as he transferred wide brown eyes to my face. "You are Signorina Mancini?"

"Sì."

"Mi dispiace," he said and lifted the rope for me. "I didn't know, signorina."

I guess word had gotten around about Giulio's engagement. I didn't know whether to be horrified or grateful. "Grazie," I said and went up the stairs.

Toes screaming with pain, I reached the landing and glanced around. No Giulio. That was odd. He said he'd be up here. Had I missed him downstairs? Looking over the railing into the crowd below, I didn't see him there either. Hmm.

When I turned, I noticed a darker section that looked like it wrapped around the side of a small room. An office maybe? I hope Giulio wasn't beating some guy up back there. Or worse, I hope he wasn't being beaten up.

I decided to take a peek. The dark narrow hallway was empty, but I saw something even better. A dimly lit exit sign. I held my breath, my heart pounding harder than it had on the dance floor. No one was around. I could slip out that door and disappear into Siderno, away from the Ravazzanis.

Did I dare?

My feet were moving before I could stop myself. In my bones, I knew this was my best chance at escape. I slipped along the edge of the wall and very carefully pushed on the heavy metal bar that would operate the door. It cracked open silently, the cool night air washing over my bare legs. I edged into the darkness, muscles poised to flee—and came to an abrupt halt.

Giulio and another man were locked in an embrace on the fire escape, kissing each other like the world was about to end. Both of their dicks were out and rubbing together, their hips grinding and churning.

Holy...shit. Giulio liked men.

I tried to step back inside without making a noise, but I must have failed because the couple looked over. Horror flashed on Giulio's face. "Minchia!" he hissed and lunged to yank up his pants, but I was already hurrying through the door and back into the club.

"I'm sorry!" I blurted before the door shut behind me.

Was Giulio going to be mad at me for interrupting? I raced through the VIP area, trying to put distance between me and a potentially angry mobster. It was none of my business if Giulio liked men or women, or both. I honestly didn't care.

Did his father know?

Likely not. While the LGBTQ+ community had made strides in recent years, the mafia was not exactly woke. They were still very old school, and gay members were quietly murdered so as to not embarrass their family. We'd heard whispers in Toronto about various soldiers killed because of their sexual preference for men.

Would Giulio kill me now that I had learned his secret?

I swallowed hard and went down the stairs, fear giving me speed. I didn't think Giulio would hurt me—not after he'd saved me in the dungeon—but what did I know? These men were strangers and cold-blooded killers. He could cause me to disappear and never leave a trace.

At the bottom of the stairs, a hand grabbed my arm from behind, pulling me to a halt. "Frankie, wait."

I turned and saw the utter devastation on his face, what appeared to be fear and shame. I held up my hands. "It's none of my business. Seriously, Giulio."

He glanced around us, clearly worried we might be overheard. "Not here. We'll talk back at the castello. Let's go."

There was no chance to plead my case or ask what he intended as he tugged me along behind him. We found Marco and the car not far from the entrance. Giulio held the door for me and I slid onto the smooth leather seat. Marco said nothing as we drove to the castle, and

Giulio was silent, as well. I clenched my knees together and tried not to panic.

He can't kill me without explaining this to his father.

Then again, Giulio could lie and invent a transgression that would necessitate getting rid of me. It wasn't as if his father actually liked me.

Oh, God.

By the time we arrived, I was in a full panic. As soon as the car stopped, I tore out of the car, ready to put distance between the Ravazzani heir and myself. Unfortunately, Giulio came around too quickly and caught my hand before I could get away.

He didn't speak as we walked. We continued to his bedroom, and horrible thoughts ran on a loop in my brain. What was he planning?

"Giulio," I started, but he cut me off with a swipe of his free hand.

We ended up in his bathroom. Dropping my hand, he shut the door and flicked on the overhead fan. Were we being listened to? Or was this to cover my screams?

He must have noticed my growing hysteria because he held up his palms. "I'm not going to hurt you. The castello has many eyes and ears, and I'd rather not be overheard."

Could I believe him? "This isn't necessary. You don't need to worry that I'll tell."

He grimaced and dragged a hand through his hair. "Frankie, if anyone found out...if my *father* found out, I would be dead. This is worse than a secret. This is my life we are talking about."

"I know. Which is why I'll never breathe a word of this, no matter what. You saved me from that dark cell when you didn't need to. I owe you."

He stared at his toes. "This hardly compares."

"Giulio, I understand and I am not judging you. Also, I genuinely like you. During this nightmare, you've been my only ally. So please, don't think this matters. If you like men, who cares?"

"Everyone cares, Frankie. Literally everyone I work with and live with would care. The last gay member of the 'ndrina had his dick cut off and shoved in his mouth before they dumped him in the ocean. Alive."

Holy shit. "I don't want that to happen to you."

"Enough to lie about it? Enough to marry me, knowing I'll be sleeping with men behind your back? Eventually you'll grow resentful and want to punish me."

"I won't," I promised. "But Giulio, I don't want this. I don't want to marry you and live here as a mafia wife. I'll never stop looking for a way to escape."

"Including blackmailing me into helping you, I suppose."

My jaw fell open. I actually hadn't considered that. "You could just as easily kill me."

We stared at one another, each trapped and wondering who would lash out first. Or, would we become allies in this nightmare?

He slipped his hands into his trouser pockets. "My father will be very angry if you leave. He'll never stop hunting you down."

"Is that your way of telling me you plan to kill me?"

"I'm not going to kill you, Frankie." He gave a grim laugh and rubbed his eyes. "I probably should. Cazzo! I hate this. I have prayed countless times to prefer women, to be like all the others."

"So you aren't bisexual?"

"No, I am one hundred percent gay."

"See, I like the D, too. We have that in common."

That got a small laugh out of him. "Strangely, it is a relief to tell someone—even if it is the woman I'm going to marry."

We weren't going to marry, but I didn't bother correcting him. "You've lived with this secret a long time."

"Since I was nine. The hardest part has been lying to my father. All he cares about are future generations of Ravazzanis to carry on the family legacy."

"He cares about you, too. Otherwise, why come all the way to Toronto and kidnap me?"

"Because of your mother. He thinks you and I will make beautiful Ravazzani babies together."

I pressed a hand to my stomach, feeling my dinner unsettle. "The man you were with? Does he know who you are?"

Giulio nodded. "He's a low-level foot soldier. We've been together for a year or so. I...." He clenched his jaw, his eyes darting away. I sensed his need to confess, though I had no idea what he might say.

"You can tell me, G."

"I love him," he blurted, the lines of his face deepening. He looked ravaged by guilt and secrecy. "We talk about running away all the time, going to America and leaving the 'ndrina behind."

But he couldn't. He was the Ravazzani heir, the only male child. His father would never allow it.

There were no words to make this any less painful, so I stepped forward and gave him a hug.

CHAPTER EIGHT

Fausto

BEADS OF SWEAT cascaded off my body, dripping onto the belt of my treadmill. I ran every morning in my gym, but today I couldn't seem to stop, punishing myself for no reason.

While I had forced Giulio and Francesca to go to dinner last night, I hadn't expected them to stay out so late. Upon their return, I studied the footage and saw my son take her to his bedroom. They remained there for some time, and then Francesca had emerged, barefoot, her heels in her hands, with her hair mussed. Had Giulio fucked her?

I sneered. Boys. If my son had fucked her, he'd done a piss poor job of it. If I had her in my bed, I'd keep her there all night, giving her more orgasms than her body could handle. I'd have her in every position—up against a wall, from behind, under me and over me. And I wouldn't stop, doing every depraved thing my mind could conjure up, until she screamed, unable to handle any more.

Cazzo, why couldn't I stop fantasizing about her?

I cranked up the speed, running faster, my muscles screaming from the effort. Sweat rolled down my bare chest and into my shorts. She was becoming an obsession, one I could not afford. Even fucking Katarzyna hadn't purged Francesca from my mind, this constant dark need that crawled inside me like a junkie craving a fix.

I should send them away after they marry. As much as I liked having my family here, I wasn't sure I could watch them together, a happily married couple, knowing he was fucking her on the other side of the house. Watching her grow round with his children. I might as well put a bullet in my brain.

Slapping the stop button, I slowed and finally stepped off. My chest heaved from the effort to breathe and I went to take my shower. There were many unpleasant tasks awaiting me today, including finding the discrepancy with Giulio's shipment two nights ago. Then at some point, Francesca would choose her wedding dress and I'd need to return her things. That meant seeing her again, which I both desired and dreaded at the same time.

I allowed myself one more fantasy while in the shower. One more daydream of fucking my son's fiancée. She was tied up on my bed, her bratty mouth gagged as her eyes remained angry and hot. Her naked body undulated with pleasure and frustration, her sex swollen and wet, begging to be filled. My erection was so hard, it hurt, and I jerked myself furiously, a man possessed as the images continued. Finally, I moaned while thick ropes of come washed away down the drain.

As I dried off and dressed in a dark gray suit, I vowed this would be the last time. I would focus on the issues at hand instead of panting after a girl young enough to be my daughter.

Resolved, I sent word for Giulio to dress and meet me in my office. I needed answers. Zia was unusually quiet when I arrived in the kitchen, perhaps sensing my dark mood, so I didn't linger. Once I had coffee, I settled in my office and began to work.

My son arrived an hour later.

"Come in," I told him and pointed to a chair. "I need to speak with you."

He held a cup and saucer, which he sat on my desk as he took a seat. "Is something wrong?"

I leaned back. "Is there something you'd like to tell me about the other night?"

He blinked, his body going still. "Which night?"

"The delivery. The one you oversaw."

He seemed to relax as he picked up his espresso. "What about it?"

"It's light."

"That's impossible."

"Are you saying Gratteri is lying?" Gratteri was one of my most loyal men, which was why I had Giulio learning under him.

"No, but there must be some mistake. I counted it myself before I left."

"And you were the last to leave." He shifted in his chair and suspicion prickled on my skin. "Were you the last to leave, Giulio?"

"Papà," he started, and I recognized the tone from when he was younger and trying to talk himself out of trouble.

"I am not speaking to you as your father. I am speaking as the boss. Were you the last to leave, or did you shirk your duties?"

He exhaled slowly. "I was supposed to stay, but I left early. Sergio and Rocco finished up."

I knew the two boys. They were Giulio's age and not very responsible. Anger at my son's stupidity tightened the tendons in the back of my neck. "Why?"

"I had plans," he mumbled.

"With who?"

"A friend. It's not important."

"It is important." I slapped the desk with my palm. "You have a job, you do it. You don't leave two idiots to do it instead so you can go get some pussy."

His cheeks flushed as defensiveness settled in the lines of his face. "It wasn't about pussy. It was a friend."

I smothered an aggravated sigh. He was clearly lying. No one would leave their responsibilities for a football match and beer with a friend. "You have to set an example, Giulio. As a Ravazzani, you have to be better than the rest. More loyal, more bloodthirsty, more accountable. One day, this will be yours and the men must both fear and respect you."

"I know, Papà. You've told me this since I was old enough to hear it."

"And yet I am missing four hundred grams of uncut cocaine."

"I will get it back."

"No, you won't. I will handle this with Gratteri. You will pretend nothing is amiss."

"What will you do to Sergio and Rocco?"

"I haven't decided. But stealing from the 'ndrina cannot be tolerated. You know this."

A muscle jumped in his jaw but he didn't plead for the other two men. It wouldn't do any good anyway because I made the decisions in this family. If I decided to kill them for stealing from me, there was nothing Giulio could do or say to stop it.

I couldn't help but ask about last night. "How was dinner?"

"Fine."

"Marco said you took her to a club after."

"Yes."

One word answers? He knew how much I hated that. "Did the two of you get along?"

Did you fuck her after?

"Of course. I like her a lot."

I tapped my pen on the desk and tried to resist stabbing myself in the thigh with it. "Good. She's choosing a wedding dress today, but I want your crew out making collections. We need to clean up the books before crimine."

"I heard. Are we done here? I haven't had breakfast yet and I need to get going."

I nodded once and he left quickly, leaving me feeling unsettled. Something about his "friend" bothered me. Who was this woman he was seeing, one who caused him to go against orders? I would need to find out and put a stop to it. Giulio's first and only priority needed to be this family.

Marco came in a few minutes later and I filled him in. My cousin appeared as confused as I felt. "That's not like Giulio, to leave a job for some random woman. He's never one to play with the girls at the clubs or the waitresses. He's always very respectful. Never even accepts a blow job."

I hadn't ever worried about who Giulio was fucking before, but now it had interfered with business. Which meant I had to get involved. "Let's find out who she is. Have him followed for a few nights. Discreetly."

"All right."

I rubbed my eyes, exhausted and weighted down by responsibility. Some days this life threatened to drag me under, to steal the little slice of humanity I still possessed.

But I knew nothing else. I'd been raised from birth to sit exactly in this chair and direct one of the biggest criminal empires in Europe. And I was fucking good at it. My gut told me something was off with Giulio—and I wouldn't rest until I found it.

"Did you sleep last night?" Marco asked.

"Three hours or so." It was the usual amount. I hadn't had a good night's sleep since I was fourteen years old.

"Rav, you can't keep going like this. You'll have a heart attack at your desk."

"Then I'll expect you to cry at my funeral."

"I'll be sure to wear white."

"*Coglione.*"

The insult made him grin. "You love me."

I did. He was the one person I trusted implicitly. Speaking of.... "Celestina arrives today at noon. I need you to handle it. Set her up in the ballroom and make sure Francesca chooses a dress."

"Sure you don't want to oversee the dress selection? Maybe watch her try them on?"

I did, and that he read me so well only infuriated me. "Fuck you."

"He didn't fuck her last night."

I tried not to let my expression change. "Oh? And how would you know?" They'd been in Giulio's bedroom and she came out without her shoes on.

"No beard burn, no swollen lips. She looked pensive, not satiated."

I hated admitting it, but this news eased something in my chest. Cristo, I was pathetic. "Fucking her before the wedding would be disrespectful and my son knows his place. Besides, I am not certain why you think I'd care."

Marco smirked. "Sure, Rav. Anything else?"

"Get out of here so I can get to work."

LATER THAT AFTERNOON, I heard the yelling all the way from my office.

I instantly knew who was causing trouble. Cazzo, this girl.

Grinding my teeth together, I rose out of my chair and tugged on my jacket. I'd avoided her all day, knowing I'd have to deal with her after she chose a dress. But I couldn't have her annoying Celestina, who was an old friend.

A steady stream of Italian curses echoed all the way down the corridor. Celestina had a foul mouth and a short fuse. Probably why I liked her.

I strode into the ballroom. The two women were facing off near a row of dresses and Celestina was cursing Francesca's ancestors. I didn't allow myself to look at my son's fiancée. "Ciao, Tina," I called. *"Come stai?"*

The tiny dark-haired designer spun around. *"Dai!* This girl, *bello*. I cannot take it. She has no fashion sense. She is turning her nose up at every dress. My dresses!"

I kissed her cheeks. "But that is why I've brought you. Because you are the best and we must teach her what it means to be a Ravazzani, no?"

"What are you two saying?" Francesca snapped, her Italian not strong enough to keep up with us. That was probably for the best, when it came to Celestina and her colorful language.

"We are saying," Tina spat in English, "that you have no fashion sense and are a pain in the ass."

Francesca gasped, her creamy skin flushing. "All I said was that I didn't want to wear white."

Tina made a noise and gestured to me as if to say, *see?*

"There are a few ivory dresses," I pointed out. "Perhaps you could try those on."

"No. I want to wear black. Or red." She set her chin stubbornly. Here was the spoiled mafia princess, the piccola monella. Her father had clearly allowed her too much latitude.

That stopped now.

I looked at Tina. "I need a word with Signorina Mancini. Would you mind taking your assistants to the kitchen? Zia will give you caffè and biscotti."

"Of course, bello." Tina herded her team out of the ballroom and Marco disappeared as well.

Then we were alone.

Strolling to the dresses, I slowly examined them. Tina was the most sought-after wedding dress designer in Italy, and each gown was unique. There were four racks of at least fifteen dresses each. Plenty for Francesca to choose from.

"I thought we had a deal," I said, continuing to shift through the gowns.

"You said I am allowed to choose my own dress."

"No, I said you had to choose a *suitable* dress. No member of the Ravazzani family will wear black or red at a wedding."

"Then perhaps I shouldn't become a member of the Ravazzani family."

I dropped the gown in my hand and advanced on her, the soles of my leather shoes slapping angrily on the wooden floor. Francesca began backing away from me, but it was too little, too late. While I admired her spirit—and yes, it turned me on—there were times when she needed to obey orders. This was one of those times.

Fear flashed in her gaze when her back hit the wall. I kept coming, closing the distance until I crowded her into the plaster. She looked up at me, pulse pounding at the base of her throat, her chest rising and falling quickly. She wore a simple strapless sundress, and I was proud that my eyes remained on her face, not drifting to the bare skin on display.

I braced my hands on either side of her head and leaned in, my body caging hers. "Do you know what happens to those who disobey my orders?"

She lifted her chin. "Giulio won't allow you to hurt me."

I sneered. "You think to use my son as a shield against me? I am the ruler of this family—and Giulio answers to me. I can do whatever I wish, whenever I wish. You would be wise not to cross me, Francesca."

"Stop threatening me. If you are going to kill me, I wish you would just do it and put me out of my misery."

"Kill you? I would not make it so easy. No, I would marry you off to some other member of my 'ndrina instead. There are plenty of old men who would love to break in a new young bride."

"You wouldn't dare. My father—"

"Your father isn't here now to coddle you. He gave you to me as payment on a debt. It is by my favor that you are marrying my son and bearing future generations of Ravazzanis." The desire to touch her overruled my good sense. I dragged a fingertip down her soft cheek, not stopping until I caressed her jaw. "If you spit on that favor, I will find you another husband. And I guarantee you won't like him half as well as my son."

She licked her lips and stared up at me with unreadable eyes. "I don't want to marry anyone."

"That is too bad, bellissima, because you will become a bride. The choice of groom is up to you."

As we stared at each other, I noticed she smelled like earth and olives. Sun and plants. Like my estate. The comforting scent sank into me like an aphrodisiac, boosting the simmering lust I already felt for this gorgeous spirited creature. I wanted to fuck her outside in the rain, in the dirt, with the grape vines all around us, her silken hair spread out like roots on the ground while I coated her in my come.

She must have sensed the shift in my thoughts because her lips parted on a swift intake of breath. Her gaze darted to my mouth and for a crazy moment I wondered if she was thinking about what it would be like to kiss me. *Madonna*, I wanted that. I wanted to taste her, to feel her lips on mine. Drink her sighs and swallow her whimpers. I wanted to *inhale* her.

Disgusted with myself, I pushed away from the wall. I spun and tried to collect my composure as I walked back to the racks of gowns.

"I hate you."

I didn't doubt it. But I didn't need her to like me. I needed her to obey me. "Accept your fate and do as you're told."

"Does no one ever stand up to you and win?"

"No." I found a simple ivory satin gown that would show off her tits. "What about this one?"

She didn't even look at it. "Fine. Who cares?"

"Excellent. I'll have Marco fetch your things. See how accommodating I can be when you do what I ask?"

"Yes, very accommodating," she mumbled as she walked to a chair, where a floppy hat rested on the seat. She grabbed it and tugged it on. At that moment, she looked so young. Too young for me, that was for certain. But it was hard to remember her age when she was staring me down better than a hardened criminal.

She started toward the door. "Are we done here? I'd like to go back outside and help Vincenzo."

Ah, so that was why she smelled like the estate. "Sampling wine?"

"No, I'm learning how to make it." She glanced over her shoulder. "Do you know there are over two thousand varieties of grapes in Italy?"

"I do, actually." Wine has been in my family for generations. I'd helped with the harvesting and crushing many times. "Which wine is your favorite?"

"The rosé, I think. Or the ciró."

The ciró was my personal favorite, and I had a brief fantasy of pouring the dark red wine all over her pale skin and licking it off. "I'll tell Celestina you prefer this gown, if you'd like to return outside." See? I could be nice.

"Whatever. I expect to find my things on my bed, Ravazzani." She disappeared into the hall.

The lack of respect and sharp attitude made my dick twitch. She took any gesture of kindness from me and threw it back in my face. No one else would dare. Would Giulio hold it against me if I spanked his fiancée?

You'd never stop at just a spanking.

Which was why I needed to keep my distance from her. She made me crazy.

CHAPTER NINE

Francesca

I STAYED AWAY from the castle for the rest of the day.

Instead I spent the hours with Vincenzo, learning about grapes and wine. I did ask about the borders of the estate, but he said they weren't walkable, that I would need a car to reach them. Apparently Ravazzani owned quite a lot of land, damn him.

I told myself I kept outside to find a way to escape, but that was a lie. My encounter with the elder Ravazzani in the ballroom had left me shaken...and aroused. He'd been so angry, yet so unbelievably hot as he cornered me, his large body caging me in as he'd tried to intimidate me. Except his touch had been gentle, while his gaze burned with an intensity that flicked a switch inside me, making me ache and soaking my panties. There was a moment where I could have sworn the attraction was mutual, but that was insane. Wasn't it?

It had to be. I was here to marry his son. And I was anything but sweet around Fausto. He hated me.

But I was woman enough to admit I was attracted to him. It was the way he moved, the way he talked, his gorgeous face and strong body. How he wore his suits. The thick dark hair and lush lips. His hot and cold personality. Everything about him, actually.

Older men didn't normally do it for me, but Fausto Ravazzani was the exception, it seemed.

He is my kidnapper. What's wrong with me?

Not so much a kidnapper, considering my father had given me to Ravazzani as payment on a debt. More like a jailer. Still, Fausto needed to let me go. I didn't want to marry Giulio—and Giulio definitely didn't want to marry me.

All of this made me more determined to find a way to escape.

Hat in hand, I strolled toward the castle after dusk. The cool night air caused my skin to pebble, and I longed for a sweater. Just as I rounded the corner, two cars raced into the drive.

Not wanting to be seen, I darted behind a tree as the castle's front door opened. Ravazzani emerged, his fit body clad in just trousers and shirtsleeves, which he'd rolled up high on his forearms. The lights of the house illuminated the firm set of his mouth as he came down the stone steps. This was angry Fausto, which was only slightly less hotter than annoyed Fausto. I could barely tear my eyes away from him.

Three men got out of each car, though the youngest two guests appeared reluctant. They were shoved forward by the older men, and the group followed Ravazzani toward the side of the house. Toward the door to the dungeon.

Holy shit. Trepidation hollowed out my stomach. Was he planning to hurt someone down there?

They all disappeared and I bit my lip. I had no desire to enter the dungeon ever again, but maybe I needed to hear more of Ravazzani's cruelty and ruthlessness to remind myself of why I could not be attracted to him. The man was a cold-blooded killer. A sociopath. I shouldn't be fantasizing about licking him from head to toe.

Yes, this was what I needed.

Before I could talk myself out of it, I edged quietly through the bushes until I reached the door. I took my time on the latch, moving slowly so as to not make a sound. When the door opened enough for me to squeeze through, I slipped in and paused on the landing, cracking the door with my foot so I could still see outside.

They were quiet for a few minutes. I suspected Ravazzani was letting his prey sweat it out, building the fear. It seemed like his style. When he finally spoke, it was in slow, measured Italian, but one word was in English. *Cocaine.*

Had someone stolen from Ravazzani? Double crossed him? Something had definitely gone wrong or they wouldn't all be in the dungeon.

Whoever he was accusing repeatedly denied it, saying "no" over and over again. Ravazzani grew angrier. "*Mi prendi per scemo*, Sergio?" he shouted.

A fist smacked against flesh, twice. Then again.

From there, it was a series of pleas, grunts, and moans as the beatings continued. Was Ravazzani doing the hitting or did he delegate the job to one of his men? I pictured him, sleeves rolled high and muscles bunching as he delivered punch after punch, sweat rolling down his face. Instead of repulsing me, it made my heart race and sent heat twisting through my belly.

I was a terrible person.

I chewed the edge of a fingernail and tried to focus on the violence, the wrongness of whatever was happening below, but it didn't work. I was getting more turned on the longer I stayed here.

A snap echoed followed by a yelp, and I knew a bone had been broken. A finger?

One of the men began sobbing at that point. "Mi dispiace, Don Fausto," he shouted, his voice racked with pain. Then it sounded like he was begging.

The tone of Ravazzani's voice changed then. It went from angry to resigned, almost paternal. "Va bene. *Dimmi*, Rocco." *Tell me.*

Rocco began speaking, his voice hitching occasionally, probably from the pain. I couldn't understand the words, though. Was he explaining why he took the cocaine?

Ravazzani responded, which prompted both Rocco and Sergio to plead some more. Ugh, what were they saying?

I only caught the word, "*esempio,*" which I think was *example.* Damn, I really needed to improve my Italian.

Two shots rang out into the empty space. My hand flew up to cover my mouth, stifling my gasp. Oh, my God. He just killed two people down there. Murdered both Sergio and Rocco.

Fuck. I shouldn't be here. I didn't want to be a witness to an actual crime.

I bolted from my spot on the landing, letting the door close behind me as I raced for the castle. Fear clogged my throat. My only thought was to reach the relative safety of my room and lock the door. I would skip dinner and come down for food after everyone had gone to bed.

Or maybe I'd never leave my room again.

The kitchen was dark when I entered, my feet moving quickly across the tiled floor. All of a sudden, arms grabbed me from behind and pulled me to a halt. I struggled, but the hands only tightened as I was pulled into a strong warm chest.

"Where are you going in such a hurry, piccola monella?"

Ravazzani. Shit. Did he know I'd been listening? I licked my lips and tried to keep my voice even. "My room."

He felt like a wall behind me. A tall muscular wall that had just *murdered* two people.

I began trembling, emotions rioting inside me. He was brutal and beautiful, like those jungle cats on the nature channel I sometimes watched, and I wanted to hate him. I wanted to scream and run away. But there was a darkness within me, too, some part of my soul that relished violence and power, and found it exciting. That shameful side was drawn to this man. I found him fascinating and sexy as fuck.

Again, what was wrong with me?

His rough hand clamped around my throat, holding me tightly. Instead of scaring me, his touch caused slashes of heat to race down my spine and settle between my legs. He surrounded me, his strength on magnificent display, and my body softened as fear shifted to need and hunger. Could he feel my pulse pounding under his fingertips?

I heard him suck in a breath, so I assumed he'd noticed my reaction. Then his voice grew low and sensual, his lips near my ear. "What were you hoping to see in the dungeon, Francesca? Hmm?"

"I don't know what you're talking about," I said, my voice barely above a whisper.

"Liar." The hand not on my neck cupped my hip, almost caressing me. "Do you know what happens to girls who spy on me?"

"Let me go. You're scaring me."

"No, I'm not. You are not frozen in fear or fighting me off. Instead, you are relaxed against me while your heart is beating so fast. Do you know what that tells me?"

I was almost afraid to ask. "What?"

"That you don't mind the danger. That you might even thrive on it." He inhaled near my neck, as if smelling me. "As I do."

Moisture flooded between my legs, arousal so swift and fierce that my knees nearly buckled. In fact, I probably would have collapsed if Ravazzani hadn't been holding me up.

"Yes," he murmured. "That is exactly what I thought. Do not ever try to tell me you weren't made for this life, that you weren't born to rule as a queen."

I closed my eyes. God, please don't let that be true. "Fuck you. I will never marry your son."

"You will, *bellissima*. And if you curse at me again, or use such foul language in my house, I will return you to the dungeon—whether it's been cleaned or not."

I shivered, imagining the blood and brain matter on those dank walls. I never wanted to be down there again—ever. "This is the twenty-first century, Ravazzani. Women curse."

He let me go abruptly, and I had to brace myself on the countertop to keep from toppling over. I looked over my shoulder and saw him run his hands through his hair. His eyes were bright and wild, almost feral, like an animal caught in a trap in the woods. "It may be the twenty-first century out there, but here in Calabria, in my house, it is very much not. We honor tradition, and that means you will also honor our traditions. Because if you don't, I promise you won't like the consequences."

Turning, he strode to the door. "And let this be a warning—do not spy on my business again. The less you know, the better."

He disappeared into the night, leaving me shaken and confused. It seemed like Fausto Ravazzani might understand me better than I did myself, which was an absolutely horrifying thought.

I couldn't let that be true.

Looking at the door, I made a swift decision. Fuck this. Fuck the engagement, fuck this castle, and fuck Fausto.

Tonight I would escape.

Fausto

SOMETHING TOLD me she was going to run.

I knew the wedding dress, combined with whatever Francesca saw in the dungeon, would overwhelm her and force her hand. I was looking forward to the challenge, actually. She had no chance of escaping, but it would be fun to see how she tried.

I kept working late into the night. As usual, guards patrolled outside and two men monitored the security feeds. There was a complex system of tunnels that connected the castello to hideouts in the surrounding mountains, and if she found them she would be able to get deep into the forest. While she wouldn't get away, it would take us some time to find her.

She was unaware of that option, thankfully, and I meant to see it stayed that way.

Giulio had returned an hour ago. Francesca would wait until she assumed everyone was asleep before making her attempt. Which meant any minute now....

I was checking over a contract we had secured for a government building when I heard the creak of the floor above me. Ah, yes. The monella was on the move.

My lips curved into a smile. It was so satisfying to be proven right.

I flicked off the light in my office, just in case she came down this corridor. More likely she would go the other way, through the kitchen to gather supplies, then out the back door, but I wanted to be cautious. When I didn't hear her footsteps, I assumed she had gone toward the kitchen, so I followed.

My feet were silent on the old floors as I approached. The refrigerator door opened and closed, and I waited out of sight as she rifled through the cabinets. Looking for food, no doubt. Packages rustled, then her steps took her toward the back door.

I didn't try to stop her. The best way to break her was to give her a tiny sliver of hope—and then crush it. Prove to her there really was no escape.

The latch on the back door clicked shut, ever so quietly. A second later, my phone buzzed in my pocket. As I moved into the kitchen to peer out the window, I swiped to answer. "Pronto."

"Don Fausto, the girl has left." It was Benito. "What do you want us to do? Should we grab her?"

"No," I said immediately. "I need to teach her a lesson. Let her go."

"She is headed toward the front. Out toward the road."

Even better. If she'd gone through the estate, she could have hidden in a dozen places and caused more aggravation. The road was a true waste of her time. "Call our friends at the *carabinieri*," I said, letting the local police be of some use. "Have someone pick her up and hold her there on the road."

"Okay," Benito said and hung up.

I strode back to my office. There was nothing to do now but wait.

Part of me admired her for running. She was strong willed, which would be good for Giulio. When I died, my son would need a formidable partner, a woman who could handle the risks of life in the mafia. In fact, many women were running 'ndrine nowadays, as their husbands sat in jail.

My father had been arrested once, but released within hours. The witnesses had recanted their testimony and moved away, up to some Scandinavian country where the food was shit. Then my father made certain to infiltrate every level of government, including the police and the judicial system, as insurance against future arrests. That foresight meant I hadn't been charged with any crime to date because most everyone was on my payroll. There were rumblings about a crackdown on a bigger scale, but I had yet to see it.

So Francesca's bravery was actually beneficial to the family. I merely needed to prove to her that my power superseded anything she might ever plan.

Benito called twenty minutes later. "They have her. It's about a half mile along the road to the east."

"Excellent." No doubt she was spitting mad. "Come, you'll drive me."

He paused for a half-second. "Should we call Marco? He won't like it if you leave the estate without him."

I considered this. Leaving was a risk, but a slight one. The road was close to the castello, well within the area my men routinely patrolled. Also, I couldn't wait to see the look on Francesca's face when I arrived.

Decision made, I said, "We'll be fine. We aren't going far."

"I'll meet you out front."

I disconnected and grabbed one of the pistols I kept in my office. I didn't expect trouble but it didn't hurt to have extra firepower. As I went through the castello, I briefly considered waking Giulio. She was his fiancée, after all. But I quickly discarded the idea. Right or wrong, I wanted to handle this. Whatever punishment she received would come from me.

Benito waited in the heavily fortified SUV I used when I left the estate. I got in the back and we drove off. Speaking of punishment, what would I do to her? I knew what I *wanted* to do, but it was impossible. I wanted to spank her ass red until she cried and begged me to stop. But that would ignite the attraction simmering in my belly for her, the precise reaction I was trying to prevent.

No, it was better if I didn't touch her.

When we approached, the lights of the *carabiniere's* Land Rover were flashing. I could see a lone figure in the rear of the dark vehicle, while the carabiniere stood outside, leaning against the driver's side door. I recognized him, so this would be easy.

"Buona sera, Paoletti," I greeted when I got out. "I hope we did not trouble you." Walking over, I handed him two hundred Euros.

"Never trouble for you, Signore Ravazzani. She put up quite a fight, though. Said she had been kidnapped."

I grinned and slapped him on the shoulder. "Women. You don't give them enough diamonds and they cry big crocodile tears." Paoletti laughed, as I knew he would, and then I thanked him. "I'll take her with me now."

"Of course, signore. A moment, per favore."

He disappeared into the back seat to uncuff Francesca. I met her angry gaze as she was pulled from the Land Rover. Surprisingly, she didn't speak, just continued to burn holes in my skin with her eyes. I tried not to grin as Paoletti marched her toward me.

"Here you are, signore."

Now that she was closer, I could see the tear tracks, evidence of where she'd been crying. I squashed any guilt I might have felt. Taking Francesca's arm, I kept a tight grip on her even as she tried to pull away. I said, "Grazie, Paoletti. My best to your wife and daughters."

"*Arrivederci*, Signore Ravazzani."

I led her to the SUV and Benito opened the rear door. She tossed her head back, long wheat-colored strands of hair whipping over her shoulder, to stare at me. Her expression was a mixture of stubbornness and defeat, like a person who knew they'd lost but could not stand to admit it. "Let me go, Ravazzani."

"Never. Get in the fucking car, Francesca."

Muttering to herself, she did as she was told. I followed and sat directly beside her, so close that our thighs touched. I wanted her uncomfortable.

She shoved at me. "Do you mind? Move over."

"Is it wise to order me around after you tried to escape tonight?"

"Can you blame me? You kidnap and intimidate me, you are forcing me to marry someone I hardly know, and you killed two men in cold blood tonight. I would be insane not to try to escape from you."

Benito started the engine and we headed back to the estate. The car was silent, and I thought about what she'd said. She believed I killed those two boys tonight, which meant she hadn't been watching but listening in the dungeon. So she didn't know that while I had shot them, they were both very much alive. I decided not to correct her. Better she think me a monster, a killer, and be afraid to cross me.

The drive was short. When we pulled up to the castello, Benito turned the car off. I told him to leave us, so he got out and strode toward the surveillance room on the back side of my home.

I said nothing, just waited.

"I should have known," she snapped, "that you have all the police here on your payroll. The two of you were laughing like old friends."

"The police are helpless, too weak to stop our organization. They know it is better to work with me than against me. A lesson you would be wise to learn, as well."

"I don't want to work with you." Her voice hitched, as if she were holding back tears. "I don't want to be part of your horrible family full of murderers and criminals. You're all psychopaths. I want you to let me go."

This from the woman who had nearly melted in my arms after hearing me interrogate and shoot two men?

I didn't believe it. She was scared because she might not mind it. She might even *like* it.

I reached into my coat pocket, took out the pistol and rested it on my knee. "Do you want to kill me, Francesca?"

She grew very still, her gaze darting between my face and the gun. "What?"

I grabbed her wrist and forced the gun into her palm. Then I aimed the barrel at my chest. "Go on, then. Shoot me." I stared directly into her dark eyes, showing her how comfortable I was with violence. "Pull the trigger, dolcezza," I said in a low rasp, like I was seducing her.

Licking her lips, she tried to edge away. "You're insane. What are you doing?"

Putting my hand on the door behind her, I caged her in. The lights of the castello illuminated the interior of the car, and I could see the pulse racing on the side of her throat, the flush to her skin. No fear, however. Whatever she was feeling was something different, something that confirmed all my suspicions about her. "You want to kill me, no? This is your chance. Pull the trigger and watch my blood spill out all over your lap and onto the seat, spray against the glass of the windows. Then you'll be free," I whispered.

"Until your men catch and kill me."

"Don't think about that. Think about how good it will feel to pull the trigger and take my life with your own hand. To watch the light fade from my eyes until I am nothing. What power you will feel in that moment."

The barrel of the gun shifted against my sternum, and her mouth parted slightly on an exhale, her pupils dilating. I bet if I looked at her nipples, they would be poking through the fabric of her clothing. Dio, this woman. She was extraordinary. I had to curl my hands into fists to keep from touching her.

"You're crazy," she said quietly. "It's like you want me to do it."

"I want to prove that you are not frightened of me. That you are just as crazy, just as wild as we are."

"I'm not. I'm a good person. I don't want any of this."

"A good girl would have stayed at home instead of sneaking out of her father's house, just to find a man to fuck her. A good girl would not have stabbed a man like me in the hand with a pen. A good girl would not be turned on by holding a gun on a man." I leaned in. "You are definitely not a good girl, Francesca."

"You're wrong." Her voice was weak, unsure.

"Go on then. Pull the trigger."

CHAPTER TEN

Francesca

THIS WAS INSANE. It was like he was seducing me into killing him.

His voice, rough and low, filled the car and my head, luring me deeper into his web. I was mesmerized, not frightened, which worried me.

You are definitely not a good girl, Francesca.

Was that why I hadn't fought when Ravazzani's soldier shoved me back into the car? Or why my stomach fluttered when Ravazzani himself showed up to retrieve me from the police?

Was that why my panties were soaked right now?

No, I could not let it be true. I had to remain strong and remember I wanted a normal life. The life my mother had wanted for her daughters. I was not turned on by this man or the violence he represented.

I shoved at his shoulder, which I couldn't help but notice was solid and strong, and handed him the gun back. "Stop fucking with my head."

Smirking, he put some distance between us and pocketed the gun.

I hated that smug look on his face. "Don't think for one second that this proves anything. I'm not stupid enough to shoot you when I know I'll be caught. I'd much rather wait until you let your guard down."

"My guard is never down. You'd be wise to remember it."

That sounded like a horrible way to live. But I didn't feel pity for him. This man had chosen this life, even if his fate was preordained by family. We all had choices to make, and he clearly made his a long time ago. Just like my choice was to not marry a criminal.

But his comment made me wonder. "How did you know I left?"

"There are eyes and ears everywhere. It's how I keep my family safe."

The cameras. Of course. Giulio said I would never see them, so I had to learn where they were to avoid them next time. "Why aren't you angry I tried to escape?"

"Because I suspected you might and I like to be proven right. Especially when it comes to you, it seems."

The light played across his cheekbones, as well as a lush mouth that could be so cruel but also teasing. He hadn't shaved recently, and a dark scruff covered his sharp jaw. There was something about his hard blue eyes, along with the power he exuded, that caused me to shiver.

I had to get a hold of myself. The man had put a gun in my hand and told me to shoot him. He was straight up certifiable.

"You knew I wouldn't get away," I said. "You knew there was no chance I could escape."

His mouth curved into a smile so sexy it would tempt a nun into breaking her vows. "That is true."

Frustration burned my skin, an embarrassing combination of anger and hopelessness I didn't bother to hide. "I hate you."

"I know. It will get easier, though, once you have accepted your fate."

"It's not fate. You are forcing me into this. My fate was to go to college and choose my own husband."

He threw his head back and laughed. "If your father allowed you to believe this, he is a bigger fool than I imagined. Women in our world do not have choices such as this. He would have married you to another family's son to strengthen his position. It's what is to be expected. And deep down you know it."

"No, I don't. What I do know is that I will continue to defy you, Giulio, and anyone else who gets in my way of escaping this nightmare."

"Nightmare? You should feel honored that I am willing to marry you to my son knowing you are not pure. You should be bowing and scraping at my feet in gratitude."

I gaped at him. "Not pure? Are you serious? You have some nerve judging me, considering you banged your girlfriend inside the house."

One dark brow rose. "You almost sound jealous."

"Don't be ridiculous," I said, putting as much indignation as I could muster into my tone. "I don't care if you screw her sideways against the kitchen wall, but you can't slut shame me for having sex outside of marriage when you are doing the same."

"Yes, I can. The rules for daughters are different, as you well know. And Katarzyna likes it when I fuck her against the wall."

Great. Now I had *that* visual in my head. I shifted in my seat, suddenly very warm. "At least she tells you she likes it. She's probably very good at faking it."

"Oh, there's no need to fake with me. Italian men are very attentive partners, Francesca. Making a woman come is necessary to men here, like breathing air."

Unbidden, my gaze darted to his mouth. Did he give oral? David hadn't been a fan and I'd always wondered what it was like. Something told me Ravazzani loved to eat a woman out. My thighs clenched, and I had to get the hell out of this car. "Are we done?"

He produced the gun again. "I don't know. Are we?"

Was he threatening to shoot me? It didn't matter. I had to remain strong and never show this man any fear. He would crush me if I did. "I won't marry your son. So go ahead and do your worst, Ravazzani."

Reaching over me, he flicked the handle and the car door opened. His smile was all teeth when he said, "Do not worry about that, piccola monella. I most definitely will."

I hurried from the car and didn't look back.

WHEN GIULIO ASKED if I'd like to take the boat out two days later, I eagerly agreed. Being off the estate meant the possibility of escape, and I would grab every opportunity presented.

I expected one of those deep sea fishing boats. Or maybe a sleek speedboat. I did not expect a gigantic 30-meter mega-yacht with split-level decks and a pool.

Dark tinted windows ran along the side, hiding the interior from curious eyes. Perfect for mafia business, I supposed. The name on the back read, *Il Destino*.

Great. Even here I couldn't escape the Ravazzani concept of fate.

"This is your boat?" I asked as he helped me aboard.

"It's my father's. Don't you like it?"

"What's not to like? This is a floating five-star hotel."

Giulio chuckled. "Come on, I'll show you around."

He briefly spoke with one of the crew members and then we set off. Each deck was more impressive than the last. Large living spaces, lounges, lush cabins, and a beach club pool area in the rear. In the front was a master suite complete with jacuzzi and helipad, plus a glass bottom window to the ocean below. I tried not to drool as we walked around, but it was a struggle.

"I would never leave if this yacht was mine," I said, dragging a finger across the soft leather chair. We were already headed into the blue waters of the Ionian Sea, the salty breeze in our faces.

"Then you should prepare to stay because this will be yours some-day. Ours, actually."

That significantly dampened my enthusiasm. I didn't want to think about our pending marriage or Fausto Ravazzani. I'd managed to avoid him by working outside in the vineyard and with the animals. The castle staff was kind and patient with me, especially considering the language barrier. Giulio had bought me a book on how to learn Italian, though, so I was slowly getting better.

Do not ever try to tell me you weren't made for this life, that you weren't born to rule as a queen.

I closed my eyes, unwilling to consider it. That couldn't be true. It couldn't. I had a life in Toronto, a family that I missed. I wanted to go to school and choose my own husband. Marrying into my father's world—Fausto's world—was out of the question. I would never have any independence if I did.

"Are you feeling ill?" Giulio touched my arm. "We have medicine for that."

"No, I'm fine. I won't get seasick."

He smirked down at me. "Just like you won't get sick from drinking?"

I couldn't help but smile. "You are the one who let me drink so much grappa."

"As if I could have stopped you. Now let's go have some lunch and get some sun."

We went to the beach club area on the bottom deck. Lobster salad, fresh bread and crisp white wine had been laid out on the table near the pool. Giulio whipped off his shirt, leaving him in just a pair of tiny swim shorts and sunglasses. He was all bronze skin and lean muscles, with several tattoos on a torso with very little body fat. God, he was gorgeous.

Good genes obviously ran in his family, and I wondered what the elder Ravazzani looked like under his clothing. Probably just as ripped, but with more body hair and bulkier. Stronger. Thicker....

"You have the strangest look on your face right now." Giulio frowned at me. "Do you not like lobster?"

I mentally shook myself and removed my cover up. A tiny bikini had been waiting in my new closet, and it was a relief to feel the sun on my whole body. "I love it. This is perfect."

His eyes swept down my body. "You are bellissima, Frankie."

"Grazie. You are quite bellissimo yourself."

"Thank you." He smirked. "I am thinking whoever purchased that bikini for you should be arrested. It is criminal how good you look."

I glanced around to make sure we were alone. "You are gay, right?" I asked in a whisper.

"That does not mean I cannot appreciate beauty when I see it."

"Is that how you're planning on creating the next generation of Ravazzanis?"

Giulio grimaced, his teasing forgotten. "I am hoping to delay that as long as possible. No offense."

"None taken. I am also hoping to delay that." Like never. "But you'll have to make babies some day, right?"

"Of course, yes."

"Will we be overheard while onboard?"

"Not here. It's already been swept for bugs and my father doesn't have cameras installed. I think it's because he uses the boat with Katarzyna." His phone suddenly pinged several times from where it rested on the table.

"Should you get that?"

"Would you mind?"

"This isn't a date, Giulio."

He grinned and lifted his phone. "I like you, Frankie. You make this easy." Whatever he read on the screen caused him to frown.

"Trouble at work?"

"My father. He didn't know I was bringing you out today."

"Why would he care?"

"I stopped trying to understand him years ago." He put his phone back on the table. "He is acting strangely. I can't explain it, but he's very interested in your whereabouts at all times."

"No doubt worried I'm going to escape." Which I would. My first attempt had failed, but it was only a matter of time before I succeeded.

"No, it's more than that." Cradling his wine glass, he leaned back in his chair. "I caught him looking at footage of you and Vincenzo in the winery."

I straightened. "What?"

"It was so strange. He closed the window quickly, like he didn't want me to know."

Ravazzani was watching me? Why? If I was on the estate then I hadn't escaped. "He's probably worried I will seduce Vincenzo and ruin his plans to marry us off."

Giulio laughed. "Vincenzo is at least sixty years old. You'd give him a heart attack if you tried to seduce him."

I would never. Vincenzo was like the grandfather I never had. In a very short time I'd come to really like him.

Unfortunately, there was a lot I liked about Italy and the estate. I was learning tons about grapes and plants, wine and oil. They even had bergamot trees, a citrus species native to Calabria that I hadn't seen before, and the fruit tasted sour and bitter and delicious.

And I couldn't handle the baby lambs and their cuteness. I'd already given them all names, and I looked forward to feeding them every day.

We finished lunch and a crew member cleared our plates, while we took our bottle of wine to the deck chairs by the pool. The yacht had stopped in an inlet, a tiny cove with crystal clear water and no one else around. "We can swim here, if you'd like," Giulio said. "Pool or sea?"

"The sea, definitely."

We swam for a long time, jumping off the back of the boat into the water, splashing and floating, while music blared from the speakers. Giulio was a lot of fun and it turned out we had similar taste in music, preferring old school hip hop to anything new.

Finally we flopped onto the deck chairs and asked the staff to make us fancy tropical drinks. I rubbed suntan lotion all over while Giulio checked messages on his phone. It seemed like he had a lot of them, but I didn't pry.

When we were sipping mai tais, Giulio asked, "Did my father ever return your things?"

"Yes." My satchel had been waiting on my bed when I returned from the dungeon fiasco. "Though he still won't let me have a phone."

Giulio chuckled. "I am not surprised. He's probably worried you will call the Guardia and report us."

I frowned, disappointed I hadn't considered it. I only thought about calling my sisters. For someone so eager to escape the clutches of the Ravazzani men, I wasn't trying too hard. Instead I was lying on a megayacht, sipping cocktails on the Mediterranean.

Real rebellious, Frankie.

"I just want to talk to my sisters," I told Giulio. "I'm not used to being out of touch with them for this long." Has it only been a week? It seemed like forever. But I was used to talking to my sisters every day.

Giulio reached over, grabbed his phone, and handed it out to me. "There. Make any call you like."

I stared in amazement. "Are you serious?"

"Of course."

I snatched the phone quickly, before he could change his mind. My eagerness only caused him to laugh. Then he surprised me again by standing up. "I'll give you some privacy. I have to speak to the crew about our return anyway."

"You are leaving me alone with your phone?"

"Why not? You already know all my worst secrets, Frankie. And my father pays the Guardia enough to ignore any hysterical phone calls from Canadian tourists." He winked, then strolled away and left me with his phone.

Oh, my God.

I started dialing Emma before I could blink. I called her because Gia often misplaced her phone and didn't answer. My sister answered after the first ring. "Hello?"

"Emma, it's me."

"Oh, my God. Frankie! Tell me you're okay."

My entire body sagged in relief, so happy that tears sprang to my eyes. "I'm okay. I'm in Italy."

"Daddy told us what happened. We've been worried sick. Are you really marrying that man's son?"

"No. It's complicated." I didn't want to say anything more than that, just to be on the safe side. "How are you? How's Gia?"

"We're fine. I'm trying to get ahead in my advanced chemistry class this summer, so I've been a mess."

I smiled. Emma took school very seriously. She was the smartest person I knew. "That's good, but don't forget to enjoy your break, too."

"I will, but this is more important. I want to get into a good—" She bit off the word but it hung there between us, unsaid.

I swallowed hard. Once I had also wanted to get into a good school. "You will, Em. You will. Is Gia around?"

"Yes." I could hear her moving, probably walking to Gia's room. "But before I let you go, tell me. Are you hurt? Are they mistreating you? Because I will tell Papà and he will come and get you."

I pressed the tips of my fingers to my mouth, trying hard not to cry. Papà couldn't fix this. He couldn't stand up to Ravazzani, not even with all the Toronto muscle behind him. Ravazzani was too powerful.

Despite my misery, I couldn't worry Emma. "I'm fine. No one is hurting me. In fact, I'm on a yacht in the middle of the Ionian Sea right now and drinking a mai tai."

"No way!"

"I know, right? I'll send you a selfie when we get off the phone."

"Please do. I miss seeing your face. Okay, here's Gia. I love you!"

"I love you, too, Em."

"Holy shit, sis," Gia exclaimed. "What the fuck happened to you?"

Direct and to the point. Exactly like Gia. "Hey, Gigi. How are you?"

"Tell me what happened. Papà said that man caught you escaping and took you to Italy. Did he hurt you?"

I thought about Fausto's hand gently brushing the hair off my face, the way he'd gripped me carefully in the kitchen. He hadn't hurt me, at least not after drugging me. Still, I wouldn't give my sisters anything to worry about. "No one has hurt me. I'm fine."

I heard Em in the background as she told Gia about the yacht. "You're on a fucking yacht right now?" Gia asked into the phone. "I told you they were loaded. Is the castle amazing?"

My face felt like it was going to split apart from my wide smile. "Yes, it is amazing. They have olive trees and a vineyard. There are pigs and cattle and the most adorable little lambs."

"Oh, I can't wait to see it. Papà said we are coming to your wedding in a few weeks."

The smile instantly fell from my face. "We'll see." I didn't want to say more, not on Giulio's phone.

"Is this your new number?"

"No, this is Giulio's phone. He let me borrow it."

"Giulio is your fiancé?"

"No. Yes. Well, sort of. For now."

"Oh, shit. I know that voice. You are planning something."

Was I? Yes, I was planning to escape, but the planning part hadn't really started. "Don't worry about me. I'll figure it out."

"You always do," Gia said. "Hey, did you hear what happened to David?"

A weird knot settled in my stomach. With the kidnapping and Ravazzani's general hotness causing my brain to malfunction, I hadn't thought of David much. Something told me I wasn't going to like what came next. "No. What?"

"That Ravazzani guy beat the shit out of him. I guess they saw David crawl out of your window that morning."

I sucked in a breath and closed my eyes. Fausto had hurt David? That asshole! He had no right to do that. David didn't deserve to be beaten just for being with me. "Is he all right?"

"He's fine, Frankie." She snickered. "Though I hear he pissed himself in fear."

"That's not funny," I snapped. "Please tell him I'm sorry if you see him."

"I will, I will. Jeez. Calm your tits."

Giulio emerged from the depths of the salon and I knew my time with my sisters was over. "Love you, Gia. I'll speak to you and Em later, okay?"

"Love you, too. I hope those bastards let you have a phone soon."

"Me, too. Talk soon. Bye."

I hung up, then snapped a quick selfie of me, the boat, and my drink then sent it to Emma. Once it went through, I handed the phone to Giulio. "Thanks. That meant a lot."

He stretched out on the deck chair. "You're welcome. Your sisters are well?"

"Did you know that your father beat up my boyfriend?"

Giulio rolled his head to the side and pulled down his sunglasses to look at me. "He caught your boyfriend sneaking out of your bedroom. So I assumed so, yes."

Mafia thugs. I crossed my arms and stared out at the beautiful water. No matter the tempting trappings of a vineyard and a yacht, I had to keep reminding myself these people were dangerous. Ruthless killers. I couldn't be blinded by broad shoulders and a chiseled jaw. Underneath Ravazzani's ruggedly handsome package was a monster.

Wasn't I supposed to be afraid of monsters?

CHAPTER ELEVEN

Francesca

WE HEARD the helicopter before we saw it.

"I cannot fucking believe it," Giulio murmured as the sleek black helicopter approached the yacht.

"Who is that?"

But even as I asked the question, I knew. I *knew*.

He was here, though for what reason I couldn't say. Giulio and I hadn't done anything wrong and I hadn't tried to escape.

"Come on." Giulio stood and held out his hand to help me up. We walked to the front, toward the helipad, and waited for the helicopter to touch down.

Fausto emerged first, all rugged windswept Italian beauty, but then he turned to help another guest climb out. Katarzyna.

Despite my best efforts to remain unaffected, my stomach knotted painfully. I had a sinking feeling that knot was jealousy, which was absolutely unacceptable. There was no need to complicate this situation with a reality-show level of unnecessary drama. I was merely upset that our private day had been ruined by the man I least wanted to see.

Liar.

Dressed in a gauzy see-through wrap, Katarzyna clung to his arm as they approached. Fausto was still dressed in his usual suit. Did the man ever wear anything else? I couldn't see his eyes behind his sunglasses, but I could feel the weight of his stare on me.

"Ciao!" Katarzyna said brightly as she leaned in to kiss my cheek. "Hope you don't mind that we've come to join you."

Giulio frowned at his father, not saying anything, so I forced a smile for the other woman. "Not at all. It's not like the boat isn't big enough for everyone."

Giulio asked his father for a word, so the two of them moved aside and began speaking rapid Italian. I could tell Giulio was angry, but Fausto's expression was unreadable.

"I hate when they do that," Katarzyna said. "Let's go get some drinks and sit by the pool."

She walked through the yacht as if she'd been here a hundred times before, which I supposed she had. The crew all seemed to know her as she waved at them. I followed, unsure why I didn't like her when she'd done absolutely nothing wrong to me. I vowed to get along today even if I couldn't stop thinking about her in bed with Ravazzani.

When we reached the pool area, she whipped off her cover up revealing a body that models in Milan would kill for. Long limbs, a flat stomach, and no cellulite or extra flab to speak of. Has she eaten a single carb since puberty?

Stop being so petty. What is wrong with you?

"Your suit is gorgeous." I gestured to her black one piece with cutouts on the side.

"Thank you. It's La Perla. A gift from Fausto."

A sour taste in my mouth made it hard to speak. "How nice."

"Yours is nice too. You can never go wrong with a plain bikini. Let's get drinks. Alex makes the best margaritas."

Alex? I stretched out on my deck chair and tried not to feel intimidated. After all, I might have years of dealing with Katarzyna ahead of me. Depressed at the thought, I tilted my face toward the sun and pretended I was alone.

A few minutes later Giulio returned and retook the chair beside me. "Ciao, Katarzyna. *Come va?*"

"Good. What about you, Giulio? Are you behaving today?" She smirked like she had a secret, but her attention was diverted when a crew member arrived for drink orders.

Giulio scowled and stared at the water, so I nudged his leg with my foot. When he looked at me, I sent him a questioning glance. He leaned over and said quietly, "My father was worried that I would take advantage of you out here. That I would anticipate the wedding night."

My jaw fell open. "You've got to be joking."

"I wish I were."

"Aw, you two are adorable," Katarzyna said, pointing at me and Giulio. "I can't wait until the wedding. I have already picked out my dress."

That sickening feeling returned in the pit of my stomach and I reached for my melted mai tai. It was then that movement out of the corner of my eye caught my attention, and all the air left my lungs in a rush.

Clad in only small white swim trunks, Fausto walked toward us, the rest of his incredible body on full display for the first time. Muscles roped across a lean frame covered by golden skin, while wide shoulders sat atop a broad chest decorated with the perfect amount of dark hair. His stomach was trim, his legs long. He moved gracefully, confidently, the king of everything around him, the bulge between his legs shifting with every step.

I. Was. Deceased.

It was too much. My heart was pounding like I'd just run a race, and thank God I was already sitting down. As it was, I shifted on my deck chair, feeling a rush of heat all over that had nothing to do with the sun. I swear his gaze dipped to my breasts, and when I glanced down I could see why. My nipples were poking through the thin fabric of my suit. I swallowed and focused on my drink.

"There you are," Katarzyna cooed at Fausto. "I was just telling Frankie and Giulio how adorable they are."

He lowered himself to the open deck chair, mouth flat and unforgiving. "Were you?"

Katarzyna grabbed the sun tan lotion off the table and crawled onto his chair. "Let me put some lotion on your back, baby."

Fausto didn't argue, merely leaned forward and made room for her behind him. I swore he looked directly at me the entire time Katarzyna slathered his body with slick lotion, her hands rubbing it into his skin like it was a life-saving antidote. Envy crawled its way into my throat. I had to force my eyes elsewhere, or risk saying or doing something really stupid.

"I'm going swimming," Giulio announced, then stepped to the side of the yacht and dove off into the water.

Nice. We weren't even married yet and he'd already abandoned me.

Wait, *yet*? What was I thinking? I would never marry Giulio. I would escape Italy and I would never see the Ravazzanis again.

Closing my eyes, I tilted my face to the sun and tried to block out everything else in my life. I was on a beautiful ship in the most beautiful place in the world. Who knew when the opportunity would arise again once I left Siderno?

"Francesca," Ravazzani snapped. "When was the last time you put on lotion?"

The first words he spoke to me today were about my suntan? "I'm good," I said without opening my eyes.

"That was not what I asked."

I lifted my sunglasses to pin him with an annoyed stare. "Why do you care?"

That apparently wasn't the right answer because his face darkened as his body went still. Even Katarzyna appeared shocked. "I care," he said, "because I do not want you sunburned for the wedding."

Everything inside me longed to scream and throw things at him, but I would lose in any fight with this man—for now. So I dropped my sunglasses back in place and closed my eyes again. "You don't need to worry about that."

"Do as I say or—"

He didn't finish because crew members arrived with our drinks—margaritas for Katarzyna, Giulio, and me, white wine for Ravazzani. I ignored the other couple while Katarzyna chatted on, though I noticed his responses were limited to only one or two words. Why did she put up with him? He couldn't be *that* good in bed.

Please. You know he's a god in bed.

Ugh. I couldn't start imagining it, not here. Not ever.

Giulio finally returned and shook like a dog, raining water down on me. I yelped, the cold droplets surprising me, and tried to push him away. "You rat!"

Katarzyna chuckled. "See? Cute," she said and draped her arms over Ravazzani's shoulders.

I hated watching them together. I had no claim on him—and I definitely hated him for trapping me in Italy—yet I wanted to slap Katarzyna's hands off his body. How in the hell did that make any sense?

Standing, I pushed Giulio over the side of the boat in retaliation. He hit the water with a splash and came up sputtering. I smirked down at him. "That's what you get, G."

He grinned. "Come swim with me again."

"Fine—but first promise not to pull me under any more."

"*Te lo prometto.*"

I sprinted toward the end of the platform and jumped into the water.

Fausto

I made a mistake in bringing Katarzyna.

Needing this to look like a social outing, I had asked my mantenuta to come along. I hadn't seen her since the night at the castello and she always loved the boat. Yet it was clear from Francesca's expression that she didn't care for Katarzyna.

Jealousy, perhaps?

That seemed unlikely, given Francesca's general dislike of me. More likely Katarzyna's habit of never knowing when to be quiet had rubbed Francesca the wrong way. But I noticed the way Francesca's nipples had puckered when I walked out on the deck in my swim trunks. She might not like me, but she was attracted to me.

Something changed between us the night she tried to escape. I read the lust in her eyes, saw the flush on her cheeks. She'd practically been panting when she held the gun on me. My talk of fucking against a wall had aroused her even more.

She was no innocent, and my suspicions about her proved to be correct at every turn. I had a feeling that this girl liked it rough. Just as I did.

And I was dying to find out.

As much as I tried to tell myself otherwise, I was burning with the need to possess her, to keep her for myself. Two days I had avoided her and it wasn't working. I was just as obsessed, just as desperate to have her as before. I couldn't concentrate on anything. My days were spent watching video of her in the winery, the stables. Even with the damn lambs.

Basically, I was fucked.

She was supposed to be for my son, the woman who would bear the next generation of Ravazzani leaders. So I had hoped seeing them together today would change my mind. That it would convince me to stay away from her and stick with my original plan of marrying her to Giulio. Rid me of this shameful craving for a girl young enough to be my daughter.

And then I saw her in that tiny bikini.

Cristo santo, her body was incredible. Soft rounded curves of creamy skin and an ass that I longed to bite. The small triangles of her top barely covered her glorious tits, and I wanted nothing more than to peel back that fabric and suck on her nipples. It was more than her body, however. Her fearless attitude, the way she stood up to me, turned me on. I wanted to control her, to make her beg for me.

Katarzyna pressed against my back, regaining my attention. "Do you want to go in and fuck?" Direct and to the point. That was what I liked best about her.

Did I want to fuck Katarzyna? As I watched Francesca splash in the water with Giulio, I knew the answer. "No."

"Then do you mind if I go swim?"

"Of course not. Have fun."

I pulled out my phone and pretended to work as the three of them swam in the water. Katarzyna mostly took selfies from the edge of the platform for her social media, while Giulio and Francesca laughed as they played together. The two didn't treat each other like lovers. They acted like siblings, if I was honest. They laughed and teased, while maintaining a respectful distance.

It didn't make sense. Didn't he want to fuck her? It was the very reason I'd ordered the helicopter readied and joined them today, because I hadn't been able to stand the thought that they might be screwing. But he kept a friendly mood between them, joking with her like a brother—not a lover.

You're obsessed with her.

Giulio's words from earlier haunted me. First Marco, now my son. They all saw what this girl was doing to me. She was turning me inside out. Ever since I caught her climbing over that wall, I've been panting after her.

The feeling was not abating, either. The craving was growing worse by the minute, haunting my every waking thought. My dreams, too. I dreamed of chasing her through the vineyards until I caught her, pinned her to the rough earth and fucked her senseless.

Something had to give, and I knew what I had to do.

I had to keep her.

She would balk at the role of mantenuta, but I would bring her around. She wasn't interested in marriage, anyway. As my mistress, I could give her the world on a platter. Money, trips, cars...whatever she wanted. It was a coveted position in my world, with power and prestige. Not as much as a wife, of course, but she would be untouchable when I gave her my protection. Then when I tired of her, I would send her back to Toronto or wherever her sexy ass desired. I'd buy her a house or apartment anywhere in the world.

There were plenty of other women—Italian daughters of the 'ndrina—who Giulio could marry. Mancini wouldn't like it, but he wouldn't dare cross me. I was too powerful, and I could do whatever I wanted to Francesca without retribution. It wasn't like she was a virgin.

I watched her juicy ass as she dove under the water and I licked my lips. I couldn't wait to slap that bottom. To watch it bounce as I fucked her from behind.

My dick began to lengthen in my trunks. Minchia! I could not get an erection right now. Standing, I decided to go make a few phone calls at the other end of the boat. The privacy there made it easier to get work done, and if I studied Francesca any longer I was likely to do something stupid.

When I finished my calls, the light had started to fade. I decided to get Katarzyna and take the helicopter back to the castello. After I changed back into my suit, I crossed the salon and found Francesca emerging from the toilet. She adjusted the top of her suit, giving me a flash of nearly an entire globe of flesh, and lust gathered in my groin.

"Wait," I barked as she started for the pool area.

Hand flying to her chest, she spun to face me. "Fuck. You scared the shit out of me."

That dirty mouth. Most Italian women didn't curse like women in other countries, and I wasn't sure if I liked it or not. I stopped in my tracks, keeping to the shadows, where no one from the outside would be able to see us. "Come here."

She cast a glance over her shoulder. "Why?"

"Because I said so, monella."

"I don't think we should be alone in here."

Interesting response. Was she worried about hurting Giulio? I doubted it. "Don't make me repeat myself."

She nibbled on her lip and I could almost see her brain thinking it over. Despite her hesitation, her nipples puckered again, betraying her. Whereas most women would feel fear, Francesca was different. She was attracted to me despite the fear—though she probably hated herself for it.

I would change that. Soon she would beg me to fuck her and lick her pussy. To suck my cock and swallow my come. There would be no shame between us, no limits to the depravity I would show her. And she would love every minute.

She threw her shoulders back and strode toward me, unafraid. Her breasts bounced with every step, her hips swayed, and I could hardly breathe. When she reached me, she arched a brow in challenge, and my hand itched with the desire to throw her over my lap and spank her insolent ass.

But that would come. For now, I had to play this carefully.

She watched me with big round eyes, her chest rising and falling with the force of her breaths. A droplet of water rolled down her temple, and I used my thumb to gently brush the moisture from her soft skin. "Do you like my boat, dolcezza?"

Her throat worked as she swallowed. "I want to say I hate it, but I'd be lying."

I liked to think she was also talking about me. "Good. You'll be spending a lot of time here."

"You still don't understand, Ravazzani. I won't be staying."

I stepped forward, closing the distance between us, and she began backing away. I continued until her spine connected with the oak paneling, then I braced my hands on either side of her head. "Fausto."

Her brows dipped low as she searched my face. "What?"

"When we are alone, I want you to call me Fausto."

"I shouldn't. You're...well, it wouldn't be...." She huffed. "We shouldn't be alone."

I flustered her. Excellent. "We will be, though. Often."

"No, we won't. We shouldn't even be alone now. They'll be wondering where we are."

"I don't care." I dragged my eyes over her stunning features, down to her lips. They were plump and wet with her saliva, begging to be tasted. I had to resist for just a little while longer.

"I'm sure Katarzyna would love to hear that," she whispered.

That was the reminder I needed. I was a heartless bastard, but I was also fair. "I plan to handle that problem in just a few minutes."

"You're going to *kill* her?" Francesca hissed.

I shook my head, disappointed in her opinion of me. Granted, I hadn't shown her much else, but that would soon change. "No, but I've decided I no longer want her."

I watched as she tried to make sense of what I'd said, confusion and trepidation etched in her features. "Why?"

Now she was asking the right questions.

"Because I want someone else." I dipped my head closer and put my lips by her ear. "And one thing you should know, Francesca, is that I always get what I want."

Her breath hitched as I pushed away from the wall. "Buona sera, monella."

Leaving her there, I strode out to the pool area. Giulio and Katarzyna were looking at something on her phone and laughing. "Katarzyna, *andiamo*. We must go."

They both glanced up and Giulio's gaze darted behind me. I assumed Francesca had now reappeared on deck and Giulio was noticing we'd been inside together. I would need to have a talk with my son back home.

Katarzyna gathered her things and kissed Giulio's cheeks. "Don't forget to tag me," she said and then came toward me. "Everything all right?"

"I need to get back."

"Bye, Frankie," Katarzyna said to the woman standing behind me.

I kept my eyes on my son. "My office when you return." He nodded once, probably aware of what I wanted to tell him. Would he warn Francesca? I hoped so. It would make it even harder to win her over...and I relished a challenge when it came to this woman.

Soon we were in the helicopter headed back to my estate. Katarzyna was suspiciously quiet. I had learned the best way to do these things was directly, with no ambiguity. "This between us? It is over."

Katarzyna didn't appear all that surprised. "It's her, isn't it?"

That was none of her business and she knew me well enough not to expect an answer. "I'll get you that property in Portofino you wanted."

"And a diamond bracelet."

I nodded. "I wish you the best, Katarzyna. If you need help, you only need ask."

"Thank you, Fausto." She played with the ties on her cover up. "Want me to suck your cock one last time?"

The idea didn't tempt me in the least. "No, that's not necessary."

She sighed. "God, I will miss you. Well, I will miss your big dick."

My lips twitched, but I said nothing. I wouldn't miss her and we both knew it.

"I hope she is ready. You are not a man most women can handle."

Francesca was strong, perhaps stronger than she even realized. She would be able to handle me. And it would be fun to teach her how....

CHAPTER TWELVE

Francesca

GIULIO and I watched the sun set as the yacht cruised back toward Siderno. We were both quiet, lost in our thoughts.

And one thing you should know, Francesca, is that I always get what I want.

Was Fausto telling me he wanted me? That had certainly been implied as he cornered me against the wall and caged me in with his body. I hadn't felt fear in that moment. Well, perhaps a little, but not because I thought he'd hurt me. I was afraid of my reaction to him, of how excitement pulsed between my legs with just one look from him. My nipples beaded every time he was within fifty feet, like they were issuing some kind of a warning.

Except I didn't want to run away from him. Far from it.

I thought of his hand on my throat, the warmth and strength of his body as he surrounded me, and I wanted more. I wanted to drown in his darkness...and that terrified me.

I was a strong woman. Independent. I had plans for my future, like going to college and finding a normal, safe man to marry. One who didn't run drugs and extort money from others. One who wouldn't get gunned down in the street by his enemies. For God's sake, Fausto's first wife—Giulio's mother—had been shot dead on a beach.

I didn't want that life.

I didn't want to be associated with these people. I was a good person, someone who believed in right and wrong. My father was a criminal, yes, but my sisters and I weren't. We deserved better.

I'm not entirely good, though, am I?

True. By day, I had taken on a more parental role with my twin sisters, watching over them. At night, though, I snuck out of the house to find fun. To find a boyfriend and lose my virginity.

Apparently I was a rebel at heart—which was why I could not be caged here in Italy, like a meek and docile prisoner. I had to find a way out.

"He's going to try to seduce you."

Giulio's words startled me. "What?"

"My father. He is going to try to seduce you."

Tingles raced up the backs of my thighs. "How do you know that? Did he say something?"

Giulio lifted a shoulder. "No, but I can tell."

"That's crazy. I'm supposed to marry you."

"Not anymore. That's why he wants to talk to me as soon as we return."

Oh, God. I was having a hard enough time resisting Fausto as an engaged woman. What happened when the engagement was off? "You have to tell him no."

Giulio grunted and folded his hands behind his head, closing his eyes. "No one tells my father no."

"I do—and you need to stand up to him. Tell him you want to marry me."

He cracked a lid at me. "Why would I do that? I don't want to marry you."

"Giulio, please. You have to help me. I cannot get involved with your father. That would be worse than marrying you—no offense."

"None taken, but you are crazy if you think I can stop him."

"Can't you convince him we are madly in love?"

"He'd never believe it—and I don't like lying to my father." I pulled my sunglasses down and gave him a pointed look, to which he nodded. "Exactly. One lie is enough, believe me."

"Then help me escape."

Giulio sat up and turned to face me, his expression curious. "Why? You could do a lot worse than my father. You like the estate and the castello...and he would treat you with respect."

Yes, but he would also consume me. I would lose myself in Fausto Ravazzani. "I can't. Please, Giulio."

"You will have to deal with him yourself. If you don't want him, then tell him. He'll accept it. He's a reasonable man."

I thought about the man who had drugged me, had locked me in a dungeon. The capo who had killed two men in cold blood. Reasonable? Ha! Hardly.

I pressed my lips together and stared at the water. Clearly, I couldn't count on Giulio. He was too interested in saving himself. I had to do this myself.

"Do not try and escape, Frankie," Giulio said as he reclined once more. "It will only make the situation worse."

"Yeah? We'll see."

"You won't tell him, will you? About me?"

"God, no." I reached over and took his hand. "Even if that was my only way to escape, I wouldn't do that to you. I know what happens if everyone finds out."

He pressed a soft kiss to the back of my hand. "Grazie, bella. I am very grateful."

"It's probably stupid of me. I should blackmail you to help me."

"You don't want to do that. First and foremost, I am a Ravazzani. Not many would dare to blackmail a member of my family."

The threat hung between us until I finally said, "If I did, I suppose I'd be taken to the dungeon and shot dead, too."

His head whipped toward mine. "What?"

"I'd be murdered in the family dungeon...just like those two men the other night."

Giulio's body relaxed. "He didn't kill them. He shot each of them in the leg. They'll limp, but they'll live."

I let out a breath I didn't know I'd been holding. Though my relief made no sense. No one rose to Fausto's rank without killing a fair share of people. Just because he hadn't killed those two men didn't mean he wouldn't ever kill someone else.

"How did you know, by the way? Not even I knew they were bringing Sergio and Rocco to see my father."

"I saw them go into the dungeon and I followed."

Giulio's brows flew up. "You spied on Fausto? *Ma sei pazza?*"

"No, I'm not crazy. But I couldn't help myself."

"Bella, if you are going to stay with my father, you have to learn not to get involved in the 'ndrina business."

"Hello? Are you even listening? I don't want to stay with your father."

"It won't be so bad. You can share him with Katarzyna. She can have Mondays, Wednesday, and Fridays, and you can have—"

I shoved his shoulder. Hard. "Don't even fucking suggest it. He's probably so full of himself that he'd like that idea."

Giulio laughed. "I feel as if you are going to be the one to break him, Frankie."

I could only hope.

Because the alternative was *him* breaking *me*...and I could not let that happen.

Fausto

NURSING A GLASS OF CIRÓ, I kept a close eye on the clock as I waited. Work had distracted me for the rest of the evening, but it was late and a feeling of dread settled in my stomach. Giulio and Francesca should have returned by now.

Was I wrong? Did he feel a romantic attachment to her? I had to tread carefully. My instinct told me Giulio didn't think of Francesca in that manner, but there was a slim chance I had misjudged the situation.

I snorted as I stared out at the dark vineyards. I haven't misjudged a situation since I was fourteen, which is how I've stayed alive so long. No, everything told me the two of them were not attracted to each other and that she was attracted to me.

I'd soon find out.

Just as I was about to go shower, I heard Giulio's Ferrari pull into the drive. Anticipation churned in my gut. I couldn't see them from my windows, but I could hear the sound of their laughter on their way inside, then the front door slammed.

Giulio came to me immediately. He was a good son and I was damn proud of him. He followed directions and stuck to his word. He's never let me down, except for the other night. I hoped he learned his lesson. The brotherhood had to come first, always.

He dropped into a chair across from my desk, so I took my seat as well. "Have a nice time?"

His lips twitched. "You're going to ask, so just ask, Papà."

He was a smart boy, my son. "Before I do, I want to make sure you aren't attached to her. That you won't harbor resentment."

"No resentment. No attachment. I was marrying her because you ordered it."

"You don't want her." It seemed unfathomable to me, but I had to press. I had to be sure.

He shrugged, as if it made no difference to him. "I would have married her, but I don't have those kinds of feelings toward her."

It was as I had suspected. "Good. I'll find you another wife. An Italian woman who won't give you any trouble. One who knows this life."

"Whatever you say, Papà. Are we done? I have to run out for a little bit."

This had seemed too easy. "You won't mind if I take her as my mantenuta?"

One side of his mouth kicked up. "No, I won't mind—but I don't think she will agree."

"We'll see."

"She's very stubborn and still eager to escape. I don't think she'll come willingly."

"I am aware of all this—and again, we shall see."

My son stood and thrust his hands into his pockets. He seemed to be contemplating his next words. "*Allora*...just don't hurt her, Papà. She's a good person, with a good heart. She's in a country where she hardly speaks the language and is basically a prisoner here. Have patience with her."

Part of me wanted to lash out at him—I'd never hurt a woman in my life—but I understood. My son had a good heart, as well. When he was six, he rescued a baby bird and kept it alive until the creature had been healed enough to fly away. In boarding school, he fought to defend kids who couldn't defend themselves. It made sense he'd look out for Francesca, too.

"I won't hurt her. She is safe with me, *sul mio onore*." I rarely swore on my honor, so he knew how serious I was about this.

He nodded and turned to walk to the door. "Oh, I heard she spied on you the other night in the dungeon. That must have been a shock."

"She told you?"

"Yes. She thought you killed Sergio and Rocco."

"I know."

His brows climbed up his forehead. "You didn't tell her the truth?"

"Why would I, when the lie serves my purposes?"

"You want her frightened." Instead of answering, I sipped my wine to hide my smile. Giulio dragged a hand across his jaw. "I don't know whether to applaud you or pity you."

"Neither. I'll handle Francesca."

Giulio held up his palms. "I'll stay out of it. Now, if you don't need anything, I'll head over to the club."

"Go. Be safe, figlio mio."

"I'll see you in the morning." He disappeared out the door.

Now that I was alone, anticipation flooded my veins like the rush of a drug. As much as I wanted to wait, I couldn't.

I needed to see her. Now.

Downing my wine, I carefully placed the glass on the desk and left

my office. The house was quiet as I made my way into the wing opposite my own. What would I find when I entered Francesca's room? Was
she showering? Relaxing in the bath? My cock twitched at the fantasy
of seeing her wet and soapy golden skin, touching those soft and
supple curves.

I didn't bother knocking. She would tell me to go away, and I would
not be deterred from seeing her. Throwing open the door, I stopped
short.

Francesca sat on the bed with her arms crossed, glaring at me.

Oh, yes. I liked her spirit very much. She would not be easy to win,
but the victory would be sweet in the end. "Waiting on me already?"

"What are you doing in here, Ravazzani? This is my room and you
cannot just walk in whenever you feel like it."

I closed the door behind me. "Oh, but I can, actually. This is my
house. I don't need your permission to come in here."

She stood up, her body covered by the wrap she'd worn on the
boat. *Madonna*, that meant the bikini was still on underneath. I
approached her, but she didn't back away this time. Instead, she bit her
lip. "Say whatever it is you came in to say and then leave."

"Always playing tough, but I am not fooled."

"What is that supposed to mean?"

"It means you don't really want to escape. Your effort to leave was
half-assed at best. Instead you spend your time with the lambs and
Vincenzo, not searching the grounds for a wall to climb over. You
could have stolen one of the cars. Or jumped off the boat today and
swam to shore. You are resourceful and smart, Francesca. If you want
something bad enough, you make it happen."

I moved closer, almost touching her. I could count every eyelash
and freckle on her lovely face as she stared up at me. Reaching out, I
twirled a piece of her golden hair around my finger. "So I have to ask,
why are you still here?"

Her gaze locked on my face. "I was biding my time before I tried
again."

"*Cazzata*. Your life in Toronto was boring. You were dying there,
like a plant starved of water. I saved you from that loser boyfriend,

from the lackluster orgasms and sneaking around. There is so much I can show you, dolcezza. So much I want to give you."

"So you're my savior? Is that it?"

I chuckled softly. "I'm no savior. They call me il Diavolo for a reason, and that is because I am as wicked and evil as they come. But if you want to get on your knees for me in gratitude, I will not object."

Her shoulders trembled as her breath hitched. She hadn't backed away—had barely moved—since I entered. She seemed to be waiting to see what I would do. "In your fucking dreams," she finally said, but there was no heat behind it.

Slowly, I dragged my thumb across her lips, loving the feel of the slick plump flesh. She was gorgeous, but the kind of earthy beauty that burrowed under a man's skin. A woman who should be worshipped every single day with kisses and orgasms. I wanted to both take care of her and wreck her in the same breath. "That mouth will get you in trouble one day. But I'll let it slide tonight because I'd rather get on my knees for you."

"What does that mean?"

"It means I intend to have you and I'm tired of waiting."

I bent down until my knees met the carpet. Then I slid my palms up over her calves, behind her legs, with my face resting right below her full tits. My dick pulsed as it thickened in my trousers and I had to resist the urge to stroke myself. Fuck, I wanted this woman badly.

As my hands continued up her body, I lifted the flimsy piece of cloth that covered her. Francesca watched me with hooded eyes, her skin flushed. "Take this off," I told her.

"What about Giulio?"

"You are no longer engaged to my son. Take the fucking cover up off, Francesca."

She didn't argue, just whipped the thin garment over her head, leaving her in the black bikini I'd both loved and hated today.

Santo cazzo Madre di Cristo.

I couldn't breathe, and my cock was now rock hard. She was even more gorgeous up close, her skin smelling of sun and salt. Her nipples beaded behind her suit, and her chest rose and fell as she took rapid breaths. But part of winning this battle meant I needed her full surrender.

And I never played fair.

My fingers trailed up her inner thigh and between her legs, and I let my breath warm the skin of her stomach. I brushed my thumb over the slick fabric of her suit until I found her clit. I rubbed back and forth a few times, letting her have a taste of the pleasure I planned to give her.

"This is your last chance." I stroked her again, harder this time. "Tell me to leave—or I am eating this pussy until you cream all over my face."

"Oh, God," she whispered, her body swaying slightly. "We can't. You can't. This isn't...."

She was weakening, I could sense it. I kept stroking her clit through the thin suit, the smell of her arousal filling my nostrils and making me crazy. "I am dying to taste you. Aren't you dying to know how good it will feel when my tongue flicks your clit?"

Her fingers latched onto my head, clutching me closer instead of pushing me away—and I had my answer. Plucking at the strings of her suit bottom, I quickly untied them and the scrap of fabric dropped to the carpet. A small patch of trimmed hair covered her mound, her pussy lips pink and swollen, and my mouth watered. As I kissed my way down her stomach, I untied the back of the bikini top, as well, glancing up as Francesca pulled it the rest of the way off. Then she was completely naked and I looked my fill at this gorgeous creature.

Full breasts with rose-tipped nipples and dark areolas. A flat stomach and long legs. Her golden skin was unblemished and I longed to see it covered in my bite marks. Soon, I vowed. I wanted to take my time with her, explore every inch of her body, but tonight was about her pussy. "Get on the bed," I rasped, pushing to my feet.

She turned and crawled on the bed, nearly making me come with the seductive sway of her ass as she positioned herself. When she was on her back, I ordered, "Now spread your legs."

She complied eagerly, showing me the flesh between her thighs, which was already glistening from arousal. I was ready to make a meal out of this girl.

Wedging myself between her thighs, I lowered myself until my stomach met the mattress. "How do you like it, Francesca?"

She didn't answer, her brows lowered in confusion. "What do you mean?"

"I want to make you come at least twice, so tell me what you like. My tongue inside your pussy? Sucking your clit? Every woman is different."

Her mouth worked but nothing came out. Had I finally shocked her?

Then I realized what her reaction meant.

"That stronzo never ate your pussy?"

Instead of answering, she tried to roll away. I immediately clamped my arms around her thighs and held her up to my mouth. "Too late, piccola monella. You're mine now."

CHAPTER THIRTEEN

Francesca

I HAD CLEARLY LOST my mind.

Fausto Ravazzani had undressed me and caressed me between my legs. Dropped to his knees for me. Had I complained or tried to stop him? No, because the way he bossed me around turned my insides to molten lava and my brain to mush. It was like he started talking dirty and I lost the ability to think.

So help me, I wanted him.

As he kissed my inner thigh, his strong hands held me in place. Hands that had done unspeakable violence, yet could be tender, as well. I was completely bared before him, his face close to my pussy. Did I smell all right down there? I knew from watching porn that a lot of guys enjoyed it, but oral had only come up once with David, when he said it wasn't his favorite thing to do. Of course, he'd liked it when I gave him head.

The tip of Fausto's tongue touched my folds—and I jumped.

"Relax," he breathed. "Put your hands on your tits and feel what I am doing to you, bellissima."

God, hearing Italian words come out of his mouth in that low tone was like sex on a plate. I cupped my breasts, which were already heavy and aching, and squeezed my nipples. Pleasure streaked through me. Fausto dipped his head and licked me, and heat suffused my lower half. Growling, he pressed closer and tongued my entrance.

"Fuck, you are so wet for me."

Then he began moving his lips and tongue, exploring my labia, until he reached my clit. The first swipe of his tongue over that tiny bundle of nerves caused me to slam my eyelids shut and throw my head back. It was electric, like a switch to the pleasure center of my brain had been flipped. Tingles ran up and down my legs and I could only lie there as he did it again and again, flicking and circling the nub with his tongue.

His finger worked its way into my pussy, stretching me, and I moaned. "Oh, my God."

The reaction earned me another finger and a long suck of my clitoris. My toes curled and I could feel the orgasm building in my belly. How was this happening so fast? "I'm so close," I told him. "Oh, God. Keep going, please."

Unbidden, my hips started rocking against his face, my body desperate for release. I think I would have agreed to anything at that moment, but luckily Fausto didn't try and take advantage. He continued to work my clitoris and pump his fingers into my pussy.

It wasn't enough. I really wanted him to fuck me.

The thought of his muscled body, so manly and strong, pounding into me pushed me over the edge. I shouted as my walls convulsed around his fingers, my limbs shaking. The euphoria washed over me, more intense than I'd ever felt before. This wasn't the gentle waves of a self-induced orgasm. This was a tsunami dragging me to depths I had never imagined before, drowning me in endorphins.

When it finally ended, I sagged into the mattress, limp. Fausto's mouth gentled but didn't stop as he lapped up the wetness at my entrance. His eyes were closed as if he were savoring me, and I couldn't look away from his beautiful face. Why did he have to be so incredible looking? It would make him easier to resist if he were slightly less attractive.

I could still see him in those tiny swim trunks, his mature and virile body on full display. This was no boy, more interested in his own pleasure like David. This was a man who knew what he wanted and took it —and right now that thing was me. I licked my lips, a fresh shot of desire going through me.

His lids opened and blue eyes pinned me to the spot. They were wild and hungry. Feral. A little scary, even. He continued to taste me while staring up at me, as if he were gauging my reaction. I couldn't move, my muscles now lax.

Then he crawled over me, kissing my skin along the way, until he reached my breasts. I liked that I was completely naked and he was still dressed. Something about that felt naughty, as if I were seducing him. My hands were still on my breasts, so he nudged my palm aside with his nose to draw a nipple into his mouth. He sucked hard, with long pulls that echoed between my legs, directly in my clit. Everything was heightened, my body more sensitive now that I'd come, and he seemed in no hurry to move on as he lavished attention on my breast.

Soon I was writhing, my heart racing as I panted, my nails digging into his shoulders. He switched to my other breast, his tongue flicking my nipple then biting it before bringing the nipple into his mouth to suck. I was a shuddering, mindless mess, unable to stop moaning as it wore on. Was he trying to foreplay me to death?

His fingers slipped between my legs, rubbing my clit exactly like I did when I masturbated, with light steady pressure, and I came a second time. When I finally calmed, he released my breast and kissed my neck. "*Tu sei perfetta.*"

You are perfect.

A sweet Fausto Ravazzani? I was used to him being an asshole, but this side was even more dangerous. Before I could wrap my head around this change in him, he shifted and rolled off the bed. Standing, he raked his eyes along my body, an erection bulging in his trousers. Then he turned and started for the door. "Buona sera, Francesca."

Wait, what was happening? Didn't he want to have sex with me? "Where are you going?"

"To bed. Sleep well, dolcezza."

"But...."

I didn't know how to ask it. Worse, I knew I shouldn't. This man was bad for me. I should be grateful he didn't want to fuck me.

But I wasn't.

I wanted to know the feel of his dick, what it would be like to have him slide inside me. Fill me up and overwhelm me in the very best way.

You're fucked up, Francesca.

Yes, clearly.

As usual, Fausto had no trouble following my thoughts. "I'm not going to fuck you tonight. I want you to crave it. To need my cock so badly that you beg me for it. And when I do fuck you, you're never going to forget it." He opened the door and something akin to panic filled me.

"Wait," I called as he started to leave.

"Yes?" He looked bored, perfectly under control. Nothing like the ravenous lover of a few moments ago.

"This was a one-time thing. Just tonight."

The edges of his mouth curled. "If you need to believe such nonsense in order to sleep tonight, then by all means, lie to yourself. But I will fuck you as much as I want, whenever I want. And you'll enjoy every second, I promise."

He left without another word. I stayed there on the bed—naked, my body humming from two fantastic orgasms—and resolved to make him eat those words. I would resist him. If he thought to make me the next Katarzyna, he was sorely mistaken. I had no interest in being his fuck toy.

I needed to come up with a better escape plan than sneaking out the back door and walking to find help. No, I had to find a true way off the estate and out of Fausto Ravazzani's life.

———————

A KNOCK WOKE me way too early.

I'd taken to sleeping in the last few days, not eager to see anyone at breakfast. And last night I stayed up late after Fausto's double orgasm fest, thinking about his promise. Was I so weak as to sleep with the man who'd almost been my father-in-law? The man who wouldn't let me go home?

No, I was strong. A Mancini. We were not weak and we were not quitters. So as attracted as I was to Fausto, I had to resist him.

"Signorina, are you awake?" It was one of the Ravazzani staff.

"Yes?"

"Signore Ravazzani requests your presence for breakfast."

What the fuck? Did he think he could just order me around because he made me come twice? "Tell him I'm sleeping."

The door opened and the maid peeked inside, her eyes apologetic. "He said you might say that, and to tell you that if you are not downstairs in ten minutes he will come up and get you himself."

The sad part was that he would absolutely do it, the stronzo.

"Fine." I was starving anyway, having skipped dinner last night. "But tell him I need fifteen minutes."

"He won't be happy, signorina."

I smiled sweetly as I pushed up out of bed. "He'll get over it."

She seemed horrified by my cavalier attitude, but I didn't care. Fausto needed to learn that I was not at his beck and call just because he'd given me head for the first time. I took my time in the bathroom. I showered and brushed my teeth, then applied mascara and sunscreen. I chose a pair of tiny shorts and a halter top that showed off my boobs and the lower part of my stomach.

I was not dressing to entice him. I was dressing to show him what he would never have again. Last night was a mistake, a moment of weakness on my part that would not be repeated, and Fausto could find someone else to jump into bed with.

I bounded down the stairs and went into the dining room. When I opened the door, he put his phone on the table and frowned at me. He wore a white dress shirt with no tie, the first two buttons at his throat undone, revealing off the thick column of his throat. His eyes swept my outfit, lingering on my bare legs, before returning to my face. Not about to give in, I selected a seat far away from him, even though the only other place setting was on his right.

"No." His voice rang out in the cavernous room. "You will sit by me."

"I want to sit here."

He flicked his fingers and the two maids in the room scurried out, leaving him and I alone. "You don't seem to understand. When I give an order, I expect it to be obeyed."

"I am not a dog or your toy. I will do what I want."

I could see the smoldering challenge in his cool gaze, the ruthless determination. Still, I would not back down.

"Come here."

"Are you not listening to me? You cannot order me around."

He put his elbows on the table and steepled his fingers. "If you do not come here, I will pull you over my lap and spank you. All the staff and probably Zia will hear. Is this what you want?"

I glared at him, trying to see if he was serious or not.

Shit, he looked serious.

"Fine," I grumbled and went over to the empty seat on his right. "I'll sit here."

"No." He pushed back from the table a bit. "You'll sit on my lap."

My skin grew hot. "That's—"

"Would you rather have the spanking, monella?"

I flicked my eyes toward the door, hoping someone would come in and save me. Where was Giulio or Zia? This man was a tyrant and everyone just let him get away with it.

"I am losing patience, Francesca."

I swallowed, but forced myself forward. What was the big deal? I could sit on his lap for a few minutes. We'd been more intimate last night, so where was the harm in this?

I slid sideways onto his lap, his thighs hard under my legs. He was warm and smelled like an expensive cologne or aftershave, the kind that could mesmerize you if you got too close. My whole body was aware of where he touched me, like he was a magnet for my blood cells.

Instead of letting me sit to the side, he quickly repositioned me with my back to his front, throwing my legs on the outside of his thighs. In seconds I was spread open, my body reclined against his.

When he tried to unfasten my shorts, I put my hands down to stop him. "What are you doing?"

"Grab the armrests." When I didn't move fast enough, he gave a light slap to the inside of my thigh. "Do it."

Heat spread from the spot he struck me, but it wasn't pain. It was a rush of excitement, and I put my hands on the armrests. After unbuttoning the shorts, his hand slid directly into my panties, reaching down until he cupped my pussy. The cloth didn't give him a lot of room to maneuver but he shifted his fingers over my clit. I gasped, sparks racing along my spine. "Stop," I said. "Someone will walk in."

"Then that means you had better come quickly." He kissed the nape of my neck then sank his teeth into the flesh and tendons there. Wetness flooded between my legs, aiding his movements over my clit. He licked over his bite marks. "I want to bite you everywhere, Francesca. Mar that beautiful skin with my teeth."

Then he began speaking a long string of Italian I didn't understand, but the sexy words along with the low, gravely way he said them filled me with fire, like he'd struck a match inside my belly. Soon I was rocking my hips, seeking, chasing, grasping at the orgasm just another few strokes away, the pleasure coiling as my muscles tightened. Fuck, yes. I needed this so badly.

All of a sudden, he paused, his fingers sliding away, not touching where I needed them most. What was he doing? I squirmed, trying to get him to finish me. "Fausto," I whined, on the precipice. "*Please.*"

His lips traveled up my throat to my ear. "Whose toy is this?"

Oh, God. Why had I ever said I wasn't his toy? Now he had to try to prove me wrong.

I couldn't answer. Instead I rubbed my ass against his very hard dick.

He grunted and shifted to hold my hips still. "Tell me, dolcezza. Whose toy are you? Who does your pussy belong to?"

"No, I can't. Please."

He moved his fingers along my labia, but not over the swollen center that begged for friction. His free hand came up to circle my throat. "I'll give you what you want. Just tell me. I want to hear the words."

My body screamed even as my ears rang with denial. But I was weak, so weak, when he touched me. It was like I had no control over my movements, no willpower. I was an animal who needed to come. Reason had long since departed.

The words tumbled out of my mouth. "I'm your toy, Fausto."

"Who does your pussy belong to?"

I dug my nails into the wooden armrest. "You, Fausto. My pussy belongs to you."

He moved his fingers to my clit and the hand at my throat squeezed lightly, but it was enough. I detonated, my body trembling against him as I came, and the world blanked out as the orgasm went on and on. I was floating on a sea of color and air, far away from mafia bosses and castles. Nothing mattered, except this glorious feeling.

But nothing good ever lasted. And when the orgasm subsided, shame instantly filled me.

How quickly my show of bravado had crumbled. A few pets of my clit and he had me panting, begging, practically drooling for him. I was pathetic.

My eyes started to fill, but I would not cry in front of him. What had happened was humiliating enough. I couldn't stand it if he saw my tears, too.

I started to shove off his lap, but strong arms held me in place. "Do not regret what happens between us. You like what I do to you, so don't question why."

"Do not tell me how to feel. You might control my body, but you don't control my mind, Fausto."

"You are strong willed, which makes my dick hard. But you will find I am strong willed, as well. Just remember that I will always win."

I pushed up off him and he let me go this time. I buttoned my shorts without looking back at him, then I grabbed a corentto off the table and walked out of the dining room. He and his hard dick could go fuck themselves.

CHAPTER FOURTEEN

Fausto

WORK WAS A WASTE OF TIME. I couldn't concentrate, my mind still stuck on Francesca. I hadn't slept last night, even after jacking off in the shower. This morning I made myself come again after what happened in the dining room, standing in the bathroom and furiously stroking myself. My cock would chafe if I kept this up.

I had to fuck her soon.

She would have let me last night. Or this morning. But I wanted her ready for it. She hadn't liked giving in to me in the dining room, but it was a lesson she had to learn. As my mantenuta, she was at my disposal, our relationship at my whim. I'd never had a mistress who lived with me before, but I figured that only made things more convenient. I could have Francesca whenever I wanted, no waiting required.

"Are you paying attention, Rav?"

Marco's voice snapped me out of my thoughts. "Yes."

We were on a conference call, but our side was muted. The discussion about what to do with the Avellinos now that D'Agostino died was droning on. Most of the upper-ranking bosses of La Provincia were on the call, where we always talked in code, but my opinion carried the most weight. The Ravazzanis had issues with the Avellinos in the past and I stood to lose the most if the peace fell apart.

They were discussing the Avellino's newest venture, computer fraud. Apparently, the eldest son had set it up and the family was raking in money hand over fist. I could hear the jealousy from the other capos over the phone line.

"Isn't there a sister?" I asked Marco. "Eleven or twelve years of age?"

"She is fifteen," Marco answered. "What are you thinking?"

"We could betroth her to Giulio now that I've decided to end his arrangement with Francesca. Merge the future of the two families."

"A lot could happen in three years, though."

"So, marry them now? He could wait until she was of age to consummate it."

"Sure, but how do you know she isn't already spoken for?"

"I don't, but I could convince Enzo D'Agostino to see things my way."

"Every other capo is probably thinking the same," Marco noted, tilting his head to the phone.

"Probably, but none of them have access like we do." He knew I meant access to the drugs that came in through our ports.

"True. So should I reach out?"

"Yes. Ask Enzo to the yacht with his woman. I'll bring Francesca and we'll make a day of it."

Marco's brows lifted. "So Francesca has agreed to be your mantenuta. That was fast."

Marco thought I should have punished Francesca after her escape attempt. He hadn't been happy that I let her off so easily. While he didn't say it outright, he clearly thought I was soft when it came to her —and capos could not afford to be soft. Ever.

"We are still negotiating her role, but yes. She'll accept the position." Based on her reaction to me in the dining room, I believed there was very little I couldn't get Francesca to agree to. I pushed out of my chair but didn't reach for my suit jacket. "Set it up and text me. I'm going outside for the rest of the day."

My cousin's jaw fell open. "You are leaving this call? And what about the rest of today's work? You never take off like this."

"I am today. Finish up for me on the call. My decision has already been made, but tell them we are thinking over the next course of action. No one needs to know about the D'Agostino girl."

I reached the door, but Marco wasn't done with me yet, apparently. "You are going outside to find her."

The sun was high up in the sky and it was a glorious day, not a cloud in sight. I knew Francesca would be either in the vineyards or with the animals. I wanted to taste the sun on her skin and see the Siderno dirt beneath her feet. "Try not to be too jealous, cugino."

"*Brutto figlio di puttana bastardo*," he cursed behind me as I left.

I chuckled and headed to the rear of the castello. Giulio's car was still not in the drive, and I wondered if he'd come home last night. I sent Marco a text, asking about the information on Giulio's girl. I needed to know who my son was spending time with, especially after leaving the drop early the other night. Then I put my phone away and walked the path I'd traveled hundreds of times, over the land that had belonged to my ancestors. I loved every bit of it.

My wife hadn't cared for the estate. She'd preferred shopping in Milan and Rome to staying in Siderno. When she was in town, she liked showing herself off at the beach instead of "playing the farmer" here on the grounds. I hadn't minded. We hadn't loved each other and slept together infrequently after Giulio was born. I wanted more kids and assumed we had time. Then she'd been killed, and all my efforts went into raising my son.

Giulio didn't seem to care much for the land, either. He had played outside as a young boy, but now showed little interest in the businesses on the estate. Of late, he preferred the clubs and posh lifestyle in the city. Someday I would need to train him on how to oversee all this. It would become his responsibility when I died.

"Signore Ravazzani," one of the workers said, tipping his cap at me.

"Buona sera, Adelmo. Have you seen the signorina?"

"Sì. I saw the signorina a quarter of an hour ago by the stables."

"Grazie. How is your wife's foot?"

"It is better, signore. The infection has cleared up and she's back on her feet."

"I am glad to hear it. Let me know if she needs anything else."

"Thank you for sending the doctor, signore. We are so grateful to you and your family."

I clapped him on the back. "No need to thank me. Unless she wants to send over some *sfogliatella*. Do not tell Zia, but your wife makes the best I've ever tasted."

Adelmo nodded, his smile wide. "Of course, Signore Ravazzani. It would be our pleasure. I'm headed home for *riposo* anyhow."

Most of the estate staff returned home between the hours of one and four o'clock during these hot summer months for a riposo. Then they would return and work until after sundown.

"Give her my regards," I said as I walked away.

The stables were not far from the barn and the farm animals. I was surprised Francesca wasn't in the vineyards, as she seemed to enjoy plants more than most people. Except for the lambs, I didn't hear of her often on this side of the estate.

I could see Zia in the gardens, tending to her aubergine and lettuce. She grew much of what we ate in the castello, and though I worried about her in the heat, she loved being outside. I didn't call out, however, as I didn't want to explain why I wasn't in my office.

That was no one's business but mine. And soon to be Francesca's.

I found her leaning against the wooden fence of the paddock, watching as a groom exercised one of the stallions. The sun had warmed her skin to a golden color, and my mouth watered. She still wore the tiny top and skin-tight shorts, and I could only imagine the thoughts of the men on the estate as they watched her today. Probably the same thoughts I'd been having about her since breakfast.

I leaned close to her ear. "Ciao, bellissima."

She started, her body jolting into the fence. "What the fuck, Fausto? Don't sneak up on me like that."

I wanted to spank her ass for ordering me around with that filthy mouth, but I figured that could wait until we were alone. There were too many eyes, even at one o'clock. "Are you having a nice day?"

"Do you ride?" she asked instead of answering my question.

"Yes. Do you?"

"I used to. My sister Gia was always more into horses than Emma and I."

"Do you miss your sisters?"

She sighed and placed her chin atop her hands on the railing. "I do, but they are closer to each other. They're twins," she explained as if I didn't already know. "It's like they can communicate without talking."

"I've heard some twins can do that."

"Giulio let me call them on his phone yesterday and I loved hearing their voices."

I blinked at this revelation. I hadn't meant to cut her off from her family forever, but giving her a phone so soon was a risk. Still, a sliver of guilt worked its way under my ribs. "I will let you call them whenever you like, dolcezza."

She turned, put her back to the fence, and faced me. The tip of her nose had turned pink. She bit her lip as she stared up at me. "I want a phone, Fausto."

I couldn't resist. I leaned down and took her mouth, needing to sample her lips. They were warm and soft, and I thrust my tongue inside, eager to taste every bit of her in this moment. I wanted her sighs and moans, her adoration and her tears. I wanted to own her, body and soul.

My hands found her hips and I let my fingers rest on the sun-kissed skin above her waistband, her tits pushing against my chest. When she rose on her toes to get closer, I cupped her ass with both hands and lifted her up. Long legs wrapped around my hips and I rested her against the fence as I continued to eat at her mouth. Fuck, she tasted so good, like wine and olives. Salty and sweet, exactly like her. I angled my head, trying to get deeper, sweeping my tongue over hers.

I was already hard, my body primed for her the instant our mouths touched. It would be so easy to drag her shorts down her legs and sink inside her body. Fuck, I wanted that. Could I make her beg for my cock and have her not regret it yet?

Her arms twined around my neck, her little whimpers driving me crazy. She was the hottest, most responsive piece of ass I'd ever had—and we hadn't even fucked yet. I swear, she was going to kill me.

She drew back, her fingers threading through my hair. "I think we should find an empty stall so I can suck your cock, capo."

I froze, every muscle clenching. Was she serious? Or was she trying to gain the upper hand with me? Something about the bold offer, so out of character for her, struck me as false.

But God, I wanted it. Despite the reason for her request, I still craved having her lips wrapped around my cock, sucking me down. I closed my eyes and prayed for strength. Soon. I had to remain strong. I needed to win over her mind as well as her body.

I stepped back and lowered her to the ground. With little regard for who might see, I slapped her ass. Hard. "Later, monella. I want to show you something first."

Francesca

FAUSTO WAS SUSPICIOUSLY CHARMING.

Over the next hour, he took me around the estate grounds, pointing out various places and trees, showing me where he'd played as a boy, and I tried not to fall under his spell. I couldn't allow him to worm his way under my skin. I was still angry with him for what happened in the dining room this morning, not to mention horrified by my wanton behavior. How easily I'd given in to him, with just a few strokes of his magic fingers....

I had to gain the upper hand with him. The only way I could do that was through sex. I had no other leverage—and he knew it. So if I had to give a few blow jobs, I would if it meant getting a phone or finding a way to escape.

Though I hadn't been entirely lying. I did want to suck his cock. I don't care what it said about me, but I liked giving blow jobs. I was good at it—at least David had said so—and it made me feel powerful.

I'd spent enough time rubbing up against Fausto's crotch in the last twenty-four hours so I had a pretty good idea of what he was pack-ing...and I needed to see it. Touch it. *Taste* it.

God, I was hopeless.

A kidnapped mafia princess who could only think about getting into the pants of her kidnapper. Was this Stockholm Syndrome? I learned about it in school last year, how some captives could become enamored of their captors. Has my brain already twisted that far?

He treated me like a doll, not like a person with a mind of her own. He'd degraded me, made me come three times, and asserted his domi-nance over me at every turn. So why did I find that so fucking hot?

Because you are messed up, Frankie.

It was the same reason I snuck out to find David and gladly offered up my virginity. I had a darkness inside me, a desperate need for excite-ment and danger. Fausto had somehow recognized it in me and was using it to his advantage.

"Where did you go, Francesca?"

I looked up at him, his beautiful face radiant in the warm Italian sun. The estate workers were on their afternoon break, leaving us completely alone. My heart raced, every bit of me alive in his presence, yet I felt at peace, too.

It was comfortable between us, walking with our hands clasped through the rows of grape vines back toward the castello. He'd taken me to a small stream where he played as a boy. We skipped a few rocks together, though mine never went as far as his.

"Why did you decide to break my engagement to Giulio?"

He chuckled and fingered a grape leaf. "You are just asking that now?"

Bastard. I pressed my lips together, knowing he was right. I should have asked it last night before I let him strip me naked and lick my pussy, but I lost the ability to think around him. "That is not an answer."

He flicked his fingers dismissively, a move I was coming to learn was the Italian version of shrugging a shoulder. "Because I decided I wanted you."

"Why?"

"Because you make my dick hard and I get what I want. There was nothing keeping us from exploring what it is we feel for the other except for the engagement. And there are many Italian girls who can marry my son. So...."

God, the absolute ego of this man. "How do you know what I feel for you?"

He smirked, his lips curled in male satisfaction. "You eye-fucked me on the yacht when I came out in my trunks. Your breath hitches every time I get close. Should I tell you how wet your pussy gets when I touch you?"

No, he needn't bother. I was well aware.

"If I'm not marrying Giulio, then let me go back to Toronto."

"Not yet."

I cast him a hard glare. "My father won't like you keeping me here for no reason."

"You have a very specific reason for being here and that is to take care of my needs. If your father wished a different life for you, then he should have ensured you remained a virgin."

Jerking my hand out of his grasp, I stopped in my tracks and gaped at him. I didn't even know which part of that was more horrifying. "Fuck you, Fausto. I will not become your mistress."

I could see the anger brewing behind his light eyes, the tightening of his jaw. He stalked toward me until he was looming over me, blocking out the sun. "How many times have I made you come in the last twenty hours?"

I lifted my jaw, not about to answer such a stupid question. "That doesn't matter."

"The fuck it doesn't. Three times, Francesca. You haven't put up a fight or even tried to stop me. Three times you've offered up that pussy because you wanted me to touch you."

"You left me no choice!"

He lifted his hand and traced the outline of my hard nipple with his thumb. The halter top didn't need a bra, which meant my nipples were obvious to everyone, including Fausto. "I haven't forced you. I think you like what I do to you. I think you like the darkness as much as I do."

I closed my eyes. Damn this man's perceptiveness.

His thumb continued to stroke my nipple and I swayed toward him. Electric sparks raced through my body, and wetness pooled between my thighs.

"That's it," he crooned. "See how good it will be between us? I will take such good care of you."

"I don't want to be your mistress," I breathed, grasping at anything to keep me from reaching for him.

"We want to fuck each other. Who cares what the label is?"

"I do." I stepped back and slapped his hand away. "It matters to me."

He thrust his hands into his trouser pockets, all traces of teasing wiped from his expression. This was the man who'd kidnapped me, who'd studied me like a piece of meat in my father's study. "You were given to me as repayment on a debt owed. I can return you and declare that debt unpaid. Perhaps take one of your sisters in exchange. Or, I could kill your father for giving me a woman who has fucked half of Toronto. It's your choice."

I sucked in a huge gust of air, outrage smacking into every cell and pore like I'd run into a wall. The absolute nerve! How dare he drag me for having one sexual partner? "I slept with *one* man! One, you asshole! How many women have you slept with, hmm? In case you haven't been told, this is the twenty-first century, not the ye olden days. Women are allowed to have sex before marriage."

His mouth curved. The bastard actually looked...pleased by my outburst, which made no fucking sense. I threw up my hands. "God, I hate you. I will never stop trying to escape you. No matter what happens, I will leave here. Somehow, some way, I will get away from you."

In a flash, his hand shot up to cup the back of my neck, holding me still. His face drew closer until he was inches from my mouth. "It pleases me to learn that only one man dared put his cock inside you before me. It pleases me very much."

I put a hand on his chest, already feeling my anger fade into something far more dangerous. Why did his possessiveness turn me on? "You're a barbarian."

"Very much so. Which is why I am the most powerful man in Italy. You would be wise never to forget it."

"How can I when you never stop bragging about it?"

"Cristo santo, that mouth." He dragged a thumb over my lips, making me shiver. "I wonder if you are ready to get what you asked for earlier."

The stables. His cock in my mouth.

"I'm not in the mood any more," I lied, even as my pussy clenched in excitement.

"Cazzata," he whispered. "If I unzipped my pants, you'd drop to your knees in the dirt right here."

I hated that I found the visual totally appealing. He must have read it on my face, too, because he grinned, his gaze turning soft and adoring. "Yes, I think you might."

"You're the worst."

"Yes, but you like it rough and mean, just like I do." He stepped back but grabbed my hand. "Come on, dolcezza. Let's see if I'm right."

CHAPTER FIFTEEN

Francesca

HE TOOK me to the stables.

I paused outside, unable to take the final steps into the building. Was I really doing this? *You teased him with it.* God, I was an idiot. How had I ever thought to gain the upper hand with this man? He saw through my every move and turned it back around on me.

He slapped my ass. "Get inside a stall. Show me how much you want my cock in your mouth."

The words melted my insides and weakened my resistance. I desperately wanted to suck him off. I wanted to be on my knees, choking on Fausto's dick. Just the visual was enough to soak my panties.

He wants it, too. Show him what you can do, Frankie.

I would do this once. Never again. I was not Fausto's mistress.

"I am not your mistress," I repeated over my shoulder as I started inside.

He said nothing and watched my ass in the tiny shorts. I put a tiny bit of sway into my hips, hoping he enjoyed the show. Somehow, I would win this battle between us.

Two grooms were working in the stables—and Fausto immediately ordered them to get out. The men scurried from the building without a word, eyes averted, clearly terrified of the capo. That only turned me on even more, which I found both telling and terrifying.

Do not ever try to tell me you weren't made for this life, that you weren't born to rule as a queen.

No, I couldn't allow that to be true. This was a game, a few days of fun before I left this place.

But I could think about that later. Not now, when I was about to give Fausto the blow job of his life.

The place smelled of hay and leather, the horses moving quietly in their stalls. When I found an empty stall, I went in. As soon as I spun around, he was on me, kissing me like he was starving. Fausto was a good kisser, better than David. My ex's kisses were sloppy, his mouth too wide. But Fausto used the perfect amount of suction, not over-whelming me with his tongue. It was a mature kiss, like Fausto knew what he wanted and would take it from me whether I gave it or not.

He'd surprised me with the kiss earlier by the paddock. I supposed everyone would know I was fucking the boss now. What would they think of me? Did I even care?

Fausto broke off and dropped his hands from my shoulders. "Show me, monella. Show me how much you want my cock in your dirty mouth."

His stare was almost a challenge, as if he expected me to change my mind. If so, he would be disappointed. I was every bit as stubborn as him. I lowered to my knees slowly, never looking away from his bright gaze. He held still but I could see the muscle in his jaw working. *Upper hand, Frankie.*

Once I was on my knees, I reached for his belt. He grabbed my hands. "Untie your top. I want to see your tits bounce as you suck me."

I should have known he wouldn't make this easy. But if he thought showing my breasts would feel degrading, he couldn't have been more wrong. I liked the idea of being partially undressed while servicing him in the stables.

Lifting my hands behind my neck, I pulled the strings loose. Then I lowered the top completely, allowing my tits to spring free. Fausto's chest rose and fell rapidly as his eyes tracked my movements. "Now, Francesca. Suck me."

I took my time, sliding my hands up his thighs to skim his cock over the fabric of his trousers. He growled. "Do not play with me. *Succhiami il cazzo.*"

I knew *cazzo* meant dick in this instance, so it didn't take a genius to figure out what *succhiami* meant. God, I loved when he spoke dirty Italian. I flicked open his belt, then unfastened his gray trousers. His black boxer briefs were made from a thin expensive material that was several notches above the plain cotton kind David owned. I let my fingers trail over the ridge near the head through the silky fabric as I watched Fausto's face. His expression twisted in agony, his cheeks flush. "I will spank you," he threatened. "No more teasing. Your mouth, now."

I took him out of his clothing and got my first look at the thick glorious length of him. He was definitely bigger than average, and sized more like the men in the online porn I had occasionally watched growing up. Veins ran along the sides and the bulbous head was red and smooth.

Fausto must've lost patience with me because he put his hand on my head and grabbed the base of his shaft. "*Succhialo.*"

I opened my mouth and he thrust inside, the warm salty taste of him gliding across my tongue. Fuck, I liked that. I closed my eyes, but he snapped, "Eyes on me. Clasp your hands behind your back."

My clit pulsed in happiness, my body drunk on him, completely turned on by his dominance. I complied, keeping my gaze on his and putting my hands behind my back as he started to tunnel in and out of my mouth. I tried to keep my jaw and throat relaxed, and Fausto took advantage, thrusting deep until I gagged. "That's it," he said. "I want to see tears streaming down your cheeks from having your face fucked."

I couldn't help it—I moaned. His nostrils flared. "Tu sei perfetta. Cristo santo, tu sei perfetta."

He didn't hold back any longer, fucking my mouth with rough

strokes, his hand still on my head, guiding me. "Relax your throat, bellissima. Let me in."

He pushed and I gagged, but he didn't withdraw. Instead, he waited until I recovered and took another breath. Then he advanced a tiny bit more. Tears spilled over my lashes and I struggled to breathe.

"I won't choke you. Take another breath then let me in. We won't stop this until my pelvis meets your nose."

Oh, God. Could I do it? I wasn't sure. Fausto was bigger and longer than David, and sometimes that had been a struggle—and I'd never deep throated before. I started to shake my head no, but Fausto just smirked down at me as he held me in place.

"You can do it. Fill that filthy mouth with my cock." He shoved in deeper and I tried to relax and breathe through my nose. "Sì, sì. Swallow if you can."

It took a few tries but then I swallowed and he slipped in deeper. Then I couldn't breathe at all and I started to panic, my eyes searching his face. His expression was soft, pride shining in his eyes as he watched my mouth. "Almost there, Francesca. Almost there. You're such a good girl, aren't you? You're going to make me come so hard. Just a little more."

One more flick of his hips shoved him all the way into my throat, and my nose pressed against his skin. He held my head, his fingers tightening as my throat flexed involuntarily against the intrusion. I could hear him moaning and talking but I couldn't pay attention. My entire focus was on not panicking and staying relaxed. *I can do this.*

He drew back to allow me to take a grateful breath. Then he returned to my throat and my ability to breathe departed me again. I stayed there, my nose against his belly, and tried to swallow. It sort of worked, and then I felt him swell even more. He shouted and I could feel him pulse as he came down the back of my throat.

After a few seconds, it was over and he withdrew until just the tip remained in my mouth. I stared up at him, knowing he wanted to see the spit and the tears, the mascara probably running down my face. He would want to know that he'd wrecked me...and I was right. The edge of his mouth hitched as he swiped at the moisture on my cheek, my lips still curled around the softening girth. "You are stunning."

When he slipped free, I made no move to stand or pull away. My throat was raw and sore, like I had been yelling for hours, and my naked breasts were heavy and aching. I kept my arms behind my back, eager to keep playing this naughty game in the stall. He didn't immediately tuck himself back into his trousers, either, but looked down almost as if he didn't know what to think of me.

After a few seconds, he said, "Now, kiss the tip and thank me for fucking your mouth."

I nearly smiled. Fausto liked to degrade me, but I was beginning to learn how to play his game. My compliance drove him wild.

Leaning in, I held his gaze as I pressed a kiss to the foreskin that covered the head of his penis. "Thank you, Fausto, for fucking my mouth."

His throat worked as he swallowed. "Good girl. Now lie back so I can reward you."

Fausto

I ORDERED her to come down to dinner that night.

Zia was here, as usual, and Giulio decided to eat at home tonight, too. He often ate out with friends or at the clubs, so it was nice to have my only son at the table. Francesca had changed into a dress, her long blond hair swinging down her back. Her nose and cheeks were pink from the sun today, giving her skin a healthy glow. She looked young and innocent and totally fuckable. My cock perked up, even though I'd had the orgasm of my life this afternoon.

Madonna, she was going to kill me.

After we left the stables, Francesca barely spoke. I still hadn't fucked her, and her silence upon getting dressed proved she wasn't ready. I wanted her begging for it, free of guilt. I wanted her willing to be mine for as long as this lasted.

It wasn't easy, though. Especially after that blow job. Cazzo, that woman could suck a cock. Never had a woman taken me so deep on the first try. She was perfect in every way.

Eyes burning resentfully in my direction, she strode to the seat next to Zia. I couldn't resist saying, "You look beautiful, piccolina."

"I am so happy you find this acceptable, il Diavolo."

That smart mouth. I wanted to hate the disrespectful way she spoke to me, but I couldn't. She was still pissed that I ordered her to eat with us.

Zia chuckled, then covered her mouth, as if to hide it from me. Giulio wasn't so circumspect. He laughed as he looked between Francesca and me. "This is nice. I think I'm going to like having Frankie around."

"Francesca," I corrected.

"Friends call me Frankie," she told me, like I wasn't already aware. "You may call me Francesca, however."

If she thought that offended me, she had a lot to learn. I'd call her whatever the fuck I wanted. After I rang the tiny bell on the table, the women I paid to oversee dinner every night emerged. All three were trusted friends of Zia's, older widows I could be sure weren't trying to poison me.

Platters of seafood pasta, stuffed artichokes, and a leg of lamb were placed on the table. We began serving ourselves while Imelda began carving the lamb.

A strangled gasp from down the table caught my attention. Francesca was as pale as flour, staring at the leg of lamb. Her eyes were glassy, horror etched on her face, like she was watching a friend being slaughtered in front of her.

I looked at Imelda and the platter. It was just lamb. What on earth could be—?

Allora. I understood. In Italian, I said, "Imelda, no lamb tonight or any other night. Remove it, please."

Imelda paused, uncertain. Refusing the food was a serious insult, but I would not have Francesca upset, thinking we are eating one of the baby lambs she visited every day. "Va bene," I said. "Just bring something else."

"There is only soup, Signore Ravazzani," she said.

"Sì, va bene, *capisco.*" I told her I understood and she removed the lamb, shaking her head on the way back to the kitchen.

Silence descended but I focused on my food. No doubt Giulio and Zia thought I had lost my mind.

"Grazie, Fausto," Francesca said, her voice shaky but I heard the relief. She dabbed at the corner of her eye with her napkin. She had a big heart, this girl.

"I cannot save them all, dolcezza. But I can prevent them from appearing on our dinner table."

She bit her lip but nodded, and I wanted to...I don't know. Kiss her and touch her, bring a smile back to that gorgeous face. Then I wanted to hold her down and fuck her, while I spanked her ass until she cried. I gave myself a mental shake. These were hardly appropriate thoughts for dinner.

Zia couldn't resist commenting. "*Sto vedendo cose che non avrei mai pensato di vedere in vita mia.*"

I am seeing things that I never thought I'd see in my lifetime.

"Basta," I told her sternly.

"What did she say?" Francesca asked, glancing between all three of us.

Giulio opened his mouth to answer, so I shot him a glare. He held up his hands but I could see the amusement dancing in his eyes. My family was a pain in the ass.

"I really need to improve my Italian," Francesca said as she took the platter of artichokes from Zia.

Part of me liked the idea of having her helpless and dependent on me to understand the language. But the practical side longed to hear my country's words coming out of that beautiful mouth. "I can hire someone to help you learn."

"You would do that?"

"Of course."

Francesca didn't realize her face showed her every thought. To me, she was transparent, an open book. I recognized the sly satisfaction she was now feeling, no doubt believing that learning Italian would help her escape. Except there was no escape, not from me. She'd had her chance when Giulio took her into Siderno, yet she hadn't run. Now, I would never let her go until I was good and ready.

As we ate, conversation turned to other topics. We kept it in English, translating for Zia when she couldn't think of the words except in Italian. It was the first time all four of us had eaten together since Francesca's arrival. Normally I'd never have my mantenuta eat with my family, but Francesca was different. She was living here and had been about to marry my son. There was no bothering with keeping my two lives separate at this point.

She and Giulio started laughing about some television show they both knew. He told her about recent things he'd seen on some app, a celebrity who had been canceled—whatever the fuck that meant. As much as I told myself I wasn't jealous, I was a bit envious of their friendship.

Popular culture had, for the most part, passed me by as the 'ndrina took up all of my time. I stayed off social media and the internet, and I rarely left the castello unless I had to. My father had been murdered on his way to a meeting, dying in the streets of Siderno like a dog. My wife had been shot and killed on the beach. Death stalked me every day, the same fate awaiting me the moment I let my guard down.

"*Dovresti sposarla*," Zia said quietly to me. *You should marry her.*

"*Falla finita*, nonnina," I snapped. I didn't want to hear it.

I had married once when I was young and foolish. I would not be so stupid as to repeat that mistake, no matter how much I loved a woman's pussy. And there was no reason to marry Francesca. She was not a virgin and I already had her here in my home, available whenever I needed. No one would dare stop me from having her, not even her father.

The only person who could stop me was Francesca. But she wouldn't. She liked what we did, too.

Zia remained quiet, though I knew she had more to say. No doubt she'd give me an earful later. Considering my mother died when I was young, Zia was always more mother than aunt to me. Still, she wasted her breath if she thought to advise me on the topic of Francesca.

Once the dinner plates were cleared, Giulio left for an appointment, which I happened to know was a delivery at the waterfront. Zia went into the kitchen to help clean up, and Francesca and I were alone with our espresso. I waved her closer. "*Vieni qua,* dolcezza. Come here."

"Why?"

"Because I told you to."

Surprisingly, she didn't fight me. Instead she picked up her cup and saucer and moved into Zia's abandoned chair. With my foot, I angled her chair even closer, so our legs were nearly touching. "There. That's better, no?"

"Thank you for the lamb." She tucked a strand of hair behind her ear. "I couldn't bear the thought of eating it."

"You are tender-hearted. I understand."

"What if you didn't sell them—?"

"Francesca, Ravazzani lamb is prized all over Calabria. I cannot keep them as pets instead. That isn't how the farm works."

"Could I have one?" She blinked at me, her gorgeous eyes adoring and hopeful.

"Yes," I said, unable to refuse. I'd give her almost anything, if she looked at me in such a manner. "Pick one and I'll let the staff know."

"Grazie."

"*Prego.*" I sipped my espresso. "I like hearing you speak Italian."

Her mouth hitched. "Funny, I like hearing you speak Italian, as well."

Oh? This was something new. And by the way her cheeks turned pink, I had an idea of what she meant.

Putting my elbows on the table, I leaned closer. "Does it make you wet, piccolina?"

She had the audacity to roll her eyes. "A gorgeous man speaking a romance language in a low sexy tone? Hmm. What do you think?"

Gorgeous? I liked this new honest side to her. Perhaps I should take her to the stables for riposo each day.

Because I wanted to torture us both, I started speaking in Italian, telling her every dirty thing I longed to do to her. How I was going to touch her, fuck her. Lick her. Have her sit on my face. Make her suck my cock again. That I would spank her ass then fuck her in that dark hole.

By the time I stopped she was nearly in my lap, breathing hard, with her chest rising and falling quickly. The movement caused her tits to nearly spill out of the top of the sundress, and I considered pulling the fabric down to suck on her nipples right here in the dining room. I trailed my fingers along the soft skin inside her thigh, desperate to feel how wet I'd made her....

"Do you want to know what I said?"

"It's probably better that I don't."

I reached her panties. The fabric was soaked. I stroked over her seam, and her breath caught. "Oh, my beautiful girl. Do you need me to take care of you right here?"

A throat cleared in the doorway. I glanced over but didn't remove my hand. Marco stood there, looking unapologetic at the interruption. "Rav, a minute."

I smothered a sigh and pressed a soft kiss to Francesca's mouth. "We'll finish this later." I stood and walked out, knowing Marco would give me shit for what he just saw.

Surprisingly, I didn't care.

CHAPTER SIXTEEN

Francesca

I CLIMBED over the railing and held out my hand. "Vieni qua, Lamborghini." My little lamb came tottering over to me and bleated, clearly happy to see me. At least, that's what I believed anyway. I loved her to pieces.

Tommaso, the man in charge of the sheep, said I had to speak Italian to the lambs. He said it was what they knew, but I didn't complain because it would help me practice. I had to admit, he was right. It was easier to speak Italian to an animal than a human who might criticize my pronunciation or verb conjugation.

Lamborghini ate the tiny pellets out of my palm, her soft mouth and tongue teasing my skin. According to Tommaso she was three months old, and would have been killed and sold sometime in the next two months if not for my intervention. As much as I hated being grateful to Fausto for anything, I was relieved that Lamborghini wouldn't end up on a dinner table.

She finished the pellets and nuzzled my arm, then crawled into my lap. I laughed and wrapped my arms around her, scratching behind her ear. "*Sei così bella,* Lamborghini," I cooed.

"That is a ridiculous name for a pet," a familiar voice said behind me.

I shifted toward him. I hadn't seen Fausto in two days, as he'd been busy with business. At least, that's what Zia said last night at dinner. I didn't want to care, but part of me had wondered where he went, considering he never left the estate.

I shaded my eyes from the sun and ran my gaze over him. He looked delicious. Tall, dark, handsome and decked out in an expensive three-piece gray suit, he was both roguish and elegant. "Buongiorno, signore," I said. "Come stai?"

He gave me a lopsided grin that would melt the hardest of hearts, and I couldn't help but return it with a grin of my own. He said, "I see your tutor has arrived. Do you like her?"

My Italian tutor, Maria, was a friend of Zia's. Apparently, they played a card game called *briscola* with some other women every Tuesday. A former schoolteacher, Maria was thankfully very patient with me during our daily lesson. "Sì," I answered.

Fausto's expression turned predatory, much like a wolf that would devour these poor little lambs if given the chance. "Come here."

I knew what that look meant. Fausto wanted to kiss me. I bit my lip, tingles breaking out all over my skin. "*Dopo,*" I said, telling him later.

His gaze glittered dark and dangerous in the morning sun. "Now, Francesca. Or do you wish for Lamborghini to see you get spanked right here?"

I let Lamborghini go and got to my feet. I sauntered toward Fausto, annoyed that I was happy to see him. "These threats of a spanking are losing their bite, il Diavolo."

As soon as I was close enough, he reached out to pull me close to the fence. "I'll show you bite," he growled and sank his teeth into the side of my neck. Then he slapped my ass, hard. My arms came up around his shoulders, my body singing from the stimulation.

I should be pushing him away, running in the opposite direction, instead of craving his touch, but I had missed him. Missed this crazy game we were playing. *God, Frankie. You are a mess.*

"Come inside with me," he whispered in my ear. "I want to take a riposo with you."

"It's only ten o'clock, Fausto. And aren't you usually working at this time?"

"Yes, but I need to talk to you. So let's talk while we're in my bed, naked. After I lick your pussy and make you come."

I had to swallow before I could speak. "Shh. Not in front of Lamborghini."

He chuckled, his big shoulders shaking. "Get out of there before I climb in and strip you naked in the dirt and shit."

Was I doing this?

My breasts ached with the need for him to touch them. I was already wet, my sex pulsing between my legs. Resisting him was becoming impossible, especially the more I got to know him. I still considered him my enemy, but he was right: I wasn't trying all that hard to escape. And I went to him willingly. I knew he would never force me, and my submissive compliance drove him wild.

Still, I didn't want to make this too easy for him.

"If I do, will you teach me all the dirty Italian words?"

"No." He smacked my butt again. "You know all the English ones and that's already too much. I am not letting you use the Italian ones, too."

"Just one, per favore?" I nipped his jaw with my teeth.

"Cazzo, you are killing me. I am coming in there." Despite his designer suit and fancy leather shoes, he started to climb the fence. Was he insane?

"No! Stop." I put my hand up. "I'll get out."

When I was finally on the other side of the fence, he stepped close to cup my jaw with one hand and hold onto my hip with the other. *"Terre e sole,"* he murmured before giving me a long, deep kiss in full view of the estate staff. I couldn't worry about who was watching, though, because I was spinning, lost in the maelstrom that was Fausto's attention. He was all I could focus on as his lips moved against mine, the warmth of his body sinking into my flesh. Fire skittered along my veins, a ball of want and need erupting in my belly as the kiss wore on. I was helpless, clinging to him as he commanded my entire being with just his mouth.

He broke off and whispered, "Let's go before I fuck you here."

Fear dimmed a bit of my enthusiasm at those words, but I didn't have time to ask for clarification because he was tugging me toward the castello. "Wait," I called to his back.

"No waiting. I am tired of waiting."

My mind whirled as he pulled me after him. I didn't want to have sex with Fausto. Did I?

My body was one hundred percent on board. I'd masturbated in the shower this morning just picturing it, imagining what it would feel like to have his big cock filling me up over and over. But the reality had implications I wasn't certain I could handle. Letting him fuck me meant I had agreed to be his mistress.

You're already his mistress, dumbass.

No, I wasn't. We had messed around a few times. That wasn't a huge deal. A few orgasms here or there from oral was more of a friends-with-benefits thing, not a mistress thing. I did not want to be Fausto Ravazzani's kept woman.

So why was I letting him lead me into the castle and through the entryway?

Because I was weak. I was a slut who liked it dirty and rough, and I couldn't resist Fausto's good looks and sexy charm. The aura of danger and power he wore like his expensive suits appealed to me, too. I guess being raised in the mafia life had rubbed off on me more than I'd thought. I had been around these types of domineering men since I was born. For some reason, I craved Fausto's darkness. I was obsessed with it, fantasizing about what he might do to me.

Except I suspected the reality would be a thousand times better, and once I had a taste I'd never be able to stop.

NO ONE WAS AROUND as we finally entered his side of the castello. I hadn't been over here before, and the bare walls surprised me. No family photos. No drawings Giulio had done in school. No famous paintings or posters. Just a blank surface on all sides, like someone had recently moved in. Hadn't his family lived here for more than a hundred years?

Worn eastern carpets covered the stone floor, with the same elegant lights overhead from our wing. He strode to the end of the hall and threw open a door, not letting go of my hand as we went inside. The door closed and then I was lifted up, my legs dangling as he carried me through the sitting room and into the bedroom.

It was nothing like I expected. If I had to guess, I would have imagined black sheets, dark walls and a mirror over his bed. This room was...romantic. Soft, almost feminine. With pale walls and an enormous bed that bordered on ornate. Plants dotted the windows, a vase of fresh flowers on a small table. The furniture looked old but made from sturdy pale oak.

I didn't have the chance to see anything more because he dropped me on the bed. "Get naked."

Pushing up on my elbows, I scowled at him. "Just like that?"

"Just like fucking that, piccola monella." He ripped off his suit coat and tossed it onto a worn leather chair. Then he started unbuttoning his vest. I could see the outline of his erection through his trousers. God, I wanted that thick cock so badly.

"Do not deliberately disobey me. You will not like the consequences."

Or maybe I would.

The part of me that loved to push him, that wanted more of his sternness, pouted up at him. "I thought we were going to talk first."

His vest hit the floor and he unfastened his cufflinks, one at a time, his eyes never leaving mine. I was caught, mesmerized, hardly able to breathe as I waited to see what he would do.

He unbuckled his belt slowly, the leather whispering as he pulled it free from the loops of his trousers. "Have you ever been spanked with a belt?" His voice was like honey, slow and seductive through his accent, and I stared at his elegant hands as they cradled the leather.

"No."

"I will not lie to you. It will hurt. But it will feel so good afterwards when I reward you. Would you like to try?"

Indecision warred inside me. Fausto slapped my ass all the time. Would the belt feel the same? Or better?

He dropped the belt. "Dio, I can see the answer on your face. Another day, dolcezza. I cannot have your ass purple this afternoon, as much as I'd love to see it."

"Why?"

His shirt came off next and I saw all his muscles on glorious display. He was large with broad shoulders and a firm stomach. Dark hair dotted his olive skin between his pecs and then into his trousers. This was no gym rat, with a smooth body crafted from protein powder and supplements. Instead, Fausto was all rough man, barely leashed power, and I needed him to surround me, to fill me with that strength.

After toeing off his shoes, he unfastened his trousers and stepped out of them. He stood there with only tight boxer briefs covering his mouth-watering body. The erection pushing its way out of the expensive fabric was nearly obscene. I swallowed, my limbs vibrating with excitement.

"Get on the side of the bed," he rasped as he moved to the nightstand. "Now."

He reached inside the drawer and took out a bottle of lube. Wait, wasn't that for anal sex? David had begged me for anal but I'd always refused. Did Fausto think I would allow such a thing right away? "You're not putting your cock in my ass."

Fausto paused, his mouth hitching as he tossed the plastic bottle on the bed. "I like the way you think, but no. That is not why I have it. But someday you will beg me to take your ass, to put my cock in there and fuck it."

I wanted to scoff, to tell him that would never happen, but Fausto was a man who thrived on challenge. Refusing meant he'd try all the harder.

"Come here." He pointed to where he stood, his face taut with desire. For me.

Whatever he had in mind, I was more than ready. A few more

orgasms, I told myself. This wasn't such a big deal. What sane woman would turn this down?

I rolled to my hands and knees and crawled to him, never looking away from his dark gaze. He tracked me, like a panther watching its next meal, a hunter eager to rip apart its prey. His nostrils flared as I reached him. "Take your dress and panties off."

Coming up on my knees, I reached behind my neck to unfasten the straps that held the top of the sundress in place. Instead of immediately bringing the cloth under my tits, I unzipped the lower part of the dress. Then I lifted the bottom and removed it in one swift motion.

"I can see how wet your panties are from here. Take them off, dirty girl."

I shimmied the silk off and pushed the panties down my legs, leaving me naked. He stroked his cock over his briefs. "Lie back."

Again, he was working his magic on me, building on this insane attraction we had together. Before I lost all sense of reason, though, I needed to tell him the situation. "This doesn't mean anything."

His hand snatched my jaw, holding me tight. "We shall see, won't we?" He kissed me hard, his lips brutal and demanding, and I yielded, only too happy to give in. Something inside me welcomed his domination, his aggressiveness feeding me like a plant in the sun. I bloomed in his hands, feeling more alive, more powerful than I ever had before.

He let me go. As soon as my back hit the mattress, he was on me, pushing my legs apart, spreading me wide for his mouth. He ate me like he was starving, as if my body was the only sustenance he ever needed. He was so good at this, knew what I liked and how to make me come quickly. In no time at all he had me panting, straining, as I rocked my pussy onto his mouth. My muscles pulled tight as the pleasure built, I was so close....

And then he stopped.

"No," I said, grabbing to bring him back. "I was right there."

"I know."

With a graceful flick of his hands, he took off his briefs—and all rational thought left my brain. I stared at his dick, so thick and hard, the smooth skin, and forgot what we had been talking about. God, I wanted that thing inside me, driving me into the mattress while he whispered filthy Italian words in my ear.

He grabbed the bottle of lube and crawled over me, not stopping until his knees were on either side of my ribcage. Popping the cap, he poured some of the cool liquid on my breasts. "Rub it in, all over. Make them slippery for me."

Oh. So this was what he'd wanted.

I did as he asked, making a show of it as I rubbed the lube on my chest. I pinched my nipples, squeezed my tits, and the stimulation caused more wetness between my thighs. I was ridiculously turned on and we'd barely started. "How's this?"

"Va bene." He squirted a tiny bit of lube into his palm and coated his erection. "Now I fuck your tits." His cock slapped between my breasts and he got into position. "Hold them. Press them tight."

I squeezed my boobs around his cock, and he groaned. His stare was fixed on my chest as his hips started to move, his stomach muscles flexing. "Tighter," he rasped. "Pinch your nipples like I would."

I did as he asked, gasping at the electricity that jumped in my veins as a result. It was like I was stroking my clit without using my hands. I pinched harder and my head rolled back as the bliss washed over me.

"Madonna, these tits."

He pushed a thumb into my mouth and I sucked, swirling my tongue over the rough skin like I couldn't get enough. Which wasn't really an act. I was desperate, my sex throbbing for relief, and I craved his touch everywhere.

"Look at me when you suck," he ordered and I instantly obeyed. His bright eyes burned fire while they watched my mouth and he reached to stroke two fingers over my clit. I tensed and made a desperate noise in the back of my throat. He continued to pet me, and I could feel how wet and slippery I was, the sounds of my slickness as loud as my breathing. The climax was right there, just a few seconds away....

God, yes. I had to come, right the hell now.

The fingers between my legs disappeared and I let out an angry growl around his thumb.

"Up," he told me, retreating down my body until he stood on the floor.

I rose up on my knees, mindless to anything but having this craving satisfied.

"Allora, put your feet on the floor." His Italian accent was more pronounced, which made it even sexier.

I scrambled to do as he asked, and his hands positioned me between his legs as I leaned over on the bed. My elbows dug into the mattress and Fausto reached for the bottle of lube again. I tensed, coming up on my hands. Was he seriously—?

"Relax. Not today. I want to shoot all over your ass."

A tiny drizzle of lube trickled between my ass cheeks. Then he smoothed it over my skin, brushing my hole. I froze.

"I never go back on my word," he whispered as he touched the same spot again. "My cock will not fuck your ass today, te lo prometto."

No one had ever touched me there, but I trusted Fausto. I sagged onto the bed and let him do as he wished. His slick erection slid into the crevice between my cheeks, which he pushed together. Then he was sliding between my ass cheeks the same way he'd fucked my tits. His strong hands held me still while his rough thighs met the backs of my legs. It was like he was fucking me from behind, but without the stimulation.

God, I needed the stimulation.

Miserable, I shook my head back and forth, shoving my ass higher. Hair covered my face and I could feel the sweat on my temples. I cupped my breasts and squeezed, pulling on my nipples.

"Roll your hips," he panted. "Work my cock and I'll reward you."

He didn't need to ask twice. I started rolling my hips, giving him friction while he held still. I was gyrating and sliding my flesh over his, that thick rod hot and heavy between my cheeks. I barely felt his hand leave my skin before he slapped my ass, fire exploding under my skin.

I sucked in a breath and lost my rhythm. *Fuck*, that hurt.

"Don't stop." Another slap. "Keep going and make me come."

The pain from the slaps turned into heat, the kind that made my knees go weak. My clit throbbed in response, and the slickness between my thighs ran down my legs. I kept moving, and he spanked me again and again, his palm landing blows all over my backside. Then he switched sides, starting over on the other cheek, and I was an incoherent mess. My body burned, but there was no pain. My skin sang with pleasure, sensitive and bright, and as if on instinct I slid my fingers down between my legs, the need to come undeniable.

"No," he said, pinning my arm down as he covered my back. My sore ass pulsed against his cool skin. "Not yet, Francesca."

I humped the mattress, my urges uncontrollable. This caused his tip to skim the entrance to my pussy. We both froze, the temptation right there. Oh, God. All he had to do was push a tiny bit forward and he would fill me. Stretch me. Give me every bit of his hard cock.

I couldn't stand it. I needed him like I needed air. "Please, Fausto."

"Allora, *tu sei mio?*"

"What?"

"Are you mine?"

I knew what he meant, but I couldn't say it. I couldn't admit to being his mistress. I pressed my lips together, unable to say the words, while I clawed and tore at the comforter, my miserably body at war with itself as my lust remained unfulfilled. The wanting was painful, like I was on a knife's edge, my mind screaming for release. I didn't know how much longer I could hold out.

"I will not fuck you until you tell me. I want to hear the words."

"No, please. Just once."

"Say it, and I will fuck your pussy. You will come so hard." He teased me with a shift of his hips, the tip of his erection skimming my entrance again. "I will make it so good for you."

My resistance folded. "I'm yours," I blurted. "Please. I'm yours."

Before I could blink, he shoved inside me, my walls stretching to accommodate his girth. It wasn't easy. He was large and I hadn't been prepared, so it took a few pumps of his hips before he was fully seated.

I clutched the duvet, my fingers sinking into the plush fabric, the sensation of having him inside me even better than I'd imagined. I could feel him everywhere, from my swollen lips and aching breasts, to my sore ass and full pussy. It was like an overload for my nerve endings.

Then he started moving, and it felt even better. It was indescribable, this euphoria. Fausto fucked me like he was punishing me, each punch of his hips slapping into the skin he'd spanked a moment ago. He drove deep, holding my hips still so he could pound as hard as he wanted. I loved it. He was rough and unforgiving, everything I needed.

The bed rocked, the frame creaking as he worked himself in and out of my body. His fingers slipped between my legs and found my clit. He pinched the swollen nub then circled it, and the world exploded. Sparks shot through my limbs as they convulsed, and my brain completely shut down, the pleasure almost brutal in its intensity.

As the orgasm subsided, I slumped on the bed, weak as a kitten, but I could feel Fausto's rhythm faltering. With a roar he pulled out of my channel and hot jets of liquid landed on my ass. He grunted, one hand holding my hip as his come coated my skin.

I relished the feeling, the knowledge that I'd made this powerful man come so hard. But as the sweat cooled on my skin, I thought about what I had said. I'd given in, admitted I belonged to him. Even in the afterglow of the best orgasm of my life, I knew I'd made a mistake.

What piece of my soul had I just traded away?

CHAPTER SEVENTEEN

Fausto

AFTER I CLEANED HER UP, we stretched out on the bed. Francesca was quiet as I held her, and I knew what she'd said was weighing on her. But it was inevitable. The sooner she came to terms with the nature of our relationship, the better.

"I am clean, by the way," I said. I hadn't ever fucked a woman without a condom before and was tested regularly. And I knew Francesca's health report was clean, because I'd reviewed it as soon as I brought her to Siderno. With her being sexually active, I'd needed to know if she had any diseases.

"Oh. Right. Thank you."

I stroked her hip. She was sprawled half on top of me, her tits smashed into my chest. If I allowed myself a riposo each day, this would be exactly how I'd want to spend it. I normally did not give a lot of my time to my mistresses, but I liked the idea of being with Francesca. In fact, I was strangely reluctant to let her go.

I should keep more of a distance, considering her age and inexperience. Younger women were clingier, the ones who texted me at odd hours with bizarre emojis I couldn't decipher. It was why I usually slept with women in their late twenties or thirties. Otherwise, we had absolutely nothing in common.

It didn't feel that way with Francesca, though. She'd been raised in the life, albeit sheltered from her father's activities. But unlike my first wife, who'd also been raised in the life, Francesca and I liked many of the same things. Being outdoors, the farm and vineyard...not to mention the way we fucked. I liked control and she loved to be on the receiving end of it. A perfect match.

I kissed the crown of her head. "You are coming with me on the boat this afternoon."

She sighed. "You can't order me around, Fausto."

Back to this? "I can and you will do as I say."

"No, fuck that." She pushed away slightly to frown at me. "I have a mind of my own. I'm not at your beck and call."

She could not have been more wrong. "You are, for as long as we are fucking. Or do I need to make you admit it again?" It would not be a hardship, that was for certain.

She glared at me. "You are the absolute worst."

Pressing up, I kissed her, shoving my tongue in her mouth until she softened. Then I kissed her some more just because I liked it. When she gave me one of her little whimpers, I broke off. "I am demanding and a stronzo, but I will make this worthwhile for you."

"By letting me go?"

"When the time is right, yes. If that is what you want."

"What about now?"

I chuckled and slapped her ass, which I knew had to be sore. "When we tire of each other and not a second before."

"Actually I'm pretty tired of you at the moment."

"Lies." I cupped her tit and pinched her nipple, kissing her until she writhed against me. My insatiable piccola monella.

Her gaze was unfocused when I finally pulled away. I smiled. "Come. I'll wash you in the shower and tell you about this afternoon."

She didn't argue and I took that as an encouraging sign as I led her to the bathroom. As soon as the water was hot, I tugged her into the shower with me.

"Your shower is bigger than mine," she said as I nibbled on her neck under the warm spray. "I like it."

"You are welcome to use it any time you like." For a brief insane moment, I considered moving her into my suite. But I hadn't shared my living space with a woman since my marriage, and even that hadn't lasted long. As soon as Lucia became pregnant, she moved to the opposite end of the castello, into the room Francesca currently used.

I did not want to repeat my mistakes.

Taking the soap, I worked up a lather in my hands and pulled her back against my chest. I soaped her breasts, massaging them and pinching her nipples. She wound her arms around my head, giving me her weight and full access to her luscious body. *Cazzo*, she was gorgeous. Any runway in Milan would be lucky to have her. I knew many designers and could get her a job with the snap of my fingers, if she wished.

I reached for her clit, stroking and circling with two fingertips, loving the way she responded to me. Never had a lover been so in tune with what I needed, her cravings a perfect match to my own. Francesca's submission was the sweetest I'd ever experienced. I felt like a god every time she gave in.

Soon she was panting, her ass rocking against the semi-erect cock between my legs. If she kept that up, I'd fuck her again in the shower, and I knew she had to be sore.

I maneuvered her into the spray and let the water cascade down her sun-kissed skin, while I soaped my own body. Her gaze darted between my legs as I washed my cock and balls, and she started to reach for my groin. "Later," I rasped. In fact, I planned on fucking her all night, if she had recovered by then.

She inspected my shampoo, bringing the bottle to her nose. "This smells amazing."

"*Che buon profumo*."

Her lips tilted. "Are you teaching me Italian?"

"Yes. Do you have another lesson today?

"No, tomorrow."

"In *Italiano*."

She began washing her hair, so I reached and moved her hands out of the way so that I could do it. "*Dimmi*."

"You are being so extra right now."

I knew what that meant from my son, so I smacked her ass lightly. "Tell me or I will put you over my knees and spank you harder," I said in Italian, knowing she'd never know what I was saying.

"It's not a punishment to hear you speak Italian and not understand you."

I liked that she found my language arousing. I decided to help her. "No, *domani*."

"No, domani," she repeated in an accent far more Canadian than Italian.

"You'll learn. You will be ready to tell me to fuck you in Italian very soon."

"Teach me how to say that," she said as she moved under the spray to rinse her hair.

"*Ti prego, scopami. Sono la tua puttanella.*"

"You said more than 'fuck me.'"

I grabbed her waist and pulled her wet body flush to mine. I said, 'Please fuck me. I am your little slut.'"

"Oh, God." Her fingers threaded through my hair, her eyelids hooded. "Why is that so hot?"

"Because you like it dirty, just like I do." I pushed her against the tile and ate at her mouth, devouring her as I thrust my tongue inside. She kissed me back, meeting me eagerly, and my balls were heavy again with the need to have her. *Cristo santo*, what was she doing to me? If I weren't careful this girl would make me weak.

Besides, I didn't have time for this. The break I had taken to fuck her earlier was already pushing it. I couldn't stay longer. There were arrangements to be made for the meeting this afternoon.

With regret, I broke away but didn't let her go. I stared down into her beautiful eyes, her lashes like wet spikes, and held onto her jaw. "On the boat today is a meeting. It is supposed to be friendly, which is why I am bringing you. But this man is no friend, capisce? He will have a woman with him, as well, so I need you to be respectful at all times. This is a test, Francesca."

The haze of desire faded from her expression, her gaze growing hard. She didn't like what I was telling her, which is what I had expected, but I didn't care. She gave herself to me, and there was no going backward.

"What if I fail your test? Will you send me home?"

"No. I'll take you down to the dungeon and let you spend a few hours there until you learn your place."

She gasped, a flash of fear crossing her face. "You wouldn't."

I wouldn't, but she didn't need to know it. "I told you, I am keeping you until I am done with you, Francesca Mancini."

I pushed through the glass door and stepped out of the shower, wrapping myself in a towel. I heard her mumbled curse words all the way out to my closet. "You have an hour to prepare yourself, monella. And do not wear the black bikini."

Only I was allowed to see her in that tiny scrap of a suit from now on. Francesca was mine, and I'd kill any man who tried to take her from me.

Francesca

WE TOOK the helicopter to the yacht this time, and I was both excited and scared. Fausto smiled indulgently at me, while Marco ignored me from his seat next to the pilot. The ride was so much fun that I forgot all about how I was now officially Fausto Ravazzani's mistress.

It could be worse. You could be married to his son.

True. At least now I got great sex and then he'd set me free. Who cared what label he put on it? Afterwards, I'd return to Toronto or New York, get a degree and live my life. As used goods, my father wouldn't be able to marry me off to anyone else, which meant I had my whole future ahead of me.

It was perfect, actually. Why hadn't I thought of this in the first place?

I slid a glance at Fausto, wondering if I could get him alone on the boat after the meeting ended. I might want to try deep throating him again.

He flicked a switch and his voice entered my headphones, "Whatever you are planning, my answer is yes."

He could read me so well.

I slid my hand up his thigh, toward his crotch. He didn't stop me, just arched his brow. I found his dick and squeezed, pleased when his head dropped back and he closed his eyes. "Cazzo, you are making me hard again."

"Isn't that the point?"

"Not before my meeting. Afterward you may do whatever you wish." He took my hand, kissed my fingertips, and placed it in my lap.

"Can we stay on the boat a little while?"

"If you'd like. We could even sleep out here. Marco can retrieve us in the morning."

That sounded like heaven. "I like when you spoil me with sex and outings."

"Then prepare for more of both. I like to see you happy, Francesca."

He dragged a fingertip along my jaw, and my chest squeezed. The fierce il Diavolo, feared mafia boss, wanted to make me happy. Was he softening toward me?

The helicopter started descending, and I nervously grabbed Fausto's arm as I watched out the window. The yacht's helipad was underneath us, blue water on all sides. It was beyond extravagant, a luxury even my family couldn't afford.

When we touched down, Marco got out first and opened our door. Fausto stepped out then helped me to the ground, making sure I kept my head down until we were safely away from the spinning blades. Six crew members, including the captain, were there to greet us, and they all bowed saying, "Buona sera, Signorina Mancini." I doubted they remembered me from my trip with Giulio, so this must have been Fausto's doing.

News of il Diavolo's new mistress has traveled fast.

He took my hand and exchanged a few words in Italian with the captain. Then Marco, Fausto, and I went into Fausto's suite. He dropped onto the plush cushions and spread his arms and legs, the king of everything around him. Marco took one of the chairs, but I wasn't certain what to do. Should I leave them alone? Should I sit?

"Come here," Fausto told me, patting to the cushion next to him.

I didn't like being ordered around, but I supposed this was hardly the time to take a stand. Not in front of Marco. Besides, Fausto had said this was a test. I didn't really think he'd send me into the dungeon...but I didn't want to risk it, either.

When I slid onto the cushion next to him, his arm wrapped around my shoulders, and for the next thirty minutes he and Marco talked in Italian, ignoring me. I wasn't sure if I felt grateful or irritated, but soon I yawned, feeling the day's activities catch up with me.

Fausto's hand landed on the back of my neck and he squeezed. A simple gesture, but one my body clearly loved because heat bloomed between my legs. A gentle roll of desire that was never far when this man was around.

He put his mouth near my ear. "There is wine and food on the patio deck. You can go out and enjoy yourself, if you like. Our guests should be here imminently."

Our guests. Such an odd way of phrasing it, when nothing here was mine. "All right."

I started to get up but he didn't release me. "Aren't you forgetting something?"

Glancing over, I could see he was in his full mafia king mode. Power came off him in waves and I could have jumped him right there. I wasn't sure what he wanted, but I decided to play his game. Leaning in, I kissed his cheek. "Grazie, Fausto."

This must have appeased him because his eyes softened and he released me. I put extra swing in my hips as I walked out, hoping he could see the outline of my ass through my thick cover up.

The pool deck had tables of food set up, with bottles of prosecco and wine already on ice. I helped myself to a glass of prosecco and some raw shrimp. I'd skipped lunch to have sex with Fausto—a decision I didn't regret—but now I was starving. There was an antipasto board, so I loaded up on various meats and cheeses before relaxing on one of the lounges. My ass was still sore from Fausto's hand, but the reminder made my nipples perk up. I was definitely not complaining about his moves in bed.

A small motorboat approached. Three people were seated on board, two men and a woman. These must be the people meeting with Fausto. I shielded my eyes and watched as they pulled alongside the yacht. The crew rushed over to help secure their boat and assist them. Fausto and Marco appeared from nowhere, their smiles not quite reaching their eyes as the guests climbed onto the deck.

One man was likely a guard, considering he was huge and had a gun poking out from under his jacket. The other man, who was probably in his early thirties, was incredibly handsome. He wore light linen pants and a tight t-shirt, managing to look both casual and expensive at the same time. The woman at his side was in high heels and a gorgeous sundress.

"Enzo," Fausto greeted, shaking the younger man's hand. He spoke rapid Italian, his sexy mouth moving quickly as everyone was introduced. Then he turned to me and held out his hand. No words, just held out his hand.

I knew what that meant.

Rising, I threw back my hair and strolled over to him, right into his side, and he slipped his arm around my waist. "Enzo, this is Francesca. Dolcezza, this is Signore D'Agostino and Mariella."

"Ciao," I said with a small nod. "Mariella, would you like some prosecco?" I held up my glass. Fausto gave me a squeeze, which I supposed meant he approved.

Mariella looked at Enzo—which made me want to roll my eyes—and he nodded, saying a few words in Italian. All I caught was, "*d'inglese.*" Then Enzo gave me a tight smile. "She doesn't speak much English. I told her to practice with you."

Fausto pressed a kiss to my temple. "And Francesca may practice her Italian with Mariella." He released me and I took this as my cue to entertain the womenfolk so the menfolk could talk business. "We won't be long," he said, and pressed a brief, hard kiss on my mouth.

The men left us alone, and so we went to the pool and got drinks. Mariella seemed sweet. She knew more words in English than I did in Italian. "Big Bang Theory," she explained. "I love Sheldon."

I just smiled. "How long have you and Enzo been married?"

"No, we are not married. He has a wife in Napoli."

Open mouth, insert foot. "I see."

"Like you and Signore Ravazzani," she continued, as if I needed further explanation.

"No, I get it." Mafia men were not known for their monogamy. "More prosecco?"

Standing, I brought the bottle over to our lounges and refilled our glasses. *Just two mob mistresses, hanging out on a yacht, drinking together. Happens every day, right?*

Mariella took her sundress off, and I could see why Enzo would cheat on his wife with this woman. She was flawless. Tall and thin, with long perfect limbs and olive skin. Her hair was dark brown, which hung down past her shoulders to showcase her fine features. I felt like a dowdy frump next to her. She reminded me of Katarzyna. What was it with these mobsters and their stick-thin mistresses?

She looked at me. "Are you not wearing a suit?"

The stubborn Mancini in me wanted to show her that I wasn't embarrassed of my big boobs and plump ass. I whipped off my cover and was instantly reminded that I'd deliberately worn the suit Fausto had ordered me not to. Whoops.

Didn't he know how I felt about his orders? Outside the bedroom, at least.

Mariella smiled. "You are gorgeous."

"Grazie. You are also gorgeous."

She shrugged. "I try to stay thin. Otherwise Enzo find someone else."

"So let him," I said. "No man is worth starving yourself for."

"Enzo is worth it." She held up her hands and measured out what had to be nine inches. "Very worth it."

I collapsed into a fit of giggles. Who said women from two different countries couldn't speak the same language? "Yes, that might be worth it!"

"Fausto is the same, no? Women talk of him all over Calabria."

Really? I sucked back the rest of my prosecco. "Let's just say he is definitely worth it."

Mariella laughed. "See, I knew. You can always tell a man with a big dick. He's very sure of himself."

"We call that BDE. Big dick energy."

We both broke out laughing, and I suddenly had to pee really badly. "I must use the toilet. I'll return in a few minutes."

She nodded and closed her eyes, face tilted toward the sun, so I refilled my glass and carried it inside with me. The men were seated near the bar, Fausto on the sofa next to Enzo, with Marco and Enzo's guards in chairs. Everyone turned my way as I came in. "Just using the toilet," I announced, and kept walking toward the corridor.

My skin prickled in the silence and I glanced over. Fausto's eyes were narrowed on me, his jaw tight. Was he annoyed that I interrupted?

Then I remembered my bikini.

Shit.

Well, that was too bad. I was allowed to wear what I wanted. If Enzo wanted to gawk at my boobs, who cared? I'm sure he'd seen plenty in his time. Mine were certainly nothing special. And if Mariella was anything to go by, he preferred flat-chested women who modeled on the weekends.

I lifted my chin and continued to the bathroom. Not going to lie, I was pretty buzzed right about then. I didn't care about Fausto's anger...unless he was going to spank me. And then I was definitely up for it. I chuckled as I locked the door behind me and did my business. Then I washed my hands and checked my front and back in the mirror. I looked pretty good, actually. The time I was spending in the sun had given my skin a slight glow and today was a good hair day.

When I walked back through the seating area, I waved at the men. "*Mi scusi!*"

Enzo's deep voice uttered a string of Italian I didn't understand, except for the last word, "puttanella."

Slut.

I nearly tripped. Was he saying that about me? That asshole. Slowing, I waited to hear Fausto put Enzo in his place. Pull a gun or smack the back of his head. Whatever Fausto did, I knew it was going to be bad.

Instead, he laughed.

That motherfucker actually laughed.

Enzo had called me a whore and Fausto had laughed, like it was a big joke. Like I was a joke. Just a warm pussy to stick his dick in at the end of the day.

Fuck. Him.

I would make him regret that laugh if it was the last thing I ever did.

CHAPTER EIGHTEEN

Fausto

SHE WORE the fucking black bikini.

After I explicitly told her not to.

I was boiling with rage, seething inside. Enzo and his man ran their eyes all over Francesca's body, ogling her like starving wolves when she'd sauntered through here. The small scraps of fabric did nothing to cover her ample tits and ass. She might as well have walked through naked.

Cazzo madre di Dio, I was going to paddle her ass raw when I had the chance.

Enzo made some remark that I barely heard through the fury ringing in my ears. How could I concentrate on this meeting knowing what she had done? We were supposed to all dine together once Enzo and I were done discussing our agreement. That clearly could not happen, as I'd likely stab anyone who dared look at her twice.

"We should finish," I said abruptly. "The women are bored without us, no doubt."

A splash and a giggle belied my words, and every muscle in my body clenched. Francesca would pay for this.

"I thought you wanted to discuss your son," Enzo said.

We'd spent the first part of the meeting talking business, instead of the true purpose. A fact I was now regretting, as I wanted to be done. "Yes, I understand you have a younger sister."

Enzo blinked. "She is only fifteen."

"I understand. Giulio will wait."

"These things might be common here in Siderno, Ravazzani, but we have evolved in Napoli. I do not adhere to the old ways, as you might have heard."

"Old does not mean bad. Many of our traditions have lived on because they serve a purpose."

"Like the merging of two families for political gain."

"Precisely. Giulio is my only son and heir. Everything I have will belong to him one day."

Enzo stroked his jaw. He would be a fool not to take this offer—and rumor held he was not a fool. Hot-headed, but not a fool. "What would I get in return?"

"I would partner with you on your computer venture."

His right eye twitched, but he gave no other outward sign of displeasure. "We need no partner. In case you haven't heard, that has become quite lucrative."

"I can make it more lucrative. As well, perhaps some of my San Luca imports can be rerouted to Napoli."

"I should hope so," he had the balls to say. "All I am gaining is an alliance with the man who replaces you."

Interesting way to talk about my son. "Your sister will become a Ravazzani."

He brushed his trousers, smoothing the fabric with his fingers. "I'll need to think about it. Violetta is my only sister and I hadn't thought of betrothing her so soon."

"I understand," I said, though I really didn't. This was the way things were handled in our world. D'Agostino was kidding himself if he believed otherwise. And he would not get a better offer than mine. "If you agree, we would betroth them and hold off on the ceremony until she is of age."

"Generous of you," Enzo said, though I sensed a hint of sarcasm. "I'll consider it. Shall we join the women?"

"Of course." I rose and strode toward the patio deck. At this point, it was no use telling Francesca to put her cover up back on, but I wanted to. I hated the idea of Enzo D'Agostino seeing what belonged to me.

It hadn't bothered me with Katarzyna. In fact, she had paraded around topless during many of my business meetings on the yacht, and it had amused me to see the way the men coveted her.

This was not the case with Francesca.

I could not say why, but I didn't want anyone seeing her bare flesh but me. She was mine.

Francesca and Mariella were in the pool, hanging onto the side and drinking. Mariella was exactly what one expected: thin, beautiful, and boring. Compared to her, Francesca was a radiant burst of sunlight, one that glimmered and sparkled. She was ripe and sexy, with no bony angles, and a body that was made for fucking.

Which was precisely why I didn't want any other man seeing it. They would only be thinking about one thing.

I approached the pool and thrust my hands in my pockets. "Are you having a nice time, Francesca?"

Her barely-covered tits bobbed in the water as she reached for her full glass. "I am, Fausto. The best time."

Was she drunk? I didn't want her too inebriated for what I had planned. "That's enough prosecco. You should eat something."

She rolled her eyes. "So bossy. I already had some salami, Fausto."

Then for some reason, she and Mariella broke out into a fit of hysterical giggles. Cristo santo. God save me from drunk women.

Marco walked up behind me. "A phone call, Rav," he whispered. "Sounds important."

I sighed and told him, "I'll take it. No more prosecco for her. Make sure she eats something." I excused myself to Enzo and went into my office on the yacht.

For the next fifteen minutes I was on the phone with one of my men who oversaw the incoming shipments at the Siderno port. A group of pirates had seized some of our product, which meant I needed to reach out to the pirates on my payroll to find out the persons responsible. My contact said he didn't know but would look into it and report back to me.

Hanging up, I rubbed my eyes and leaned back in my chair. I suddenly wished that this was all over. How had my day turned to shit so quickly?

Standing, I went back outside to the pool deck—and stopped in my tracks. Francesca was laying on her stomach on a chaise, the ties of her suit top hanging loose. Enzo and Mariella were cuddling on a nearby lounge, but Enzo's eyes were locked on Francesca's ass.

My hands shook and I had to shove them in my pockets to keep from punching the wall. It was incredibly dangerous to tempt a man like Enzo D'Agostino. And what of the crew or D'Agostino's guard? Had she no respect for me at all?

Figlio un cane.

"I'm afraid I must cut our day short," I announced tightly. "There is something that needs my attention." Punishing Francesca, but they need not know that. "Perhaps we can do this again soon, D'Agostino."

Francesca struggled to tie the strings of her top and I wanted to roar with frustration. I wanted to go over there and throw a towel around her so no one ever saw her but me. I wanted to fuck her until she followed orders.

Enzo stood and helped Mariella to her feet. "We'd like that, Ravazzani. Thank you for your hospitality. We'll be in touch about that other matter."

He shook my hand then I kissed both of Mariella's cheeks. "Thank you both for coming. Marco will assist you back into your boat."

Francesca was now on her feet, the triangles of her top slightly askew. She rushed to hug Mariella. "Ciao, Mariella. It was nice spending the day with you."

"Ciao, Francesca. I hope I see you again someday."

Do not count on it. I would not trust Francesca at another meeting for a long time. Perhaps ever.

Everyone left but I never took my eyes off Francesca. I was too angry to even speak. It was like when she had stabbed me with the pen, but worse. That had been a personal injury to just me. Today was an insult to me and my business, the very family.

As she stood facing me, her defiance wilted bit by bit the longer I stared at her. Finally, she bit her lip. "I know you're mad because I wore the bikini."

I remained silent, still trying to get a grip on my temper.

"I like this suit! Why shouldn't I be able to wear it?" She glanced down at herself. "I look hot in this suit, Fausto."

When I continued to stand there, she blurted, "I'm sorry, all right? I shouldn't have worn it. I didn't think it was a big deal."

Disobeying me, not a big deal? She was mine, my responsibility. Everything she did as my mantenuta reflected on me. Did she think I invited just any woman to the yacht during sensitive business meetings?

"Please, don't be mad. I said I was sorry."

I dragged in a breath and let it go slowly. "Are you sorry?"

Lines formed between her brows as she slammed them together. "I just said I was."

"If you are sorry—truly sorry—you will go to my suite, lay on my bed with your ass in the air and wait for me."

"Fausto—"

"This is your only chance to prove it, Francesca. Because if you are truly sorry, that will lessen your punishment. Allora, are you truly sorry?"

The slim column of her throat worked as she swallowed. "Yes, I am truly sorry."

"Then you know what to do, no?"

———

Francesca

I WALKED to the master suite like a prisoner going to the gallows. Fausto was livid. In fact, I think he might be angrier than the night I stabbed him with the pen. He looked like he wanted to strangle me.

Fear slid down my spine, causing my skin to break out in a cold sweat.

Would he hurt me?

No, he wouldn't. I knew it in my bones. He might spank me, but we would both enjoy that. No doubt he would tease me until I admitted I belonged to him. I just needed to comply with whatever orders he gave to prove my apology and then he would forgive me. Hopefully that involved some naked time.

The bed was perfectly smooth, not a crease on the gray duvet. I slid onto the mattress and folded my legs under my hips, shoving my ass in the air. The buzz from the prosecco had faded as soon as I caught sight of Fausto's furious expression on the patio deck. Too bad I hadn't allowed myself one more glass. Then I might not be so nervous for whatever he had in mind.

I waited there for a long time, what felt like hours. My legs started to cramp and I thought about moving to shake them out, but then I heard his footsteps. I held my breath.

The bed dipped and his scent teased my nose. He didn't touch me, nor did he speak.

Another few seconds and I cracked. "Fausto—"

"Do not speak, Francesca. When I am done speaking you may explain yourself, capisce?"

I pressed my lips together and waited, feeling like a small child who had disappointed a parent. I didn't like it. Why was he so angry? Why was he humiliating me like this?

"That man was Enzo D'Agostino. He is the head of the Napoli 'ndrina, a powerful but tenuous ally of mine. We were at war for many years, and my father brokered peace after both sides suffered terrible losses, including losing two of my uncles and six cousins. Enzo has recently become capo, and he is known for his unpredictability. His hot-headed temper."

He shifted restlessly, like he was too mad to sit still. "I want to merge some of our business interests, but more importantly, I also want his younger sister to marry my son. This was a critical meeting today, one I had to cut short because you did not do what I asked."

Oh, shit.

How was I supposed to know? He said the man was no friend, but he hadn't shared any of this backstory.

"All I asked was that you not wear this suit. Simple, no? You had others to choose from, suits not so revealing of your tits and ass. Yet, you disobeyed me, even after I told you this was a test. Were you trying to fail?"

I clenched my hands and blurted, "No, of course not. I told you, I didn't think it was a big deal."

"Yes, but what I haven't heard is why you wanted to disobey me. Why did you wish to defy me, after all that's happened today?"

After admitting I belonged to him.

"I don't know. I really like this suit, I suppose."

"No, I do not accept that. Tell me why."

I still hadn't seen his face and it was starting to annoy me. "Can I sit up?"

"Not until you tell me why you wore this suit. Was it to tempt me? To distract me? To distract my guests?"

"No! I wasn't thinking about any of that."

"Then what were you thinking, Francesca?"

He hadn't called me "dolcezza" or "piccola monella" once since emerging from his meeting, only Francesca. I missed playful Fausto, the one who kissed and teased me. "I don't know."

"I do not believe you. A conversation happened in your mind where you went against my wishes. Tell me what it was."

This was ridiculous. I could tell he wasn't going to drop it. But saying it out loud would make me sound immature and silly.

So I turned the tables back on him.

I sat up and glared at him. "I heard Enzo refer to me as a puttanella when I walked through your meeting and you laughed. You didn't stand up for me at all."

"Francesca, I do not explain myself to you. That is not how this works."

"Wrong. Just because we are sleeping together does not mean you can treat me like trash."

"And how is giving you orgasms and bringing you on my yacht treating you like trash?"

"He called me a slut, Fausto!"

Something fierce and frightening shone in his eyes as he closed in, his voice low and tight. "You are a slut, Francesca. *My* slut. But if you must know, I wasn't listening to Enzo because I was too angry over your choice of bathing suit. He could have called you anything, said anything about my mother, and I would have reacted inappropriately. Because I was too fucking furious," he ended on a roar, and I shrank back.

Shit. He was beyond mad.

Fausto took a deep breath, like he was struggling to compose himself. When he spoke, it was at normal volume. "Allora, I'll ask one more time. Tell me why you disobeyed my one order for today?"

I swallowed, unable to take any more. "Because I don't like being told what I can and cannot wear."

Fausto nodded, as if this was what he expected. "Thank you for admitting it. I think we can both agree this won't ever happen again. If I give you an order, I expect you to obey it, Francesca."

He stared at me, waiting for a reaction. I blurted, "I'm sorry. I won't do it again."

Rising, he put his hands into his trouser pockets. "I am glad to hear it. But I am still going to punish you."

"Why?" I lifted my hands and let them fall on my bare thighs. "I said I was sorry. There's no need to drag this out." Must he be so dramatic?

"I told you today was a test, Francesca, and you failed. Now my meeting was cut short and Enzo D'Agostino has an inkling of how possessive I am over you. Instead of a casual afternoon, we've given more information than we received. Do you understand?"

"Yes." I pushed my loose hair behind my ears. "Just tell me what the punishment is and let's get it over with. Then we'll go back to the castello."

"You are not going back to the castello. You are staying here tonight."

I didn't like the way that sounded. "We're staying here?"

"I am still too angry, and I will never touch you in a mood such as this. As much as I want to spank that ass—and I want to very badly—I will never hit you out of anger. Your punishment is to stay here alone tonight."

My jaw dropped open. Was he serious? "You are leaving me here on your yacht? What, so I can billionaire lifestyle myself to death?"

"Enjoy it, then. I hope you and your bikini have a wonderful night. The crew is at your disposal and will give you anything you need." He turned and started for the door.

"Wait, that's it? You're leaving? Just like that?"

"Yes, Francesca, just like that." He paused and glanced over his shoulder. "Perhaps this separation will be necessary for both of us."

What did that mean? Was he reconsidering our arrangement? Well, if so that was fine with me. He could put my ass on a plane and return me to Toronto.

So if I didn't care, then why did my chest suddenly feel hollowed out?

I swallowed the lump in my throat, not above begging for him to reconsider. "Fausto, stay. I'll make it up to you, I promise."

The resolution in his expression didn't change at all. His features remained hard and implacable, the capo feared by all southern Italy. "I'll send Marco for you in the morning."

And with that, he walked out the door. I was still sitting there, dumbfounded, when I heard the helicopter's rotors start turning. They were leaving me here.

Instead of banishing me to the dungeon, he'd banished me here.

CHAPTER NINETEEN

Francesca

I WAS certain I would die that night.

For the first few hours, I explored the yacht. The ship was amazing, with no detail or expense spared. I saw all the bedrooms, the living areas, the bathrooms. Only one room remained locked, and I assumed that was Fausto's office. The crew nodded politely, and I came to quickly realize they didn't speak much English. When I asked for a snack, they brought me more prosecco.

I ended up back on the pool deck where I found bottles of water in the mini fridge. They brought me dinner, which was some amazing shrimp and lobster pasta dish that I wanted to eat every day for the rest of my life. Then I watched the sunset over the water, wishing I had a phone to call my sisters.

Wait, there had to be a phone on the boat, right? Fausto had taken a call at one point.

Wandering to find a crew member, I asked about a phone, holding my hand to my ear. He shook his head. "No, signorina. *Sta nell'ufficio.*"

"*Ufficio?*"

He waved me forward and led me to the locked door near the master suite. Fausto's office. Shit. "*Grazie,*" I said, inwardly sighing. Then something else occurred. "Television?"

"Ah, sì." He nodded and motioned for me to follow. In the master suite, a television was hidden in a cabinet. I clapped my hands, beyond giddy to be saved from total boredom.

"Is there a remote?" I moved my thumb to mime a remote.

He lifted his hands and shrugged, his expression saying he had no idea. Then he pointed to a drawer under the television. Ah, that made sense.

I pulled open the drawer and I found a remote there, along with stacks of DVDs. Old movies? I examined the titles, hoping to recognize at least one.

They were all Italian porn.

Jesus Christ, Fausto. One track mind much?

At least it would save me from silence...and maybe help me learn Italian. Especially dirty Italian, the kind Fausto would like. Not that I cared what Fausto liked at the moment, that asshole.

I chose one featuring two men and one woman. The slot for the disc was on the side of the TV. It took some time to figure out, but I finally got it playing. The production values were hilarious, the plot ludicrous. Nice to see that Italian and American porn were similar in that regard. It wasn't particularly arousing, so I wondered what Fausto liked about it.

Then the men began to dominate the woman...and it all became crystal clear.

Of course, he liked watching her being tied up and held down, flogged and teased. I added the captions and tried to study the words, but I found my eyes fluttering. I fell asleep to the sound of moaning.

A jolt woke me sometime later.

The TV had turned off, so the room was pitch black, and the wind was howling. The yacht moved as though we were at sea, and my stomach lurched. Had we left the inlet while I was asleep?

Someone pounded on the door. "Hello?" I called.

It opened and one of the crew members peered inside. I could barely see his face, but his expression did not reassure me. "Signorina, *si fermi qui.*" He gestured to the bed. I understood the word *here*, and I assumed he was telling me not to move.

"Are we in danger?"

He gave me a helpless shrug that said he didn't understand. "Si fermi qui, per favore."

"Okay," I said, practically being drowned out by the sound of the wind and waves crashing outside the yacht. The boat rose and fell, and I dug my fingertips into the mattress as best I could. Holy shit. Were we going to sink?

The crew member disappeared, leaving me alone in Fausto's big bed. Rain pelted the glass, sheets of it coating the deck beyond. The wind was louder than I'd ever heard, a fierce roar so strong it was a wonder the roof didn't blow off. I didn't have any personal experience to compare this night with, but I couldn't help but wonder if this was a tropical storm. Worse, a hurricane?

Fear turned my blood to ice. I couldn't move, my body frozen in dread as the waves rocked the yacht. Should I be searching for a life preserver? I stared out at the black water and shivered. Unfortunately, I wasn't a great swimmer. I certainly couldn't swim to shore, which meant I'd either drown or become shark food if the boat sank.

Oh, God.

The waves seemed to be getting larger. Angrier. I tried to think of it like a roller coaster, a ride I had to endure for a little bit, but it didn't work. The longer it went on, the worse it became. At one point, my stomach revolted and I had to rush to the toilet to vomit. I had no one to hold my hair, no one to tell me this was all going to be okay. I was in the middle of a terrible storm all alone in a place I barely knew. If we died tonight, I would never see my sisters again. I would slip under the waves and disappear.

That scared me like nothing else.

As the waves continued to batter the yacht, I clung to the bed and prayed, queasy and miserable. I could only wonder, had Fausto known the storm was coming? Was this his way of punishing me?

Fausto

When the storm abated at daybreak I was in the helicopter, flying toward the water. The wind hadn't completely died down, and the pilot struggled to keep the craft righted. I didn't care. I had to get to the yacht.

There had been no way to reach her last night, or I would have gone. But the wind had been too fierce, too sudden to risk a small speedboat or the helicopter. I hadn't even been able to reach her by phone to reassure her, as we'd lost service early on in the storm.

I knew the yacht was sound. Nothing, not even a category five hurricane, could capsize a boat that big, equipped to handle rough seas. But for someone not used to the ocean, a storm such as the one last night could be terrifying. I hated that I put her through it. Instead of letting her come back to the castello, I'd left her on the yacht, alone and with no way to reach me, surrounded by a crew that spoke little if any English.

Bastardo! What had I been thinking?

The night had been a sleepless one. I paced and worried over Francesca. At dinner, Zia had given me an earful about my treatment of Francesca, hissing, *"Vecchi peccati hanno le ombre lunghe."* It was true. Old sins did have long shadows, and I knew that what I'd done would have long-lasting repercussions.

While I regretted leaving Francesca the instant I departed the yacht, I could not weaken and reconsider. I intended to live with the consequences, good or bad. Of course, if I had known about the storm, I would have handled things differently. I prayed she would forgive me.

As we approached, the yacht was still, the waters once again calm. I held onto the door handle, tossing my headset onto the seat next to me, and as soon as the helicopter touched down, I was out and racing along the deck.

A lump of fear lodged in my throat as I opened the suite's door. Francesca was sprawled out on top of the bed, limbs askew, asleep in one of my dress shirts. My shoulders relaxed slightly, until I got close enough to see the dried tears on her cheeks.

Something in my chest turned over.

I found a soft blanket in a drawer. Carrying it to the bed, I crawled next to her, gathered her to me and covered us both. She sighed and nestled closer, her eyes never opening, and I sagged into the mattress, exhausted. I should have been here last night, as we'd planned. Or we should have been in my bedroom inside the castello. My anger over her disobeying me was not an excuse for isolating her and scaring her half to death.

Marco had tried to tell me as much on the ride back to the estate yesterday, but I hadn't listened, so full of my own importance that I couldn't see reason. I closed my eyes, determined to make this up to her. I wanted my sweet girl back.

Though I meant to stay awake, I must have slept because movement at my side brought me out of a deep fog. I felt her edge away, and I instinctively reached for her. "No. *Non muoversi*," I mumbled, telling her not to move.

"I have to use the bathroom," she said, her voice distant, and I released her.

She was gone for quite some time. I was beginning to worry when I heard the latch. I pushed up to my elbows as she emerged, her face clear and freshly washed. She stood by the side of the bed and crossed her arms. "When did you arrive?"

"At daybreak, when the storm abated. Dolcezza—"

"No, Fausto. You do not get to call me that. Not anymore. You left me here. I was all alone," her voice cracked as it trailed off, and I was on my feet instantly.

Crossing to her, I pulled her tight to my chest. She pushed back, trying to get away, but I didn't let her. I held her tight, whispering, "I am sorry, Francesca. Mi dispiace. Perdonami, bellissima." I repeated it again and to my astonishment she broke out into tears, her fingers clinging to my shirt.

The sound of her misery tore me apart. I kissed the top of her head and sat, holding her on my lap. "You're safe now," I told her. "You are safe. Nothing will ever hurt you."

"I was so scared."

"I know, but you were not in danger. This boat could never capsize."

"That is what they said about the Titanic," she said, her face buried in my throat.

The Titanic hadn't capsized, but I didn't say as much. "You were safe, though I know storms on the water can be very scary."

"I was terrified. And I got sick. Twice."

"Oh, piccolina." I squeezed her, hating myself even more for not being here. "I am so sorry."

"All because I wore a bathing suit you didn't like." She pushed off my lap and stood, glaring down at me. "I hate this. I don't want to be your mistress or your prisoner or your daughter-in-law. I want to go home."

I would never allow it, not yet, but I suspected she didn't want to hear that at the moment. I had to use honesty and finesse to coax her anger away.

I rubbed her hip. "You don't mean that. You are angry—and you have every right—but I am asking for your forgiveness. I should not have left you here alone. I let my temper and jealousy control my tongue. If there had been any way for me to get to you last night I would have tried, but the wind was too strong."

She slapped my hand away. "I don't believe you, not after you said the separation would be good for both of us. What the fuck did that even mean?"

"It meant I was angry, Francesca. I was trying to spare you my temper. But I regretted leaving the second we lifted off."

"Bullshit."

"I will never lie to you. I am many things, most of them terrible, but I am not a liar."

"If you regretted it, then why didn't you come right back?"

"I had to stand by my decision. Changing my mind is a sign of weakness."

She gave a humorless laugh and dragged a hand through her long golden hair. "I am not one of your soldiers, Fausto. Mistress or not, you cannot treat me like shit."

"I want to spoil you and treat you like a goddess, if you'll let me."

"Until the next time you get angry and put me in your dungeon. Or leave me in the middle of a hurricane."

There was no hurricane, but I didn't bother correcting her. "I promise I won't banish you to the dungeon or the yacht the next time you piss me off."

"Or anywhere else. You won't banish me anywhere, Fausto."

She was forgetting who held the power in our arrangement, and I would need to remind her as soon as her temper cooled. "Or?"

"I'll stab you with something sharper than a pen."

I couldn't help it, I laughed. "Many have tried, Francesca. I wouldn't recommend it." Rising, I cupped her jaw in my hands. "The devil cannot be killed."

I pressed my lips to hers, moving softly, letting my body convey my apology. My regret. I needed to reassure her that I would never let her down again. And I craved reassurance that she was still mine.

Her lips parted and my tongue swept inside, desperate to taste her. She was warm and slick, and so sweet I could feel blood pumping to my dick. The boat rocked gently, our bodies swaying ever so slightly, pushing her tits into my chest, and I hoped this meant she had forgiven me. We could spend all day on the boat, fucking.

I reached under the dress shirt hanging down her thighs to cup her ass—and she wasn't wearing panties. I sucked in a breath. "Cazzo, you are so sexy."

"I had no clothes to change into after I puked on my black bikini."

I gave her ass a slap. "I like you in my clothing."

"I can tell." Her eyes dipped to my crotch. "But I am not fucking you today, Fausto." I trailed my fingers to her seam, but she edged away. "Did you not hear what I said?"

"I feel as though you need a reminder as to how our relationship works."

"And after last night, I feel as though you need a reminder that this pussy belongs to me, until I decide you've earned it."

The back of my neck itched, my chest hot. "Not even close, Francesca." I started toward her and she retreated, step by step, until I had her pinned against the wall. Then I slid my hand between us and cupped her. "This pussy is mine until I decide it isn't."

She started to argue, so I grazed her folds with my fingers, brushing over her clit. Her body softened, relaxing into the wall and into my hand. "You are not playing fair," she whispered.

"I never do. This is mine—and I will fuck it raw until I've had enough."

"You are an asshole."

"The biggest." But I didn't want her to regret giving herself over to me. While I craved having her again, her submissive compliance was a thousand times more satisfying. Was I growing soft when it came to her? Possibly, but I couldn't seem to help it.

I let her go.

"Come. Let's return to the castello. Zia is worried sick about you. Not to mention that Giulio nearly punched me when he learned where you were last night. They deserve to know you are all right."

"I wish he would have punched you. You deserve it."

When I took her hand, she said, "Wait, what am I going to wear? I don't have any clothes."

"I'll find you something to cover your legs. But keep my shirt on, because I love the way your tits look in it."

She rolled her eyes and walked to the television. "Fine, but I am taking some of your porn back with me."

I smothered my grin. "I see you were busy exploring. Which one did you like best?"

"I'm not watching them to get off. I am trying to learn Italian from them."

Madre di Dio. Learning dirty talk in my language from porn? This girl was going to be the death of me. "Bring four or five. Just for variety."

CHAPTER TWENTY

Francesca

GIULIO APPEARED in my doorway after I had showered and dressed. "Cristo santo, Frankie. I was worried about you last night. Are you okay?"

He was dressed like a fashion model, expensive fabrics carelessly draped over his lean frame, his hair perfectly styled. His features were softer than Fausto's, handsome in a more classical sense. His mother must have been beautiful, too.

I sighed and waved him in. "Barely. I was scared shitless."

"I can believe it. That was a bad storm." He shook his head and closed the door. "My father's temper is a fearsome thing. He must have been very mad at you to leave you out there."

I figured I could level with Giulio. "He asked me not to wear the black bikini during his meeting with Enzo."

"And you wore it?" Giulio winced. "Bella, that was asking for trouble."

"I know, and he later explained why. But I didn't know any of that at the time. I should be able to wear what I want."

"You don't know many Italian men, do you?"

"There are plenty of Italian men in Toronto."

"No, there are Italian-Canadian men. I mean, true Italian men. It is a much different thing. They can be very domineering."

"You're not like that."

He gave me a wolfish grin. "Not with women, I'm not."

I laughed. "You're all assholes."

"That's true." The smile dropped and he stared at me soberly. "Is he...? I mean to say, are you okay with this? With him?"

How to answer that? I had so many conflicting emotions. I wanted to go home, but I also craved Fausto's body like air and water. And living here wasn't so terrible. The castello and the estate were beautiful, and I was in Italy. Other than a lack of a phone and laptop—and Fausto's refusal to let me leave—it was the perfect summer vacation.

I could see Giulio was truly worried, so I had to be honest. "I'm okay. For now. It's weird telling you this, but I'm insanely attracted to your father. We're having fun hooking up."

"Fausto, fun? I don't believe it."

I bit my lip, remembering our little games. Fausto's dirty mouth, my compliance, his rewards. It was a vicious cycle I was becoming addicted to. "I won't traumatize you with the details, but yes. He's intense and a total dick sometimes, but what we are doing together is fun. At least it was, until he had to go and ruin it last night."

"I definitely do not want details," he said, holding up a hand. "But I am glad you are happy."

"He said he would let me go when we got bored of each other. Then I'll go back to Toronto and start college." Hopefully Columbia would still take me, as I'd already been admitted once. If not, I'd find another school in America, far away from my family and the 'Ndrangheta.

"He takes good care of each mantenuta. He bought Katarzyna a house on the water in Portofino."

I blinked. "What? A house?"

"And a diamond bracelet."

"Holy crap." Talk about parting gifts. But I didn't want jewelry or a vacation home. I wanted my freedom. To go to college, study, and live like a normal young person. My father hadn't allowed any independence growing up, and I had hated it, using every chance I could find to sneak out.

Is that what Fausto thought, that I expected a payout when this was done? I was sleeping with him because I wanted to, and because he was a beast in bed. I didn't need his money. My family was wealthy, too. I haven't ever wanted for anything in my life.

Suddenly, the door opened and the devil himself walked in.

I couldn't help but feel conflicted. He looked gorgeous, already put together in one of his designer three-piece suits. He'd shaved since I saw him last, his handsome face now smooth. But I was still angry with him, so my hormones needed to sit the fuck down.

"Do you mind?" I said, attempting to sound stern. "You're supposed to ask if you can come in first."

He jerked his chin at his son and Giulio immediately strode out, closing the door behind him. Fausto turned his attention to me, the edges of his mouth curling slightly. "I thought we covered that, dolcezza."

"I'm still furious with you. What do you want?"

He stalked toward me and put one hand behind my head, the other on my hip. He surrounded me and I wanted so badly to lean into him. To kiss and touch him. As if he could read my thoughts, his nostrils flared as he stared down at me. "I come bearing gifts."

The conversation about Katarzyna fresh in my mind, I recoiled. "I don't want gifts. I want to go home."

The lines around his eyes deepened, but he continued as if I hadn't spoken. "You will want this one. Reach into my left coat pocket."

He was wrong. I didn't want it, but I couldn't tell him that without seeing it first. I reached into his coat pocket and a thin rectangle met my fingers. I gasped and pulled it out. "Oh, my God. A phone!" The relief I felt was overwhelming. I could call my sisters whenever I felt like it. My friends, too. I could watch cat videos and catch up on celebrity gossip.

"This pleases you, no?"

I would gladly take this gift, seeing as how it was one of life's necessities. Like food. "Yes, it does. Thank you." I couldn't help it. I pushed up on my toes and kissed him on the mouth. He didn't deepen it, and I was glad. I still hadn't forgiven him.

"Prego. Now reach in the other coat pocket."

I wasn't sure I would like another gift, but curiosity got the better of me. I reached in and felt a small piece of plastic. "What is this?"

"Pull it out and see."

It was a credit card, the exclusive black color. I stared at it like it was a snake. "I don't need this. I have my own money, Fausto."

"I know you do, but I would like to spoil you today. Giulio will take you to Rome this afternoon. Buy anything you like. Then I'll see you tonight."

Rome? Oh, my God. I've always wanted to see Rome. How did Fausto do this to me? It was like he plucked every thought inside my brain and used it against me.

But taking his credit card meant I was signing on as his full-fledged mistress, didn't it? I wasn't certain I was ready for that step, especially after last night. "I will go to Rome but I will use the money I brought in my satchel."

His thumb rubbed back and forth across my neck, causing tingles all along my spine. "Use my credit card. Let me do this for you to ease my conscience, okay?"

"Fausto...." I couldn't even finish the thought. My resistance was melting in the face of his sweetness. Was there really harm in accepting his generosity this one time?

"Please. Just today."

I closed my eyes and gave in. "Fine, but just today. And fair warning, I will spend until I'm no longer angry at you. I hope you have a high limit on this card."

He bent to kiss me, softly on the lips first then along my jaw. I arched against him, like a needy cat starved for his touch. His lips reached my ear. "That card has no limit, la mia piccola monella. Do your worst, then forgive me and let me fuck you tonight."

The walls of my pussy contracted, the greedy bitch. "We'll see," I breathed, desperately clinging to my dignity.

He stepped back and released me slowly. "Have fun, bellissima. Feel free to text me pictures. My number is in your phone."

"That was presumptuous," I said smartly. "How did you save it? Il Diavolo?"

Fausto's mouth curved into a wicked smile. "*Il Trombamico*. It's what all the kids say these days."

"I'm afraid to ask what that means."

"Fuck buddy," he answered.

"I think I'll change it to stronzo. What am I in your phone? Piccola monella?"

"No, you are *La Bella Figa*."

I frowned. "Beautiful...fig?"

Fausto bent to whisper in my ear. "Beautiful pussy."

I don't know why I found that so hot, but I did. I swallowed hard and tried not to let him see how I felt. "How will you keep all your bella figas straight in your contact list?"

"There is just una bella figa, Francesca."

He let that statement sit between us for a long second, and I have to admit that I was relieved. At least in the short term, he was mine, too.

He stepped back, releasing me and heading for the door. "Now, go and spend my money. Buy something sexy I can tear off of you later."

"Dio santo! More gelato?"

I ignored Giulio as I accepted my pistachio gelato. "Grazie. He's paying," I hitched a thumb in Giulio's direction, a small bit of revenge for mocking me.

Giulio handed some of our bags to one of the guards and dug out his wallet. "I have never seen one so tiny eat so much. Where does it go?"

"To my boobs and ass, obviously."

I held up my gelato and snapped a selfie, then posted it to my social media. Gia and Emma had been commenting on my photos all day, and I was so happy to connect—even virtually—with my sisters. Giulio refused to get in any of my photos, saying it wasn't a good idea for him to be seen online. I wasn't sure if that was because of the Italian police or his boyfriend. Whatever the reason, I respected his wishes.

"Where to now, G?" I licked the creamy goodness off the spoon. "I don't know how many more dresses and shoes I can buy."

"We are going around the corner next. You'll see."

A man riding a sleek compact motorcycle buzzed by us. "Do you think Fausto would let me buy a Ducati?" I'd always wanted one but my father refused, saying they were too dangerous.

"I think he would never permit you to ride it. He was very angry when I bought my Ferrari. He would rather I was driven around by the guards in one of the protected vehicles he uses."

"I'm not surprised. You are the only heir."

"Do not remind me."

"What did you tell him about marrying Enzo D'Agostino's sister?"

He sighed, a pinched expression flashing over his handsome features. "I said she was a child. But he reminded me that the wedding wouldn't take place until she was of age, so that at least buys me some time."

"That sucks. Maybe something will happen and you won't have to marry her."

"My father will only find someone else. It is inevitable and not surprising for a man in my position."

"Will you be happy?"

"Does it matter?"

I glanced back at the guards following us. They were close, but not within earshot. "Of course, it matters," I murmured. "Hiding and lying your whole life? That sounds miserable."

"I have had years and years to come to terms with my future. And all men I know cheat on their wives. I will just need to be more discreet."

"All married men you know cheat on their wives?"

"Except Zio Marco. He is the only one."

"When your father was married, do you think he cheated on your mother?"

"Without a doubt. They were not happy together, but even if they had been, I doubt Fausto would have remained faithful."

"Why?"

"Because a man in his position, in our world, it is a sign of strength, of manliness, to have more than one woman."

My stomach cramped around the gelato. I hated that the mafia bred misogyny and infidelity. It was toxic masculinity on steroids.

I elbowed Giulio. "What about more than one man?"

His olive skin colored slightly. His voice was quiet. "No, we are exclusive. I would kill anyone who touched him."

"Possessive and monogamous. Who would have guessed such a thing was possible for a Ravazzani?"

He gave me a dazzling grin then pointed to the right. "Over here."

Rome had the most amazing boutiques and shops. Spending Fausto's money had been easier than I thought, probably because Giulio encouraged me at every turn. I tried not to dwell on the whole mistress thing too much. Fausto had kidnapped me and wouldn't let me leave, so it seemed only fair that I purchase things just this once to make me feel more at home.

"There it is," Giulio said, crossing the quaint cobblestone street. "Let's go."

La Perla resided in a charming yellow building on the corner, decorated with gold accents around the windows and doors. The storefront managed to look both expensive and rustic. I tugged on Giulio's arm to make him stop. "Wait, are you sure you want to do this? Watch me buy lingerie to wear in front of your father?"

"It's better than buying it to wear in front of me. And are you forgetting that I have impeccable taste?"

He really did. Giulio had selected most of the outfits I had purchased today. Italians had the best fashion sense of anyone in the world.

"Also," Giulio continued, "except for last night, my father has been relaxed since you two started up. It is nice to see. Refreshing. Even some of the guards have commented on it. I think you are good for him."

I bit my lip, ridiculously pleased by that statement. No doubt Fausto's mood was a result of having a new and shiny toy to play with, but he was my toy, too. I tossed my paper cup into a bin and took Giulio's arm. "Fine, but don't say I didn't warn you if this gets awkward."

Inside, Giulio spoke rapid Italian with the saleswomen. Soon I was in a dressing room, being told to take my clothes off. "But I haven't picked anything out," I told him.

"They will bring the things back and you try them on." He studied my face, putting a finger under my chin to tilt my head this way and that. "You should wear red, I think. Italian men love red lingerie, and it will look hot on you."

Back home, I had a few pieces of fancy lingerie, but David hadn't seemed to care what I wore. Fausto, on the other hand, struck me as the kind of man who would like it when a woman paraded around in front of him, dolled up in silk and lace.

Actually, I liked the sound of that, too.

The saleswomen began bringing me bras and panties, camisoles and silk pajamas. Some red, but some white and black, too. There was a black lace corset that was to die for. I didn't try on any of the panties, just selected the ones I liked. When a red lace bodysuit was added to my stack, I paused and stared at it like I was a heart-eyed emoji. It was delicate and sexy, with a little bit of stretch. The underwires and padded cups would thrust my tits sky high.

I had to try it on.

When I adjusted the straps and had it the way I wanted, I turned to the mirror. Oh, I *liked* it. I looked like a naughty pinup girl. Would Fausto like it, too? Suddenly, I couldn't wait to find out.

Whipping out my new phone, I held my arm up high, getting the best angle of my boobs, then snapped a picture. I texted it to Trombamico without any text.

I hadn't even set my phone down when a reply came in.

Cazzo

Your tits in that thing make my dick hard

Buy four of those

No—five

Smiling, I took off the bodysuit and hung it up. I looked at the other things Giulio had sent back. Perhaps Fausto could help me decide.

I began trying on pieces and sending him photos. He responded quickly and succinctly, telling me what he was going to do to me in each of the outfits. The thong and bustier were for when he wanted to spank my ass. The sheer slip dress with embroidered tulle was for when he wanted me to sit on his face. The black lace pushup bra was for when I sucked on his cock. The silk nightgown was for grinding his cock into my ass from behind.

The more he texted, the hornier I became. I was breathing hard, my heart racing, standing alone in a dressing room. It was like he was touching me, though he was still back in Siderno.

I decided to torture him.

Placing my phone on the small stool in the dressing room, I angled the camera so it could see most of my body. I was wearing a simple violet bra embroidered with lace and no panties. Then I started recording.

Looking into the camera, I slid my hands over my chest and cleavage, cupping my breasts. The image reflected back at me was a wanton creature, a seductress with long blond hair and sultry lips. I barely looked like myself.

Feeling braver, I slipped my hands down my belly, coasting my hips, until I reached my pussy. Closing my eyes, I let my fingers skim my seam, gasping when I brushed my clitoris. I was soaked and the touch felt unbelievably good, like I would die if it stopped.

I eased my legs apart, giving my fingers more room to explore. I tried to put on a show at first, but it soon became about my pleasure instead. The pads of my fingers circled my clit, working it as I panted, my body coiling with hunger. At some point I didn't care who would see this—I just needed to make myself come.

I bit my lip to keep from moaning, keeping as silent as I could manage as I stroked myself. The lust doubled and tripled, my toes curling into the plush carpet, my fingers coated with my wetness. I wished Fausto was in the room with me, his hot glare devouring me while he gave me orders in his sexy Italian voice....

The orgasm slammed into me, my back arching as I trembled and shook. Light and heat exploded, carrying me off on a wave of bliss that went on and on. When it finally subsided, I gave the camera a dreamy smile and blew it a kiss. Then I stopped the video and hit send.

CHAPTER TWENTY-ONE

Francesca

TODAY HAS BEEN PERFECT. Before shopping, Giulio had taken me to see the Coliseum, Papal Basilica, and Trevi Fountain. But more than the tourist locations, he'd shown me his favorite spots—the charming side streets and gardens, the fruit stands and cafés. It was better than any tour I could have asked for.

"You come here a lot, don't you?" I asked as we strolled.

"As much as I can. It's easier here than in Siderno. Here we can blend in."

"But you still have to be careful."

"Yes. My father's reach is vast and our enemies are everywhere. There is no truly safe place for me."

"I'm sorry, G."

"Things are changing, slowly. Perhaps the next generation of our brotherhood won't judge a man for his preferences."

I doubted it, but didn't say it. Progress in the mafia never matched progress in the real world. From what I had seen, the mafia was still stuck in the nineteenth century.

Giulio pointed to a four-story cream stone building with black shutters on every window. A bakery occupied the ground level, the smell of coffee and bread filling the air. "We'll stop here."

At the door, he punched in a code on a keypad and the lock opened. I followed inside. "Where are we?"

"Technically this apartment belongs to my father, but he never comes here so I use it."

Fausto had a Roman fuck pad? Of course, he did. Why was I even surprised? My feelings were a bit hurt that I hadn't heard a word from him since I sent that video. Was he angry that I'd gotten myself off? From romance novels, I knew some domineering men didn't like their women to come without them.

If that was the case, then that was too damn bad. I was my own person and I wasn't about to stop masturbating when I felt like it just because I was sleeping with him.

We climbed the marble stairs, the guards following us, until we reached the top floor, where Giulio entered another code and held his thumb on some sort of scanner.

The Ravazzanis took their safety seriously.

We walked in and my jaw fell open. The apartment was gorgeous, light and airy, with huge rooms and, like the castello and yacht, tastefully decorated. The double-height living room opened directly onto a balcony, so I immediately went outside and marveled at the views.

It seemed like all of Rome stretched out before me, with brown tiled roofs and domed church bells every way I turned. A marble dining table with iron chairs awaited, and planters filled with lavender ran the length of the balcony. Unable to help myself, I bent to inhale the clean scent. This place was unreal. Why didn't Fausto use it?

"Would you like a tour?" Giulio came up beside me. "Or do you just want to stand here a little longer?"

"I think I could stand here forever. It's absolutely gorgeous." We both stared out at the buildings. "When I thought of Rome, this right here was exactly what I pictured."

"It is beautiful, no? I love the combination of the old and the new."

"Me, too."

"Signore Ravazzani," a voice behind us said.

Giulio and I turned at the same time to find a guard standing in the doorway. "Eh, Paolo?"

They exchanged rapid Italian I couldn't understand, so I turned back toward the city. Why didn't Fausto ever come here? It was too beautiful a spot not to be appreciated.

"Frankie, this is Paolo." Giulio nudged my arm until I turned around.

"Ciao, Paolo," I said quickly. The guard had been with us all day, so I wasn't certain why we were just being introduced now.

"No, you don't understand," Giulio said, his voice low and soft. "This is Paolo, *il mio ragazzo*."

His boyfriend.

"Oh, my goodness." Hurrying toward the other man, I held out my hand. "Nice to meet you. I'm Frankie."

He blushed slightly, his expression turning sheepish as we shook. "Ciao, Frankie."

"He's embarrassed because you saw his dick at the club," Giulio put in, his tone amused. "I told him that you were too busy admiring mine to even look at his."

I held up my palms. "It was a blur of dicks, to be honest. I don't really remember either." I also didn't remember Paolo. I guess I hadn't been looking at their faces at that moment.

Giulio translated and Paolo smiled, his large shoulders relaxing slightly. He was handsome, in a rough and tumble sort of way. I could see him strangling a man with his bare hands, which were the size of hams. Was Paolo hoping to get Giulio alone?

I sent a nervous glance into the apartment, but Giulio said, "No one else is here. The other guards are downstairs."

"Let me guess. Fausto owns the entire building."

Giulio grinned and leaned against the stone surrounding the balcony. "*Sì, certo*."

"Would you two like to be alone?"

Giulio shook his head. "No, Paolo needs to go sit with the guards downstairs. Otherwise, it attracts attention."

"Oh. I suppose that makes sense."

"Give me a moment, bella." Giulio strode purposely toward Paolo and cupped the bigger man's jaw. Giulio pressed his mouth to Paolo's and began devouring him with a kiss, so I turned away to give them privacy. They whispered in Italian for a moment and then Giulio returned to the edge of the balcony.

"You two are cute together," I said.

"I worry for him. If we are caught, he will suffer more than I will."

"So don't get caught."

"Of course. It is so easy. Why didn't I think of that?" His phone pinged and he glanced at it. "What should we do now? We could make bellinis."

"Do you have the ingredients?"

He made a sound that said I was an idiot for even suggesting he didn't. "We freeze the white peaches, so they are always on hand. Come on. I'll show you."

"Can we drink them out here?"

"Is there another way to drink them in Rome but on a gorgeous terrace such as this? Then we will get ready for dinner."

I followed him inside. "Where are we going for dinner?"

"It's a surprise."

"That sounds fun." We entered a modern kitchen with marble countertops and white cabinets. A huge island rested in the middle, with stools on one side. I dropped onto a stool and took my phone out of my back pocket. I checked for a text, but Fausto had left me on read, the asshole.

"Missing someone?" Giulio teased, nodding at my phone.

"*Baciami il culo.*" *Kiss my ass.* I had been busy translating today on my new phone when not buying clothes.

Giulio laughed as he went to the freezer. "We will make a true Italian of you yet, bella."

Soon Giulio blended peaches into puree and poured it into a pitcher with prosecco. He told me where to find two flutes and then we were back on the terrace, watching the sun drop in the sky over Rome as we sipped bellinis. "I don't hate this," I said, swallowing more of the cocktail. "I could do this forever."

"Ask my father to give you this apartment when you part, and perhaps you can."

"Ew, gross."

"What is gross?"

"I don't want him to give me gifts or pay me off. Even though Enzo D'Agostino called me a puttanella, I'm not."

Giulio's face darkened and he grew serious. Scary serious. "Che palle! Did he say this to your face?"

"No, he said it to your father, who laughed."

"I will have a word with him. He should have put D'Agostino in his place."

"Perhaps as D'Agostino's brother-in-law, you can put him in his place."

"Do not remind me. But my father should not tolerate such disrespect."

"That is what I told him."

Giulio looked confused. "What did he say?"

"That he was too angry over the black bikini to even hear what D'Agostino said."

"I bet this was true. He's very protective of you. Another man seeing all your gorgeous skin must have driven him crazy."

"You saw me in that bikini."

"Which was why my father arranged that trip with Katarzyna in the first place. He thought you and I were fucking on the boat."

Fausto, jealous over other men? Ridiculous. He was gorgeous, powerful and wealthy, and had a big dick. What other man could possibly compare? Not that I would ever tell him as much.

"What's up there?" I pointed to an upper terrace.

"That is part of the master suite. There is a jacuzzi and more seating."

Wow. "You Italians really know how to live."

Giulio lifted his glass. "Indeed we do, bella. So, why would you ever want to leave?"

As I sipped the cocktail, the Roman sun warming my face, I had to agree. This was about as close to perfection as I could imagine.

But perfection never lasted. Losing my mother at such a young age had taught me that. You had to appreciate what you had in the moment, because who knew when it would disappear? This summer, I was in Italy and I had a smoking hot boyfriend who was incredibly wealthy. For now, that was enough.

ONE THING I learned since staying here was that Italians like to eat dinner late. It was almost nine o'clock when Giulio and I left the apartment. He still wouldn't tell me where we were going, but he did insist on picking out my outfit.

He chose the red lace La Perla bodysuit and a red wrap-around dress we had purchased today. "You should always wear red," he said with a smirk.

"Why?"

"Because of your coloring, bella. And I have a feeling my father will like it."

Giulio held my arm down the stairs. While I loved the black heels he paired with the outfit—Louboutins with a scalloped edge along the sides and a sky-high heel—they did not allow for going up and down stairs easily. Still, I adored them. They made my legs look long and I reached Giulio's height with them on.

Three guards followed us, including Paolo. It must have been strange for him to follow his boyfriend as Giulio escorted a woman out to dinner. I wondered if they would find a way to be together tonight when we returned to Siderno.

We didn't go far. The restaurant was directly across the street from the apartment, a small trattoria that looked charming from the outside. Giulio held open the door and I went in. The restaurant was empty, the tables and chairs completely vacant. Was this place even open?

A woman emerged from the back. She had silver hair that was cut into a sleek bob. "Buonasera, signore, signorina. Follow me, please."

I trailed her toward the rear of the restaurant and out a small door. A stone patio stretched out in front of me, twinkling lights strung overhead, illuminating the lone table on the stone patio.

And the man waiting there.

I couldn't move, my feet rooted to the ground, as Fausto stood and buttoned his jacket, looking more delicious than any of the gelato I'd eaten today. I gaped at him as he came toward me. "You're here."

He slid a hand onto my hip and cradled my jaw with the other. I was coming to learn this was his favorite way to hold me, not that I was complaining. His mouth touched mine in a soft kiss full of promise. "Ciao, dolcezza."

"I can't believe it." I skimmed my hands up his chest until I could wrap them around his neck. He smelled like his fancy Italian soap, a combination of lemon and bergamot. "When did you get here?"

"Not long ago." He moved a hand lower to cup my ass, bringing our hips together. "I left just after you sent me that video."

Oh. I bit my lip. "That explains why you never responded."

"Never has a man wrapped up his work so rapidly to get to his woman as I did this afternoon."

His woman. I liked the sound of that. Probably too much.

I looked over my shoulder. "Did you—" No one was there. "Wait, where did Giulio go?"

"Where does any young man go in Rome after his father tells him to go away?"

"You told Giulio to go away? That's not very nice."

Fausto trailed his lips over my jaw and down my neck, my skin pebbling everywhere. God, he was here five minutes and my panties were already soaked.

"I want you to myself tonight," he whispered. "I plan to take my time while I punish you for teasing me."

I knew his punishment would really be a reward. "Did you like watching me masturbate, capo?"

He growled deep in his chest. "I came twice while watching it over and over today. You are the sexiest woman I have ever seen."

"I will happily do it for you live any time you like."

"Not to worry. I will have you do that soon. But not tonight. Tonight I plan to fuck you until you can't take any more."

He kissed me then, not the gentle greeting of a moment ago, but an attack on my mouth. He devoured me, robbing me of breath while he thrust his tongue deep inside to tangle with mine. I sagged against him, caught up in the give and take between us, the frenzy that had pushed us together in the first place. I needed him desperately. My head was spinning with chemicals and endorphins, a purely physical reaction that only this man had ever caused within me.

"Cazzo, Francesca," he said when we broke apart. "I want to strip you naked and fuck you right here on the stone and dirt."

"The apartment is across the street," I panted, clinging to him.

"Later. First I want to spoil you with the best food in Roma. Come, let's sit." He took my hand and led me to the small table. Wine had already been poured and a small candle sat in the middle. Fausto helped me into my seat and then took his own.

Leaning in, he said, "*Sei mozzafiato.* I like you in red."

Something occurred to me. "Did you tell Giulio to have me wear this?"

"My son has been keeping me updated throughout the day. Did you think I wasn't interested?"

I picked up my wine glass. "I thought you were busy."

"I was, but I am never too busy for you. Especially when I know what you are wearing underneath that dress."

"Maybe I won't let you see it," I teased.

His lips curved in the most sinfully arrogant way. "I could order you to strip right here and deep throat my dick and we both know you would do it gladly."

I tried not to choke on my wine as I swallowed. God, that sounded hot.

Fausto chuckled at my reaction and relaxed in his chair just as the woman from earlier returned, a plate in each hand. One was parma ham and the other fried anchovies, which I'd never had before but were surprisingly delicious.

"Tell me what you think of Roma," Fausto asked as he poured more wine. "Giulio said you liked the apartment."

"I love the apartment. I don't know why you don't use it more often."

"It is not easy for me to leave the castello."

Right, I'd forgotten. Mob boss. "So why come today?"

"Because I couldn't wait another minute to see you."

I bit my lip and focused on my plate, trying to hide how happy that made me.

Fausto refused to let me. With a finger, he lifted my chin to meet his gaze. "I have never, not once, neglected my duties for a woman before today. But seeing you here, so beautiful while drinking wine with me in one of my favorite restaurants...how could I ever regret it?"

I loved that I affected him as much as he affected me. I nuzzled his palm like a cat. "I am very, very glad you came."

He pushed his finger past my lips and onto my tongue. Locking eyes with him, I sucked hard, swirling my tongue around the digit. He watched, his gaze growing dark. "Remember that when I fuck your three holes tonight."

I let his finger fall from my mouth. "Three? Aren't you getting a bit ahead of yourself?"

"I want all of you, places you never let that stronzo have. I want you to feel me everywhere until there's no room for anyone else."

The woman returned with our next course, leaving me to contemplate his words. How did he know just what to say to both turn me on and make my heart swell? It was as if Fausto had a window into my brain.

We ate spaghetti with crispy pork cheek and zucchini, as well as fettuccini with pecorino cheese and pepper. There were veal meatballs on the side. "This is too much food," I said.

"You don't have to eat it all. Just try a little bit of each. The meatballs are the best in the city."

After tasting them, I concurred. "Do you come here a lot?"

"Every time I am in Roma. I own the restaurant."

"What?" My voice rose two octaves. "You do?"

"I do own some legitimate businesses, you know. And it's run by the widow of one of my men killed about five years ago. I helped her get started."

Fausto, benevolent? The layers to this man never ceased to fascinate me. He was like the ground. The more you dug, the more things you found underneath.

We finished with tiramisu and crème caramel. And espresso, of course. Fausto asked for a splash of sambuca in his, but I took mine plain with lots of sugar. I was still getting used to the bitter taste.

The whole day had been perfect. From shopping and bellinis, to dinner with Fausto. "Thank you," I told him simply, knowing he would understand.

His expression softened. "I will give you the world if you let me, piccolina. But I am glad you had a nice time. Does this mean you have forgiven me for last night?"

Had the storm on the yacht been only last night? It seemed like weeks ago. And as much as I wanted to torture him, I couldn't lie. "Yes."

"Thank fuck." He threw his napkin on the table and pushed back. "Because I need you now, Francesca. I'm so full of come for you that I am practically choking on it. Let's go."

CHAPTER TWENTY-TWO

Fausto

I CARRIED her up the stairs to the apartment.

Though the heels made her legs look long and sexy, they would not allow her to hurry up the steps. And I needed to hurry. My dick had been hard since the second she walked onto that patio, her body wrapped in red. Cazzo, she should always wear red.

My men went to the apartments on the floor below while I continued to the top. After opening the door, I put her on her heels and grabbed the ends of the ties holding her dress together, pulling on them to unwrap her. This was the best gift I'd ever received.

"Wait," she said, stilling my hands. "Go sit on the sofa."

Impatient but willing to indulge her, I dropped onto the sofa, spreading my legs wide to ease the ache in my balls.

Francesca smirked at me as she slowly untied the dress she wore. My hands tightened into fists on the back of the sofa. "I'm not sure teasing me is a wise idea."

She turned away from me as the dress dipped off her shoulders. I could see the straps of the red bodysuit and my mouth watered. I made the decision to come to Roma as soon as she sent me the photo of her trying it on. I knew I had to have her right then. The video only made my departure take longer, because I had to jerk myself off twice while watching it.

"Piccolina," I warned when she let the dress fall too slowly.

In one quick motion, she spun toward me and dropped the dress— and the world stopped. Dio, she was gorgeous, sexy as fuck. My nostrils flared as I tried to drag air into my lungs, every muscle in my body tight, ready to pin her down and thrust. To rut and grind and give her my seed. She turned me into an animal every time, the need so overwhelming I thought I would lose my goddamn mind.

Tonight would be no different, apparently.

"Come here."

She obeyed, swinging her hips as she drew closer. I hadn't turned on the lights, so the city and the moon illuminated her luscious curves in the tight lace and silk. Her tits were pushed in and up, her small waist flaring into generous hips. She was a wet dream come to life...and she was mine.

And I knew what I needed first.

Stretching out on the couch, I pulled her closer. "Sit on my face. Right now."

"Wait, what?" Her brows pinched together.

I slapped her ass. "Your pussy needs to find my mouth in the next few seconds or I am going to spank you."

She climbed onto the sofa and adjusted her knees until she strad-dled my head. She was already wet—I could smell it. Reaching between her legs, I unfastened the body suit, and jerked her hips down until her pussy slammed onto my face.

"Goddamn, Fausto. Holy shit," she breathed, curling slightly to brace herself on the arm of the sofa.

I ate at her like I was starving. Like the world was ending and making her come was the only way to stop it from happening. I sucked and licked her, relishing every roll of her hips, every whimper.

Francesca loved sex as much as I did, and she never faked it. Her reaction to me was one hundred percent real every time.

She was so slippery and wet, the flesh of her cunt swollen and needy as I lapped at her. I shoved two fingers inside her roughly, knowing she could take it. And she moaned, rocking back to fuck herself on my hand. When I drew her clit between my lips and suckled, she climaxed. Her fingers threaded my hair and pulled, her body jerking and trembling as she came on my face. I could barely breathe, but I didn't care. There was no better way to die, not for a man like me, than to be smothered by pussy.

La mia bella figa.

Finally she slumped and moved off my face. I stared up at her, still ravenous, my cock hard in my pants. "Take me out and put me inside you. If I do it, I'm liable to break this sofa."

She licked her lips, her hooded gaze darting over her shoulder to my crotch. "Should we go to the bedroom?"

I began unbuckling my belt. "I want inside you now, Francesca."

When I had my pants undone, she reached behind her and found me. I closed my eyes to enjoy the feel of her touch, quickly shoving my pants and briefs down before maneuvering her toward my cock. I was too far gone to wait. Too impatient for our games. I needed her pussy strangling my dick, now.

She put one hand on my chest and took me in hand with the other. My tip found her entrance, and she began lowering down, the wet heat surrounding me as I tunneled inside her body. I bucked my hips, eager to get all the way in but her cunt resisted my size. "Cazzo, *come sei stretta.*"

"What does that mean?" she panted, her dark gaze glazed with lust.

"It means you are so tight."

"God, I love when you talk to me in Italian when we fuck."

"Then start fucking me and I will."

"If your dick wasn't so big, I already would be."

Cristo, that sassy mouth. I would take pleasure in filling it later.

Bracing my feet on the cushions, I thrust up while dragging her hips down, impaling her fully. I had to close my eyes and grit my teeth, it felt so goddamn good.

"Jesus, Fausto," she gasped. "Give me some warning next time."

"Your pussy should always be ready for me." I grabbed her by the back of the neck and pulled her head down to where my mouth reached the shell of her ear. *"Sei la mia puttanella, no?"*

"Oh, fuck," she whispered, her hips rocking. "Why is that so hot?"

"Because it is," I told her. "Now you tell me. In Italian. Tell me who you belong to."

"Sono la tua puttanella."

My balls instantly tightened, lust shooting straight to my groin like a lightning bolt. "Good girl," I crooned, my voice rough with the need to come. I gathered her hair in my fist and pulled hard, her neck arched for my mouth. "Now ride me while you say it."

I held her, not giving her much room to move, but she rolled her hips, churning to slide my dick in and out of her pussy, her tits smashed against my chest and nearly escaping the lace. I bit her neck, sinking my teeth into her perfect skin. "Dimmi, Francesca."

She gasped, her lids screwed shut. "Sono la tua puttanella."

Fuck, yes.

I let her go and rewarded her with a stream of filthy Italian because I knew she liked to hear it. I told her how I was going to fuck her all night and every dirty thing I planned to do to her body. She continued to work herself on my cock, her gorgeous curves encased in the red bodysuit except for her pussy. I could feel her legs trembling, her muscles tightening as she readied to come. Francesca fucked with her entire being, held nothing back, and it was one of the things I liked best about her. I'd never had such a strong physical and mental connection with a woman in the bedroom before.

I needed to see her come on my dick.

Reaching down, I found her clit with my thumb, but I only brushed it lightly, teasing her. "Beg me," I ordered. "Ti prego, Fausto."

"Ti prego," she panted, sliding her hands into her hair as she leaned back. "Ti prego, Fausto. God, ti fucking prego."

With my other hand, I tore open the front of the bodysuit and let her tits spill free. Full breasts with dark nipples bounced as she moved and I grabbed one with my hand, squeezing hard. She moaned, her pussy constricting around me. Madonna, she was so fucking hot.

I strummed her clit with my thumb, rubbing and pressing while she rocked, and it only took a minute until she began coming, her walls clamping down and milking my cock. Her gorgeous face was frozen in ecstasy, her moans filling the empty apartment, and my balls couldn't hold back any longer.

"*Guardami*," I told her, forcing her eyes to mine. "Watch as I shoot inside you, Francesca. I am going to mark you, fill you up. Because you are mine." Never had I wanted to coat a woman in my come like I did with this one. I wanted to break her, to conquer her. To use her whenever I wanted.

"Sì, Fausto," she whispered dreamily, her body lax and sated. "Ti prego."

The begging did it. My body seized as my cock swelled inside her, the orgasm rushing over me as come shot out the tip and into her cunt. I shouted, the world going dark while climax dragged me down. It was so good. Better than I'd ever experienced before. I never wanted this feeling to end.

She collapsed on top of me when it was over, and I tried to catch my breath as I wrapped my arms around her. Cazzo, this woman. She turned me into a caveman. A slavering beast. It got better every time.

And now that I knew how good we were together, I wasn't certain I ever wanted to give her up.

Francesca

I COULDN'T MOVE. I sprawled on top of Fausto, my muscles quivering like jelly. That had been the best, most intense sex of my life. It was like he knew what I wanted better than I did.

You like it rough and mean, just like I do.

Yes, I suppose I did.

It was more than that, though. It was Fausto. He turned me inside out, made me do and say things I never would otherwise. Then he rewarded me in return. There were no losers, because I made him crazy, too.

His hand swept down my back, removing the ruined bodysuit. I smirked against his chest. "You weren't kidding when you said to buy four of those."

"I ordered you to buy five, but Giulio said the store only had three in stock. So the others are being shipped to the castello."

I blinked up at him. "You had Giulio order more lingerie for me?"

"Of course. Do you think this embarrasses me?" He huffed, his lips quirking. "My son knows we are fucking, Francesca."

"Maybe it embarrasses *me*, you stronzo."

He pressed a quick kiss to my mouth. "It shouldn't. The entire estate knows you belong to me."

God, how mortifying. I had known it, but hearing him say the words had my skin going up in flames. "You really know how to ruin a moment, don't you?" I pushed up and he let me go.

I got to my feet and his come started to run down the insides of my thighs. Of course, Fausto didn't miss this, either. Sitting up, his mouth curved wickedly as he reached out and ran a finger through the mess. "See? You belong to me."

He held the same finger up to my mouth, and without thinking I opened my lips, allowing him to slide it inside. The salty taste flooded my tongue and I sucked his skin clean. Something dark and possessive flashed in his eyes, the same look he got when I said I was his little slut.

I can play your game, too.

I wasn't the only one drowning in whatever was happening between us. Fausto was equally caught up.

"And you belong to me," I said when his finger left my mouth.

"My dick belongs to you, monella. Now, let's shower and sit in the jacuzzi."

Taking my hand, he led me to the master suite. He left me in the large tiled bathroom while he warmed up the jacuzzi on the terrace. I slipped into the shower after using the toilet and began soaping up. A naked Fausto soon joined me, his body on glorious display. "How do you stay in such good shape?" I asked as I rinsed my hair.

"I run every morning."

"You have a gym?"

"I do. You're welcome to use it any time you like. There's a pool, too."

"Why didn't I know this?"

He moved me out of the way so he could get under the spray. "Because you spend most of your time outside with the plants and lambs."

True, I did.

"I like learning about the vineyard and the farm. It's fascinating."

"I hadn't pictured you as a gardener and a farmer. I thought you'd prefer the indoors."

I smoothed some conditioner on my hair and told him the truth. "I accidentally locked myself in a closet when I was nine. Though I screamed and yelled, it took hours for someone to find me, and I was terrified." I'd wet my pants because I couldn't hold it any longer, convinced I was going to die in there. It was the worst experience of my life. "After that my mother started taking me outside as much as possible. She taught me about plants and flowers, and I loved spending time outside ever since. I have an entire flower garden at our house in Toronto."

Fausto paused, his luscious mouth turning into a frown. "This was why the dungeon frightened you so much, no?"

I nodded. "Yes."

He wrapped his arms around me, the spray hitting his back. "I am so sorry, Francesca. Forgive me."

I slid my hands around his waist, hugging him in return. "I begged you not to leave me down there."

"I have fucked up twice with you, but I promise there will not be a third."

Warmth wrapped around my heart at his sincerity. Fausto never bullshitted. He never said anything he didn't mean. I pressed a kiss between his pecs. "Thank you, baby."

He nudged my face toward his and gave me a tender kiss, one so soft and sweet that my knees nearly buckled. "I like this word on your lips," he said. "I like it a lot."

I had to think back. Oh, the endearment. It had slipped out of my mouth naturally, as if I'd called him that for years. Sliding out of his arms, I grabbed for the soap, hoping to hide my embarrassment and horror. It was way too soon for me to be calling him names like that, names that people in serious loving relationships used. I wasn't staying and this was not a loving relationship.

Thankfully, he didn't push it.

Soon we stepped out and dried off with thick towels. Strangely quiet, he took my hand and led me toward the terrace. I dragged him to a stop. "Don't we need suits?"

He grabbed my ass and squeezed. "No, we don't. No one will see."

I soon discovered why. One half of the upper terrace was surrounded by Italian cypress trees, giving privacy to the jacuzzi. Probably countless women had been here to soak with him, and an irrational jealousy swamped me as I slid into the warm water.

"Is it too hot?" he asked as he climbed in next to me.

"No, it's perfect."

"Then why are you frowning, piccolina?"

I had nothing to lose by asking him. Perhaps in learning how not special I was to him would help prevent any feelings from developing. The last thing I needed was to fall in love with Fausto Ravazzani. "Do you bring women here often?"

He reached over, lifted me and settled me on his lap. "Why? Would it bother you?"

"No, but I am curious. It seems like the perfect fuck pad."

"Fuck pad?"

"Place where you bring women to fuck."

He shook his head, his chest shaking with suppressed laughter. "Francesca, I don't need a special place fuck women. I can fuck wherever I like."

Hadn't he already proven that with me? The stables, the dining room.... "I get it. You're a man whore. Congratulations." I tried to push him away, needing space.

His arms tightened around me. "Wait. I did not mean to upset you." He kissed my neck, my jaw. Then he nibbled on my earlobe. "I haven't brought a woman here in a long time. Not since the last time someone tried to kill me."

Gasping, I leaned back to see his face. "Kill you! What? When?"

His expression said I was naive for even being surprised. "There have been four attempts to kill me since I took over, the most recent six years ago. It's why I stick to the castello as much as possible."

"Jesus Christ," I muttered. Four attempts on his life? "Were you hurt?"

"My car blew up, but the detonator went off early. I was thrown back and suffered a concussion, nothing more."

I gaped at him. "Oh, my God. That is terrible."

The edge of his mouth hitched. "I like to see you worried about me. It makes my dick hard." He kissed me, long licks of his tongue against mine, and sure enough his cock thickened underneath me. How could he get aroused so soon? Didn't men of a certain age need some sort of recovery period?

When we broke apart, I said, "Everything makes your dick hard."

"True. But only around you these days, it seems."

"If people are always trying to kill you, then why did you come to Rome?"

"To see you. I couldn't wait." He put his arms on the back of the jacuzzi and closed his eyes. "Believe me, Marco had a fit. He nearly restrained me to keep me in Siderno."

"He's right. You shouldn't have come, if it's dangerous." I would never forgive myself if something happened to him here.

"If I die, it would have been worth it to see you in that red bodysuit."

"Fausto! It's not a joke."

He slid a hand to cup my breast, his eyes still closed. "It is no joke. You are the sexiest, hottest woman I have ever had. If I died tonight, I would go happy, with no regrets."

How was he so evil and so sweet at the same time? I couldn't take it. I wasn't strong enough to resist this man. He was undoing me, bit by bit, unraveling me and putting me together as someone new. Someone stronger, more confident. I wasn't certain I liked it, but I also didn't hate it.

I melted against him, clinging to his big body as the bubbles swirled around us. Emotion filled my chest and wrapped around my heart, so much that I felt ready to burst.

Leaning in, I kissed his neck. "Baby," I whispered near his ear, letting that one word hang, the sound filled with everything I dared not voice aloud.

"Dolcezza," he whispered back, and I swore I could hear emotion in his voice, too.

We stayed there until our skin wrinkled. When I yawned, he lifted me and stood, water cascading off our bodies. "Come. Let me put you to bed."

"We're staying here tonight?"

"I thought you might like to stay in Roma one more day. We can go back tomorrow afternoon."

I liked the idea of sleeping together in the same bed. Was Fausto a cuddler? He set me on my feet and dried me off with a towel first, wrapping it around me carefully before he found a towel for himself. His muscles shifted and bunched as he moved the cloth over his fit frame. He was the hottest DILF I had ever seen. I would have to search for a comparable nickname in Italian, a pet name I could call him during sex.

I found my phone and brought it into his bedroom, where I discovered him frowning at whatever he was reading on his phone. "What is it?" I asked, the knowledge that someone had tried to blow him up with a car bomb fresh in my mind.

"Nothing," he muttered as he typed back. "Something I will deal with tomorrow." Then he set his phone on the nightstand and stretched out on the bed.

"Do you ever get a day off?" I plugged my phone in to charge and set it on the nightstand closest to me before laying down.

"Over here," he ordered, holding his arm out, his eyes closed.

He knows I'll obey.

And God help me, I did.

I scooted to his side and sighed when he nestled me close to his warm, hard body.

"No, I don't," he answered. "Too much depends on me. But I can take a break every now and again, like tonight." He kissed my forehead. "I'll get up early and work a few hours before you wake up. Then I'll bring you caffè in bed and fuck you again."

I grinned and closed my eyes. That sounded like heaven.

CHAPTER TWENTY-THREE

Francesca

TRUE TO HIS WORD, he nudged me awake, the strong smell of coffee filling the room.

"Bellissima, you cannot sleep all day."

God, that sexy, accented voice. He could make a killing as an audio-book narrator. "How are you already awake?" I struggled to open my lids.

"I have been up for three hours while you laze about in bed, neglecting your duties."

"And what duties would those be?"

He squeezed one of my butt cheeks. "Presenting me with that ass to fuck."

I shot up in bed, uncaring that I was completely naked. He was on the mattress next to me, smirking. "No, Fausto. You promised. Remember? Te lo prometto."

"And what did you promise me in return?"

I didn't want to say it. I pressed my lips together, hoping he forgot.

"Do I need to spank you to make you say it again? Allora." He motioned with his hands for me to get up.

"No, no, no." I did not want him near my ass. "Fine. I said I was yours."

Reaching out, he stroked my jaw with his knuckles. "And as such, you will trust me to take care of you. I won't ever do something you do not enjoy."

"What about making me deep throat you in the stables?"

"Francesca, you were so wet after deep throating my cock that my tongue slipped off your pussy." He clutched my tangled hair in his fist and pulled, causing me to gasp as my head tilted back. "You like submitting to me, just as I like dominating you. Don't fight me. I promise you will love it."

"If I don't, will you stop?"

"Of course."

I reached for the small espresso waiting on the side table. "Fuck, I need to be caffeinated for this."

He chuckled and stood, his hands beginning to remove his clothing. God, was I really doing this? As he pulled off his shirt, my fingers itched with the need to explore that sculpted chest. Maybe it wouldn't be so bad....

Then he dropped his pants, and the outline of his dick inside his briefs mesmerized me. Yum. Yes, I wanted to submit if it meant I got his cock.

"I know that look," he murmured and stroked his thick length through the briefs. "Cristo santo, you were made for me."

I finished my espresso and reached for his waistband. "Let me taste you first." Maybe he'd come in my mouth and forget all about my ass.

He shoved his briefs off his hips and I eagerly swallowed him down. "*Cazzo!*" he shouted at the ceiling. "You are too good at that."

I worked my tongue and lips over his erection, worshipping him with my mouth until his thighs trembled. Then he pulled out, much to my disappointment.

"You'll get more soon," he said, noting my pout. "Roll over on your back."

I slid onto the mattress as he went to a wardrobe in the corner.

Inside were two drawers, and he opened both, pulling out various items. Lube, condoms, and a dildo still in plastic packaging. He tossed the lube and condoms on the bed, then tore the plastic packaging on the dildo.

"What is all this?"

"Preparation. I could use a plug, but that would take time and I'm greedy for you. Start rubbing your clit, piccolina, like you did in the lingerie store."

I slid my hand between my legs and stroked using the pads of my fingers. Fausto watched me instead of what he was doing, and nearly dropped the package. Once he had the dildo out, he reached for a condom. He had the sexiest hands I'd ever seen on a man, with long fingers and veins running along the back. Maybe it was because I knew what those hands were capable of, but I thought they were hot.

I moaned, rolling my hips.

His nostrils flared but he continued rolling the condom onto the dildo. When he finished, he crawled onto the bed. "Open your legs."

I obeyed, but I asked, "Is this going to hurt?"

"Absolutely not."

I doubted that, but I didn't argue with him. He promised we could stop if I didn't like it. "Okay, *paparino*."

He froze, his lips parting in surprise as he looked up from between my thighs. "What did you say?"

Had the internet let me down? I'd searched for the perfect word earlier, when I woke up to use the bathroom. "Paparino. It means a daddy in the bedroom. Like, a benevolent older man that takes care of you. At least that's what I was told."

The translation hit a little close to what I'd been trying to avoid, that Fausto was my sugar daddy. I didn't like how that made me feel outside the bedroom. But inside the bedroom, the name definitely fit him. Here, he could be my paparino.

"I know what it means. I just never.... Madonna, you surprise me at every turn. I like this name very, very much." To prove it, he growled and buried his face in my pussy, eating me out with abandon.

My back arched, pleasure rocketing through me at lightning speed. "Holy shit," I whispered, my fingers threading through his thick hair.

He used his tongue on my clit, circling and flicking, until that was all I could feel. He was everywhere, surrounding me. The room fell away and all I knew was Fausto's mouth driving me out of my mind.

Then there was pressure at my hole—but not the one I was expecting. He spread my legs wider, and I could feel the slick tip of the dildo as he used gentle pressure, circling the tight ring of muscle no man had ever breached. He didn't push, however, just massaged, and my body eventually relaxed, loosened up, until he was able to slip it inside.

I gasped, unsure about this invasion. It didn't hurt, but it was strange.

"Relax. This is not as thick as my cock, and you will need to take it all first. Let me stretch you out." He returned his lips to my clitoris, suckling on the little bud, and I could feel him working the dildo deeper. It was so much sensation, but it all felt amazing.

"Hold behind your knees," he told me as he shifted. "Lift your legs."

I did as he said, and the dildo slid in even more. "Oh, fuck," I moaned, the orgasm gathering in my spine and toes.

Still, he didn't rush. Fausto was being very careful with me. His hand rocked back and forth, the slick toy tunneling deeper each time. Soon I was meeting his thrusts, needing more than he gave me. I was so close to coming, my thighs shaking. My mouth hung open, my entire world suspended as what I needed remained just slightly out of reach.

Then his hand met my skin, the toy as deep as it could go.

The fullness. Oh, God. So dirty. I needed more.

Suddenly, it was too much. I came hard, my shout echoing in the room as I bucked and rocked under his mouth and hands. It was more intense than anything I'd ever experienced, my lower half clenching around the toy inside me. I loved it.

When the pleasure ebbed, I started to drop my legs. Fausto came up on his knees and kept my left leg in the air, still holding the long toy with the other. "Stay," he said. "I am not done with this ass."

To prove it, he fucked me with the toy, his mouth glistening with my arousal. His bright gaze followed the movement of the toy, his skin flush with lust. "Yes, you like this, don't you? You need a big cock in your ass, no?"

I licked my lips, my chest heaving. How was I so turned on again, immediately after having an orgasm? I whispered, "Only if it's yours, paparino."

Cursing, he removed the toy and tossed it onto the floor. Then he flipped me in one motion onto my stomach and pulled me to the edge of the bed, with my legs dangling over the side and onto the floor. He grabbed the lube while he stepped between my thighs, spreading me wide. "I cannot wait to be inside this tight little hole."

I heard him slick up his cock then felt the tip of him at my back entrance, circling as he'd done with the toy. Several seconds later the head popped inside. I hissed through my teeth. "You said it wouldn't hurt."

He stroked my back, petting me. "That is the worst of it. Relax, baby."

I liked hearing the English endearment from him. It was almost as sexy as when he called me "dolcezza." The burn ebbed and again I was left with fullness. Fausto began moving then, slowly pressing forward, rocking back and forth, while he reached between us to stroke my clit. My whole body tingled as he stretched me out. I panted, a light sweat breaking out on my skin, but there was no pain. Just a pressure that I couldn't tell if I liked or not.

"You are being such a good girl," he praised, smoothing his palm over my buttock. He straightened and grabbed my hips with both hands. "Look at you letting me inside. Sucking me in. Madre di Dio, it is the sexiest thing I have ever seen. Do you like it? Do you like taking your paparino's cock in your asshole?"

God, his filthy, filthy mouth. When he talked to me like that I would do anything he asked. And he probably knew it.

He drove deeper, making me gasp. "Yes," I whispered, dragging the word out on a long whine. "I like it very much."

"My dirty piccola monella." He gave a real thrust of his hips this time and it drove him all the way in, his hips meeting my asscheeks. "I knew you could do it. There, now doesn't that feel good?"

It did. Fuck, it really did. I was full of him, my body hyper-sensitive. I nodded, unable to speak.

He started fucking me then, rough slaps of his hips that sounded obscene in the quiet space. I could do nothing but lie there and take it, which made the whole experience even hotter. My nipples scraped against the sheets as he worked himself in and out of my body, his grunts mixing with my gasps.

"So tight. You are squeezing me so hard." He pulled out slowly, leaving in just the head, and then plunged forward once more until he bottomed out. We both groaned.

"Tell me who is fucking your ass, Francesca. Tell me who you belong to."

"You, Fausto." The words fell from my lips, partly because I knew they would drive him wild. And partly because I loved this game we played. "Sono la tua puttanella."

He spanked me, hard. "Play with your clit and make yourself come. Quickly."

He didn't need to tell me twice. My hand shot between my legs and I circled my clit. Fausto spanked me again and again, his palm raining slaps on my butt cheeks. The heat spread from my skin through my groin as my fingers worked over the taut nub. When he wrapped my hair around his fist and pulled, using it to jerk me back onto his cock, riding me, I came so hard, the orgasm deep and intense. I clenched around him and he thickened inside me, his hips growing uncoordinated as I heard him suck in air. Then he groaned and held me still, his body jerking slightly as he came inside me.

When it was over, I couldn't move. He seemed equally undone, panting and holding onto me like a life raft. He made no effort to pull away, just leaned on my back while remaining buried inside me.

Finally, he kissed my spine and slipped out. I winced at the soreness, and he immediately swept me up in his arms.

"Let's clean you up, baby," he said softly, in a tender tone I hadn't heard before. One that settled into a permanent place in my heart, marking it as his. What was happening to me? I knew better than to develop serious feelings for this man.

For once, I was incapable of words, so I dropped my head onto his shoulder and let him carry me to the bathroom.

Fausto

AFTER FEEDING FRANCESCA BREAKFAST, I took her for another soak in the jacuzzi. Then I fucked her slow and sweet one last time before we left the apartment. I could not get enough of this woman.

In fact, I considered keeping her in Roma for another day. But these wishes were foolish. Too much demanded my attention in Siderno and it was dangerous for me to be away for so long.

My life was not my own.

It never had been. From the time I was born, my destiny was set—just as Giulio's had been. And his sons as well, and so on. It was the way our brotherhood worked. And I wouldn't change it. Our traditions were how the 'Ndrangheta had grown and maintained a stronghold throughout the world. We were more fearsome and powerful than the Cosa Nostra or the Camorra, and my 'ndrina was near the top of the pyramid.

And despite the high probability that I would one day be murdered or arrested, I still loved my life.

When we walked inside the castello, Marco was waiting in the entryway. I could tell by his face that I had annoyed him by staying away so long. But I didn't answer to my cousin.

"Buona sera, Francesca. Cugino," he said tersely.

"Buona sera, Marco," she greeted and tried to pull away from me.

"*Fermati!*" I held onto her hand, dragging her toward me. I didn't care if Marco watched, I was not letting her scurry away like she was embarrassed. Francesca was a queen—my queen—and she should never worry over anyone else's perception of her. Other than mine, of course.

"Fausto," she snapped, her gaze filled with annoyance—and the sight still managed to make my dick hard after coming so much today. "Let me go."

"Not yet." I held her face and kissed her deeply, using my tongue to make a point, until she softened against me. "There," I said when I pulled back. "Now you may go."

She tried to huff like she was angry, but I knew she wasn't. She liked my bossy side. Even if I couldn't read it on her face, her wet pussy told me every time.

As she was hurrying up the stairs, I called after her, "Try to stay out of trouble."

Lifting a hand, she gave me the middle finger.

I shook my head and chuckled. Madonna, this girl. She was never boring, that was for certain.

Marco folded his arms over his chest. "Are you finished?"

"You act as if I have been on holiday for two weeks." I started toward my office, where we could have privacy. "I was gone for only twenty-four hours."

"Rav, this could be very bad."

I told him to be quiet, not wishing to discuss this where anyone might overhear. Once we were closed up in my office, I said, "You are worrying for nothing. I will handle Mancini."

"He's pissed. You didn't hear his voice. He learned that you took Francesca as your mantenuta, that you have no intention of marrying her to your son."

It was inevitable that Mancini would hear of this information. I hadn't tried to hide my relationship with Francesca and people talked. So I would not lie to him—but I did not need his permission, either. If I wanted to keep Francesca tied to my bed forever, then there was nothing Mancini could do about it. "Get him on the phone."

I slipped off my suit coat and rolled up my sleeves while Marco dialed Mancini on the secure line. I paid a fortune for the privilege of privacy here, and even then, it was risky. We tried not to use phones for our illegal operations, unless they were the disposable kind.

Mancini picked up on the first ring. "Yes?"

"Ciao, Roberto."

I heard shuffling on the other end, like he was moving to a place where he wouldn't be overheard. "You stronzo," he snarled into the phone. "You had no right to turn my daughter into a whore."

"Your daughter was no innocent. We caught a man sneaking out of her bedroom window that morning in Toronto."

"You lie. Francesca would never—"

"His name was David and she had been fucking him for months. Have you no idea what goes on in your household at all?" This was an insult to a man such as us, that we are not the rulers of our homes.

I could tell the news did not sit well with Mancini. He was thinking this over, probably trying to see if what I said was true and how he could work it to his advantage.

I wasn't about to give him the chance.

"Allora, I should be furious that you gave me damaged goods for my son, Roberto. I expected a pure bride, one to bear the Ravazzani heirs. Instead, I have taken Francesca to my bed and now she is well cared for and respected."

"As your mantenuta," he spat. "Hardly a position of respect."

"It was the best she could hope for, considering. You are lucky I did not send her back to you and demand payment in full on our debt." He couldn't afford to pay me, not with money. "Or, I could have asked for one of your other daughters for my son."

"They are only sixteen. Hardly ready for marriage."

"That is not uncommon here," I said, even though I would have waited, as I planned to do with D'Agostino's sister.

"I would never allow it."

I laughed, but it was cruel and without humor. "There is not much you can prevent, if I wish it. Do not forget who it is you are speaking with."

"This is an insult to my family," Mancini said. "My other daughters will have a hard time finding husbands because of the shame you have inflicted upon Francesca."

"That is not my problem. If you had kept better control of your oldest daughter, then she would be marrying my son, as we originally discussed. The insult was against my family in that you gave her to me in the first place, knowing she was not innocent."

"I want her to come home. Immediately."

Though Mancini couldn't see it, I let my lips curve into a malevolent grin. "Absolutely not. I am keeping her. When I decide I am through, then I will let her go wherever she wishes."

I could hear him breathing on the other end, the fury evident in every exhale. He was like a dragon, ready to spew fire. But he had no leverage over me. While he might be powerful in Toronto, I was a hundred times more powerful all around the globe. My name inspired fear in the hearts of hardened criminals from Berlin to Brazil, Colombia to New York. "Now, are we done? I have things to do."

"For now, Ravazzani."

The line went dead. I wasn't thrilled that he hung up on me, but I was in too good of a mood to care. Marco was frowning at me when I looked up. "What is it?" I asked.

"You were very calm during that call. Perhaps too calm?"

I threw up my hands. "You are normally chastising me for my temper. Which is it? Do you want me to be calm or angry?"

"I don't know." He shook his head. "But after that kiss in the entryway and now this call with Mancini, I have to wonder if Francesca is good for you."

"What the fuck are you talking about? Good for me? She isn't red meat, Marco."

"You have been obsessed with her for weeks. Then you tear off to Roma to see her without any regard for proper security. And you walk in looking like a lovesick puppy."

"You'd better take care," I said softly, trying to hold onto my temper. "You are my cousin, but that does not mean you may treat me with disrespect. My relationship with Francesca is none of your concern."

"It is when it affects the business, the brotherhood."

"There is no reason to worry. You have merely forgotten what it is like to fuck a new woman."

"I am very happy fucking my wife, Rav. I don't need new pussy to feel like a man."

My entire body went hot at the insult and I shot to my feet. I angled down and snarled, "Get out of my office before I do or say something I might regret."

He held up his palms. "I am sorry. I didn't mean it as it came out. But I will leave." Standing, he slipped his hands into his pockets. "Please, just be careful. She is not from here, Rav. She has different ideas of what her life looks like. We don't know that she is entirely trustworthy."

I did. I trusted Francesca down to the marrow of my bones. She had given me everything I'd asked of her, had put her life in my hands, and I would not allow her to regret it. As my mistress, she would be given the world at her feet.

Anyone who didn't like it would answer to me.

CHAPTER TWENTY-FOUR

Francesca

MY BEDROOM LOOKED the same but I felt completely different. Instead of the usual dread I experienced while inside these walls, I was relaxed. There were little touches of me everywhere, from the lipstick on the side table to the bra I'd flung onto a chair. It was familiar, and I realized I didn't hate being here any longer.

Was that because of Fausto and Rome? Had I let his charm twist my mind into accepting this?

Or was I as dark inside as he believed?

Was he also experiencing this insane connection between us, the burning need for each other that felt too big, too important to be only lust?

I'd spent my life searching for something more, a way to find myself outside of my father's orbit, as my mother had wanted. And I never felt more like myself than when I was with Fausto. It was like he was peeling away the unimportant layers and helping me learn who I was underneath. Not to mention I was discovering my gorgeous devil in a three-piece suit could be tender and sweet, as well.

Mine? Was I really thinking Fausto belonged to me?

My dick belongs to you, monella.

If that's what he was offering, I would take it. Grinning to myself, I plugged in my phone to charge and noticed a voicemail. It was from a Toronto area code, but I didn't recognize the number. Not many people had my new cell number. Was this one of my sisters?

I hit play.

"Frankie, this is your father. Call me right away, but wait until you are alone." Papà had found my number? Gia or Emma must have given it to him.

Biting my lip, I called him back. He answered on the first ring. "Frankie. Are you alone?"

"Ciao, Papà. Yes, I'm alone."

"Good." I could hear him breathing hard, like he was angry. "I cannot believe you have dishonored this family and let him turn you into a whore. Are you so selfish as to not consider how your actions affect anyone else?"

My mouth dropped open and my stomach burned with embarrassment. Was he serious? "I am not a whore."

"You were not pure. You gave your most precious gift, your only worth, to some stronzo here in Toronto. This boy was caught crawling out of your window."

My only worth? Rage coiled in my throat and I had to swallow it down to speak. "I am more than just my virginity. I want to go to school—"

"You stupid girl," he snapped. "You are worth nothing. You are disgraced, and your sisters will suffer for this. Who will marry them now?"

I hadn't intended for this to affect Emma and Gia, but my sisters didn't want mafia husbands either. We were all better off choosing our own husbands. "Plenty of men outside your business will marry them. Which is what they deserve—a life outside all of this. And I don't care what I am worth to you. I never wanted to be used like a commodity, traded to some man for him to own."

"That is exactly what happened, you foolish slut, except you've let him have you without marrying you. He's made you his mistress, and everyone will soon learn of it."

I'd never heard him speak such hurtful words, calling me stupid and a slut. I hadn't ever thought he'd treat me with such little respect, but clearly he didn't care about me or my happiness. Perhaps he never had. "It is a temporary thing. I am still planning to come home and go to school." I would find a way. Somehow.

"There is no school for you, certainly not now."

He couldn't mean that. This was all I had talked about for years. "But you promised Mama."

"I promised her I would send you for a semester of school. After that I planned to bring you home and find you a husband."

A semester? What the hell?

I gripped the phone tightly, my entire body locking in horror. "How could you do that? All Mama wanted was for us to get an education before we married."

"Your mother is dead, Frankie. I am your father and you should have done exactly what I said. Instead you disobeyed and dishonored me. Now I must cut you off from our family to try and save it."

"Cut me off? What does that mean?"

"It means you are a stain on our family's honor. The only way to repair it is to remove that stain. You are no longer my daughter."

I dropped onto the bed, unable to believe what I was hearing. Tears stung the backs of my eyelids. "This is unbelievable. You are disowning me? Just because I slept with two men?"

"I could have overlooked the boy here. We could have taken care of him and no one ever would have known. But Ravazzani is too powerful. Everyone will learn of this shame. I cannot risk your sisters' futures. They are the ones who matter now."

Because I no longer mattered.

I struggled with how to respond. This was unreal. Was anything I believed true?

He snarled, "I hope you are happy with Ravazzani, Francesca. Because you are his problem now." Then he hung up.

My father hung up on me.

I sat there, numb, my mind reeling from his fury and cruelty. I was disowned. What did that even mean? That I was no longer welcome to the Toronto house? Would he try to keep my sisters from me?

Oh, God.

I rocked slightly and covered my mouth with my hand. I'd fallen under Fausto's spell like a complete fool and now I had no family. No place to go. Nothing. I was stuck here, alone.

Would I ever see Gia and Emma again?

I couldn't breathe. I couldn't cry, either. I felt shell-shocked, like everything had turned upside down and twisted inside out. My heart was racing, my lungs constricted, and the edges of the room blurred. I had to get out of here. I had to get outside, where I could get air.

Why was there no damn air in here?

I lunged for the door knob and pulled. The corridor stretched out in front of me and I stumbled as fast as I could toward the stairs. I didn't stop, flying down the steps until I reached the first floor. Moving blindly, I hurried toward the kitchen and the back door.

Except I ended up going in the wrong direction. When I looked up, I was standing at Fausto's office door.

I waited there, staring at the ornate wood and wondering why I was perpetually drawn to him. Was I so intent on self-sabotage? Did I hate myself and my family so much?

Before I could turn away, the door opened. His brows were pinched in confusion. "Francesca, what is it?"

I looked up at him, unable to even form words. The hurt and fear strangled my tongue and robbed me of breath.

Whatever he saw on my face caused him to tug me inside. I didn't even bother to fight, just let him lead me to his desk chair, where he sat and pulled me onto his lap. I leaned into his warmth and tried to get a handle on my emotions. How was I going to survive this?

He stroked my back with one hand. "Dimmi."

His laptop was open, a complicated spreadsheet on the screen. The numbers all blurred together as I stared at them, my eyes filling with water. Still, I tried to force out the words, needing to purge them from my heart. "My father...."

I couldn't even say it.

Fausto's hand stilled. "Your father, what?"

"He found out about us and disowned me."

Tension radiated off his body, and I knew he was angry without even looking at him. "What did he say? Tell me every word."

I took a deep breath and recited the entire conversation, including the names Papà had called me. Not seeing Fausto's face as I spoke made it easier. Then I didn't have to see the truth in his eyes, that what Papà had said was a fact. That I was shameful and a disgrace. A foolish slut.

When I finished, he didn't speak. His hand continued to stroke my back, his strong body cradling me like I was important. Like I mattered to him. I knew I didn't, but at this moment I needed the lies. I'd never felt more alone, as if I had absolutely nothing and no one.

So yes, I'd take whatever kindness I could.

The tears came then, pouring from my lids to soak his shirt. I held onto him tightly, clinging for all I was worth, grateful that at least I had this.

At some point I think the door opened, but I wasn't paying attention. I just cried and thought about how I'd never see my sisters again.

"I am sorry, dolcezza," he said when I quieted. "I am not sorry you are here with me, but I am sorry that your father has hurt you."

"My life is ruined," I whispered shakily. "I'll never go to university. I'll never see Emma and Gia again. I'm totally alone."

"This is not true. You wanted a life outside of your father's world, and now you've been given it. You're not foolish or stupid. You're very clever. I am certain you'll find a way to see your sisters again."

He made it sound so easy. But then, to a man like him, everything was easy. I shook my head. "I cannot see how. He'll keep them from me, then marry them off to men who will keep them from me."

"You forget that you now have a very powerful man in your life who can do almost anything. I can help you."

"How?" I nearly screeched. "You are here and they are in Toronto. Plus, you know nothing can supersede a husband or father in this life. If they want to keep me away from Emma and Gia then they will."

"Trust me, no? I will help you with your sisters. And if you want to go to school, take classes online. Plenty of students attend virtually these days."

Right, sure. What an easy solution! "With what money? He will cut me off. Not to mention that school was supposed to start in two weeks. I don't even have a laptop."

"I will give you the money and you'll have a laptop by tonight."

I leaned back to see his handsome face. The light in his blue eyes was soft and tender, and I let myself get swept away by the affection there. "You would do that for me?"

The edge of his mouth hitched. "Francesca, I like taking care of you. Haven't you realized that by now?"

"But it's expensive."

"I have the money. Let me pay for your classes and books."

Could I do this? Could I allow Fausto to pay for my school? I considered it, thinking through everything that could go wrong. "What happens if we stop sleeping together? Then I won't be able to continue. That would almost be worse."

"Then I'll set aside the full amount into a trust that only you can access."

I studied his expression, but he looked completely serious. Good lord, that was a lot of money. If I accepted it, did that mean I really was a whore? I hadn't wanted a big payout at the end of this relationship, like his other mistresses, but what choice did I have?

Be your own woman, Francesca. Don't make my mistakes.

My mother's words haunted me. The only way to do that was to get an education and make a life for myself outside of the mafia.

I was proud, but not stupid. "Okay, but I will pay you back. Every euro."

"Can you not consider it a gift?"

"No. Then I'd feel like I was in it only for the money."

His eyes narrowed. "The position of mantenuta is important here, Francesca. You have more access to me than anyone, even Marco. Everyone knows this and will treat you with respect or they will answer to me."

"So you're saying it's not just about the money."

"Exactly. It's about power, as are most things in this world. And you have a lot of it. Haven't you realized that yet?"

No, I hadn't. It didn't feel like it when my father hurled hateful insults at me and I would never see my sisters again. "Isn't it also about orgasms?"

He pressed his mouth to mine and gave me a deep kiss that made me dizzy. "It's especially about orgasms."

That I could handle.

I leaned my forehead against his cheek and inhaled his familiar comforting scent. "Thank you, baby. I will pay you back and whatever you can do about my sisters would be very much appreciated."

His lips found my forehead. "See? Now was that so difficult? I like to make you happy."

I was coming to believe it, and I had to admit this felt good. He understood me better than anyone and had gone out of his way to stay with me in Rome. More than anything else right now, I needed to forget all the shame and hurt in my heart. I didn't want to think about the future, my family, or what anyone was saying about me.

This man could make me forget.

I kissed his throat. "Is it too early to drag you upstairs so I can have my wicked way with you?"

He caressed my thigh, in no hurry to break our connection. "Why don't you sit here and keep me company while I catch up on work and calls? Then I'll take you upstairs and fuck you."

OVER THE NEXT THREE WEEKS, life settled into a normal pattern—or as normal as could be expected when one was a mafia don's girlfriend. Yes, girlfriend. I had convinced myself that Fausto was my boyfriend, because that was preferable to the real situation, that I was his mistress. Everyone knew the truth, however. The only person I was fooling was myself.

Most days, my inner lie worked. Everyone on the estate treated me with kindness and respect. Whatever I asked for was granted, and I felt like part of the family. The only person who hadn't quite warmed up to me was Marco, and I found that troubling, considering his closeness to Fausto. Marco's attitude remained polite but cold towards me. I told myself I didn't care, but the question of why dug under my skin like a splinter.

My classes started next week and I couldn't wait. I found a college with a good agricultural program that had online classes, and as promised, Fausto gave me the money in a trust and bought me a laptop. Meanwhile, on my phone I set up a secret account that allowed me to chat with my sisters every day. I showed them the vineyards and the castle. Gia thought I was the luckiest woman alive, but Emma was more concerned with my happiness. Did Fausto treat me well? Was I safe? Did I mind not being married?

The truth was I didn't care about marriage. I knew what it meant to be a mafia wife, waiting at home with dinner on the table for a man who cheated on me every chance he got. My mother had given up her career, her whole life, for my father. Then she'd died from cancer in her mid-thirties, regretting the choices she'd made. I never wanted that. I wanted independence and a career of my own. No mafia husband would ever allow that, which meant I had to make my way outside my father's world.

Besides, this fling with Fausto was a short-term arrangement. Whenever the fire between us burned out, he would let me go and I would start a life in Toronto or New York. I would think fondly of this as the summer I studied abroad in Italy and dated a sexy older man who had more money than God. And who was incredibly talented in bed.

Like, how was that a bad thing?

I wouldn't think about my father and his hurtful words. Instead I kept busy. Except for my daily Italian lesson, I spent my time outside, mostly with Vincenzo. He taught me more and more about the grapes and the vines. How to care for the plants and the soil. It was better than any hands-on college course I could have taken. Vincenzo loved the outdoors as much as I did, and I peppered him with questions all day long, taking note of his answers in a journal Fausto bought me.

The evenings belonged to Fausto. Unless work demanded his attention, he ate dinner with me, Zia and Giulio. After that, he and I went up to his suite and he fucked me desperately, wringing every drop of pleasure from my body before we collapsed into bed. There was no shame between us and I loved the little games we played. I learned so much about myself, like what I found arousing, and quite a bit about Fausto, as well. He liked me bratty, a little bit resistant, and a lot naughty.

I was more than happy to comply.

Today I was in the outdoor garden with Zia. Fausto's aunt had offered to teach me about vegetables. She didn't speak much English and my Italian was only so-so, but we were muddling through. The August sun was overbearing, even this early in the day. It never seemed to bother Zia, though.

Zia's garden was laid out with carefully defined beds and a network of trellises. There were climbing beans, tomatoes, herbs, eggplants, potatoes, artichokes, onions, and more. She handled each plant with care. She reminded me of my mom, giving each leaf and bloom careful attention, pouring her love all the way down into the roots and dirt. It made my heart ache with bittersweet memories.

"Viene qua, viene qua," Zia said, waving me over. When I came closer, she showed me the tiny green bug crawling on the leaf. "*Un afide. Molto male.*"

I recognized the aphid, a species of insect which were bad for gardens. "What now?"

She reached for a spray bottle on the ground and began spraying the liquid on the plants. "Soap. Water. *Il pepe di Caienna.*"

"Cayenne pepper?" Zia nodded and I wrote this down. Fascinating.

She imitated a choking, gasping sound and sure enough the aphid stopped moving.

We walked along, looking for more aphids and checking on her plants. She told me when each vegetable would be ready to harvest, and let me eat a tomato right off the vine. I swear, it was the best tomato I'd ever put in my mouth.

When we passed a trellis full of pea pods, she pulled one off and handed it to me. "*Fa bene al bambino.*"

I blinked. Wasn't bambino....? Did she mean *me?* Wishful thinking for her nephew, no doubt. I smiled and shook my head as I accepted the pea pod. "No bambino, Zia."

"Sì, bambino." She gestured with both hands toward my belly. "Fausto's bambino."

I nearly choked on a pea. Most old women were obsessed with babies, and she considered Fausto a son. However, there was no way I was having Fausto's baby. I answered the best way I knew how. "Molto molto no bambino."

She just smiled and tapped her temple. What did that mean?

"Ah, my two favorite women out in my Italian sun. What could be better?"

I turned and saw Fausto edging toward us. He was dressed shockingly down for the daytime, wearing jeans and a simple gray t-shirt. Was he not working this morning? By the time I got up, he'd already dressed and left for his office. The sun caressed his golden muscular skin, like he was a Roman god sent straight from heaven.

He kissed Zia's cheeks first, then got close to me. "Dolcezza, you are never more beautiful than when you are outside on my land." Bending, he pulled me close and gave me a deep, lingering kiss on the mouth. "Mmm, terre e sole."

Land and sun. He loved to smell my skin when I came in from outside.

"Now, you must stop eye-fucking me," he murmured, "or you won't get your surprise."

Thankfully Zia had wandered away, busy in another part of her garden. I slid my hands over his chest. "I can't help it. I've never seen you in jeans and a t-shirt. Very sexy, paparino."

He squeezed a buttock. "Behave. I cannot walk around the workers with a hard dick and still maintain their respect."

"Maybe they'd respect you more, if they could see what you're packing."

Rolling his eyes, he dragged me out of the garden. He spoke to Zia over his shoulder, probably telling her he was taking me somewhere, so I waved good-bye. Fausto wrapped his arm around my waist and tucked me into his side. We headed toward the southwestern part of the estate, away from the vineyards and toward the farmland. "Any guesses as to your surprise?"

"Are we going to clear out the stables again for an early riposo?"

"Hmm. Maybe after. I have very fond memories of that day."

The first time I had deep throated his cock. "Me, too. Can I take a selfie with you? Please? I like the casual mafia boss look. I won't post it anywhere. It'll be just for me." He always refused to be in pictures with me, much as Giulio had in Rome.

"No photos, Francesca. I can't risk it ending up online or someone hacking your phone."

"Are you saying the Italian government doesn't know who you are?"

"Of course, they do. But that doesn't mean I want to remind them."

We went into the stables. This time, he didn't order everyone out. Instead, he led me to a stall in the back. On the wall was a brass plate that read *La Piccola Monella*. "You're moving me out to the stables?" I joked.

"Not yet," he smirked and slapped my ass. "Look inside."

I peeked into the stall and a huge brown head appeared. It was a chestnut-colored horse with a patch of white on its face. She nuzzled toward me, curious. I reached out and stroked her muzzle. "Hello, girl." She shifted and bobbed her head, like she was saying hello, too. I laughed.

"I think she likes you," Fausto said, his chest at my back. "Not that I ever doubted it. You are far kinder to animals than you are to me."

"I was very kind to you last night. Twice, in fact." I continued to pet the horse. "She's beautiful, Fausto."

"I am glad you think so. She belongs to you."

I cast a glance over my shoulder. His brown gaze smoldered with heat and affection, a look I was coming to know well. "You bought me a horse?"

"Sì. I took the honor of naming her, though."

"So I can ride whenever I like?" I liked to walk the estate, but that could be exhausting. Plus, I missed riding. We had grown up taking lessons as girls.

"Of course. You must wear a helmet, however."

My paparino. Always looking out for me. I bit my lip as happiness coursed through my chest. "I promise. May I go now?"

"Yes, as long as I may come with you."

Now the casual clothes made sense. He'd planned time away from work to take me riding. Grinning, I threw my arms around his neck and wrapped my legs around his waist, clinging to him like that aphid on the leaf. "Of course. Grazie, Fausto. This is the very best surprise."

He held me under my ass and kissed my mouth. "I'm glad you are happy. Let me have both horses saddled and then we'll go."

CHAPTER TWENTY-FIVE

Francesca

"I THINK MY ASS IS SUNBURNED," I said as we rode back toward the stables.

He smirked, looking very pleased with himself. And why wouldn't he? I had just fucked him stupid out in a pasture under some olive trees. Between my legs was a sticky mess, but it had been worth it.

"Or perhaps it is red from the spanking I gave you last night."

Right. Of course, he would remember that.

I grinned and tilted my face up toward the sun. It was hot but there was a nice breeze, which Fausto said came off the ocean.

Today has been one of the best days in a long time. I loved being on a horse again, and Fausto explained the various plots of land and the animals they raised as we rode. His knowledge of the estate never failed to impress me. It was clear that he loved the land, and from the stories he told he'd obviously spend a lot of time out here.

We had stopped for a bite to eat, which Fausto produced from a bag tied to his horse. There were olives and figs, cured meats and cheeses. And one of Zia's pastries, because he knew how much I loved them. We shared ciró from a bottle, except for when Fausto dribbled some on my naked breasts and licked it off.

He undressed me slowly, then put me on top of him. I had a thing for being naked while he was clothed—a kink that was no secret from Fausto. After we came, he closed his eyes and I relaxed on top of him, just breathing in the scent of lemon soap and sex.

"I wish we could do this every day," he whispered into my hair.

My toes had curled into the grass, the flutters in my chest nearly an earthquake. I was so happy with him—and he seemed happy, too.

Now we were headed back to real life.

"Are you returning to work this afternoon?" I asked him.

"Yes. I have a few important calls. Will you miss me?"

"No," I lied.

His expression said he didn't believe me. "Since you are in a good mood, I must tell you that I'll need to skip dinner tonight."

"Oh." Disappointment crashed through me. I liked eating dinner with him and his family. "It won't be the same without you."

"I like to hear you say it, dolcezza."

"Do you have late calls?"

"No, I must go out for a meeting."

I pulled Piccola Monella to a halt. "You are leaving the estate?"

He leaned forward on the saddle, bracing his forearms on the horn. "Yes."

"Where are you going?"

"You know I cannot tell you that."

"Why?"

Bringing his horse closer, he reached out to touch my face. "You cannot ever know details of my business. I won't risk getting you sent to prison."

"The police won't care if you tell me one tiny thing, Fausto."

"No, Francesca. The only person who goes to prison is me."

"I don't want you to go to prison, either."

His expression softened. "There is an expression in Italiano: 'Hai voluto la bicicletta? E adesso pedala!'"

"What does it mean?"

"'Did you want the bicycle? Now ride it.' I wanted the bicycle, Francesca. Whatever the consequences, I will face them alone."

I pressed my lips together and stared out at the cows grazing in the field. "Will you be safe?"

He dipped his finger inside my shirt, then inside my bra, to graze my bare skin. "I will take every precaution, if only to return back to this." He fingered my nipple. "Will you wait up for me?"

"Yes." I knew I wouldn't be able to sleep, worrying about car bombs and bullets instead. "Are you taking guards with you?"

"Of course. And Marco."

"Good."

The horses grew restless and we started toward the stables again. Worry had settled in my stomach, but I tried not to let it show on my face. The thought of losing him....

Something that had been bothering me popped into my mind. "Why doesn't Marco like me?"

He tried to cover his surprise but failed. "What makes you say such things?"

"I can tell he doesn't like me. You don't need to hide it, Fausto. I just don't understand why. We've hardly spoken two words to each other since I arrived."

I hadn't ever seen Fausto uncomfortable before, but he clearly was now. He studied the ground and fidgeted with the reins. "He believes my attention is lacking, which is not true. But he blames you for it, for distracting me."

My jaw fell open, but I closed it quickly. "You work more than anyone else I know." Certainly more than my father or uncle.

"Still, I have taken more time away in this last month than ever before. But it doesn't matter who likes you, piccolina. Only if I like you."

"And do you? Like me, I mean."

I sounded needy and insecure, but I didn't care. Chuckling, he grabbed the reins of my horse and pulled us both to a stop. Then, he held me by the back of the neck and brought our mouths together, kissing me deeply. It felt like a stamp of possession with no respite, no escape, and I reveled in every second.

"What do you think? Do I like you?"

My grin nearly split my face. Who needed words when he treated me like a queen and kissed me like his life depended on it? "Yes, I think you do."

"See? And they say Canadian girls aren't smart."

I smacked his shoulder. "You'd better be nice or this not-smart girl won't suck your dick again."

He made a dismissive hand gesture. "You could never resist my dick, even if you tried. You're practically panting every time I take my clothes off."

"True. I'll have to think of something else to threaten you with."

I was smiling as we rode into the stables and dismounted. Fausto returned to the castello, leaving his horse with a groom, but I insisted on unsaddling and brushing Piccola Monella myself. Once she was settled, I decided to go in and shower. I smelled like sex, horses and Fausto.

In my room, I saw something green on my pillow. What on earth? Were those caterpillars?

They were pea pods. Zia had obviously stopped by. Shaking my head at her, I started to get undressed while munching on the peas. The poor woman. Giulio would give her great grand nieces and nephews, but probably not anytime soon. And I knew I wasn't—

I paused mid-chew. Wait, when was my last period? Had it been three weeks ago? No, that was Rome. Was it a week before that?

Had I even bled since coming to Italy? Yes, when I first came, because I had been relieved to find tampons in the bathroom.

Panic started building in my chest, but I forced it down. It was too soon to be pregnant, right?

I snatched my phone and opened my calendar app. I usually tracked my cycle, but my phone was back in Toronto. With the kidnapping and everything going on here, I hadn't even thought about it. My shot should still be effective, right?

Shit. I hated that I was now doubting myself. I was always so careful.

I looked back and tried to remember when I'd had my last period. Six weeks ago.

My stomach dropped. This couldn't be. It couldn't be. I used the birth control shot, which had never failed me before. I'd never even had a scare with David. My cycle was as regular as rain.

I searched my brain for the date of my last shot. It was supposed to last for three months, so I should still be covered. My heart raced in my chest, my breath coming faster as I remembered that my last shot was four and a half months ago.

That shouldn't matter, right? I should be okay. This was not happening. I wasn't pregnant. I was late because of the stress of being taken from my home and kidnapped, then seduced by a sexy older Italian man.

I opened a browser and began searching to see if the shot remained effective after the three-month timeframe elapsed.

The results had my eyes welling with tears. The effectiveness plummeted when the three-month period ended.

Okay, don't panic, Frankie. You can handle this.

Could I get a morning after pill? *It's not the morning after, you idiot.*

I took a deep breath and texted the one person I thought I could trust to help me.

Emergency. Come home ASAP.

Fausto

The club's basement was sparse and musty. There wasn't much down here to speak of, just a table and some chairs. A metal storage box in the corner housed the equipment needed to work over unwilling captives. While I didn't like having meetings outside of the castello, these weren't the kind of men I wanted anywhere near my home—especially with Francesca there.

Two men were strapped to chairs, their eyes burning with hatred but also fear. They knew they would die here tonight, but also it would not be an easy death.

It had taken time, but we finally located the captain and first mate of the ship that stole my product a few weeks ago. The coke had long disappeared, sold off to one of the Sicilian families I couldn't touch. We had an agreement with the Cosa Nostra not to interfere or intrude in their business, and vice versa, unless absolutely necessary. And this theft was hardly worth breaking peace over.

But I would have answers and vengeance.

I'd already removed my suit coat and rolled up my sleeves. I sat in the chair opposite the two men and spoke in Greek, knowing these two wouldn't understand Italian. "Do you know who I am?"

One of the men closed his eyes and began reciting Greek Orthodox prayers.

Yes, they knew me.

"That boat you hijacked last month? It and everything aboard belonged to me."

The man not praying swallowed loudly.

I continued. "The pirates in my waters know to leave my ships alone. They know the risks of interfering with my business. Which means you were new to this, hired by someone else. Before I leave this room, you will tell me who."

The captain shook his head. "We don't know, I swear."

I didn't believe him for a second. "We will see, won't we?" I nodded to Marco, who handed me my favorite weapon of choice—a long hunting knife. I could carve a man from mouth to ass with this thing without breaking a sweat.

I fingered the sharp tip, pressing hard enough to pierce my skin. A tiny drop of red ran down the blade. Darkness crept into my soul like vines, preparing me for what needed to be done.

Flipping the knife in my hand, I drove the blade into the captain's leg. His scream filled the sound-proof room. I left the blade in, both for shock value and to prevent blood from coating the floor too soon. "Who hired you?"

"I don't know!"

"Bullshit. Someone paid you to rob me, gave you information on where to find my ship. Tell me who."

He was trembling, eyes dull with pain. "We don't know."

I ripped the knife out of his leg, and blood surged down his calf and onto the ground as he screamed again. Then I plunged the knife into his partner's leg. I knew exactly where to stab to avoid bone. "I will continue to do this until I get answers from one of you. Whoever answers me will die quickly. Whoever doesn't...."

The first mate shook his head, breathing hard through the pain. "Please, il Diavolo."

"Tell me."

The captain's head was hung low, saliva dripping from his mouth. "We-We saw him once. He was Italian. No names."

"Young? Old?"

"Young. Early twenties, maybe."

"And?"

When he didn't answer, I jerked the knife out of the first mate's leg and put it into the captain's non-injured thigh. When the screams died down, I said, "What else can you tell me?"

"He sounded different than you. From a different region. North, maybe."

"His shirt," the first mate added. "It had a round circle, blue. With an N in it."

I glanced at Marco. Sounded like the Napoli football club, *Gli Azzurri*. My cousin and I were both thinking the same, that D'Agostino was likely behind the theft.

I stood and began rolling my sleeves down. Then I put my suit jacket back on. The two men begged in Greek for their lives, but I didn't reply. I instructed Marco and Benito to deal with them and then I went back upstairs into the club.

It was packed, as usual. Gratteri, my man who ran all the night-clubs, had turned this old warehouse into Siderno's latest hot spot. My son did a lot of work here, as well. I headed to the VIP area to see if either Gratteri or Giulio was here.

Gratteri was in a booth with some of our men. They all had women on their laps, champagne bottles on the table. "Rav!" Gratteri yelled when he saw me, waving me over. "*Vieni, unisciti a noi!*"

I wasn't in the mood for women and champagne. "*Ha un momento?*"

He got up and came to where I waited. I shook his hand and

slapped his back. "The place looks fantastic. And the numbers are even higher than that club last year. You've done very well."

"Thank you, Rav. Are you all finished in the basement?"

"Marco and Benito are still down there." I filled him in on what we'd learned. I had always liked Gratteri, which is why I trusted him to teach my son. He was older and had seen a lot over the years, so I didn't hesitate to ask his opinion on how to handle D'Agostino.

While Gratteri talked, I saw movement from a back hallway over his shoulder. It was Giulio and another man, one of Gratteri's lower foot soldiers. My son looked to be in a hurry, his eyes on his phone as he texted furiously. I swear, I didn't know how he and Francesca did it. I've never seen anyone text so fast.

Just as I was about to look away, I saw the foot soldier's hand swipe across Giulio's back. It was a familiar touch, one that spoke of intimacy and affection, and lasted a shade too long. Like how I might touch Francesca as I quickly walked past her.

It happened in a blink and I thought maybe I imagined it.

But I knew I hadn't.

Italian men were demonstrative, even sometimes with other male friends, but this had been different. This touch had been more than friendly. I knew it in my bones.

He's never one to play with the girls at the clubs or the waitresses. Never even accepts a blow job.

What did this mean? That my son...preferred men?

No, that wasn't true. It couldn't be. He was my son. The Ravazzani heir. He was not gay. I would know it if that was the case, wouldn't I?

I watched as Giulio strode across the floor, still texting. He'd never seemed attracted to Francesca, which was a miracle in itself, considering her looks. Instead they had played in the ocean like siblings.

I shook off these thoughts. If he were gay, someone would have noticed. There would have been talk. Rumblings. The men gossiped worse than Zia and her friends when they were playing a game of briscola. Marco would have undoubtedly heard and brought this news to me.

Still, the back of my neck itched as I finished up with Gratteri. I gave him half of my attention, while the other half remained on my son as he left the VIP area and went downstairs. He never noticed me, which was probably for the best.

Bidding Gratteri goodbye, I went to find Marco.

The bodies were being dismembered and shoved into drums for disposal. Marco and Benito were laughing and chatting, unaffected by the grisly work. "Marco," I called.

He came over, his gloves covered in blood. "What is it, Rav?"

For a moment, I hesitated. I trusted Marco with my life, but this was my son. If Giulio were gay, I could not even begin to fathom the repercussions.

Still, I needed my cousin's help.

"I saw Giulio come out of the back hallway off the VIP lounge with one of Gratteri's soldiers. The boy seemed overly familiar with Giulio." I let that sink in, and Marco's eyes went wide.

"You think? No, Rav. It's impossible. Your son?"

"I'm sure I am wrong, but I have to know."

"As far as I know there aren't cameras outside that exit, just on the inside of the door. I can put one outside if you want."

"Do it. No one is involved but me and you. Not even Gratteri. And no one sees that footage but me. Capisce?"

"Of course. I'll get it up tonight, when no one's around. We have those new tiny cameras the Guardia uses. I'll put up one of those."

"Good." I dragged a hand through my hair. "Grazie."

"Rav, don't worry. Maybe they were out there doing blow. You never know with kids these days. I'm sure it's nothing."

I nodded and clapped his shoulder. "God willing."

Because the 'Ndrangheta did not tolerate gay men. They were feared and distrusted, and usually one of their family members killed them to save face.

I could not even contemplate what this meant for my son if it were true.

CHAPTER TWENTY-SIX

Francesca

I WAS PACING in my room, on the verge of hysteria, by the time Giulio returned from the pharmacy.

"Here," he said, handing me the bag. "I bought five, just like you asked."

"Thank you. I'm sure it's nothing. It has to be stress."

Giulio held up his palms. "I know nothing about a woman's cycle, but I think you should check. Just for peace of mind, no?"

I swallowed. "I know. Will you stay?"

"Of course. Go. We'll check together."

I went into the bathroom and opened the first box. The instructions seemed fairly simple. Hold the stick in the pee, let it sit, and read the results. Maybe I should take two tests, just to be sure.

Hands shaking, I unwrapped another box and peeled open the paper on the stick. Holding both, I sat down and peed, making sure to wet each stick thoroughly. Then I set them on the counter, cleaned up, and called Giulio in.

He entered carefully, like he was afraid of startling me. "Well?"

"Set the timer on your phone for five minutes. Then we'll have our answer."

Giulio started the timer and then peered at the sticks. I smacked his shoulder. "Don't check early. You're making me nervous."

His expression serious, he leaned against the wall. "What result are you hoping for?"

"Negative, obviously."

"Not obviously. Many women would love to get pregnant with my father's baby, you know."

"I am not many women, and they can have his babies for all I care. I cannot be pregnant, G. Not now, and not by your father."

"Why not? He has been a great father to me, and he would see that you are well cared for. You'd want for nothing."

I pressed my palms into my eye sockets and tried to control my breathing before I hyperventilated. "I don't want to be tied to him for the rest of my life. Plus, I'm not ready to be a mother. I want to go to college and get a job. Have a normal life."

He made a dismissive sound. "Normal is boring, Frankie. You were not made for that life, punching a time clock in some menial job for little money. You are better than that."

"I'm sure my mother thought the same thing, but she gave up her whole life for my father. Her career, her freedom." *Be your own woman, Francesca. Don't make my mistakes.* "I can't do that. I promised myself I would have a different life." Tears welled in my eyes, the terror overwhelming me.

"Frankie," Giulio said softly, pulling me into his arms. "Don't cry. We don't even know if it's positive yet."

Deep in my bones, I knew. I was pregnant. I'd never gone this long without a period, and the shot was no longer effective. Fausto had knocked me up.

What was I going to do if it were true?

I stayed there, praying, nestled in Giulio's embrace, until the timer went off.

He turned off his phone and held my shoulders. "We look together. All right?"

I nodded, my mouth as dry as dirt. "Okay."

We turned and looked down. Both tests were positive. "Oh, shit," I whispered and sank to the floor. I buried my face in my hands. "Oh, shit."

I couldn't help it—I started crying. Giulio sat next to me and wrapped an arm around me. He didn't say anything, his strong hand just stroking my back.

I was having Fausto's baby.

Why? Why did the universe hate me so much? What had I ever done wrong in life to deserve this? Kidnapped and brought here, engaged then not. Seduced by stupid vineyards and stupid Fausto. And now the worst has happened.

A baby.

"If I run away, maybe he'll never know," I choked out through my tears.

"You have to tell him."

I shook my head *no* against his shoulder. I didn't need to tell him. I could run away, have the baby, and give it up for adoption. He would never know.

Giulio tilted my chin so he could see my face. "Frankie, if you don't tell him, I will. He's my father."

"But you're my friend. Bros before hos."

"I'm not sure any of that applies in this case." He kissed my forehead. "I think this is a good thing. It is fate. You were destined to come here and give me a baby brother or baby sister."

"Oh, my God." I rolled into a tight ball and started rocking. I was having Giulio's half-brother or half-sister. How fucked up was that?

And like an idiot I had called him for help. Of course he'd want me to stick around and have the baby. Another Ravazzani boy would take the pressure off him to have his own children.

But any boy child raised here, my child, would be in the mafia. And a girl wouldn't fare any better. She would be married off at an absurdly young age to a man she didn't know, and he would probably be in the mafia.

No, no, no. This was not happening.

I cried harder. I wanted to die. This was the end of everything as I knew it.

I heard Giulio put his phone down, but I paid no attention. Maybe Fausto didn't want a baby any more than I did. After all, he was almost middle aged. The diapers and late-night feedings were long in his past. If he learned I was pregnant, he'd probably send me back to Toronto. Then I could decide whether to have this baby or not.

"You can do this, Frankie," Giulio said. "Any child would be lucky to have you as a mother. And I think this will be good for my father. I can tell he cares about you very much."

That made me feel worse. Fausto didn't love me. I was a puttanella, a convenient hole. Eventually he'd tire of me—just like he tired of Katarzyna—and send me and the child away. I'd always be the woman who was stupid enough to let the head of the Calabrian mafia knock her up. And my son or daughter would pay the price.

How could I bring a child into this fucked up situation?

Tears began falling in earnest again, and I could hardly catch my breath. Giulio's shirt was a mess, but I didn't care. He handed me tissues occasionally but I was crying too hard to stop.

"What is going on?" Fausto's voice echoed in the tiny washroom. "Francesca, why are you crying?"

I couldn't even look at him. I wanted to both throw myself in his arms and strangle him with my bare hands. This was all his fault. He'd kidnapped me and prevented me from getting another birth control shot. Then he'd filled me with his super sperm and impregnated me.

Giulio and his father began speaking rapid Italian that I didn't even try to understand. I no longer cared. This whole country sucked. I hated everyone and everything in it.

Giulio started to get up, but I grabbed his arm. "Don't go. Please."

He gave me a half smile. "It's going to be fine, Frankie. I promise. This is fate."

Traitor.

For all I knew he'd texted his father to come in here.

I let him go like he was burning my hand. "Nothing is fine. Nothing will ever be fine again."

Standing, he exchanged a look with his father and then walked out.

Fausto peeked at the two pregnancy tests. "And this is what has you crying?"

"Yes, Fausto," I snapped. "That is generally what happens when someone who doesn't want to get pregnant gets pregnant."

"You had to know it was a possibility, no?"

Anger flared to life in my chest, the burning hatred replacing the sadness. "Something about being kidnapped, drugged, almost forced to marry your son, brought to a country where I don't speak the language, and seduced by you made me forget that I was overdue for my shot. How silly of me! Yep, stupid, stupid Francesca." I dropped my head in my hands. "Fuck you, Fausto."

He grabbed my wrist, tugged me to my feet and began leading me out of the bathroom. I resisted, pulling away from him. "Don't touch me. I hate you—and I definitely don't want to have a baby with you."

Sighing, Fausto bent and scooped me up in his arms. I squirmed and shoved at his chest. "Put me down. I don't want to talk to you right now."

"That is too bad."

He sat on the bed and then twisted until we were both flat on the mattress, our heads on the pillows. I was too furious to speak so I folded my arms and stared at the ceiling. Fausto rose up on an elbow. "Tell me what you are thinking."

"I'm thinking I should have smothered you in your sleep while I had the chance."

The bastard chuckled.

"I am sorry to tell you, then, that I'll definitely be sleeping with one eye open from now on." His hand gently rested on my belly. "Piccolina, this does not displease me. I like the idea of you round and big with my child."

I glared at him. "What if I don't want to be round and big with your child?"

He lifted a shoulder in a small shrug. "I won't allow you to abort it, if that is what you are thinking. But you needn't be involved after the child is born, if you don't wish."

My mouth fell open. While I had been thinking of adoption, something about his phrasing made me think this was not what he was talking about. "What does that mean?"

"This is not an uncommon occurrence. While I've never had a child out of marriage, many mistresses have babies in our world. I can find someone to help raise it."

Was he serious right now? This was how he was attempting to make me feel better? *Get in line, Frankie. All the mafia whores have bastards.* And who would help raise it? His next mantenuta?

Over my dead body.

Fausto clearly didn't want me around for the long haul. He was already planning how to raise this child without me. Weren't men at least supposed to offer to marry the woman they knocked up?

You don't want to marry him. You were planning to go back to school.

He kept talking. "Though not an heir, this child will be treated like a king because he is mine. Another Ravazzani for the brotherhood."

"How do you know it's a boy?"

"I don't. But either a boy or a girl will serve in their own way. It is how things are done here."

Was he listening to himself? Already signing our child up for a lifetime of misery and violence. I didn't want this—for me or my child.

I rolled off the bed in a flash and pointed to the door. "Get the fuck out, Fausto."

He made no effort to move. "We need to talk about this, Francesca."

"I'm done talking. I don't want to talk to you anymore. This is my body. I will decide what happens in the future. Not you."

His expression twisted into something dark, something frightening. I hadn't seen him this angry since I had stabbed him with a pen. "If you harm yourself or that child, there will be hell to pay. Do you understand me?"

"Do your worst! Whatever you do can't be any worse than kidnapping me, keeping me here, getting me pregnant and stealing my future from me. I don't want to have a baby, especially not with you!"

Very carefully, he got up off the bed. He came over to me but didn't touch me. "It is too late for immature tantrums. You let me fuck you and come inside you. In fact, I remember several times you begged me to fill you up with my come. Do not blame this all on me, monella."

Oh, I would absolutely blame this all on him.

Lifting my chin, I said, "I want to go back to Toronto."

"No fucking chance," he snarled. "You and my child will stay here."

"For how long? Until you get tired of me? What then?"

"I will always take care of you and this child, Francesca."

That was an evasion if I'd ever heard one, and it didn't reassure me in the least. I wanted to be alone so I could contemplate an escape plan. "Get out."

He stared down at me, his blue gaze inscrutable and hard. I couldn't tell what he was thinking, and I was too mad to care.

Before I could tell him to get out again, he grabbed my wrist and began bringing me toward the door. I dug in my heels. "What are you doing? Let me go. I'm not going anywhere with you!" Silent, he picked me up and began carrying me. "Fausto, goddamn it. Put me down."

I continued to struggle all the way into his wing. When we arrived in his bedroom, he finally placed me on the floor, but he didn't let go of my hand. Instead, he dragged me to the wardrobe where he kept his sex toys. Was he planning on spanking me? Worse, gagging me? I tried to pull free.

"Stop," he said, his voice tight with fury. "I am not going to hurt you."

"I don't care. And whatever you are getting out of that drawer is a waste of time because I won't have sex with you."

He lifted a pair of handcuffs. Before I could tell him to go fuck himself, he had the bracelet secured around my wrist. I hid my other hand behind my back. But I needn't have bothered. The other bracelet went around his own wrist and clicked into place.

The asshole handcuffed us together.

"You will stay here in my room from now on. I'll have your things moved tomorrow."

I gaped at him. "Have you gone insane? I am not staying here, handcuffed to you. I want to go back to my own room."

"Absolutely not. Now, do you want to get ready for bed or shall I do it for you?"

Fausto

I woke up first.

Francesca slept next to me, her luscious body pressed tight to my side. Even angry, she wanted to be close to me.

I hadn't lied—I was not unhappy about this child. I'd always wanted more children, but Lucia and I never had time before she was killed. Then I never found the right mantenuta to trust with raising a child. But I trusted Francesca. As furious as she was now, I had seen her with Lamborghini and the other animals. She had a gentle heart. She would make an excellent mother.

My cock thickened just thinking about her round belly and swollen breasts. Stretch marks from my child increasing inside her. I could not wait to dote on her hand and foot. Zia would be thrilled, as well. My aunt loved babies.

Clearly, my stubborn piccola monella would not go easily into this situation. She would fight this, keep demanding to go back to Toronto. I had to convince her to stay—for her sake and the baby's. I would not have my unborn child upset by discord between its parents. It wasn't healthy.

Lucia and I had been separated while she was pregnant with Giulio. She had moved to the other wing, and we never had regular sex again. Instead I had found a mantenuta and left my wife alone, as it seemed she preferred.

I didn't want that for this pregnancy.

Besides, I wasn't certain I was capable of leaving Francesca alone. I needed to have her close, watch all these changes and be present for my child's birth. I needed to fuck her and make her come, ensure she was happy and healthy for the entire nine months.

I would treat her like a queen.

She had no idea of the financial gain she'd receive for giving me a healthy child. Many women had begged me to fuck them without a condom over the years and I always resisted. I never risked a baby with a casual fuck.

I wasn't sure why I'd been so careless with Francesca. Fucking her raw had been a risk, one I well knew, but I hadn't been thinking straight when it came to her pussy. Probably because Francesca was more than a casual fuck to me. I cared for her. In fact, I was perfectly happy to keep her here at the castello for the rest of her life.

Not that she was ready to hear as much.

I slid my hand over her flat stomach, resting it where my child was growing. Cazzo, I liked that. She would be so beautiful, full of life. Full of my baby.

After I had handcuffed us together last night, I cut off her shirt and bra, so she was deliciously naked against me right now, warm and soft from sleep. I knew the best way to keep my girl happy was to give her orgasms. Francesca liked sex as much as I did, and she craved the dirty and dark. Just as I did.

My fingers trailed between her legs, parting her folds to stroke her sex. She was already wet for me. Lust twisted in my belly, so I closed my eyes and breathed deeply, trying to remain gentle. I found her clit and stroked it lightly, loving the feel of her slick heat. Her breath quickened and I could sense her coming more fully awake.

I continued to pet her until her hips rocked slightly, seeking. Pulling her leg over mine, I spread her wider, giving me better access. Her arm came up to wind around my head. I had unlocked the handcuffs last night after she fell asleep, so I now had full use of both hands to pleasure her.

Remaining silent, I kissed her throat and pinched her clit. She gasped at the pain then moaned at the resulting pleasure after I let go. Then I slid two fingers inside her, and her walls sucked me in greedily. Yes, I needed that so badly, her tight cunt gripping my cock and milking my come from me.

Shifting her leg, I lined my tip up at her entrance and shoved inside. I went about halfway before I met resistance, so I gave her a moment to adjust, my fingers returning to her clit. When she rolled her hips for more, I slid the rest of the way home. I tried to go gently with her, to fuck her slowly, but she dug her nails into my backside, pulling me roughly toward her. "Fausto, please."

That pleading voice did me in. I gave up trying to fight it.

I got her up on all fours and began riding her hard. She clutched the sheets. "God, yes. Harder. *Fuck!*"

"Am I hurting you?" Were pregnant women allowed to be rough in bed? I would need to ask the doctor.

"Stop talking and keep fucking me."

I froze. Even though my balls screamed for release, I didn't move. No, this was not how things went between us. It was very much the opposite, with me giving orders and Francesca obeying them.

She tried to rock back onto my dick, but I held her hips still and pulled out. As expected, she snarled, "What are you doing?"

I lifted her up until her back met my chest, her knees on the bed. My erection slid between her thighs, close to her entrance but never inside. I thrust gently, teasing her. "I am reminding you whose bed you are in right now. Who is fucking you?"

"You bastard."

She was still furious with me, but I didn't care. I would wear her down through pleasure.

I squeezed a breast in each hand, molding them, then I rolled her nipples between my fingertips. My tip skimmed the entrance to her pussy. "Who?"

"I hate you."

"No, you don't. You wish you did, but you don't. And you'll get my cock if you answer me." I let her feel the thick length between her legs. "Won't that feel good, baby?"

She whimpered, her head thrashing on my shoulder.

"I want to fuck you so badly," I told her. "I dream about fucking you, Francesca. I have never wanted anyone more. Tu sei perfetta."

"Fausto, please. Fuck me."

I angled her hips so I could slide inside. Shivers wracked my body as I drove deep, the bliss so intense. She dropped onto her hands and I bent over her back, grinding and thrusting, rutting like an animal. I'd never been so wild, so out of control with any other woman. I craved her like a drug, wanted to get as deep inside her as possible.

"There you go," I growled against her shoulder. "Do you like that? Is that what you need?"

"God, yes. More, paparino."

The name had my balls drawing up tight, ready to spill. "You are so fucking sexy, taking my cock like the best girl. Taking my come from me. I am going to take such good care of you, my dirty piccolina."

She whimpered, and I could tell she was close. I needed her to come because I couldn't hold on much longer.

Lifting slightly, I slid my fingers between her ass cheeks and let my thumb find the hole there. I circled with gentle pressure. She bucked and the tip of my thumb slid inside. That did it. Her body locked and her pussy clamped down on me, strangling me as she came.

My orgasm didn't wait, instead rushing over me, stealing my breath as come shot out the head of my cock. We climaxed together, a mass of trembling limbs and incoherent words.

When it was over, I pulled her close, until she rested half on top of me. I stroked her back as we tried to catch our breath, sweat cooling on our skin. I kept silent, letting her work through whatever was in her mind.

"You aren't going to let me go, are you?" she finally asked.

"No."

"Can I move back into my room?"

"No." I didn't care if this made me a bastard, I wanted her close to me.

"Why not?"

I figured I owed her the truth. "As soon as Lucia became pregnant with Giulio, she moved into the other wing. I never got to see the little changes in her, the signs of my son growing in her body. I always regretted that. She didn't even let me inside the delivery room." I kissed her hair. "I don't want to miss that this time around. And I want to help you and take care of you."

"Did you have a mistress when your wife was pregnant?"

I debated how to answer this. "If you are asking whether I will sleep with another woman while you are pregnant with my child, the answer is no."

"You had fucking better not, but that wasn't what I asked."

"Francesca, nearly every married man in my world has a mantenuta, especially when their wives are pregnant. Lucia knew this, as she was raised in our culture. It was not a surprise." I gave a small laugh. "She was likely relieved."

"Because?"

Were we really discussing my marriage? I never did, not to anyone. It felt disloyal, considering my wife was dead and could never share her side of the events. Furthermore, what was the point? But as the mother of my next child, Francesca deserved to know. "Because I think I scared her. She was...delicate. Timid. A proper Italian wife for the head of the Calabrian mafia. She would never refuse me, but I don't think she enjoyed what we did in bed together."

"I find that very hard to believe."

"You shouldn't. Not all women are like you." I cupped her ass, then moved my fingers between her legs, where my seed mixed with her juices. I played with her, pushing my come back into her cunt. "You need this. You crave it, the dirtier the better. We like the same things."

"Which is why I ended up pregnant."

She sounded despondent again, so I rolled her onto her back to see her face. Pushing her hair out of the way, I stared into her eyes. "This is not the end of your life. If you do not want to be a mother, I will understand. I have Zia and Giulio, and I can hire women to act as a nanny to my child. But I would like for you to stay, to raise this baby with me. To love him or her as much as I do, and to make a home here."

She studied me, her expression skeptical. "Until you get tired of me and start sleeping with someone else."

I flopped onto my back and moved my free hand in an aggravated gesture. "Basta, Francesca! How many ways can I say this will not happen?"

"Words are not enough, not any more. I want some sort of contract. A legal agreement between us that outlines what happens if things go wrong. Then I'll consider staying."

"Is this what you need to feel safe and secure with me?"

"Yes. Clearly, we aren't getting married, so I need some security for what happens down the road. For me and the child."

"Fine."

She gaped at me. "You're really agreeing?"

I frowned at her. "Are you doubting my word?"

"A capo never goes back on a decision once it is made," she recited in a bad Italian accent, rolling her eyes.

I smacked her ass in retaliation. "Was that supposed to be me? You must practice more, dolcezza. Enunciate like a true Italian and roll your r's."

She laughed, and it was a joy to see her relaxed and no longer furious with me. I cupped the back of her neck and brought her mouth to mine for a long kiss. She gave me her tongue and I took full advantage, in no hurry to let her go. When we broke apart, I said, "See? All looks better after a good night's sleep and a good fucking, no?"

"I'm still not happy about this, Fausto."

"Allora, let me be happy enough for both of us until I can convince you." I kissed her again. "Okay?"

Tears suddenly welled in her eyes and I didn't know why. Panic filled me as I examined her face. "What did I say? Francesca, baby. Please, I didn't mean to make you cry."

"I can't help it. You're being very sweet and I don't know how to handle you when you are sweet."

My muscles relaxed and I pulled her close. "Do not worry, then. I'll soon return to being a stronzo."

"Good, because that I am definitely used to."

CHAPTER TWENTY-SEVEN

Francesca

WHEN I CAME DOWNSTAIRS for breakfast, I found Zia in the kitchen. Fausto had retreated to his office an hour ago, and Giulio was probably still sleeping.

"Buongiorno, *la nipote,*" she said, giving me a sly smile from the range.

What did that word mean? Pregnant mistress? Stupid woman who forgot about her birth control shot and let a mafia king impregnate her?

With Zia, it was hard to say. The crafty old woman.

I went and kissed her cheek. "Buongiorno, Zia."

When I tried to make a cup of espresso, she smacked my hand. "*La caffeina fa male al bambino.*"

"Ouch, Zia. I need coffee." I pointed at the espresso maker. "Per favore?" I put my hands together like I was praying and shook them, pleading. I might die if she didn't let me have coffee.

"No. Fausto's bambino." She pointed at my stomach, as if I needed a reminder.

Pouting, I dropped onto a stool. "How did you know?" When she frowned, I thought about the Italian I'd learned. *"Come...sapere...bambino?"* "Sapere" was the verb "to know" but they couldn't expect me to start conjugating this soon.

Zia came closer and lifted my chin with one of her bony fingers. She tilted my face this way and that. *"La tua pelle bellissima."*

When she went back to the stove, I used my translation app and learned "pelle" was skin. Huh.

I still couldn't believe I was pregnant. I was going to have a baby. Fausto's baby. I felt too young to be a mother. I wasn't even nineteen. I barely knew how to take care of myself, let alone someone else.

Let me be happy enough for both of us until I can convince you.

Of course, Fausto was happy about this. He didn't have to do the hard part, which was to grow and then push a watermelon out of his vagina. Plus, he had all the money in the world to hire nannies and tutors, and pay for private schools. I could leave the child here in Italy and return to Canada.

My hand slipped to my belly. Could I do that? Move away and leave my child here in Italy?

I remember the twins after Mama died, how confused and sad they'd been, the nightmares and tantrums that had followed in the months after the funeral. Papà had been no help whatsoever, so I did whatever I could to give them stability and care. To make sure they felt loved.

The answer to my current dilemma was obvious. I couldn't do it. I would never want this baby thinking I had abandoned them. No matter what happened with Fausto, I would raise this child.

I needed to think about the conditions of our agreement. Once he agreed and signed off on them, then I could relax a little over my future.

Zia put two cornetti and juice in front of me and gestured that I should eat.

I was starving, so I didn't argue.

Giulio came in the back door, whistling, dressed in last night's clothes. "Someone got laid," I murmured through a mouthful of cornetto.

He smirked and went to kiss Zia's cheeks. She began speaking in rapid Italian, clearly cross with him. Then she gestured to me. "What is she saying?" I asked.

He exchanged a few words with Zia, then said, "She is berating me for staying out all night. Saying the bambino needs calm and stability in the house, not a boy out at parties and coming home at all hours."

My stomach sank and the cornetto turned to dust in my mouth. Thanks to Fausto's sperm, my days of parties and staying out all night were over, clearly.

Giulio sat next to me. "Do not look so sad, *la matrigna*."

Zia chuckled and I cast a suspicious glance at him. "I'm almost afraid to ask, but what does that mean?"

His smile was playful and slick. "Stepmother."

I shoved his shoulder. "Fuck off. That is not even funny."

"He will marry you, Frankie. Mark my words."

"No, he won't. He told me that it's not unusual for mistresses to have babies in his world."

Giulio pursed his lips and said something to Zia, who nodded several times as she answered. "What?" I asked.

"Zia agrees with me. He will marry you eventually."

Had no one even considered what I wanted? "Maybe I don't want to marry him. Maybe I want to take my child back to Toronto."

"He will never allow that to happen, *bella*."

Fausto had said as much, but maybe he'd change his mind. Once the diapers and late-night feedings started, he'd probably be glad to get rid of me and the baby. "I hate you both."

"No, you don't. You love us both."

I drank my juice and tried not to react. Love Fausto? No way. I couldn't. It would be awful, loving him when he didn't love me in return. Eventually he'd take another mistress and that would kill me. I was the jealous type. No way would I be able to share him with anyone else.

You're jealous because you love him.

Ugh.

Zia set an espresso in front of Giulio and I eyed it hungrily. Did they make decaf espresso? I would need to research that ASAP.

Actually, I knew nothing about being pregnant. I would have to research all of it ASAP. Weren't there special vitamins and doctor's appointments?

Oh, God. I put my head in my hands. How had I let this happen?

"How did he take the news, by the way?"

I looked up at Giulio. "He's thrilled."

Giulio grinned. "I knew it." He exchanged words with Zia, then filled me in. "Zia is not surprised, either. She said he will right the wrongs of his past with you."

Great. Just what I wanted.

I never got to see the little changes in her, the signs of my son growing in her body.

Hard to feel sorry for him when he was off fucking another woman during Lucia's pregnancy.

My phone lit up and I saw Gia's name on the screen. Why was my sister calling me from Toronto at—I glanced at the time and did the math—three thirty in the morning? "Scusci," I said and swiped to accept the call as I stood up. "Gia? Why are you up so late?"

When I started to leave, Zia pressed my uneaten cornetto in my hand. "Per il bambino."

I rolled my eyes but took the pastry. "Grazie," I told her and then walked outside to the terrace. A stone table with an umbrella was already set up, casting shade in the morning heat.

"Are you there, Frankie?" Gia was speaking quietly.

"I'm here. What is going on? Why are you calling me so late?"

"Are you really Fausto Ravazzani's goomah?"

Suddenly, I lost my appetite. I set the cornetto on the table. "How did you hear?"

"Papà is losing his mind. I heard him yelling about it with Uncle Reggie. He is pissed." She paused. "It's really true? You're his mistress?"

There was no use lying about it now. And I hadn't even told her the worst part. "Yes, and brace yourself, Gia. It gets worse."

"Oh, my God. Spill it."

"I'm pregnant."

"Holy shit! But you've only been there barely two months. That was fast."

Yes, because of Fausto's stupid virility. "I forgot about my shot. Normally the doctor's office calls to remind me to make an appointment, but I left my phone in Toronto. With everything that happened, it just totally slipped my mind."

"You're having a baby. I can hardly believe it. I'm going to be an aunt!"

Hearing her excitement, I pinched the bridge of my nose between my thumb and forefinger. "This is not a good thing. This is a nightmare, actually."

"Frankie, if you had married his son, you'd probably be having a baby anyway. That's the way these stupid mafia marriages work. They like to keep us uneducated and pregnant."

A knot lodged in my throat. I didn't want that future. I wanted to go to college and live like a normal young woman. Have fun and go to parties. Get drunk and hook up with random guys. My eyes started burning, tears gathering behind my lids. "Gia, what am I going to do?"

"Oh, sis. I'm sorry. He didn't...force you, did he?"

"Definitely not. I wanted to sleep with him. I just didn't mean to get pregnant."

"Well, what did he say about it?"

"He's beyond happy. Apparently, it's common here for mistresses to have babies. No one has batted an eye so far." At least Giulio and Zia hadn't. Who knew what everyone else would say?

"Papà will seriously flip out if he learns of a baby."

"You can't tell him. Please, Gia. You can tell Em, but don't mention this to anyone else."

"I won't. He's already pissed because you are a quote 'whore,' sleeping with a man you aren't married to. He's been screaming that you've brought shame to the Mancini family, whatever the fuck that means."

I could almost hear him ranting, calling me a disappointment. "I'm sorry. I know this might affect you and Em, too, since you're still unmarried and living at home."

"Are you kidding? I don't want an Italian husband. I hope no one in this stupid 'ndrina wants to marry me when the time comes."

I sighed and traced the edge of the stone table with my fingertip. "I've made a complete mess of my life."

"You said you liked it there, so maybe it won't be so bad."

"I liked it here when I considered it a summer abroad. Now it's the rest of my life."

"Well, Em will tell you this is fate, but I will say it's shitty luck. We'll find a way to help you escape, if that's what you want."

If only.

"He'd just hunt me down. There's no escaping this, Gigi," I said, using her childhood nickname.

"Well, he better take good care of you or I will hire someone to beat his ass."

I laughed. "Gotcha. I'll be sure to let him know. Love you."

"Love you, too, Frankie. Talk soon, okay?"

"Okay. Give my love to Em."

When we hung up, I started crying, silent tears streaming down my face. I missed my sisters. This nightmare would be so much easier if I had them here with me....

Then I remembered the conditions I needed to write for Fausto. I was definitely adding "bring my sisters to Siderno" to the list.

Fausto

I SPENT the next few days setting up things for Francesca.

She presented me with a list of things she needed right away, like an obstetrician. The doctor, rumored to be the best in Calabria, would see her beginning next week. In the meantime, they recommended prenatal vitamins, which I had Marco pick up at the pharmacy.

Francesca's list also included healthy foods, pasteurized cheese, and decaf espresso. Comfortable clothes and lotion for her belly. Pregnancy books and morning sickness relief.

I bought it all and rushed the delivery. Whatever my piccolina needed, she would have it.

She seemed to come to terms with having the baby. I knew she was working on her list of conditions for our legal agreement, which I would have drawn up and signed. There wasn't anything I would refuse her, as long as it kept her happy.

I very much looked forward to the cravings and back rubs. Feeling my child move inside her womb. Seeing her tits grow larger as they readied to produce milk.

I was the luckiest man in Italy.

Of course, I had asked about sex during pregnancy, and the doctor reassured me it was totally safe for the baby. So I continued to fuck my beautiful girl every night in our bed, keeping her well satisfied.

Marco entered my office without knocking. "Rav, you're going to want to see this."

I didn't take my eyes off my laptop. "Did your wife have one of these pregnancy pillows? It says they help with sleep."

He glanced over my shoulder at the screen. "Don't buy that one. Buy the one that hugs the whole body. It fits on both sides."

"Ah." I clicked on the one he recommended. The reviews called it the Ferrari of body pillows. Excellent. I added it to the shopping cart, then glanced up. "What do I need to see?"

He held out a flash drive. "It's the camera we put outside the VIP emergency exit at the club."

My stomach in knots, I took the small drive and put it into my laptop. When it mounted, I double clicked the video file and it began playing.

"Go to the three-minute mark," Marco instructed.

I moved the player forward until I saw Giulio come outside the exit door. A man followed, the same man who I'd seen touch Giulio's back. When the door closed behind them, Giulio grabbed the other man and shoved him against the wall, then attacked his mouth by kissing him.

I froze. My son was kissing another man.

"*Che cazzo?*" I whispered. The tips of my ears burned and I pounded my fist on the desk. Still I didn't take my eyes off the screen. I had to know.

I was not homophobic. I'd seen men together before, and I was very unhappy when the last gay member of my 'ndrina had been killed by his cousin.

But we did not interfere in these things. The men in our world considered homosexuality shameful. A sign of weakness and an embarrassment for the family. And it was left to the family to handle it.

Maybe I was wrong. Maybe Giulio just liked kissing other men, but he still fucked women.

Praying this was so, I continued to watch.

When my son sank to his knees, his hands going to unfasten the man's trousers, I shut my laptop.

Neither Marco nor I spoke. The silence said volumes between us. We both knew how bad this was for the 'ndrina—and for me personally.

Giulio was supposed to be my heir. To take over everything after I died. He was my only son—and he was gay. There had never been a gay man in a place of prominence in our organization. It was pointless. He would never have been respected enough by the other men to effectively lead.

"Rav, I'm sorry."

I nodded once, but I couldn't speak as my mind raced. How did this happen? What had I done wrong? All my plans for him were now ruined. It was only a matter of time before someone discovered this information and used it against him. Or me.

"He's kept this a secret for a long time," my cousin said. "Maybe it'll stay a secret."

"Not a chance. Eventually someone always talks. An ex-boyfriend, an ex-lover. Someone."

Marco dropped into the chair across from my desk. "No one else knows. I destroyed the original video and I took the camera down. You have the only copy."

"Thank you."

"What are you going to do?"

"We could get rid of the soldier. Maybe Giulio is only attracted to this particular man."

My cousin winced. "Rav, you know that isn't how it works."

Did I? Dio cane, I didn't know anything at the moment. I felt numb. "Do you think he loves this man?" Marco pressed his lips together, hesitating, and I had my answer. "Cazzo Madre di Dio!"

"This is not a fling. They are serious. Hey, at least he's not sleeping around."

"Certo. Thank God for that."

"I meant that he isn't taking risks. The more people who know, the more dangerous it is for him."

I picked up my phone and texted my son.

MY OFFICE. IMMEDIATELY.

"What are you going to do?" Marco asked again.

"I need to talk to him. Tell him to give up this man. After he has married and given me grandchildren, then he can continue his secret affairs."

"Is that really what you want for him?"

"What is my other choice?" I hissed. "Kill him? I cannot do that either."

Marco held up his palms. "No one is suggesting that. But you're having another child. If it's a boy, then Giulio could move away. Live a life outside the 'ndrina—"

"No," I snapped. "I am not disowning my son and forcing him to live in exile. He will give up this man and get married."

Marco clearly didn't approve but he kept silent. Which was wise, considering I had already decided how this would be handled. I would not be talked out of it.

Giulio was home, so I wasn't surprised when a knock sounded seconds later. I told him to come in and then my son strode into the room. I still remembered holding him as a baby, his chubby fingers wrapped around mine as he learned to walk. I had been the one to break the news to him about his mother, had consoled him and dried his tears. I gave him his first gun and taught him how to shoot it. I was there to induct him into the 'Ndrangheta. Everything I had done for the last eighteen years had been for him.

He would do this one thing for me.

"Sit down," I barked and pointed at the empty seat next to Marco.

My cousin started to stand, but I told him to stay. He was often the voice of reason when my temper got the better of me.

I folded my hands and tried to remain calm. "I will ask you this once and only once. And I expect the truth, Giulio."

A flash of fear went through my son's gaze, but he tried to smile through it. "Of course, Papà. I would never lie to you."

"Are you gay?"

He didn't move, didn't even seem to be breathing, as he stared at me. After a few very long seconds, he swallowed. "You wouldn't ask if you didn't already know the answer."

"Still, I want to hear you say it. To my face."

His chin lifted, the Ravazzani pride and courage surfacing. "Yes, I am gay."

I pounded a fist onto the desk again and closed my eyes. I had known it, but hearing him admit it twisted the knife in my chest a little more. "How long?" I rasped. "How long have you known?"

"Since always. There's never been a time when I didn't know."

Unbelievable. He'd hidden this from me his entire life. It felt like a betrayal of the worst kind, as if everything I'd known had been flipped upside down. "Why didn't you tell me?"

Giulio's eyes bulged. "Are you joking? Because I knew you'd act like this." He gestured toward me.

"If I had known, I could have protected you. I could have made other plans. I never would have—"

"You mean you would have sent me away. You never would have made me your heir."

Yes, that was exactly what I meant.

I stabbed at the desktop with my finger. "You cannot possibly blame me for that. You know what happens to gay men in our world. I'd rather you were alive and somewhere else than here and dead. But now it's too late."

His face lost its color but he didn't look away. Resignation settled in his expression. "What are you going to do?"

"I do not want this life for you. I want you married, with children.

Whatever you want to do once you have raised your children and become capo is up to you. But first you must give up this man and get married."

"Or?"

"There is no fucking *or*, Giulio," I snapped. "You will do this for me, as your father and capo. It is a direct order."

Swiftly, his face turned red. "Why can't I secretly see him? I'll get married and have children, I swear. But I want to see him on the side."

"No, absolutely not."

"Why not?" Giulio stood and dragged his hands through his hair. "You had a mantenuta when you were married. Every married man in the 'ndrina does—"

Marco cleared his throat pointedly. Giulio sighed. "Fine, everyone but Zio Marco has a mantenuta. What difference does it make if mine is a man?"

"Because it matters!" I shouted. "If someone finds out, they'll either kill you or both of us. This jeopardizes everything I have ever done!"

"I don't care! I love him!"

It felt like a blow to my heart, a knife cut deep in my chest. "You would put this man over the 'ndrina?" I paused and took a breath. "Over me?"

"Papà," he said in that petulant childish voice I'd heard many times over the years. "Do not make me choose."

"You must, because if you don't give him up I will have him killed, Giulio."

His eyes grew glassy with unshed tears and hopelessness. "Papà, no. I am begging you."

I hated this. I didn't like hurting him, but being capo meant making hard decisions—even when it came to your own family.

I hardened my resolve in the face of his misery. "If you want to save him, you will do as I say. You can never speak to him again. And you will marry the woman I choose and get her pregnant with your babies."

His hand shook as he covered his mouth, staring at me as if he'd never seen me before. As if he hadn't known I was capable of such cruelty. And that was because I had sheltered him from the worst of why they called me il Diavolo.

But I would not shelter him any longer. It was time for my boy to grow up and understand the world of men. "It is your choice, figlio mio."

He cleared his throat. "I'll break it off and I won't see him again. You have my word."

"Good boy. You are excused."

CHAPTER TWENTY-EIGHT

Francesca

I WAS JUST COMING out of my old room when Giulio hurried along the hall, his head down. "Hey, G," I called as I shut the door. "Did you want to—?"

He glanced up and I saw tears streaming down his face. "Not now, Frankie."

When he tried to dodge around me to go into his room, I put my hand out to stop the door from closing. I slipped inside as he flopped on the bed, face first. "What's wrong?"

"You'll just take his side. You're practically his wife."

He had a fight with Fausto, obviously. "Except I'm not and never will be. So, what happened?"

Giulio whispered, "He found out, Frankie."

I knew instantly what he was talking about. I dropped onto the mattress. "Oh, shit. How?"

"I don't know. I've always been so careful."

"What did he say?"

"That I have to break up with Paolo. If I don't, he said he would have Paolo killed."

What the fuck? I sucked in a breath, my hands reaching out to steady me on the bed. "Was he serious?"

"My father does not joke, not about murder. He was very serious."

And this man was the father of my child?

Great choice, Frankie.

"Does he think breaking up with Paolo will turn you straight?"

Giulio gave a harsh humorless laugh. "If so, he will be very disappointed. He wants me to marry and have babies. When I take over as capo, he said he doesn't care if I fuck men. But until then I cannot risk all he's built."

My skin turned hot as I considered this. Instead of doing the brave thing and supporting Giulio, he was forcing his son to live a lie so the family could save face. What a coward.

What an asshole.

I looked at Giulio, who'd never asked to be gay. He just was—and why couldn't Fausto understand that? His son had struggled with this secret for so long because he knew the repercussions, and his father had proved him right.

Who cared if Giulio was gay? It was none of anyone's business.

Fausto was being a shitty father and a shitty human being.

My heart raced as I stood. "I will go talk to him."

"I wouldn't do that," Giulio said. "He will see it as interfering."

I didn't care. If this was Fausto's parenting style, then I needed to know it sooner rather than later. Because no way would I raise a child with a man who chose the mafia over his own flesh and blood.

I hugged Giulio and walked out. No doubt Fausto was in his office, probably gloating over ruining Giulio's life. I marched down there, my ears buzzing with indignation. He would listen to me. Once he calmed down, he would see reason and reconsider.

I didn't bother knocking. Instead, I threw open the door and stepped in. Marco and Fausto were in the middle of a conversation, but I didn't care. This was too important. "A word, Fausto."

My man leaned back in his chair. "Francesca, this is not a good time. Did you notice the door was closed?"

Was he patronizing me? "I will speak with you now. Alone."

His eyes narrowed ever so slightly at the corners. He didn't like when I gave him orders, but that was too bad.

He murmured a few words to Marco, who got up and walked past me on his way out. Marco hadn't warmed up to me at all, even after learning I was having Fausto's child. If anything, he'd been even colder.

I ignored him and focused on Fausto. When the door closed and we were alone, I asked, "What the hell is wrong with you?"

A muscle jumped in his jaw. "You might want to rephrase that, dolcezza."

"I don't, actually. I just saw Giulio, crying in his room. He said you learned that he was gay."

Fausto cocked his head and stared at me, his mouth flat. "Yes, I did. But I have to ask if you knew this about my son."

I answered without thinking. "Yes, I knew. He told me—"

His hand crashed onto the top of the desk, startling me. Slowly, he rose out of his chair, the air disappearing from the room as he took up more space. "You knew my son was gay? He confided this to you and you...did what about it?"

Was he worried I had told others? "He asked me not to tell anyone. So I kept it to myself."

His face turned hard and scary, his il Diavolo face. No doubt it was the expression he wore before he gutted someone like a fish.

Unwittingly, I took a step backward.

"You didn't think to tell *me* this news?"

Oh. That was what he was mad about? "No. It wasn't my place."

"Wasn't your place? Your place is at my side, doing what I say. I thought I could trust you."

"This has nothing to do with trust. It's Giulio's life—and who cares who he sleeps with?"

"I care, actually. I have to care so that I may keep him safe. But at the moment I am more concerned with your dishonesty."

"I never lied to you!" I shouted.

"Who do you belong to, Francesca?" Fausto prowled toward me in measured steps.

"Fausto, this isn't about our sex games."

He continued like I hadn't spoken. "Who has put his child in your belly? Who should you remain loyal to above all others?"

"Are you listening? This is not about you and me. This is about your son. About what kind of father you are!"

He stood close, his skin flush as he sneered down at me. "Wrong. This is about the puttanella I've had sleeping in my bed who was betraying me the entire time."

Before I could even plan it, my hand came up and aimed for his cheek. Unfortunately, he caught my wrist before I could strike him. I tried to free myself from his grip, to no avail. "I am not a whore, you dick. Let me go!"

He released me like I was on fire. "You were very much my whore —and a good one at that. You made me think you were mine, that you actually cared. What a fool I was. Marco kept saying I could not trust you, and he was right."

"Fuck you—and fuck Marco. I never asked for this!"

"Didn't you? You were so eager you were nearly gagging for it, like when you begged to suck my cock in the stables. And now I know why. When you learned my son was gay, you set your sights on me. A bigger payout, right?"

Jesus, hearing those words nearly destroyed me. My chest felt shredded by a thousand tiny cuts, each breath a struggle. Yes, we had played games and I had let him degrade me, but I never actually thought he believed it. I never thought he believed me a gold-digging whore.

And now I was carrying his child? What an idiot I was.

"You are an asshole."

"And you are a fucking liar. I cannot ever trust you again." Roaring, he picked up a glass paperweight from his desk and threw it against the wall, where it smashed into a picture. I covered my head as glass shattered everywhere, the broken frame falling to the ground.

Then I held up my hands and backed away from him. "You're crazy. Don't fucking come near me ever again."

His chest heaved, and his mouth twisted into something sinister, his eyes so cold and cruel that I winced. "You need not worry about that. I would never sleep with someone who betrayed me like this. Marco!" he bellowed.

Marco couldn't have been far, because the door instantly opened. "Sì, Rav?"

He continued in English, obviously wanting me to understand. "Take her upstairs and watch as she packs a bag. Then drive her to the beach house. She is no longer welcome here."

I stood there, reeling. He was sending me away? Again? More punishment at the hands of Fausto Ravazzani. Was he hoping there would be a tsunami this time?

This was the final straw. He'd done this too many times and I would never forgive him. "You bastard," I hissed. "Do not come apologizing to me when you realize what a mistake you've made. Because it will be too late."

"I never change my mind, not after someone betrays me. You are dead to me, Francesca Mancini."

First my father, now Fausto? Shit, why did that hurt so badly? I grabbed my chest, certain it would crack open and spill out all over the fancy eastern carpets. "Good. Now I can go back to Toronto!"

He walked back to his desk and started sorting through papers, dismissing me like a servant. "After the birth, you'll be free to leave."

"I will not let you have my child. You're a terrible father, and I'd rather raise them alone."

"Unfortunately, that will not happen. The child is mine and will be raised here. Marco." He waved his cousin forward. "Get her out of my sight."

A ball of misery lodged in my throat, burning, but I would not let him see me cry. Why would I want to stay here anyway? He'd called me a whore and said I had betrayed him.

Because you love him.

Yes, I did and what a fool I was, falling for such a terrible man. I deserved to be alone and heartbroken.

"Oh, and remove my phone from her," he added. "She takes nothing I bought for her."

Just when I thought I couldn't hurt any more, he carved out more of my chest. *He thinks I'm a gold digger.* That I was a whore who was in it for the yacht and clothes and jewelry.

Fuck. Him.

I ripped the phone from my back pocket and threw it against the wall, where it cracked open and fell. "You are going to regret this, Fausto Ravazzani. I am the best thing that has ever happened to you. And it will be too late when you realize it."

"Cugino," he said impatiently, not even looking up.

Marco touched my arm. "Signorina Mancini."

"Don't touch me." I jerked away from him and walked out, my head high. I would walk out like a queen, even though Fausto had treated me like dirt.

And he could drop dead.

Fausto

EVERYONE in my household hated me.

It had been three weeks, and Giulio still wouldn't speak to me, his eyes full of sadness and heartbreak. Zia was furious that I'd sent Francesca away. I couldn't tell her why, except to say that Francesca had betrayed me. Zia replied that it was nonsense, that Francesca was in love with me and I had ruined it with my temper.

I didn't have the heart to correct her.

Even Marco seemed to tiptoe around me, acting like I was a volcano that might erupt at any moment.

Perhaps I was a bit on edge, but wasn't I allowed? I was the most important man in Calabria, perhaps all of Italy, and I had a secretly gay son and a gold-digging traitor pregnant with my child. I increased the speed on my treadmill and my legs began to burn. I'd already logged one hour running, and I wasn't sure how much longer I could keep going.

But I couldn't stop until I was exhausted. It was the only way I could sleep.

I had removed all traces of her from the house. I forbade anyone to speak her name—a rule only Zia flaunted. I stopped eating dinner with my family, taking my meals in my office instead. And I worked around the clock. The cells in the dungeon were now full of men who needed to be taught a lesson, and though I didn't normally participate in these matters, I was more than happy to get my hands dirty these days. Only when blood ran down the drain in rivers could I forget her face, her laughter. Her soft cries when she came. The way she clung to me, even in her sleep.

Cazzo, I had been such a fool for her.

A notification popped up on my phone. I turned off the treadmill and hopped down, my chest heaving as sweat ran down my body. It was my daily report on Francesca.

There were cameras at the beach house, but I refused to watch the footage. Instead, I had guards observing her at all times, keeping her safe, and they were instructed to report back to me daily with her activities.

Awoke at eight thirty.

Sucked on ginger candies until eleven, then had coffee.

This was not surprising, as the morning sickness had started a few days ago. The ginger candies had been a gift from my son, who visited Francesca almost daily.

Took her vitamins, then went for a walk on the beach.

Read on the terrace in the afternoon.

My son had gifted her with a tablet, too.

Groceries were delivered.

Good. I made certain she had a decent selection of food for when she felt well enough to eat. I might hate her, but I didn't want the baby to starve.

Giulio arrived. He had a glass of wine and some fruit. She had sparkling water and pasta.

My son was a good man. Better than me, certainly. And she had shown her loyalty to him—not me—so let him entertain her.

I kept reading.

After Giulio left, she video chatted with her sisters.
Went to bed at nine.

Each report was similar. Dry bullet points of a life lived as my prisoner. But I would not feel sorry for her. In my world, loyalty was everything. She had known a secret that could destroy all I had built, could get people killed, yet she hadn't shared it with me. This after I had taken her into my bed, showered her with affection and gifts. The mother of my child.

And deception was how she repaid me.

So, no. I would not feel guilty. Francesca would stay there, stewing in her mistakes, until the baby was born. Then I would take my child away from her and she could go wherever she wanted. I no longer cared.

I took a cold shower. My cock remained limp, which was what I preferred. When I got myself off lately, memories of her crept in, making me want impossible things. It was better not to tempt myself.

My bed awaited, but I wasn't tired. I was wide awake, as usual. I dressed in jeans and a t-shirt and went down to my office, determined to be productive.

Behind my desk, I slipped on my glasses and opened my laptop. There was plenty of legitimate work to oversee, so I started there, going through reports and stock transactions. Years ago, Toni had bought a large amount of digital currency, and it was making us a lot of money. Everything my cousin touched turned profitable. He really was a whiz.

The camera app beckoned me. With one click, I could see her. Watch her sleep. Was she comfortable?

I told myself I did not care. She would not break me. I was not a weak man, and she would learn her place.

Minutes later, I heard a thump and a bang out in the house. Not a gunshot, but like someone was stumbling into furniture. I took off my glasses and went out to investigate.

Giulio was in the entryway, picking his phone up off the tile. He swayed and cursed, and I could smell the whiskey from where I stood.

Sighing, I put my hands on my hips. "Do you need help?"

He started at the sound of my voice, but didn't look at me. "Do not pretend like you care."

Still angry, then. "Figlio mio, there is no one I care about more than you."

"Cazzata," he slurred, straightening. "You care about your pride, your precious 'ndrina. Nothing else matters but tradition and money."

His face looked terrible. Red-rimmed eyes that were glassy and devoid of his usual vivacity. His skin was sunken, like he'd lost weight. I hated seeing him like this, broken and angry, even if I knew it was for the best. "That isn't true. You'll see one day when you have your own children."

"I can't wait. Maybe they will hate me as much as I hate you."

My chest twisted, but I remained silent. I knew I was right. He just needed time to heal and start a different chapter in his life. Then he would find happiness.

"You should be pleased, Papà. I went with the boys to the strip club tonight. I paid for several lap dances so a strange woman could shove her huge tits in my face while I pretended to love it. Just like you."

I hadn't been to a strip club in ages, not since I was still a soldier, but he wouldn't know that. "That isn't necessary, Giulio."

"Of course, it is. I should get used to tits and pussy, so I can get it up when my wife wants me to fuck her. Isn't that right?"

I glanced around, not wanting us to be overheard even though it was the middle of the night. These were the first words he'd spoken to me in three weeks, and they were bitter and angry. I hated this rift between us. In eighteen years we had never disagreed like this. "You're drunk. You should go up to bed."

"Sure. Send us all away. That makes it easy for you, doesn't it, il Diavolo?"

I ground my back teeth as heat washed over me. This was too much. I would not tolerate such disrespect from my son.

I advanced on him but he did not back down, not even when I grabbed his shoulder roughly. "You need to watch what you say to me. I am your father and your capo."

He shrugged me off. "As if I could ever forget when you are always reminding me. I've dreamed a thousand times about escaping from here, going to live somewhere you can't find me. Somewhere I can be happy."

I blinked, unable to believe what I was hearing. He'd considered running away? "Don't be foolish," I snapped, livid that my only son would even think about leaving. And panicked that he might actually do it. "Think about what you will soon have. All of this will be yours."

"I don't want it! Not if I have to live a lie to get it."

"Basta! I told you, you can do what you like after you are settled and have children."

"Why not give all this to your other child? The one Francesca is having."

"Don't be ridiculous. I'll not entrust my legacy to the bastard of a whore."

His mouth dropped open, and he stared at me like I had just stomped on a puppy. "Cristo santo. You are every bit as heartless as she said. No wonder why she cries all the time."

The daily reports had left out that bit of information and I didn't like hearing it. My stomach cramped, and an ache settled between my shoulder blades. "I know that you are visiting her almost every day."

Giulio walked unsteadily toward the stairs. "We have a lot in common, Frankie and I. Not many people understand what it's like to have your life destroyed by il Diavolo."

I watched him stumble up the steps, my mind reeling from my son's hurt and anger. Never had he said such terrible things to me. He wouldn't have dared before.

He no longer cares about the consequences.

It didn't matter. I didn't reconsider my decisions, ever. Once they were made, I never retracted them. To do so made me look weak. Ineffectual. My father had drilled this into my head time and time again as he aged. When he passed on and I took over, I vowed to rule the same way.

And it had worked. The Ravazzani 'ndrina was the most powerful in Italy. We controlled the money, guns and drugs for most of Europe, the Middle East and Central America. We were feared and respected across the globe.

So I couldn't let myself care that Giulio was angry or that Francesca cried every day.

I had an empire to run. There was no room for weakness.

CHAPTER TWENTY-NINE

Francesca

THE TERM "MORNING SICKNESS" was a lie, no doubt invented by a man to give the impression that it wasn't so bad. Newsflash to women everywhere: it was fucking awful.

I rolled over and reached for another ginger candy. While these little golden ovals didn't eliminate the nausea, they definitely reduced it. And pregnant beggars could not be choosers.

After I sucked on the candy for a few moments, I felt ready to get up.

No, wait. Not so fast.

I flopped back down and closed my eyes. I hated this. I hated being in Italy. I hated being a woman. I hated being pregnant.

And I really, really hated the father of this baby.

I no longer referred to him by name. He was either "my baby's father" or "il Diavolo" whenever I had to mention him in conversation. Which wasn't that often, considering Giulio and my sisters were the only people I spoke to.

At least the beach was beautiful. The house was predictably gorgeous, right on the water, with large airy rooms and expensive furnishings. If I had to be a prisoner, at least it was here. I could take walks on the sand, take a dip in the water, and open the windows to catch the breeze.

During the thirty minutes I didn't feel like puking my guts out, at least.

Finally my stomach calmed and I trudged to the kitchen, where I made a decaf cappuccino. Zia had sent some pastries with Giulio but I learned the hard way to let the cappuccino settle first. I sat at the island and drank my coffee, my tablet in front of me as I checked my text messages.

Emma had sent me a photo of her swimming in our pool and I was so homesick at that moment that I nearly cried. Well, most anything made me cry these days, so that wasn't saying much. But I still missed my sisters. I missed my old life.

I wanted everything to go back the way it was three months ago.

Before Italy. Before the pregnancy. Before *him*.

My eyes welled up and a tear escaped. Damn that man. I couldn't even enjoy morning coffee without getting weepy.

Grabbing a tissue, I wiped my eyes. Giulio texted that he would come by this afternoon, that he had something to tell me. I hoped it was good news, because I seriously couldn't handle any more bad.

"Buongiorno, signorina!"

I looked up and saw one of the guards standing outside in the back. "Ciao, Sal."

They never made any attempt to hide from me. I guess the father of my child wanted me to know I was being watched, just in case I considered running. Honestly, I was too tired and nauseous to consider an escape. I needed to rest and feel better, then I'd plot a way back to Toronto.

The guards were always respectful. I knew they were reporting everything back to the boss, but I couldn't work up the energy to care. He had kicked me out, so let him hear about my naps and crying fits. He wouldn't give a shit. Only the life growing inside me interested him, this Ravazzani son or daughter to help carry on his illegal empire.

"Sal, un caffè?" Just because they worked for a stronzo didn't mean I would be rude.

"No, grazie." He pointed to the chair he'd sit in until three, when Luca arrived to take over.

I flipped through the news app, hoping something would distract me. Being heartbroken was the absolute worst. Adding pregnant and alone to the mix compounded my misery tenfold. All because I hadn't shared a secret that wasn't mine to tell.

Giulio felt horrible for causing the rift between his father and me, but it wasn't his fault that Fausto was a *pezzo di merda*. And yes, my translation app had curse words, which came in handy when referring to my baby daddy.

He'd called me a gold-digging whore. If that was what he really thought of me, it would have come out sooner or later—regardless of Giulio's sexuality—and I will never forgive him for it.

After I ate, I decided to go for a walk on the sand. Though he never came with me, Sal watched me intently from his chair. I knew if I tried to run, he would be on me in seconds. If I felt better, I might risk it, just to see how fast the guard could run. *One of these days, when the morning sickness passes.*

The beach was already crowded, families and couples laughing and smiling everywhere, and I tried not to hate them for their perfect, happy lives. I stayed near the water, loving the cold spray on my feet. I didn't have the energy for swimming today. Maybe I would take a nap when I got back.

I dodged a group of people playing near the water.

"Frankie!"

I started, surprised at hearing my name in the crowd. Looking up, I found Mariella, Enzo D'Agostino's mantenuta, in front of me. "Ciao!" She grabbed my shoulders and kissed my cheeks.

"Mariella, ciao!" How strange. What were the odds of seeing her here? I thought she and Enzo lived in Naples. "How are you?"

"Good. You?"

"Okay. What are you doing here?"

"Visiting the beach." She pointed to the water. "Siderno has the best in all of Italy."

Better than Naples? I shrugged. What did I know?

"Come, sit with me!"

Before I could say no, she began tugging me toward two chaises and an umbrella. Was she here with Enzo or a friend? But seeing as how I was exhausted, I gratefully sat down.

I could see Sal getting to his feet at the house, probably coming to check on me. But once he saw me on the chaise, he retook his seat, content that I wasn't trying to escape. His eyes didn't leave us, however.

Mariella smiled brightly. "It is good to see you. How is Fausto?"

I certainly didn't feel up to discussing that asshole. "Fine. Enzo?"

"He's very good." She waggled her brows. "He is in Napoli with his wife this weekend."

"Oh." That must suck.

"Fausto is here with you?"

"No. I'm by myself."

She nodded. "It is good to take time away. Makes them miss you, no?"

I felt my stomach roll, the nausea returning. "Did you come to the beach alone?"

"Yes, but now I found you, so not alone anymore."

Covering my mouth, I hid a yawn. I didn't have the heart to tell her yet, but I was definitely not up for a wild weekend in Siderno. She chattered on, talking about the Siderno night clubs and all the hot men here. Then she told me about Naples and her life there. I guess Enzo treated her pretty well. Did he think of her as a gold-digging whore?

Still, it felt nice to have an interaction with another young woman close to my age. Mariella and I weren't friends, but we were friendly and both involved with dangerous men. Fortunately, her constant talking distracted me from the train wreck that was my life at the moment. I even laughed once or twice.

"Come, let's get a rossini!"

Though I'd never had one, I knew this was a cocktail. "I don't have any money."

"I'll buy you one." Mariella stood and led the way toward the bar near the boardwalk. I turned and saw Sal marching across the sand, following us. I pointed to the bar, and he nodded, slowing down.

Mariella didn't stop at the bar. "Before we get drinks, you must see something. My car is just over here. Enzo bought it for me. Come, come. I want to show you."

Wait, a car?

Mariella had a car—a car that could take me away from the beach, away from Siderno. Away from *him*.

My heart began pounding with possibility. Could I slip away? Sal wasn't close enough to stop me. This seemed like the perfect chance. Possibly my only chance. We could get in and drive, and I could disappear.

I would explain my situation to Mariella. As a fellow mafia mistress, surely she would understand and help me. Wouldn't she? Keeping my head down, I began walking quickly toward the parking lot, Mariella keeping pace. She approached a sleek gray four-door sports sedan at the curb. I asked, "Is that yours?"

"Sì! Isn't it gorgeous? It's a Maserati. Come see."

She didn't need to ask me twice. I approached the car, imagining my getaway. "Actually, Mariella—"

A hand grabbed my arm and I instantly tried to pull away, desperate for my chance at freedom. How could Sal have gotten to us so quickly? "No, let me go."

"Hello, Francesca."

What the hell? That wasn't Sal.

Enzo D'Agostino stood behind me, a sharp object digging into my ribs. Was that a gun? Jesus Christ. "What are you doing?"

Before I had time to think, he shoved me forward, toward the Maserati, the gun never leaving my side.

Oh, fuck. This whole thing was a setup. These two assholes were trying to kidnap me!

My adrenaline surged, and I began struggling with all my might, attempting to free myself from Enzo's punishing grip, but he wouldn't budge. I kicked at him, twisting and yelling for all I was worth, but it made no difference. He pushed my top half into the trunk.

"Enzo!" Mariella shouted, and he suddenly let me go. I straightened as Sal launched himself at Enzo, and I barely got out of the way as the two tumbled to the ground. They began wrestling for Enzo's gun, and I saw my chance. I had to get the fuck out of there.

I didn't hesitate. I ran through the parking lot and then darted around a corner heading for the crowds on the beach, my arms pumping as my legs churned. My stomach protested but I managed to keep from barfing. I was no runner, but I put all my energy into escaping.

Arms wrapped around me from behind, jerking me to a stop. "No!" I yelled. "Help! I'm being kidnapped!" The people around us averted their eyes, hurrying away like I was radioactive. "No, please!" I called. "You don't understand! I need help!"

"Shut up," my captor said. "Or I will choke you, stranza."

I didn't recognize the voice, so it had to be one of Enzo's men. Of course Enzo hadn't come alone. Goddamn it. "Let me go. Please. Ravazzani won't like this." Fausto wouldn't care about me, but he would care about his unborn child. Maybe.

"I do not answer to that piece of trash."

He half-carried, half-dragged me back to Enzo's car, with me struggling the entire way. When we arrived, Enzo was wiping blood from the corner of his mouth. A slumped figure lay on the pavement. Shit, it was Sal. Was he dead?

I tried to wrench away but the guard held firm. "Enzo, don't do this," I begged. "It's not too late. Just let me go and we can forget all about it."

"Get in, puttanella," Enzo said angrily, pointing at the trunk. "You're coming with me."

"Why? Where are we going?"

"Don't worry about that. Just get the fuck in the car."

I looked at the small trunk. Would I have enough air in there? "Please, Enzo. Don't do this. I'll ride in the back seat. Please, just don't put me in the trunk."

"Shut up, and do as I say."

He shoved me down and I fell halfway in the trunk. Kicking my legs, I yelled for help, hoping someone would stop this. In a flash, Enzo's soldier covered my mouth with duct tape. Then he used a zip tie to secure my hands behind my back, threw my legs in and closed the top.

I was locked in.

Oh, fuck. No, no, no! Panic clawed at my insides, my fear of tight spaces robbing me of breath and making my heart pound. I couldn't see anything and couldn't move my hands. I tried my deep breathing techniques but they weren't working. Was there enough air in here? Worse, what if I grew nauseous and actually vomited? I would choke to death.

The car began moving, rolling away from the beach, and I kicked at the trunk. It did nothing except make me feel more helpless and more claustrophobic. Why was this happening? Why would anyone kidnap me?

I started trembling, my mind stuck in terror mode. I couldn't breathe and no one would rescue me. Sal was dead, Fausto had kicked me to the curb, and I barely knew a soul in this godforsaken country. Who cared about one pregnant mob mistress being abducted and taken who knew where?

If they were hoping for ransom, then *ha ha assholes*! Good luck because Fausto wouldn't pay a single Euro to get me back. Probably be glad to get rid of me and his bastard kid.

Tears streamed from my eyes, and I couldn't catch my breath. What had I ever done to deserve this? They were going to kill me. Or torture me.

The darkness spun around me as I got dizzier and dizzier. I knew I was hyperventilating, that I wasn't thinking clearly, so I tried to calm down. Nothing worked, though, and my last thought was of the strangely pretty tiny red halo that shone from the taillight....

Don't miss **MAFIA DARLING**, the exciting conclusion of Fausto and Francesca's story, available now.

Want a sneak peek at the exciting conclusion?
Read on!

MAFIA DARLING
by Mila Finelli

Fausto

I often dreamed of blood.

Rivers of it, filling my mouth and choking me. Drowning me and everyone I cared about, with no hope of survival.

The dreams started back when I was a foot soldier, still being groomed under my father's watchful eye. In those days, the boss's son did not receive a pass on the more gruesome of tasks. No, they used those tasks to harden me, to turn me from a boy into a man.

A man capable of leading the world's most dangerous mafia. The 'Ndrangheta.

There had been no choice for me, no other life to consider. As the years went on, I followed instructions and never dared show a hint of weakness. Torture and killing became second nature to me, work I learned to love. It earned me respect from my 'ndrina brothers and fear from my enemies. Whispers followed me wherever I went, the tales of my cruelty spread far and wide.

This made my father proud.

He told me this often, especially after watching me at my worst. They called him in when I was too eager with my knife, the blood of our enemies staining every part of me red like the Devil. It was from this that the legend of *il Diavolo* was born. Gutting, dismembering, disemboweling . . . the pain I doled out was returned tenfold in my father's love.

It became a vicious cycle for me, more killing to earn more praise, until I hardly slept due to the nightmares. Even years later, I slept only three or four hours before I woke up in a cold sweat, a scream clawing at my throat. Then I would get up and exercise, running until I nearly dropped.

This was my life before she came along. I had more than most men could ever dream of, even if exhaustion stalked my every waking moment, so it was enough. I wouldn't ever trade my life for a clear conscience.

Then she arrived, with her fire and sass. And the bad dreams? They stopped when I was with her. For a few blissful weeks, I had a respite from the ghosts of my past, my first decent sleep in decades.

Then I sent her away.

The dreams have returned, but worse because they include her. My dolcezza, alone and scared, her body bleeding out in front of my eyes, and there is nothing I can do about it. My nightmares don't care that Francesca betrayed me, that she was not the person I believed her to be. No, my nightmares live to torture me and drive me insane night after night, pushing me to the limits of my endurance.

My son also featured in my dreams, and each time I find him dead. They always killed him before I can save him, leaving his lifeless body for me to find. My good boy, slaughtered like a pig.

So much blood. So much death.

Chi male comincia, peggio finisce.

A bad beginning makes a bad ending.

This is the life I have chosen. No matter what happens, there is no going back.

Giulio

Waiting at a stoplight, I took another hit from my weed vape and held in the smoke as long as I could. I exhaled, and the mellow sensation rolled through my bloodstream like a warm bath. Cazzo, that was nice.

I leaned against the headrest and closed my eyes. This feeling was much better than drinking alcohol, which only made me feel even more like my father. He'd taken to booze now that Frankie was gone.

Fausto and I already had enough in common; no need to add a drinking problem to the list.

A car honked behind me. I opened my eyes and gave the driver the finger. *Stronzo*. I put my Ferrari in drive and sped off into the midday beach traffic. The music pumped from my stereo, a song I hadn't heard in ages. I tapped my hands against the steering wheel, changing gears swiftly, as I sang along. Dio, I felt good. Thirsty, but good.

I wish I could fuck Paulo right now.

The thought nearly ruined my buzz, so I shoved it aside. If I wanted to keep Paulo alive then I couldn't see him again. Except I didn't want to fuck anyone else. I still loved him.

My chest tightened and my heart thumped so hard, I swear it was louder than the bass in the song. I hadn't slept with anyone in three weeks, and it was torture. Even still, my dick remained limp at the strip club last night, much to the disappointment of the girl grinding on my lap. Life would be so much easier if I liked women.

Or if I could have Paulo.

My father believed it was so simple. The great Fausto Ravazzani gave his orders and expected us all to fall in line.

I told you, you can do what you like after you are settled and have children.

Except Paulo would never wait while I knocked my wife up enough times to fill out the family tree—and I didn't expect him to.

Cristo, was Paulo fucking someone else already?

The thought turned my blood to ice, even with the herb in my system. Had he forgotten me and moved on in the last three weeks? I bet he had. He seemed sad enough when I broke things off, but maybe those tears had been fake. Has he started posting on the hookup apps and meeting other men?

I had to find out.

I pulled into the drive of the beach house, and carried a box full of Zia's cornetti and sfogliatelle with me to the front door. Frankie still wasn't eating enough, but maybe I could coax her into a few bites. At least we were miserable together. Though I hated to see her sad, being with her every day has kept me sane after my breakup. That, and the weed.

I texted Sal, her guard, to let him know I was here then used my key in case she was asleep. I headed for the kitchen first. The rooms were empty and quiet, sounds from the beach faint in the background. An old cup of coffee sat on the kitchen island, Frankie's tablet resting there. Had she gone back to bed?

"Sal," I called quietly. Normally the big man sat at the back door, not quite inside but nearby in case of trouble. Except his chair stood empty. I checked my watch. Two o'clock. Sal should be here.

Were they on the beach? I scanned the sand stretching out along the edge of the water. Frankie hasn't felt up to long walks or swims in a while. There were lots of people on the beach but none of them were Frankie or Sal.

This was strange.

I dialed Sal's cell phone and retrieved my gun from the inside of my jacket. Keeping absolutely quiet, I went upstairs to see if she was in bed.

The master bed was rumpled but empty. She wasn't in the bathroom, either. *Ma che cazzo?*

Sweat broke out on the back of my neck, every part of me now on high alert. I quickly checked the rest of the upstairs then returned downstairs. I called Sal's replacement, Luca. He picked up on the second ring. "Where are you?" I barked.

"Just about to leave the house, why?"

"Did you hear from Sal today?"

"Yes, this morning. He wanted to know if we could swap shifts tomorrow."

"He's not here." I began opening closet doors and checking behind furniture. "Both Sal and Frankie are missing."

"That is impossible," he said, and I could hear him moving in the background. "I'm coming right now, but you should call Marco. They can review the security footage at the castello."

As I hung up on Luca, I returned to the kitchen to look in the pantry. As soon as I pulled open the door, my heart sank. Sal was there, unmoving. Minchia! Was he dead?

Worse, where the fuck was Frankie?

This was bad. This was very, very bad.

I had to call my father.

Fausto

I rubbed my eyes behind my glasses. The words on the screen were fuzzy, my body too tired to focus.

Sighing, I picked up my Campari and tonic. I'd taken to drinking early in the afternoons, a habit Marco disliked immensely but one I found necessary to dull the ache inside my chest. The past two nights I had fallen into bed in a drunken stupor and passed out for a few hours.

It was an improvement over weeks of sleepless nights.

Marco sat in the corner on his phone, pretending to ignore me while really watching me closely. He wasn't fooling me.

I read the numbers on my screen again, wanting to prove I was still on top of my empire. "Toni just made us over two million Euros by shorting a tech stock."

Marco grunted.

"Maybe we don't need D'Agostino for this computer idea."

He didn't respond.

I drummed my fingers on the desk and sipped my cocktail. When I drank, my thoughts frequently drifted back to *her*, even when I tried to prevent it.

She'd made a fool of me. I'd mooned over her like a lovesick teenager with his first taste of pussy. All the while she'd been keeping a secret from me, one that could destroy everything I'd built. I would never forgive her.

I narrowed my gaze on my cousin. "Why don't you take the rest of the day off?"

"I'm fine where I am."

He was babysitting me, like I was a toddler. I didn't like it. "Marco —" My phone lit up and Giulio's name appeared on the screen. I hadn't seen him since our argument.

Swiping to answer, I held the phone up to my ear. "Pronto."

"She's not here."

I heard the panic before I understood the words. Straightening in my chair, I immediately put it on the speaker so Marco could hear. "What do you mean? Where is she?"

"The house, it's empty. No Frankie, no guards."

Marco and I exchanged a look. What the fuck? Had she run?

Or had something terrible happened instead?

My chest seized, my heart suddenly forgetting how to function, and I got to my feet. Marco began dialing on his phone, probably trying to reach the men I had stationed at the beach house, but I remained focused on my son. "Show me," I barked.

Giulio turned on the video and I saw he was in the kitchen, a gun in his other hand. "When I got here," he explained, "the back door was open. I found Sal out cold in the pantry."

He showed me Sal, pale and lifeless on the ground. "Is he dead?" I snapped.

"He's alive," my son said. "There's a syringe next to him on the floor."

"Where is she?" I shouted, yanking at the knot of my tie with one hand to loosen it. Had Francesca somehow drugged Sal and then escaped?

No matter what happens, I will leave here. Somehow, some way, I will get away from you.

"Search every inch of that house. I am on my way." I hung up and started across the room.

Marco held up a hand, talking rapidly on his phone. He grabbed my arm to stop me as I passed. "She left for a walk on the beach. Nothing out of the ordinary. Sal stayed behind at first, then went after her. Vic is watching the camera footage now."

I sprinted out the door and down the corridor. The security room was in the east section of the castello, and I ran there like a madman.

Vic was at the desk, a wall of screens in front of him. He was our best tech guy, a hacker, with skills that we put to use all over the globe. His gaze was locked on the screen with Sal in the chair at the beach house, his eyes tracking something on the beach. *Francesca.*

"She's been gone for about ten minutes," Vic said, moving the video forward. "Sal watches her and then gets up to follow."

"Why weren't you on the cameras today?" I snarled. "How the fuck did this happen?"

He swallowed but didn't meet my eye, his attention still on the screen. "I'm sorry, Don Ravazzani. I was working on a security update.

I wasn't paying close attention to the cameras." On the monitor a dark shape crept into the kitchen—a man carrying Sal over his shoulder.

"Who is that?" I leaned in and watched as a man in a black mask tossed Sal into the pantry. A few seconds later another camera caught him leaving. Was this someone she'd hired to help her? Or was it one of my enemies? "Is she still on the beach? Can we get the CCTV footage?"

Vic shifted to a laptop and began typing. "It might take some time."

I pounded my fist on the desk. "There is no time. You're supposed to be this tech genius. So find those fucking cameras. I need to know what happened to her—"

"Rav." Marco held out his phone in front of my face. "You should take this."

"Not now."

"Rav," he implored, his expression as serious as I'd ever seen. "It's D'Agostino. He says he has something that belongs to you."

Order MAFIA DARLING on Amazon.

A NOTE FROM MILA

Thank you so much for reading my very first mafia romance, MAFIA MISTRESS. I had a blast writing it. I hope it was fun to read.

With regards to the Italian words and phrases in the book, I tried to italicize only the first usage of each one. Thanks to Nadina, who helped me with the Italian translations. All the errors are mine.

Thanks to everyone who read this and told me I wasn't crazy for doing it. And thank you to those who offered helpful comments along the way. You know who you are!

Want to know when more stories are coming? Visit milafinelli.com and sign up for Mila's new release alerts.

Lightning Source UK Ltd.
Milton Keynes UK
UKHW020847230822
407709UK00010B/871